Vicious Kitten
The Insatiable Series (Book 3)
Sarah JD

ISBN-13: 978-0-9756312-5-6

2024 Cover by DAZED Designs
Many thanks to my Beta Readers: Alana, Anoesjka, & Melissa, and proofreader, Jen.

For my Beta Readers
Alana, Anoesjka, and Melissa.
Your dedication and support is absolutely everything!
I could not do this without your honest feedback
and passion to help me with my typos and lack of
grammar skills, plus picking up any plot holes.
Thank you for being so invested in helping me.
I am eternally grateful!

Sarah JD's Books

Sarah JD's Books

https://sarahjaneduncan.com/book-links/
https://sarahjaneduncan.com/my-books/

VICIOUS WARNING

It's your Kitten speaking! Welcome back to the final instalment in my dark and depraved world. Once again, I'm here to give you a heads up!

What you are about to read contains some extremely serious triggers. Please take them seriously because things are about to get brutal!

This series contains content that could be triggering to some readers, which include:

- Non-consensual Sex Acts.

- Taboo – Age Gap with a minor.

- Reverse Harem – meaning I'm worshipped by multiple partners in a sharing relationship which includes group sex.

- Humiliation.

- Fetishes such as food play, foot play, blood play, bondage and golden showers.

- Addiction.

- Blackmail.

- Suicidal Thoughts.

- Kidnapping.

- Bullying.

- The backstory includes references to grooming, molestation, and child pornography.

Are you still here, ready to be consumed by my world one last time?

Buckle up Kitten's. This ride is about to get bumpy!

CHAPTER ONE

RHYS

The rush of blood thunders in my ears as I take two steps at a time. My left cheek burns like a bitch, and my legs are still trembling, but that's nothing compared to the panic racing through me.

"Ty!" I call out as I stumble up the last two steps.

"I got you, Kitten." Shaun's firm hands grip my hips from behind, steadying me as I reach the landing.

A sob escapes me as my emotions become almost overwhelming. *No Rhys! Not yet! Hold it together for a little longer!*

Moving his grip to my shoulders, Shaun urges us forward until we reach the door, his fist banging loudly on the surface before taking a step back. My whole body is trembling now, so I wrap my arms around myself, barely covered by my t-shirt, with my legs and feet bare.

The door swings open, and there he is. Ty.

Unfortunately, his eyes barely glance at me as they lock onto the person standing behind me. Shaun's not meant to be here. It was just meant to be me. Ty and I were meant to be talking about, well... hopefully not breaking up. It was just meant to be the two of us.

"What the fuck are you doing here, Fuckboy?"

"T-Ty." I stutter, quickly gaining his attention.

When his eyes land on me, they widen, his pissed off glare plunging from his face.

"What the fuck is going on? What happened?" He steps forward, reaching out to grip my arms, his blue eyes roaming over my face and then travelling down my body.

"You gonna let us in?" Shaun hisses from behind me just as a salty drop slips from my eye.

"Kitten?" Ty whispers, ignoring Shaun as he brushes away my tear.

"I fucked up." I barely get the words out before Tyler scoops me up in his arms, carrying me into his apartment.

"Shut the door behind you." He grumbles over his shoulder to Shaun, and a moment later, I hear the door click shut.

I cling to Ty, curling into his chest as he carries me down the short passage to an open kitchen and living area. Tyler smells like home. Like a place that is safe. A place where you are always welcome. A place you are loved. It's a battle for me to remain focused and not want to melt into everything that is him when my heart has missed his closeness so much.

"What's going on, Kitten?" He sets me down on the kitchen counter, the cool stone against my bare legs momentarily taking my breath away. Tyler shifts back, his eyes locking on the spot on my cheek that feels like it's on fire. I guess there's a bruise or something left behind from Master Hill's fist. "Someone better start talking right fucking now!" He turns his glare to Shaun then, who just looks to me for help.

"Ty." My voice is a whisper, and I suck in a breath when Ty's piercing blue eyes turn back to me. "I've fucked up. Bad. I was trying to help, but things got out of hand. I couldn't go through with it, but it didn't matter."

"Through with what?" His eyes are fierce as his anger grows. He doesn't like beating around the bush.

"Master Hill made me a deal."

"What?" He steps away from me, his eyes turning to Shaun for something. I'm not sure what. "What deal?"

Shaun's lips thin, but he doesn't speak, so Ty turns back to me.

I try to smile, hoping to ease his anger, "I made a deal to return to the Feast nights with Madam Vik as my new sponsor, and part of it included that I spend an hour with Master Hill each Feast, and in return, he won't expose you… and me."

"Are you fucking kidding me right now?" Ty's face turns red. I knew he'd be upset at my revelation. He's going to lose his job when the truth about us comes out. Shit, he may even get arrested. I didn't want that to happen, which is why I made the stupid deal in the first place. But now I've gone and made it worse by refusing Master Hill.

Why couldn't you just let him have his way with you? It's not like you haven't whored yourself out in exchange for something before, Rhys!

"Why would you make that deal with him?" Ty bellows, fisting his hands in his hair, the anger laced in his tone making me flinch.

"Hey arsehole! Back the fuck off. Can't you see she's been hurt?" Shaun pushes in between Tyler and me, shoving Ty in the chest. He barely moves, but his brows come together as he frowns, and his blue eyes study me again.

"I… he didn't give me a choice," I murmur. "It was either that, or he would expose us. I didn't want him to do that to *you,* Ty. He has a video of us together."

"Kitten." Ty shoves Shaun away and steps up, cupping my face. "I don't fucking care about any evidence he has. All I care about is you and your safety."

"But… you'll lose your job. You might get arrested or something."

"That's not for you to worry about, Rhys." Moving into my space, Ty tilts my head up. "I've already resigned from my job, Kitten. Effective immediately, as of Thursday just gone. I had to choose because it was never going to work if I didn't, and I chose you, beautiful."

"What?" Did I hear him right? "You resigned?"

"Yes, Kitten. That's where I was last night. At my farewell dinner. I'm sorry I couldn't take your call. You sounded pretty drunk."

"You resigned?" Is he being serious right now?

"Yes. I understand that you're still under age, and I will wait and do the right thing until you turn eighteen and hopefully, you'll still want me."

"Ty. Why didn't you tell me sooner?" Tears spill over, rolling down my cheeks as I lean into him.

"Well. That's what I was going to tell you tonight. I needed to get things sorted out first. I'm going to move to Redfield for a bit. Lie low in the house I have there."

"You have a house in Redfield? You're moving?" I see it then in my peripheral, and I glance around to confirm. There are packed boxes lining the walls. Some still open. Newspaper on the bench. Books in piles on the floor. "Will I still be able to see you?"

He pulls back, clasping each side of my face as his blue eyes dance between mine. "It probably won't be as much as we'd like, but yeah, I'll make sure we can see each other. And once you turn eighteen, maybe it'll get a little easier since I won't be breaking any laws."

"O-ok. April better hurry the fuck up." I hiss, and he chuckles.

"You turn eighteen in April?"

"Yes. April first." I study his face for a moment. The faint lines around his eyes and the shadowed facial hair that lines his jaw are a reminder of how *man* he really is. "Are you sure you want me? I'm like 15 years younger than you. Won't you get sick of me and my brilliant ability to act like a brat?"

"I've never been more sure of anything in my life." He brushes his thumb over my lips, his eyes watching the action. "I know there's an age difference, but you feel right for me." He leans in, using his thumb to lower my chin, the movement opening my mouth as he presses his lips to mine.

His arms wrap around me, tugging me impossibly close as I hook my legs around him, ignoring the pain in my cheek as I relax into the kiss. It's one of those real kisses that isn't all about sex. It's about love.

The thought makes my heart swell inside my chest, filling me up to feel complete. It's something I never thought I'd feel and also something I never realised I needed until these five guys came into my life.

"As for the bratty part," Tyler mumbles as he pecks my lips over and over. "I'll never tire of that, beautiful."

"What about four other seventeen-year-old guys? Can you deal with sharing me with them?"

"Hmmm." He grumbles. "Now that I'm no longer a teacher, does it mean I can slap them around if they piss me off?"

I giggle. "Not too much. But maybe a little."

"Hey! Did you forget that I'm standing right here?" Shaun hisses, and I giggle as Ty rolls his eyes before turning serious.

"Now time for some more truths because I'm having a lot of trouble looking at you and seeing this bruise forming, and the patches of face paint you weren't successful at removing. Tell me *everything* that happened tonight, Kitten. Don't leave anything out."

I take in a deep breath, my eyes darting to Shaun momentarily. He nods, encouraging me, so I look back to Ty, hating that I've fucked things up so badly.

"Master Hill asked me to come early and go to the back door. When I got there, he took me upstairs to a girl's bedroom. The things he usually leaves in the barn for me were in there. He left me to get ready, and then I met him and Madam Vik downstairs. I managed to include Shaun's attendance in my deal, so Cass was there, which made it too hard to focus on being the Feast's Kitten." My eyes dart to Shaun, who is leaning against the table, his arms crossed as he listens. "I hated seeing him being touched, and I couldn't stand anyone touching me. I managed to dodge everyone for a bit, but Master must have been watching me and decided that our hour may as well start, since I wasn't fucking anyone else." My eyes fall shut, and I suck in air as the memories swarm me. It's the gentle brush of Ty's fingers on my nape that helps ease some of my tension.

"Master took me down to this creepy sex dungeon and made me kneel on the pillow again. Then… he made me crawl to him."

"Fucking arsehole!" Shaun hisses, and my eyes dart to him. He's standing by the table now, his hands fisted by his sides. "I'm gonna kill that motherfucker!"

"Get in line, Fuckboy." Tyler growls, and I shiver at the sheer menace in Ty's tone.

I force myself to keep speaking, needing to get this out. "After that, he made me stand and bend over the end of the bed. He tried to put a wrist cuff on me... like he did the night of the punishment. I wouldn't let him. I said Cactus, which he didn't like, and I admitted I wasn't going to let him do anything with me tonight. That's when he reminded me of what would happen if I didn't submit." I drop my eyes, squeezing them tight.

"I tried to renegotiate. I tried to reason with him, but he was dead set on destroying me, no matter what. He grabbed me. We struggled. He pushed me down and punched me." I point to my cheek and finally look back up to Ty. I can tell he's chewing the inside of his cheek, his eyes swimming with so much emotion that I'm not sure I should continue, yet I know I need to.

"He bound my wrists behind my back. Things got a little hazy in my head for a few moments, but I heard him say that my contract was irrelevant in that room because it's not part of the Feast. I could feel his fingers between my legs, poking me. Then he told me he was going to take my butt virginity. He... He... put his finger." I shake my head, squeezing my eyes tight as I fight off the vile memory. "I kind of lost my shit then." I open my eyes again, tears blurring my vision. "I somehow head-butted him with the back of my head, and he fell to the floor. That's when I turned around and stomped on his nuts."

"That's when I came through the door." Shaun's words gain our attention, his steel-grey eyes remaining on me. "Brock busted through after me, but Kitten bared her teeth at him like a vicious lioness and screamed. Man, you should have seen his face. He looked like he was going to piss his pants." Shaun chuckles, enticing a smile to tug at my lips. "Then Master told Rhys that the deal is off, and now the real fun begins."

"Shit," Ty whispers, looking between Shaun and me. "And how did you get here?"

"After we got Kitten's things from that creepy girl's bedroom upstairs, we went back to my place, and my brother Derek drove us here."

Tyler nods and steps back from me before he starts pacing. I look at Shaun. I'm not sure what for… help, maybe? But he just shrugs, not really knowing what to do next.

"When was this deal made with Master Hill?" Tyler turns back to me, his blonde brows raised, waiting for my answer.

"Uh… He messaged me Wednesday, and I went to see him on Thursday night."

"So, he messaged you? You didn't go to him first?" Ty frowns, and I shake my head.

"No. He reached out to me."

Ty sighs. "You didn't cause this, Kitten. I did." He shakes his head and rakes his hands through his blonde hair again in frustration.

"What do you mean?" I frown, sneaking a glance at Shaun to see him frowning, too.

"I went to see him on Tuesday." Ty admits, "He needed to know that what he did at the Feast with you, the humiliation, was *not* ok. I may have used my fists to show him how I felt."

Holy shit. That's why Ty had a bruise next to his eye last week and why Master is still banged up. And hell… why is the thought of Ty swinging fists so fucking hot?

"Jesus Kitten. Get your head out of the gutter." Shaun mutters, and I swing wide eyes at him.

"What?"

Ty chuckles. "You're easy to read when you're turned on, Kitten."

I glance back at Ty, my face heating as I suck my lips in, trying not to smile. He steps back into my space then, his gentle fingers gripping my chin as he hovers his lips over mine. "If I could rid this earth of anyone who has ever harmed you, I would, Kitten, without a second thought."

His lips press to mine, and I sink into his embrace as he tugs my body flush with his. I could easily forget my worries and get lost in Tyler, but Shaun's clearing throat reminds us that we aren't alone, and the reality of the situation comes flooding back.

With a last gentle peck, Ty pulls back and sighs.

"I need to call Master Fuckwit."

"Do you think it will help?" I look hopefully at Tyler, but he shakes his head.

"Probably not, but it's worth a try." He walks across the room to the coffee table that sits centred between a couch and the floating TV on the wall and picks up his phone, tapping something before the sound of ringing fills the room from the phone's speaker.

"Good evening, Skipper. I've been expecting your call." Master Hill's voice sends a chill down my spine.

"Kitten has filled me in on your little deal." Ty hisses, and Master chuckles.

"Oh, there's no deal now. She's turned frigid. Such a shame. She had so much potential."

My face heats at Master's words. I've never been called frigid before. It's an insult used by men to make a woman feel insufficient. To make a woman feel like she has to prove them wrong. I fucking hate that word. How many girls have gone further than they wanted because a guy has used *that* word on them? That word makes me want to go on a dick-severing rampage.

"No one cares what you think, Terence." Tyler hisses, and Master chuckles.

"They will when they see Fox Pines Catholic's reputable sports teacher fucking one of his female students. That video footage isn't even grainy. You can see everything."

I suck in a sharp breath, and Shaun takes my hand, tugging me off the counter to pull me into his chest. I wrap my arms around him, needing his touch to help me remain grounded.

"What will you gain by doing this, Terence? We would never expose you and the Feast nights, so why would you expose us and put the Feast at risk?"

"Oh, I won't risk using the footage of the two of you inside my house. That's just for my viewing pleasure. The barn session you two had is so much better for others to watch. No masks. No makeup. No one will know it took place on my property."

"What?" I whimper as his words sink in. He filmed us in the barn?

"Oh, how sweet. Your little Kitten ran straight to you. Does she visit you often in your home? Do you have private teacher-student study sessions, Tyler? Do you teach her well?"

"Fuck you, you motherfucking cunt! I'm going to fucking kill you for this!"

I flinch in Shaun's arms at the sheer violence in Tyler's tone, and I peer up from Shaun's chest to glance at Ty. His face is bright red. He actually looks like he could kill someone right now.

"As for you, Kitten. You'll do well to learn how to do as you're told. Breaking rules, and deals, has consequences. Something I hear you've been learning a lot about lately. I've been lucky enough to watch that video footage of you and your old foster dad. It's a great movie. Please thank whoever sent it to me."

My face pales as his words sink in. He's seen the video of me when I was little? With Brian?

"If you go through with this, Terence, you'd better be prepared to fight!"

Master Hill chuckles. "Go through wIth it? Oh, Skipper, it's already done." He ends the call, leaving Tyler with red-faced fury, his breathing sharp and short as he tries to calm himself down.

A sob leaps from my throat a second before a loud bang fills the room. I freeze in Shaun's arms, my eyes wide as I watch Tyler's head dart towards the passage that leads to his front door.

BANG! BANG! BANG!

There's strength and anger behind that beating fist, the door rattling with each pounding like it's going to fly from its hinges.

"Don't answer it!" I cry as Tyler stomps towards the passage, his fierce eyes flicking to Shaun as he points a stern finger.

"Keep her here."

I feel Shaun nod, and when I try to move from his embrace, his arms tighten around me.

"Let me go, Cass."

"No, Kitten. You heard Ty."

I shove him as more banging sounds, getting free in time to round the corner of the passage.

Tyler swings the door wide, and I hear the venomous bellow of a man's voice.

"You fucking paedophile! I'm gonna kill you!"

Then a fist flies through the doorway, colliding with Tyler's face.

CHAPTER TWO

RHYS

E verything happens so quickly that I hardly have time to process it. Fists fly. Blood splatters. Screams fill the air. I try to get to Ty to protect him from the hulking silhouette in the doorway, but Shaun drags me backwards.

"NO!" I scream, kicking and flailing, trying to break free of Shaun's firm grip.

The silhouette figure looks up then. I can't see his face in the dark shadow of the passage, but I can tell he's looking at me right before he looks back down at Ty, who is trying to stand up.

"I'll fucking kill you for laying your hands on my daughter!"

The voice. That voice. I recognise it now as he stalks Tyler on the floor, who isn't fighting back, just trying to get away. It's Will. My dad.

"No! Dad! Stop!" I scream, but he ignores me, leaning down to lift Tyler by the scruff of his neck and starts slamming his fist into his face. "Please stop, Dad! Please!"

I elbow Shaun, my low blow connecting with his jewels, his grip instantly releasing me as he doubles over in pain, and I rush forward down the passage and leap in between my dad and Ty, giving my dad no choice but to stop. He doesn't stop in time, though, his fist connecting with my face in the exact same spot that Master Hill landed his fist.

I scream out in pain before Tyler's strong arms wrap around me from behind, twisting me away from my dad as he covers my body with his, trying to protect me. More footsteps thump on the timber floors, but I can't see anything with the way Tyler is shielding me. He jerks over and over as more fists land on his back, my dad not letting up.

"Stop!" Shaun bellows before he yelps, and then my mum's voice cries out.

"STOP WILLIAM!"

Suddenly, the angry roar of my dad dies, and all I can hear is the frantic panting of Tyler's breathing in my ear.

"Tell me you're ok, Kitten." He whispers, and I try to talk but realise I'm crying and can't form words, so I clutch tighter to the arm he has wrapped around me.

"What have you done?" Cynthia cries, her heels clicking on the timber floors, stopping somewhere nearby. "You just hit a child, William!"

"I…I didn't know." My dad's voice is tormented. I've never heard it sound so broken.

"It's ok, Mrs R. It was my fault. I got in the way." Shaun speaks then, and it's a relief to hear his voice. "I was just trying to stop him. He was gonna hurt Rhys."

"What?" Will hisses. "I would never hurt Rhys!"

"You hit her, man! Just like you did to me. She was trying to stop you. If Ty hadn't rolled her under him, you would have been beating the shit out of your daughter!"

"You hit Rhys?" Cynthia cries. "Rhys! Rhys!" Her heels click frantically until I see them halt near my head. "Oh my God!" She gasps.

"Let's get you up." Ty rasps in my ear, and I'm still too distraught to speak, but he shifts behind me, anyway. Slowly, Ty stands, pulling me up with him. My eyes land on my mum as I stand, her eyes red from crying, black mascara running down her cheeks, her hands pressed to her mouth as she looks me over in disbelief.

"Rhys." She whispers, and I try to calm my shuddered crying so I can respond.

"I-I-I'm o-ok."

"What have I done?" My dad's voice is laced with agony, so soft it's nearly a whisper.

We turn to him then, and I watch as the sorrow on his face morphs into anger, his eyes focused on my side where my hand is entwined with Ty's. Then Dad leaps at us again.

"I saw you in that filthy video. I saw what you did to my daughter!"

We stumble back, trying to get away from my dad, crashing into some of the packing boxes as we try to flee. Something smashes to the floor as the fight tumbles past the kitchen. My dad's fury consuming him again, his eyes focused on Tyler, ignoring me at his side.

"Stop, William!" Cynthia cries again, but it's no use. He's lost to his anger again, and he only has eyes for his target.

Stumbling backwards to put more distance between us, we reach the small living area right before my dad swings his fist towards us. It misses me as Shaun tackles me to the floor, but I hear the loud smack of skin on skin, followed by the heavy thud of Tyler falling backwards again. I fight Shaun off, scrambling on the timber floor to get between my dad and Ty again, and this time, as my dad prepares for another swing, I scream at him, the same way I did to Brock at the Feast earlier tonight.

The vicious animal in me rears up, baring my teeth as a growling hiss explodes into my voice. "STOP!" My lips turn up in a snarl as my dad flinches back, the haze of his anger faltering as he realises I'm in front of him now. "You will stop hurting me!"

"W-what? I wasn't hurting you. I'm not trying to hurt you, Rhys."

I snarl at my dad again. "When you lay a hand on someone I love, you are hurting *me*!"

My dad stumbles back, and Cynthia sobs behind him as the room fills with panting breaths again. With each step backwards that my dad takes, I relax a little more, until he stumbles into a bar stool, his shoulders drooping with defeat.

"Rhys." Cynthia steps forward, but I ignore her, turning to face Ty. He's sagged back against the couch, blood oozing from a number of open cuts on his face.

"Ty." I whimper, grabbing a throw blanket from behind him and dabbing it against the gash over his eyebrow, which seems to be bleeding the most.

"I'm ok, Kitten."

"Don't call her that." My mum's voice is closer now, but I ignore her.

"Cass, can you get a wet face washer or something?"

"It's ok. No need to fuss over me." Tyler mutters, but I ignore that bullshit. As if I'm not going to fuss over him.

I hear Shaun move behind us, and I shift to a kneeling straddle over Ty's legs so I can get closer to him.

"Rhys. Get off Mr Foster now."

"Just go, Cynthia. You and Will have done enough damage." I mutter, hot tears spilling from my eyes as the reality of what just happened sinks in.

"What? No, I'm not leaving you." Cynthia whimpers.

I risk a glance at Ty's blue eyes and see that he's watching me carefully. He's too still. He should be fighting or ranting or something.

"You should go with your parents, beautiful."

My bottom lip wobbles as my emotions almost become unbearable. "What?"

"Go with them. I'll be ok." He lifts his hand to my face, the pads of his fingers brushing over my swelling bruise.

"N-no. I'm not leaving you."

"Given the situation, it might be best if you go with them." His eyes soften with sympathy then, and I feel like he's silently saying goodbye.

"You should listen to Mr Foster, Rhys. Don't make things worse than they already are." Cynthia tries to make me see sense again, but I shake my head, glancing over my shoulder at her.

"I'm not leaving Ty."

She flinches when she sees my face again, her eyes honing in on the swelling bruise.

"William didn't mean to do that." She whispers, almost as if she's trying to convince herself.

"Oh, this?" I stand from Ty's lap and face my parents, pointing to my cheek. "Don't worry, this isn't *all* on Dad. There was already a bruise there given to me by another man from earlier tonight. Dad just added to it."

"What?" Cynthia gasps, and Will's eyes widen.

"Yeah, you know that video you obviously received? The man who sent that did this because I wouldn't let him restrain me and fuck me up the arse."

"Rhys!" Cynthia cries, anger flitting across her face.

"What? It's the truth. You're always on me about being honest. Well, that's my honesty, Cynthia." She flinches at my use of her name, obviously noticing that I've stopped calling her mum. "I guess his feelings are hurt because I said *no*. So that video you saw is payback." I laugh, but there's no humour in it. "I guess the cat's out of the bag now."

"Let's go home." My dad stands from the barstool, his eyes avoiding Ty's, or Shaun's, who has come back into the room with the wet washer I requested.

"I'm not going anywhere with *you*." I glare at Will. "You're a monster!"

"Rhys!" Cynthia scolds, and I glare at her, too.

"Look what he did!" I point to Tyler, slumped on the floor. "I have a right to refuse to be around anyone that is dangerous and abusive. I'm *not* going to sit back and keep letting this stuff happen to me. It's *not* ok. People hurting me is *not* ok."

"Your Dad never meant to hurt you." She pleads with me, taking a step forward, but I take one back.

"But Will *did* hurt me." I see the way Will flinches when I don't refer to him as Dad. "He hurt Ty and Shaun too." I shake my head, trying to bite back the hot tears wetting my eyes. "I'm not going anywhere with him."

"You can't stay here, Rhys. This is illegal. You are only seventeen." Cynthia looks like she wants to approach me, but she must think better of it. Smart woman.

"Tell me, what about my life *has* been legal? Was it legal when my mum used her unemployment money on drugs and then fed me food scraps from the rubbish bins of our neighbours? Was it legal when the foster homes I lived in used my body as a boxing bag or my fear as a weapon? Was it legal when Brian convinced me that his games were normal? Was it ok for him to take my virginity? Was it legal for Julie to film me with Brian and then send a fucking copy to my school friends? How about the spit roast you found me in last month? Those guys were well into their twenties. Did you call the cops on them and report them? No, you didn't because you knew it would end up with me having to answer uncomfortable questions. And guess what? The cops would have concluded that I asked for it. I wanted to be fucked. I'm just another whore!"

"Stop it! You are not a whore, Rhys!" Cynthia cries, and I ignore the pang it sends to my heart.

"No? You don't think I'm a whore for sleeping with those teachers at Redfield High? You don't think I'm a whore for blackmailing Ty into getting me into a sex club? You don't think I'm a whore for having five boyfriends at once, one of whom is my PE teacher?"

"Stop talking like that. No matter what you do, I will never think that about you. I love you, Rhys. You're my daughter," She gestures to Will standing behind her, "You're *our* daughter. We love you unconditionally."

I have no response to that, and tears blur my eyes as my emotions take over.

"Can we just talk about things, please?" Cynthia asks, and I shrug.

"I'm not leaving, so if you want to talk, you'll have to do it here."

Cynthia sighs and starts pacing, her heels clicking on the timber floors again, so I turn back to Ty to see Shaun helping him clean up the blood on his face. I sink to my knees, taking the washer from Shaun and help.

"Tyler, is this why you resigned on Thursday afternoon? Why you said you couldn't teach anymore? Did you think if the video came out that the law wouldn't apply if you were no longer a teacher? She's a minor!"

I roll my eyes at Cynthia's questions, even though she can't see me, and I flick my gaze to Ty as he watches me.

"How often do you lure her here?" My dad hisses then, ignoring his wife's questions, asking his own.

"She hasn't been here before." Tyler rasps, his voice scratchy, probably from the beating he took. I hate that he didn't fight back, but I understand why. He's not going to fight my dad. Not unless my dad hurts me.

"Is that so? She just happens to be here now, though?" My dad's voice has an arseholey tone to it, and I hate hearing it. It doesn't sound like him at all.

"I asked her here tonight to tell her that I resigned," Tyler admits, and my dad laughs sarcastically.

"Like that makes a fucking difference. You're still an adult, and she's still a child!"

"Stop, Will!" I hiss, turning a death glare his way.

"Kitten, maybe you should go home," Tyler says once again, and I frown at him before Cynthia jumps in.

"Why do you keep calling her Kitten? You need to stop!"

"You stop, Cynthia!" I snap, and she glares at me.

"We are going. Get in the car now, Rhys."

"No!" I hiss and she hisses back.

"I wasn't asking!"

My dad moves toward me then, leaning down to grab my arm, but I swing it back out of reach before Shaun steps in between us.

"Move out of the way, boy." My dad growls, and Shaun shakes his head.

"I'm sorry I can't. She's already told you both that she's not leaving with you, and I won't let another person lay their hands on her if she doesn't want it. It's happened since she was a little girl, and it's not happening anymore."

Cynthia and Will fall silent, and I watch as their shoulders slump in defeat.

"Look, everyone is angry." Shaun tries to smooth things over. "Perhaps you should hear more from Kitten… I mean Rhys, before things get even more out of hand."

I'm too busy focusing on Ty again to pay my parents the attention they want from me. Ty's brow won't stop bleeding. He probably needs stitches or something.

"It's ok, Rhys. I can clean myself up." Ty whispers, and I roll my eyes before standing and pointing to my parents.

"I'm going in search of a first aid kit. You both stay right there. Do not make a move near Ty, or I swear I will never speak to you again."

They both frown at me but give me a nod as I leave the room to search this unfamiliar house.

"In the bathroom!" Shaun yells out, obviously getting the location of the medical kit from Tyler.

I rush down the passage that connects to the living area and see that there is a bedroom up each end, with a bathroom and laundry in the middle. I wish I had more time to explore Tyler's domain, but it will have to wait because right now, I need to stop the bleeding. In the bathroom, I find the first aid kit under the sink, and I quickly return to the living room to find Shaun kneeling by Ty's side, holding a glass of water to his lips. It's caring the way Shaun does it. I imagine he'd do the same for his brother. I'd love it if my guys could look at each other like brothers or family one day. The six of us could be happy. I just know it.

Shaun takes the kit from me when I re-appear, and he sets to work on Ty while I reluctantly turn to look at my parents, who are taking in every little thing we do.

I take a deep breath and spill the whole truth to my parents. I tell them how I blackmailed Tyler. How he avoided me at the Feasts and had rules about us staying away from each other. I tell them about the punishment at the Feast and how I was coerced into having sex with Tyler. I include the night of the humiliation and how I was forced. Raped. Then I tell them how Master Hill has always wanted to get me alone, and I've always refused, except for tonight, because I was trying to protect Ty. Then I tell them how he responded when I said no, and how if Shaun weren't there that the Master probably would have gotten his way.

"But why didn't you just leave that place? No one was forcing you to stay there." Cynthia frowns as she speaks, her dark brows pulling together as she tries to understand my world.

"You know who I am. Being banished from that place would feel like I was slowly dying. That's how I would have felt at the time, anyway. Besides, we know Master has hidden cameras. He would have already had footage of us in the same vicinity. Being coerced into having sex with Ty felt like our only option because there was no way I was going to give myself to Master, and I couldn't fathom a world where I couldn't go to the one place I could be my true self. I wasn't that upset about it, mum. I was... am extremely attracted to Ty. For me, it felt like a win."

"I knew it was wrong, but Rhys is right." Tyler rasps, "It's easy to get swept up in things when you're there. It's a completely different world."

"So, you had sex with one of your students in front of everyone? You defiled her in front of everyone?" My dad hisses, and my shoulders drop. I feel like we are going around in circles.

"Stop!" I yell. "He didn't defile me. Jesus, you have already seen me being defiled last month when we were on that trip. You know what that looks like. Are you telling me that the video you saw was the same thing?"

"Well, the video is different. There were no bystanders, but at that Feast place you're talking about, there were. How do *I* know what he did to you there in front of everyone?" Dad yells back, and I huff.

"You need to trust what I'm telling you. Tyler has never disrespected me."

"He was spanking you!" My dad's bellow is loud, echoing off the walls of Tyler's apartment.

"It's a fucking kink, Will! Don't act like you don't have dirty sex with Cin! Does that mean you're a deviate? No, it doesn't."

"But you're only seventeen." Will's voice drops as emotions take over.

"Yes, and I was eleven when I unknowingly gave my virginity away. You know this about me. You know about my sexcapades. Fucking hell, I have sex at school most weeks."

Cynthia glares at Ty. "Better not be in your office."

"No!" Ty growls, sitting up taller. "I've never been intimate with Rhys away from the sex club."

"You two don't act like fuck buddies, Tyler! You obviously have more going on." Cynthia acknowledges, glaring at Ty.

"I have never had relations with Rhys outside the property of the Feasts. But *yes,* we have formed a bond. I care deeply for her." Ty's admission fills my chest with warmth, and I dart my eyes to Shaun, who is biting back a smirk. He's loving this show of truth right now.

Will scoffs, "How the fuck can you care for her? She's seventeen!"

"Are you serious? What? Am I not good enough to be cared about because I'm five months shy of being a legal adult? Can I not feel love because I'm not old enough? Is that what you're saying? Have you forgotten that I'm not like normal girls, Will? I don't adhere to social norms. I have five fucking boyfriends, for Christ's sake."

"You said that before, but you must be mistaken." There is so much disbelief in my dad's tone that I just want to slap him.

"Five friends with benefits, you mean?" The fact that Cynthia is asking that, even after I admitted it earlier, pisses me off. Do they not believe anything I say? How can I make this clearer to her? To them?

"They aren't friends with benefits. They are *my* guys. I care about each of them. We have something special, and just because it's not a typically normal relationship doesn't mean it's not one."

"I don't think I can hear anymore today. We should go. I need to figure out what to do next." Cynthia turns to Will, who nods in agreement.

"You go. I'm staying." I snap, and their glares turn back to me.

"Like hell you are." Will snaps, and my brows shoot up.

"Unless you're willing to *try* to physically remove me, then I'm staying." I challenge Will, and he frowns.

"I'll call the police. Then this pedo will be taken away, and you will have no choice."

"Will!" Cynthia cries. And fuck am I glad she's not agreeing with him.

"You'd really do that?" I ask Will as my fists ball at my sides. "Because you know if you do, I'll never forgive you. Ever. I will never live in a home with adults that think the only way to get me to submit is by force. I've already had enough of that tonight, thanks. The last guy that did that to me is probably icing his balls right now."

Shaun chuckles, and Ty curses.

"Rhys, I'm the principal of the catholic school. I can't leave my daughter in the home of a former teacher. It's already a risk that I'll lose my job now. I mean, we don't even know if the video was sent to other people as well or just to us."

"I can't leave him like this." I look back at Ty before turning back to Cynthia. "Mum, you know Ty. You know he's a good person. He would never hurt me."

Cynthia sighs, "Even so. It's not right, Rhys."

"Nothing about me is right. Look at everything that has happened. I know you don't deserve the shit storm I bring to your life, but I'm thankful you have been so understanding. And let's face it, deep down, you know I sleep with older people. It's because Ty was a teacher, and you know him personally that this is such a big deal right now."

Cynthia's shoulders slump before she whispers. "I don't know what to do."

Chapter Three

RHYS

T ears burn my cheeks as I cry silently, slumped on the floor of Ty's bathroom. I've made such a mess of everything. I've ruined the lives of foster parents that deserve so much better than what they got when they took me in. I've ruined Ty's life. He's quit his job and could potentially get arrested if the video has leaked further than my parents' email. I broke Marcus' heart when he found out that I was sleeping with his mates. And what for?

Sex?

Love?

Chaos follows me. Sex rules me. My past haunts me. I've had enough, and I just want it to end.

For the first time, when those words flit through my mind, I don't feel the pull of my eternal death looming over me. I don't want to die. I don't want my life to end. I just want to end the chaos. I want to fix the broken parts of me. I want to fix the parts that I broke in others' lives, and I just want to be content.

Is that so much to ask?

My parents left a little while ago, and Shaun not long after. My mum was reluctant to leave me here, of course. I get it. Ty is a man, and I am a child. Ty is a teacher, and I am his student. Ty was my mum's colleague, and I am her daughter. Of course, it went against everything in them to leave me here. They could see I wasn't going to budge, though. They could see my trust in them waning.

Will's outburst scared the shit out of me. I've never seen him so unhinged like that. He was trying to stand up for his daughter. I understand that, but the violence behind his anger was terrifying. It would be better directed at Master Hill, but in Will's mind, the crime isn't with the man that sent him the video. It's with the man that starred in the video with his daughter.

Cynthia and Will promised they won't take any legal action against Tyler tonight and will think about the situation over the next few days, as long as I come home willingly tomorrow. Cynthia called it a compromise. I call it blackmail. An ultimatum of sorts. She didn't exactly say that if I don't come home, she will go to the police, but the insinuation was there. She knows I'm going to do whatever I have to, to keep Tyler out of trouble. So, I agreed to her terms, and she said she'll be back early in the morning with my uniform and stuff for exams so she can take me to school.

Swiping at my tears with the heel of my palm, I pull myself up off the cold tiled floor and turn to face the fogged-up mirror over the sink. Using the towel I had my wet hair wrapped in, I wipe over the mirror until my reflection comes into view. Sighing, I stare at myself, taking in the purple swell on my cheek. All the makeup in the world won't be able to hide it. When people ask, who will I say is to blame? Master Hill? Or my dad? Both contributed to its size and colour. Both inflicted the pain. Only one did it deliberately, though. Only one had intentions of raping me, so he will be the one I will issue the blame on.

I comb my fingers through my long, dark hair. Ty doesn't have a hairbrush. His hair is short. He probably doesn't even need to brush it, so why would he have a hairbrush? As I look through his cabinets, I notice there are no signs that a woman has ever been here. I guess I don't really know much about Tyler Foster. How can I care about a man so deeply when all I know is the taste of his kiss, and the way his muscles bunch and strain as he drives into me? I don't even know what his favourite colour is, or if he has any allergies. Does he drink coffee or tea? What sort of music does he listen to? Does he have brothers and sisters? Are his parents still alive?

I should know this stuff, right? Especially if I care for him so much. It seems strange to have formed a bond with someone I barely know. But then again, maybe I know all the important parts. The parts that matter, like that he's a good person. That he is passionate, loyal, and fiercely protective. Those parts are more important than how he takes his coffee… if he even drinks coffee.

There's time for me to learn these things about him, and I do want to learn them, which is new. I've never really cared about anything other than knowing what a guy's come face looks like. I'm not sure what to make of that. Is my so-called sex addiction cured? Am I changing into a normal girl?

I grin at myself in the mirror.

Normal girls don't have five boyfriends, Rhys. You'll never be normal.

And I'm ok with that.

I leave the confined space of Ty's bathroom, quietly padding across the timber floors down to his bedroom, where he said he would wait for me. It's weird being in his apartment alone with just the two of us. It feels very confronting for some reason. I don't hate it, though. But I'm nervous, something which I'm not used to feeling.

Stepping through the open door of Tyler's bedroom, my eyes scan the space until they land on the dark silhouette sitting in the shadowed corner. My heart flips, and my face heats as my nerves skyrocket.

Jesus Christ, Rhys. Pull yourself together.

"Come here." The deep rumble of Ty's voice meets me across the small space, and I hesitate for a moment, shifting nervously on the spot.

Leaning forward, Ty's face comes into view as he rests his forearms on the tops of his legs. "If you're not comfortable being here, Kitten, it's ok. I won't be offended if you'd rather go home."

I shake my head, licking my lips before I respond. "I'm not leaving you tonight."

"Are you scared of me?" He asks, and I frown.

"No. Why would you think that?"

"You seem out of sorts. Nervous perhaps. Are you realising you don't really know anything about me?"

How does he know that?

"Maybe." I shrug, stepping into the room a little, keeping my eyes on him. He's studying me. His blue eyes are watching my face, my every reaction, and my heart flips again.

Lifting his hand, Ty gives me two strong come here finger waves, the movement sinful in itself. I'm helpless to deny him, and I find my feet slowly stepping one in front of the other until I'm standing right before him.

"I want you to be comfortable, Kitten. So, let's get to know each other a bit more." His fingers link with mine, lifting them between us until his lips press to the back of my hand. I nod, watching the way his eyes remain locked on mine as his lips press to my skin. When he draws back, he tugs on my hand, pulling me forward so I have no choice but to straddle his lap on the armchair in the corner of his bedroom. He isn't wearing a shirt, only boxers, so I can just make out the faint bruising on his chest. It's not as bad as his face, but I don't cringe when I see the wounds and swelling my dad inflicted. I just see a man I can't live without.

"Are you comfortable?" Ty asks as I shift into position, and I give him another nod as I run my fingers over the shadows marring the skin of his chest. "I have an older sister. She's married with a daughter. A spoilt daughter. My mum died when I was twenty-three from cancer. My dad lives up in Queensland in a small fishing town. He hasn't been down to visit us in about eight years. I usually go up there every Christmas." Ty brushes his fingers through my damp hair. "Now you?"

I'm not used to talking about stuff, mainly because I have no interest in it. I've always had this 'information is power' mindset, yet with Ty and my other guys, I feel like I want to share every memory I have, even the dark ones.

"My mum died of a drug overdose when I was 9, which turns out was a deliberate overdose administered by my bio dad, who is Brian, the very man that played '*make Brian's dick feel better*' when I was a little girl." I drop my eyes and suck in a breath, trying to calm the rage that builds inside my chest when I think about what Brian did. "You know my foster parents. I've only just started calling them, Mum and Dad… tonight is the first time in a while that I've called them by their name." I clear my throat because a big, annoying lump is forming when I think about my parents. "I have an older foster sister, Charlotte, and twin foster brothers, Connor and Archie." I glance back up at Ty to see his face soft and his eyes caring as he watches me. "Your turn."

He grins. "I enjoy cooking. I try new recipes at least once a week. I use the gym downstairs to work out and help others reach their fitness goals. I have a small personal training side hustle. I have a house on the outskirts of Redfield that I sometimes stay at. I do a bit of hunting there. Fishing too." He brushes his fingers along my jaw, stopping at my chin as he smiles, and I can't help but smile in return. And blush. Let's not forget that fucking blush. "Your turn, Kitten."

"I'm not good at cooking, but I love to eat." I flash him my teeth, and he chuckles. "I'm good at taking photos. I really enjoy it, actually. I try not to think about the fact that it was Brian who got me into photography and videography. He groomed me well, I guess." I cringe and shake my head before continuing. "The only workouts I get are of a sexual nature, and I don't have a house. Or a job. And I have no idea what I want to do once I graduate from high school… Soooo, yeah, still figuring my life out, I guess."

"Maybe I can teach you how to cook? It can be fun cooking with someone." I smile stupidly at Ty's suggestion. I think I'd love to do domestic stuff with him. "Will you show me some of your photos one day soon? I'd love to see them."

"Uh. I guess. Sure. There's an exhibition happening at the end of the year, but you probably won't be able to go there now, since you're no longer a teacher." My face falls, and I drop my chin to my chest as the reminder of how I've fucked his life up slaps me in the face again.

"Hey," Ty lifts my chin back up with his fingers before cupping my face. "Don't feel bad about that, Kitten. I made the decision to leave. I don't, nor will I ever, regret it. It was time for me to move on, and now I'm going to focus on doing the things that I've always wanted to do but put off because I had to work in a job I never really connected with. It wasn't the first time I've written that resignation letter. It was just the first time I decided to hand it in. Ok?"

I nod, biting the inside of my cheek as my eyes glass over, and I'm thankful when Ty continues talking so I don't have to.

"I like to watch true crime stories and action movies. I read sometimes, and my music taste is old school. I like anything from the Beatles and Van Morrison to Cold Chisel and AC/DC."

I giggle. "Seriously? Are you like eighty?"

He grins. "Thirty-two, and I bet I have better taste in music than you do."

"So, you really are fifteen years older than me, hey? Doesn't my age freak you out?"

"No, Rhys. It's just a number. It doesn't change the connection we have."

My face heats at his words, and I feel strangely emotional all of a sudden, so I steer the conversation back on track.

"I like to watch porn and... porn. And I read smut, so it's basically porn, and my music taste is epic. You'll learn to love it."

He grins. "I'm sure you're going to try and help me love it. Can we go back to the porn?" My brows shoot up, and he chuckles. "Do you watch porn alone, or do you like to watch it with someone else? You know, like your boy band entourage?"

"No, I watch porn alone, thank you very much. And stop calling them that. They are men, just younger than you. They want to meet you, you know?"

"Yeah, I know. Next year, maybe." He grins, and my face falls as my mind flits to our reality. Nervous anxiousness twists inside my chest, and Ty cups both sides of my face, locking his eyes with mine.

"What's wrong, Kitten?"

"How can I make this right?" I whisper, feeling the weight of the ruin I've caused.

"Let's not think about it tonight. We should go to bed. You must be tired."

"Do we have to sleep? I can think of other things we can do." I throw on a fake grin, hoping the whole '*fake it until you make it*' applies when you want to change your mood.

Ty grins, "I'm sure you can think of many other things we can do in bed, Kitten. I've seen you fuck. It's always wild. I love that about you, but I'm curious. Have you ever made love?"

I cringe, and he chuckles.

"What? You don't like that term?"

I shrug. "It sounds a bit cringy, that's all."

"Maybe so, but have you done that before, Kitten?"

I shrug, remembering when Simon whispered in my ear as Garrett took me bare. M*ake love to your man*.

Ty continues, brushing his thumb across my bottom lip. "Will you let me show you what it's like?"

Will I let him show me how to make love? The idea fills me with anxiety, yet I find myself nodding.

"I'm up for it as long as it doesn't involve piss."

Ty throws his head back, laughing. "No piss, I promise."

Chapter Four

Tyler

I knew it was risky asking Rhys to be vulnerable with me. Sure, she finds the term *making love* cringy, but her discomfort isn't really with the term. It's with the act of letting me see past the walls she puts up. She's used to fucking, and at the end of the day, sex is sex. You can think of it as fucking, screwing, banging, or making love, and it still means the same thing mechanically. But emotionally, it's different. And Rhys George doesn't do emotions. Up until recently, that is.

I should probably tell my little brat that I've never done this before. Making love. I've never wanted to be that revealing with anyone before. But I want that now with Rhys George. My year eleven Health class student. My Feast Night Liege. The feisty little brat that has stolen my fucking cold black heart. That's how I knew leaving my teaching career was the right thing to do. I've never felt this way about anyone. Never has another person's soul called to mine. She may call me Daddy. Our roles may have me as the dominant controlling party, but make no mistake, Rhys George owns me. Not the other way around.

She looks nervous as I stare at her. Study her every move. Memorising each feature of her face. Her nerves show in the way her big brown eyes flick to mine, and can't maintain eye contact for long. The way she absent-mindedly sucks in her lower lip, biting it. The way her skin flushes pink from a blush, I know she can feel the heat on her cheeks.

I ignore the purple mark on her cheek. It fills me with anger each time I look at it, so I dance my eyes past it, only taking in the parts of her that aren't marred by the dark world we live in.

Reaching up, I cup her jaw and brush the pad of my thumb over her bottom lip, tugging it free of her bite. Her breathing picks up, her chest rising and falling as her eyes dart from my lips and back to my eyes. She wants to kiss me, but I'm holding her at bay, and it's making her squirm.

"Kitten?" I rasp quietly, gaining the attention of those chocolate pools again. "Would you like me to kiss you?"

We don't normally dance this dance. Our bodies normally guide us, taking what they need from each other, our animalistic needs taking over. Now, though, I'm attempting to control the animal inside us. Hold them at bay to let the true feelings break free, so instead of just going in for the kiss, I'm asking her.

"Yes." She whispers, her voice breathy as she licks her lips.

I grin, moving in closer to hover my lips over hers, all while maintaining eye contact. She's the first to look away. Closes her eyes to break the connection. I let her have it this time. Mainly because it's probably awkward as fuck to kiss with your eyes open.

When my lips finally close the distance, a needy whimper escapes her as she parts her lips and accepts my kiss. I keep it slow. Sensual. Deliberate. I nibble at her lips. I tangle our tongues torturously slow. My hand cups the nape of her neck, my fingers tangling into her hair so I have control of her head, and I give a gentle tug on the strands, showing her that making love doesn't have to be rainbows and butterflies. It can be dirty. It can be a little rough. It can be consuming.

The hair tug does the trick. Her body finally relaxes against mine, her hands gripping my shoulders with excitement as her hips do a small roll over my lap. My other hand presses into the curve of her back, needing her closer as our mouths, lips, and tongues ignite the fire between us.

I kiss her for a long time. It's amazing what a good, thorough kiss can do, getting lost in each other without even taking our clothes off. When I feel her pelvis no longer able to control her need for friction, I shift forward in the chair, gripping the round globes of her arse, and I stand, turning around and lowering Rhys back to the chair.

I break our kiss finally, pulling back to see the pink swell of her lips as she licks over them, her eyes remaining on mine, probably not even realising she's staring at me like that. Grabbing the hem of her Paramore t-shirt, I lift it over her head, revealing all of her creamy satin skin and her two handfuls, her nipples dark and straining with need.

"You're so beautiful, Rhys."

And there goes the eye contact. She doesn't do well with compliments that are so personal. That's ok, though. I'll teach her how to love herself and show her she is more than just sex.

"Eyes on mine." My command isn't a demand like I'd give her in our daddy and brat role. It's spoken gently, but she knows I'm not asking, and that's why she obeys, bringing those dark eyes back to mine. "Don't look away. No matter what. Ok?"

She hesitates for a moment but then nods, so I reward her with my fingers circling her nipple, and she arches forward a little, seeking more.

"Rhys George, you are truly beautiful." I give her the compliment again, and she darts her eyes away again briefly, but brings them quickly back to mine. I can see she wants to say something but isn't sure, so I help her out.

"You can speak, Kitten. If you have something to say to me, I want you to know you can always say it. Ok?"

She nods, and her eyes dart to my lips for a moment before coming back to mine.

"Thank you." Her words are a whisper, but they are still her words. She is thanking me for the compliment, and I can't help but smile.

"You're welcome."

She bites her lip as my fingers dance gently over her nipples, and then I lower my mouth to the pebbled buds. Her breath hitches as her chest arches towards me, her nipple pressing into my mouth with desperate desire. My tongue lashes over one nipple and then the other before I kiss a trail down her creamy skin, seeking the deep pink flesh between her legs.

I'm too hungry to hold back, and I start kissing her over the top of her panties, my tongue flicking over her clit, loving how the fabric is already soaked through. I glance back up at her to see she is watching. Her lips parted as she grinds her pelvis, pressing her needy cunt firmly against my hot mouth.

It doesn't take long for the fabric barrier to piss me off, so I shift back, tugging her panties from her body before spreading her legs wide. She has the prettiest cunt I've ever seen. It's proportionally symmetric and is flushed deep pink from the rush of blood to the area as her arousal grows. I look back up to see she is watching my every move, so I lean forward and blow over her heated flesh.

A whimper escapes her, and I grin, loving how responsive she is to me.

"Don't take your eyes off mine, Kitten. Do *not* close them."

She nods at my command, and I waste no more time, settling my face between her legs, my tongue finally making contact with the swollen, needy bud at the top of her pussy. She tastes like the sweetest nectar I've ever had as I drag my tongue down through her folds, and I revel in her desire as her fingers grip my hair, her loud moan filling the room.

She is perfect.

A gush of wetness meets my tongue, my need taking over, and I lose a little of my control, spearing my tongue as deep as I can go into her opening. She grinds on my face, and my fucking dick jerks like it's already gearing up to spill. I don't stop, though. No way am I letting my dick control this situation. Not when my very need to breathe is fuelled by pleasuring my little brat.

I shift, bringing my fingers up to join the party, sliding two into her molten heat as my tongue flicks back over her clit. Rhys throws her head back as she starts to lose control, so I nip at her clit, the action gaining her attention as she gasps, her eyes coming back to lock onto mine, wide with disbelief.

"Keep your eyes on mine." I remind her, and when she nods, her chest rising and falling quickly, I return my tongue to her needy nub.

She's already so close. I could drag this out, but I don't want to torture her tonight. I want to worship her. Give her what she needs. What she craves. And more.

Adding a third finger, because I know that's a magic number for her greedy cunt, I ease them in, syncing the brush of my tongue and curl of my fingers to send her in a frenzy. Her mouth is open, and she pants, her brow furrowed in that pleasure-pained way that tells me she is consumed by what we are sharing. She grinds her pussy harder, meeting my tongue and fingers with her insatiable hunger, and a moment later, her inner muscles begin to tighten before they start pulsing and sucking my fingers deeper as she comes over my face.

Rhys tries to keep her eyes on mine, but as her pussy contracts, she's unable to maintain the connection, her body ruling her. That's ok, though. What we shared was hot and intimate, and I'm ready to bury myself deep inside her.

"Ty." She pants, latching onto my hair at the top of my head, pulling as she tries to squirm away from me. Oh yeah. I guess I can stop lashing her with my tongue now. It's hard to stop, though. Her taste is so addictive that I'd happily drown in her.

I chuckle against her swollen clit, moving back as I slip my digits from her heat, and she slumps back in the chair.

"You ok, Kitten?"

"Legit, I think I stopped breathing." She pants, and I chuckle as I rise over her creamy flesh, peppering her skin with kisses as I trail up her body.

"You ready for round two?" I hum over her nipple, sucking it in and giving it a little nip. She arches into me, her moan the only answer I need. I rise up, hovering over her mouth as she pants, still trying to catch her breath, and I steal a kiss.

One of the things I love about Rhys George is that she doesn't shy away from tasting herself on my lips. If anything, she kisses me harder, her tongue lapping at my mouth as she moans over her own taste. There's nothing fucking hotter.

"Wrap your legs around me, beautiful." I gently demand against her lips, and she complies, her arms wrapping around my neck at the same time.

I stand, lifting her in my arms and turn, walking over to my bed. My feet hit the end as I kiss her deeply, the heat of her pussy pressing against my hard dick, only the thin fabric of my boxers between us.

Leaning forward, I gently lay my girl down on my bed. How many fucking nights have I dreamed of having her here, getting lost in her, having her scent cling to my sheets? So fucking many, and now it's finally happening.

I didn't want it to happen this way, though. I never wanted to cause her more problems in a life that has already been so hard for her. If I could change my fucking age, I would. I'd do anything for Rhys. Even walk away from her if that's what she needed. It would kill me, but I'd fucking do it.

There's still a big possibility that I'll have to do that. Hell, I may find myself in prison soon, and fuck, if that idea isn't all that bad, if I was put in the same one as that Brian fucker. Her bio dad. I'd kill the motherfucker without hesitation. Sure, I'd see the inside of a cell for the rest of my life, but it would be worth it to get that revenge for Kitten.

This right now, though, me and my little brat, here alone in my shitty apartment, is all we have for the moment. We don't know when things are going to change, so I'm intent on making the most of having her in my bed, of having this time alone together.

"Mmm, the sheets smell like you." Rhys purrs, and I grin. She fucking belongs in my bed.

"I'd really like to make them smell like you, Kitten."

She returns my grin. "Let's make it dirty, then." Her delicate hand reaches out to me, her black nails like claws, eager to dig into my skin.

That's all the invitation I need. I drop my boxers and climb on the mattress, hovering over her, my knees coming to rest in between her spread legs.

"I'm not wearing protection, Kitten. I meant what I said in that barn."

She blushes at my comment and then bites her lips. "Ah... I should probably let you know that I kinda had bare sex with the others."

My brows shoot up. "Really? I thought that obsessive fucker, Grady, was dead set against skin on skin."

"I was able to convince him. I thought you should know, in case you're uncomfortable with it." She shrugs, almost looking worried, but I chuckle.

"As long as they are clean and remain that way, then I don't have a problem with it. I just know that when I'm with you, I want to feel everything. No barriers between us."

She bites her lip again and nods. "No barriers."

I dive down then, taking her lips in another searing kiss. The time for talking is over. I want to drown in her. Taking my time, I explore her mouth with my lips and tongue, building the heat between us by the kiss alone. Before kissing Rhys George, I never realised just how powerful a kiss could be. Thirty-two fucking years old, and I didn't know that a kiss could build arousal like it does between us. Then again, I've never been this attracted to another person before. What we have is more than physical attraction. It's soul deep. It's the kind of attraction that has the ability to end me if it's taken away.

A scary fucking thought, but worth the risk. Rhys is everything.

With my dick hard, prodding her creamy skin, desperate to slide between her legs, I mumble against her lips. "I'm going to claim you now, beautiful. And you're going to claim me right back."

She moans and nips at my lips, nodding, her legs falling wider as her dripping pussy thrusts up, seeking to be filled. That's all the approval I need, so I rise up on one hand, locking eyes with my little brat, and use my other hand to line my cock up.

Then I drive in. We both moan, our eyes widening as my dick squeezes into her tight heat, and her pussy stretches with my girth. Our eyes remain locked, my blue ones hypnotised by her brown ones, and I start to move, slow sensual thrusts that make my dick weep.

"Ty." She moans, lifting her head to press her lips to mine.

I lower down, pressing her into the mattress, taking her lips as I continue my slow thrusts. I don't kiss my sex partners at the Feast. Kitten is the only one I've kissed. That first night we were made to step over the line together felt so natural to take her lips in mine. Just as it does now. Everything about her body withering against me feels natural.

I break our kiss, leaning up to get better leverage, my need to thrust harder and faster, quickly consuming me. My eyes stay on hers, though, never once looking away. I want her to see into my soul. I want her to feel how I'm entranced by her. Feel the love I have for her, and know without a doubt that she can trust me. Always.

I slip my hand between our bodies, seeking her clit because I'm close to blowing, and I want her to join me when I do.

"No." She pants, digging her clawed nails into my bare arse, and my brows hitch.

"No?" I ask, sliding my hand out as I frown in confusion.

"I don't need it. Not right now. I just need you."

Her honesty cracks my heart wide open. She's feeling it. The love. The arousal from our union is enough that she doesn't want or need extra stimulation.

"Just me?" I pant, still thrusting, my drives getting harder, causing her back to arch as her pleasure builds.

"Just you and me right now. You feel…" her eyes glass over a little, and she takes a moment to continue, her pelvis meeting my thrusts with a hungry demand. "Perfect."

I feel her walls clench, her climax building, so I give her what she wants, keeping my eyes on her as I piston deep. Her eyes flutter closed momentarily before she must remember that I wanted her eyes to remain open, and she pries them open, her lips parted as she moans and pants, accepting what I have to give her.

The moment her climax hits, my balls tighten, and I pump profusely, driving her higher as I reach my own heights and explode inside her. Her hot inner walls squeeze me over and over, milking the biggest load I think I've ever released.

It's in this very moment that, for the first time, my mind conjures up thoughts of a future with Rhys by my side, her belly round and heavy, carrying our child. I should punch myself in the head for such a thought, but why should I lie to myself? Sure, she's too young yet, but one day, I'm going to make her my wife and the mother of my children.

Chapter Five

Rhys

Hot water cascades over my head, not for the first time tonight, but this time, the fingers running through my strands aren't my own. They are Ty's. I moan, loving the feel of the pads of his fingers pressing against my skull, his deep chuckle floating up in the small shower we share.

"Stop moaning like that. You're making me hard again."

I giggle, turning in his arms to face him, sneaking a peek at his growing erection.

"I'm not complaining." I grin, and he smirks, shaking his head.

"Stop it, Kitten. We are trying to get clean so we can go to bed."

"And get dirty again?" I ask hopefully, and again he chuckles, shaking his head.

"You're insatiable."

"Yes. Insatiable for you." Standing on my toes, I slowly lick up his cheek, avoiding one of his many grazes, and he chuckles again, trying to pull away before giving my arse a good squeeze.

"So, what did you think about making love? Yay or Nay?"

Oh, my lord, he actually looks nervous. This is new for Ty. He's the older experienced guy with all the confidence, yet here he stands, looking worried that I'm going to cringe again.

"I really enjoyed it, *Daddy*, but can we call it something different?"

His lips thin at the same time as he smiles. He's reacting to me calling him Daddy again. I fucking love calling him that. "Like what?"

"I don't know. You're the teacher. Don't you know words that would better suit?"

Ty chuckles, running his hands up my back as the water falls down over us. "Well, how did it make you feel?"

"Hmmm…" I purse my lips. "It made me feel vulnerable, I guess. Exposed. And loved."

Ty smiles, his straight white teeth flashing. "You felt loved?"

I nod. "Yes."

Again, he smiles. "I felt loved too."

His admission makes me blush, and fuck if the flare of his eyes at seeing my blush doesn't make me feel good. This whole blushing thing isn't so bad, I guess.

"How about I just say, let me love you?" His tone is raspy. Raw, like there is emotion behind it. His eyes study me, looking for a reaction, and I can't hold back my smile as I nod. Is he saying he loves me?

"It's less cringy." I grin, and he chuckles. "I think I may have done it before." I study him this time for his reaction, and his brows lift to his hairline.

"Made love?" He shakes his head before correcting. "I mean, let someone love you?" He corrects, and I nod.

"Kinda. I'm not totally sure, but I think maybe the night I turned up to the Feast with no mask or invitation, and Shaun took me back to his house, he…" I bite my lip and drop my eyes from Ty's, but his fingers meet my chin, lifting my face back up so I can't avoid his gaze.

"He what?" When I keep my mouth clamped shut, Ty's face softens. "You can tell me anything, Kitten. I'm well aware I share you. You don't have to hide things from me."

A slight smile tugs at my lips. Is it really ok for me to be so greedy and have five guys while they only have one? Me?

"That night, Shaun looked at me the same way you did. It was hard for me to relax. I felt exposed, but I trusted him. It was the closest thing to what we just did." I shrug, and he smiles. I could tell him about Garrett, but that was a little different with three others in the room.

"I'll give it to Fuckboy. He really does care about you."

I giggle. "Are you ever going to call him by his name?"

Ty shrugs. "Maybe one day, but right now, calling him Fuckboy is too fun."

He leans down and kisses me then. His warm lips mingled with droplets of water is an enticing effect. I could easily drop to my knees and take his hardening cock into my mouth, but strangely, I kind of feel sated. That desperate need to fuck isn't there right now. My need to just kiss and hug him is more overwhelming than anything else.

Weird.

Ty turns off the shower and gives my arse a wet slap before pushing the door open and grabbing us both a towel. I stay inside the shower with the towel draped over my shoulders as I watch him dry off. He really is a magnificent sight. Strong, hard abs. Well-defined arms. Toned legs. He's any woman's wet dream.

Once he's towelled himself off, he wraps the towel around his waist, securing it in place before lifting his blue eyes to me.

"Come here, beautiful."

I step out of the shower, and he takes my towel before proceeding to dry my body.

"Uh… I can do that myself, you know. I graduated from shower skills in like grade one or something."

Ty chuckles. "Let me take care of you while I have you to myself."

I shrug and grin. "Suit yourself."

And he does. He slowly dries my body, arms and legs, getting down on one knee to lift my foot and dry that, too. It's intimate, what he's doing with me. Taking care of me. Almost as if he's worshipping me. My face heats at the thought, but he doesn't notice this time. His eyes focused on the area he's drying.

I want to tell him I love him. It's still a strange concept to me, but for some reason, I can't say the words to him. It's my self-doubt rearing its ugly head, trying to control me. So I try to shut it down.

I'm surprised when he uses the towel to dry off my dripping hair, and when he's done, he sweeps my long locks over my shoulder to press his lips to my neck.

"I love seeing you like this, Kitten. Your natural beauty is breathtaking."

And now my legs turn to jelly. Fuck, he knows exactly how to make me putty in his hands. I typically hate compliments, yet here I am, loving his words. Loving him.

Ty leads me back to his bedroom, going to his drawer and pulling out one of his Nike t-shirts before tugging it over my head and helping me thread my arms into it.

"I want you in my clothes." He rasps, and I grin. It's such a guy thing. Ayden does the same with Lexi. I wonder if I say I want him in my clothes if he'd comply? I smirk inwardly at the stupid thought. Maybe now is a good time to tell him I stole his red soccer jersey?

Ty turns and changes the bedsheets quickly, and I step in to help him, my heart fluttering at the domestic task we share together.

By the time we slip under the covers, exhaustion sweeps over me and Ty notices, pulling me close as we wrap tight in each other's arms.

"You ok, Kitten?" His voice is quiet, a hint of concern in his tone.

I nod against his chest, inhaling his unique Ty scent. "Is it bad that I don't want the morning to come?"

"No. Not bad. I feel the same way." He presses his lips to the top of my head, and I squeeze him tight, never wanting to let go.

I try not to think about today's events and focus on what we shared here tonight. It was perfect. The only thing that would make it even more perfect would be if I were wrapped in the loving arms of Marc, Shaun, Garrett and Sy, too.

I sleep heavily, almost like I pass out or something, and morning comes way too quickly, a loud banging startling us both from sleep. Ty sits up, scrubbing a hand over his face as he checks his phone on the table next to his bed.

"Christ. Your mum's already here. It's only seven."

She must have sent him a message. Hopefully she's not accompanied by police officers. I don't think I could handle that right now.

The banging sounds again, and I groan while Ty chuckles at me.

"I've just sent her a message to say we are getting up." Ty does just that, swinging his legs over the side of the bed and standing up into a stretch before turning his glorious front to me. Fuck. A girl could get used to seeing that every morning. "Come out in a few minutes, Kitten. Take your time." Leaning down, Ty kisses my forehead, but I loop my arms around his neck and drag him back down to the bed. Chuckling, he squirms but accepts the kiss I give him, relaxing on top of me.

"You're not helping my morning wood right now, Kitten," Ty mumbles against my lips, and I giggle.

"Can't we pretend she's not here? She might go away."

"Actually, I'm pretty sure she'd break down my door. Never underestimate a mother's fury, Kitten." He bops my nose as he rises off the bed, leaving me feeling cold and empty. I pout, and he chuckles, stepping into a grey pair of sweatpants before shooting me a wink and leaving me in his bed to let my mum into his apartment.

I take a moment to lie there in his sheets, wishing away all of our problems so we can be left alone to enjoy each other. But of course, Cynthia Rogan smashes away the little daydream as her loud voice floats down the hall to the bedroom.

"Get up, Rhys! We don't have time to drag our feet today."

Ugh! FML!

I roll out of bed and stomp out of the room, acting very much my age as I enter the living area to see Cynthia eyeing Ty as he makes coffee.

"Morning." I sing, faking a cheery mood. No one can be cheery before fucking 9am. I don't know why they make teenagers go to school so damn early.

Cynthia darts her head in my direction, looking me over and taking in Ty's oversized t-shirt and probably a bird's nest of hair on my head. She frowns, holding out a bag.

"Here's your clothes and some extra make-up. You'll need to cover that bruise."

Ah, so we are hiding truths. Fun.

Ty looks over at me and frowns, holding up a mug. "Coffee? Tea? Hot Chocolate?"

"No thanks. I'll take a joint if you have it, though." I smile, and Cynthia rolls her eyes as Tyler frowns.

"No, I don't, and you need to stop doing that shit, especially at school." He scolds, and I grin. Oooh, teacher Tyler is in the house. Cynthia's brows shoot up in surprise at Ty's words, but she doesn't say anything.

"But *Daddy*, it makes it more tolerable." The innocent voice I put on is accompanied by fluttering lashes, and Ty curses as Cynthia's eyes widen.

I'm feeling like a smug bitch until I hear Tyler's footsteps and see him round the bench, stalking towards me with fury on his face.

"Oh, shit." I turn to flee, but he grabs my arm and drags me to his side to speak quietly.

"Do me a favour, Kitten. Keep our play between us. There's no need to torment your mother even more." His words aren't harsh, even though his stance looks like I'm getting in trouble right now. I could be a brat and push the boundaries, but I don't want to. He's right. I'm only fuelling the fire with my mum by teasing her with my brattiness.

"Fine," I whisper, my eyes darting up to his. "But only if you promise to punish me for it."

He growls low and quiet, so Cin can't hear, and gives me a slight nod before releasing my arm. I bite my lip, turning back to take the bag Cin brought, and I flee to the bathroom to get ready.

I make quick work of my makeup, lining my eyes, just not as dark as I usually do, and I leave off the lipstick today. I'm just not feeling the black lip vibe right now. I feel like they should be hot pink, which is really fucking weird, but hey, my soul is a little brighter right now. No need to question it too much.

After painting my lashes and covering the bruise as best I can, I look at my hair, and instead of starting on my twisted buns, I throw my head forward and comb my fingers through my hair, scooping it together and securing it in a messy ponytail.

I feel different, and I want to look different. I don't know any other way to explain it, but once I'm dressed and entering the living area again, Cynthia's eyes widen as she takes me in. Feeling a little self-conscious—because, let's be honest, breaking that habit is going to take a long fucking time—I dart my eyes to Tyler, and he grins as he brings his steaming mug to his lips to sip whatever hot drink he made himself.

"You're going to school like that?" Cynthia asks, and I grin.

"You've been asking me to dress normally for years. I thought you'd be happy." I state, walking up to the counter and glancing at Tyler as he watches me. He looks pleased with the way I'm presenting myself.

"Well, yes, but it's a very sudden change, Rhys."

I frown and turn to her. "Not really. Those who matter have seen me like this lately. Why should I keep dressing in a way that I feel doesn't represent who I am anymore?"

Her brows shoot up again. "You feel different about yourself?"

"Parts of me. Do we have to talk about this right now?" *Or ever*, I think to myself while Cynthia relaxes her shoulders.

"No, of course not. If you're ready, I thought we could grab some breaky before we head to school."

I nod at my mum and turn my eyes back to Ty. The muscles in his arms are flexing with the way he's leaning over the bench top. Fuck, he's one sexy man. Maybe I can ditch my exam and stay here with him… forever?

"Can I have a minute with Ty before we leave? I can meet you out in the car." I mutter to Cynthia, and she huffs.

"I'll be at the end of the hall waiting at the front door. Don't be long." She shoots Ty a glare before she turns and walks from the room, her heels clicking on the timber floors until she reaches the end of the hall.

My eyes drop to the bench between Ty and me, and with it, my heart, as an overwhelming sadness washes over me. Shit, maybe I should have gone with the black lipstick after all.

"Hey. What's wrong?" Ty's voice urges me to glance back up, and my eyes burn with stupid, hot tears.

"I feel like I'm not going to see you again."

Ty's lips thin, and he rounds the bench, coming to me, cupping my face with his hands.

"Don't think like that. I'll make sure we see each other. We may have to lie low for a bit and be extra careful, but I need you, Kitten. I'm not going anywhere."

I nod because I can't manage words, and then Ty leans downs and presses his lips gently to mine. It's an emotional kiss, turning desperate like the touch of our lips and tongues are trying to say the words we can't seem to say out loud.

I love you.

It's strange to feel this way yet be crying over it. It's an overwhelming feeling. Like the slightest bit of happiness we get will be ripped away from us at any moment. My salty hot tears slip from my eyes, and when Ty pulls back, his own eyes swim with emotion I've only seen on him one other time. The night of my humiliation.

"I'm only a phone call away, ok?" He rasps quietly, and I nod, sucking in a steadying breath to try and pull my shit together. "I belong to *you*, Rhys. You own my heart. Always."

His words make me want to crumble to the floor and sob, knowing he can feel it, too. The pending doom. Something bad is going to happen, and this feels like goodbye.

I nod as I slowly back away from him, not wanting to drag my eyes from him, but as I reach the mouth of the hall, I turn and face my mum, who is standing there looking at me, probably overhearing my hushed conversation with Ty.

I walk slowly. The magnetic pull of Tyler behind me is overwhelming with each step I take away from him. When I reach Cin, she reaches back to open the door, but I can't go. I can't leave yet, because if this is goodbye, I need Ty to know how I feel.

A sob escapes my throat, and I drop my bags, turning quickly and running back towards Ty, where he now stands watching me at the other end of the passage.

"Rhys?" Cynthia calls in confusion, but I ignore her as Ty opens his arms for me, and I leap at him. He catches me, and I wrap my legs around my waist as I bury my head in the crook of his neck.

"I love you, Ty," I whisper, and he pulls back, cupping my chin with one hand.

"I love you too, Rhys. So fucking much."

"Why does it hurt so much?" A sob escapes me, and Ty's eyes reflect the same emotions.

He wipes a tear away with his thumb and shakes his head. "I don't know, beautiful. Maybe because things are so uncertain right now. But just remember, whatever happens, I fucking love you."

I kiss him, not caring about Cynthia or her huffing back down the hall. She's not going to ruin this moment for me.

There is so much difference between this kiss and our arousal kisses. It's just as powerful, but in a different way, and I know I'll die if I never get to share a kiss like this with Tyler again.

Dramatic? Fuck yes! This is emotional shit I'm not used to dealing with. Sex is so much easier. Love… is hard.

Chapter Six

Rhys

C ynthia drives us to Maccas for breaky. It takes me most of the ten-minute drive to pull myself together, and I even have to fix my fucking eye liner by the time we pull up. It doesn't help that Cynthia is staring at me like I've grown two fucking heads. I know my behaviour isn't *Rhys* normal, and she knows it too.

We walk inside, not speaking to each other, and she orders the food before leading me through the restaurant, to the back corner, away from the breakfast crowd. I have to hide my smirk because she takes a seat at the very table that I sat at last week with the guys, where Garrett made me come on his four fingers.

If I didn't actually like Cynthia, I'd tell her about that just to piss her off, but I do like her, which is why all this stuff with Tyler is so hard. I love him, and I love her. I don't want to choose between them.

I take a small bite of my hash brown when we sit at the table, while Cin stares into her black coffee.

"Why do they call you Kitten?" Cynthia's question startles me, and my eyes dart up to find her looking at me.

"It's my name at the sex club."

"So why was it used on the video that Julie sent? How does she know you are called Kitten? Does she know you go to that place?" Cynthia pushes her coffee to the side like she has no intention of drinking it, and I frown as I think over her questions.

"I… don't know. Brian said Julie has been watching me, so maybe she's done her own investigating?"

Cynthia nods, her eyes falling to her hands, where she picks at her nail for a moment before speaking again.

"I can't let you see Tyler again."

"What?" Even though I was kind of expecting to hear her say those words, it fucking hurts to hear.

"You have to wait until you're older, Rhys. It's the safest option for both you and Tyler."

"Older, as in eighteen?" My words are a whisper, like I'm too scared that she'll say thirty or something.

"I'd prefer if you wait until you graduate from secondary school. Being a student, even though you're eighteen, will still have bad repercussions."

"Bad repercussions for you, you mean?" I snap, and her dark brows lift.

"Waiting until you graduate will be more suitable for *everyone*. You obviously care about him. Do you want him to go to prison, Rhys? Because if anyone finds out, that's exactly what will happen. It will ruin his life."

Tears well in my eyes, knowing she is speaking the truth. I don't want Ty to go to prison, but the idea of waiting a whole year feels excruciating.

"So, you're not going to tell the cops?"

Cynthia shakes her head, sighing. "Not at this stage. But if we find out he's hurt you or swayed you in any way-."

I cut her off. "He hasn't. He would never hurt me. He has saved me, mum."

Her face softens as she looks at me, and she reaches over the table, taking my hands in hers.

"I just want you to be happy, and safe, and free of all this pain you have already suffered. I know it hurts to think about not seeing him for another year, but if you love him, you will wait, sweetheart. And he will wait for you. Sure, there will be gossip after you graduate when people find out you two are seeing each other, but he won't go to prison. That's the important thing, right?"

I nod, knowing she is right. It fucking sucks big hairy dog's balls. But, yes, she is right. It doesn't do anything but make my heart ache in unimaginable pain.

"Can I skip today's exam? I just want to go home." I whisper as tears spill over again.

"No. You have responsibilities, and you need to stick to them. Once you get through the next couple of days, you can stay home all you like."

I want to pout, but I can't even bring myself to be a brat right now. It just really fucking hurts. I slump back in the seat, pushing my food away.

"I'm not hungry."

Cynthia frowns. "You need to eat. You have a big exam to get through this morning."

I shrug. "I don't care. I'm not hungry."

Again, she sighs and takes the food, putting it back on the tray. I take my phone out of my pocket, seeing that it's flat. I haven't even bothered to look at it after the whole incident last night. I hope Shaun is ok after everything that happened.

"My phone is flat. Do you have a charger?"

Cynthia shakes her head and holds out her hand. "No, but I'll hold it for you. You can't take it into the exam, anyway." I nod, slowly handing it to her.

"Am I going to get it back?" I ask because I get the feeling she is confiscating it, just like the teachers do at school. They lock them in the school safe and keep them ransom. The ransom payment is good behaviour.

"We'll see. If you're not going to eat, we may as well head into school early. You can sit in my office and study for the exam."

I roll my eyes but follow her out of the booth, dread still sitting like a heavy weight in my gut.

After forty-five minutes of studying in Cin's office, she escorts me to the stadium where the exams are. All the students are congregating outside, waiting to be let in, their eyes on their phones as they wait, and there's a hype in the air that's not typical for exam day. People are looking at me, probably because I look different today. My eyes are painted with the same amount of liner and mascara as the rest of the girls, just not the same amount that I typically wear. My lips are bare, my hair basic. A hush falls over the crowd as all eyes fall to me, and I start to squirm. I should have dressed normally. The student body isn't ready for me to have a makeover.

Cynthia grips my arm when she notices my guys off to the side, and I frown at her as she pulls me in the opposite direction. I look back over my shoulder to them, noticing Shaun taking a few steps in my way, but Marcus reaches out and grips his shoulder, holding him back. My eyes meet Simon's and his lips thin, looking almost sympathetic, and then my eyes dart to Garrett who is standing rigid, his shoulders tense as he glares at me, a bruise marring his left eye.

What the fuck?

As the doors open, my mum pulls me inside while the other teachers call for students to fall in line alphabetically.

"Why didn't you let me go see the guys?" I frown, snatching my arm from Cin's grip.

"We don't have time. The exam is about to start. Go take your seat. You know which table is yours." Cynthia's cold tone makes the dread feel heavier.

I don't go to my seat and instead follow her up the front of the hall.

"What's going on? Why are you being a bitch to me?"

"Remember who you are talking to right now." Cynthia hisses, spinning on me and gritting her teeth.

"Right. Principal Rogan. I forgot I have to wait until school's over to speak with my mum." I snap, but she just glares at me. "My mistake. Not my mum, I guess. Just Cynthia."

My words are a low blow, and I can't even stop myself from saying them because I'm fucking hurting right now and confused as fuck. My words have the effect I was hoping for, though, pain slashing across Cynthia's face at hearing me take back her title as my mum. I spin on my heel, glad the crowd of students is loud enough to drown out Cynthia's voice as she calls for me, and I start weaving through the rows of tables.

"Whore." A male voice snickers beside me, and I turn to look for who said it. No one in my vicinity is looking at me, so I keep walking.

"Slut."

I spin again, trying to find who said the words. A girl's voice this time. Again, I don't know who said it. Frowning, I keep walking, wanting to get to my seat.

"Oh Daddy, does it feel better?"

I spin to glare at the voice, and this time I come face-to-face with Daniel, Lexi's ex-best friend's vile boyfriend slash forced fiancé: it's a whole fucked up story that I don't have time to get into right now.

"What the fuck did you say?" I sneer at Daniel, and he chuckles like he's all fucking that.

"Oh Patty, suck it like a lollipop."

Daniel throws Brian's words from the video at me, and I flinch back, almost tripping over and stumbling into someone behind me.

"Give it to Daddy." The deep voice of some other guy I don't know rasps against my ear, and I throw an elbow back, turning on him with wide eyes as everyone around me starts laughing.

"Sit down, please, everyone." My mum's voice fills the room coming from the speakers, and students hurry to sit, leaving me standing there in shock.

"Rhee, I got you." Marcus' voice wraps around me, and I turn to him, looking up into his brown eyes.

"What's going on?" I whisper, and he shakes his head.

"Let's get you to your seat." He whispers back, placing his hand on the small of my back, urging me forward. I let him guide me, my eyes darting around to see most students peering up at me, their heads cast low so they don't make it obvious. It's obvious to me, though. So are the words "Sick bitch," that floats to me from somewhere.

Marcus gets me to my seat, sitting me down, before darting off to his own as the exam starts, leaving me in a state of utter fucking confusion.

Something has happened, and I know deep in my gut it has to do with the video Julie leaked, and not about Tyler. That's a good thing, right? If people find out about Ty, it would be devastating for him. Not me. I don't fucking care what happens to me. I just care about him.

It's impossible to concentrate on the exam, so I accept that it is another exam failed. What's the point, anyway? What does it matter if I pass or fail at this point? My life is falling apart, and I couldn't care less about school or these stupid fucking exams.

For two hours, I sit and stare at nothing. I think about Tyler mostly because what we shared last night is my happy place right now. I felt safe there. I felt happy. The outside world didn't matter in the slightest.

When the exam finally finishes, and the hall fills with chatting students, insults assault my ears from all directions, and I can't bring myself to stand from the small desk. Marcus and Garrett reach me first, pushing through the crowd and help me out of my chair. I'm too stunned to stand by myself, apparently, and then Shaun and Simon reach us, surrounding me as the hall empties out.

"What the fuck is going on?" I whisper, finally meeting four sets of concerned gazes.

"Eric Carter won the contest," Shaun explains. "A new video came out this morning about half an hour before the exam started. Eric won the money."

My brows shoot up. "So, Julie went through with it anyway, even after I turned up at the prison?"

"It looks like it," Garrett grumbles, and my shoulders drop.

"Right. Well, that's that then." I whisper, looking at the floor and shaking my head. "You guys don't have to hang around me, you know. You don't have to deal with my bullshit." I move to step past them, but Garrett's firm grip wraps around my wrist.

"We aren't going anywhere, Rhys. This doesn't change anything between us."

I crane my head back, meeting his icy-blues. "You should reconsider. Being associated with me and my depravity isn't socially strategic."

"We don't care about anyone else, Kitten. We only care about you." Shaun wraps his arms around my waist from behind, and I feel like collapsing and getting lost in him. In all of them. He presses his warm lips to my cheek, and I briefly let my eyes flutter shut, revelling in his touch and missing the quiet moments we don't seem to be getting much of lately. Unfortunately, now when I close my eyes, all I see is Tyler's face when I had to walk away from him earlier this morning, and the centre of my chest aches.

With a frown, I pry my lids back open. "Did you tell them about last night?" I whisper, even though I know they can all hear me.

"Yeah. I told them that Master Hill sent your olds a video of you and Skipper, and they found out who Skipper is and went around to his house last night when we were there."

So Shaun didn't reveal Tyler's identity? That's good. So far, it seems that it's only my parents who know. The fewer people who know, the better.

"Cherry, I'm sorry about that happening. I know how much you care for that guy. Did your parents call the cops?" Simon's hazel eyes are filled with concern as he tucks his blonde hair behind his ear. It's gotten really long. I hope he doesn't cut it. I like the look.

"No. For now, they have agreed to keep it quiet as long as he hasn't hurt me. They want me to…" I swallow a couple of times, trying to dislodge the lump in my throat, "They want me to stay away from him until I graduate."

"But you're eighteen in, like, five months, aren't you? Why can't you see him then?" Marcus is too perceptive.

"Cynthia is worried about how it will look for the principal of a catholic school to have a daughter at the school who is dating a man."

Marcus nods, but still frowns a little, and I'm not sure if I've convinced him. It doesn't matter, though, because the clacking of heels across the stadium floor tells me that Cin is on her way over to us.

"Time to go, Rhys." She calls, and I roll my eyes, making my guys grin.

"She has my phone. I get the feeling she's not going to give it back. I'll try to message you guys from my laptop later."

Shaun squeezes me from behind, his hand coming up to grip my chin, tilting my head around so he can kiss me from the side. I want to turn in his arms and keep kissing him, but even with Cynthia still a good distance away, I can hear her huff.

Breaking the kiss, Shaun locks his steel-grey eyes with mine. "Don't worry about Eric Carter and the other fuckwits. We will sort those fuckers out for you, Kitten."

I grin, giving him a slight nod. There's nothing they can do now that the secret is out, but if they want to make heads roll, I'm not going to stop them.

Marcus steps up to me as Shaun moves away, cupping my face with both of his hands. "Rhee, I'm sorry there are so many arseholes in this place. You are better than all of them combined. Don't forget how much I love you. How much *we* love you."

I smile, losing myself in Marcus' brown gaze before he leans in for his own kiss. Even though his body is tense, radiating with anger, his touch is gentle and loving. When he pulls away, I can tell he'd prefer to throw me over his shoulder and run off with me, but he steps back, letting Simon push in to claim my lips.

I can't hold back the giggle at his enthusiasm. Sy is a ball of energy at the best of times, and right now is no different. He kisses me thoroughly, his fingers fisting in my ponytail before he pulls back to stare into my eyes. "I'll video call you later. We can play Simon Says or something."

I giggle and nod, earning myself another deep kiss from Simon before he reluctantly lets me go.

"Rhys George, it's time to go now!" My mum bellows across the hall, and I turn to shoot her a fucking dagger. Bitch better back off when a girl is saying goodbye to her harem!

"Quick, Baby Girl. Give me those lips before your mum comes over here and rips our heads off."

I turn back, grinning up at Garrett. "She can try, but I'll go ham on her arse."

He chuckles, gripping the lapels of my blazer and tugging me to his chest. "I'm not gonna lie. I'd like to see you go ham on someone. Such a firecracker."

"You gonna tell me what happened to your eye?" I ask, and his smile drops. He remains silent for a few moments, like he's trying to figure out if he should lie to me or not, but then he chooses the truth.

"My old man got home early this morning. Apparently, he was let out of prison yesterday, and he took the early train back here." Garrett shrugs, "The black eye was a reminder to me that he hasn't forgotten that I was the one who got him thrown in prison in the first place."

"Shit Gar. Are your mum and sisters, ok?"

He nods, "Yeah. He won't touch them. Not for a while, anyway. I have a bit of time up my sleeve to figure out a way to get rid of him again."

That is so fucked. Why do they let people like Garrett's dad out of prison in the first place? I hate that Garrett has to worry about my bullshit on top of his family stuff. Hell, all the guys have worries, except for maybe Marcus. Shaun's mum is sick and getting worse, plus his dad is on his case about dropping out of school to work on their farm. Simon's parents are getting divorced, and both are moving away, wanting him to go with them. Even after they have ignored him most of his life, they expect him to give up his life to move somewhere else just for them to ignore him again. My guys deserve better. So much better.

"Be careful, ok? I can't bear the thought of you getting hurt, Gar."

He tugs me closer, lowering his head as I tip mine back to match his move.

"Ok, Baby Girl. You be careful too." His deep voice is soft and raspy, and then he claims my lips in a searing kiss that my mum should probably not see, but I can't bring myself to put a stop to. It's impossible. When Garrett Cole kisses you, it's with his whole soul.

Chapter Seven

Rhys

For some stupid reason, my parents think they can ground me! Ground me! Yes, fucking ground me! I've never been grounded in my life, even after all the bullshit I've pulled, never once have they grounded me, yet here I am, wallowing in my bedroom with no phone, no laptop, and no way to contact my guys or Lexi. What the fuck do my parents think they are going to achieve by grounding me?

Will thinks I need some time to think without being consumed by sex and boys. Pfft! Have you ever heard of anything more ridiculous? Does he fucking forget who I am? Ever since the age of eleven, my life has been consumed by sex. It's controlled me. How could he think that by taking it away, it will help?

Does he think this is a version of rehab? Am I going through withdrawal now? Fuck yes, I am, just not in the typical way. My sex addiction has eased. It's the addiction to five particular guys that has me pacing my room, about ready to start peeling my skin from my bones.

I feel cut off. Like a prisoner. I have no idea if Ty has tried to contact me. Is he still in Fox Pines, or has he gone to his house in Redfield already? Does he think I'm ignoring him? I need to fucking ring him. This is making me crazy!

I'm being a total brat to the 'rents. When I got home from school with Cin earlier today, I refused to talk to her. I ignored her when she asked me to come and have lunch in the kitchen with her, and I slammed my bedroom door in Will's face when he asked me to come out of my room for dinner. I didn't even eat the food they had Connor and Archie bring me. I am on strike, damn it!

A knock at my door has me stilling and snarling. I'm about to yell go away, but the damn door opens, and Char pops her head in.

"I need to talk to you." Her green eyes lock with mine, and I nearly laugh. They are bright green, not at all a natural colour. She is wearing contacts to match her damn hair.

"Does it have to do with my escape or the new puppy you overheard the olds talking about recently?"

She rolls her eyes at me and slips into the room, quietly closing the door.

"Evie Prattle called me earlier today. She told me about the video leak from that stupid Julie bitch saying it was you in it."

My shoulders drop at Char's words, and I slump cross-legged to the floor in defeat. This shit is never going to go away. I'm going to be forever known as the little girl who fucked her dad.

"She wants to help." Char sits down on the carpet in front of me. "She even went to the CEOs of Angel Org and told them your story. Apparently, they are ruthless bitches who don't care about stepping over the line to help other women, especially with this stuff."

"The CEOs want to help me?" My brows disappear into my hairline at Char's words. "But why? I'm no one special. Surely there are others that need their help more than I do?"

"Apparently, every case is important. You have a whole organisation of badass women who want to help you bring down your old foster parents." Char is normally a grumpy bitch, so it's nice to see the genuine smile on her face.

"How can they help me?" I whisper. It sounds too good to be true.

"Well, Bec and Amanda, that's their names. The CEOs. They are strategizing on how to best approach the situation. Meanwhile, Evie said she heard about what some of the kids were saying to you in the exam this morning, and she is gathering her troops to castrate some guys."

"Really? Fuck, Evie is a badass. You'd never know it from looking at her. She looks so fucking prim and proper, but she is fucking scary. Can you make sure she destroys Daniel Stone? He had a lot to say to me, but I don't really care about that. He's fucking with one of Lexi's friends, and he needs to pay."

Abbey Delany is Lexi's ex-best friend. She ditched Lexi at a time when Lexi needed her most, and Abbey turned on her, banding together with some bitches to try and bring Lexi down when she had already hit rock bottom. It was out of character for Abbey, and it turns out that there's this whole weird, arranged marriage thing happening between Abbey's family and Daniel's. It's unheard of here in Australia, but it's fucking happening, and to make it worse, Daniel is holding it against Abbey, no longer treating her nicely. He's made no attempt at hiding what an arsehole he is to her, and she just takes it. I know for a fact that he has left bruises on her body. The only problem is that she won't speak up against him because her parents have threatened that they will be forced to marry the day of her eighteenth birthday if Abbey doesn't stay in line. Right now, Abbey is banking on the arranged marriage being held off until they finish uni. I get the feeling she would rather die than be forced into that fucked up marriage.

"Sure, I'll drop his name to Evie." Char grins. This shit excites her.

"So when will I know what's happening with the CEOs?"

Char shrugs. "I'll keep in contact with their organisation, don't worry. I'll let you know as soon as I hear something."

I'm feeling even more emotional than I already was, and I leap at Char, wrapping my arms around her neck, causing her to squeal from my abrupt hug. Then we both laugh. It feels good, but it's short-lived because all I want to do is talk to my guys and tell them about Angel Org. I fucking can't, though, because my phone is being held captive.

"I need my phone, Char," I whine as I pull back from our hug. "I need to speak with my friends."

"You mean your reverse harem, don't you?" She wags her brows, and I roll my eyes.

"Yes, them. And Lexi."

Char sighs. "Well, the olds had your phone earlier. They were listening to a voice message that Julie left some time today."

"What?" I squeak, nearly bolting up.

"Yeah. From what I heard, Julie said that Brian has been put into separation because of you, and she can't contact him, so all bets are off, and you'd better watch your back."

"Fuck. Is separation like solitary confinement or something?" I whisper, and she nods.

"I think so. It's like isolation." Char shrugs.

"Do you know if Cin went to the cops about the message?" I stand from the carpet and start pacing again.

"She did, yeah. They are sending regular patrols to drive by the house just to be safe."

"I really need to speak with my guys," I whisper more to myself than to Char.

"Oh, and the new pet? It's been put on hold. Apparently, the girl they want to bring into the family is safe right now in a good group home, and since she's only ever responded well to Cin and Will and no other foster carers, the home is happy to wait until things settle down here before releasing her to us."

"How the fuck do you know this, Char?" I'm stunned, staring at my big sister, who always has more information than she needs.

"If I told you, I'd have to kill you." She beams, standing from my floor and poking her tongue out. She giggles to herself as she slips back out my door, and I remain rooted on the spot in shock.

Brian is in isolation.

Julie knows it's my fault.

All bets are off.

I need to watch my back.

The CEOs at Angel Org, Bec and Amanda, want to help me.

Evie Prattle wants to help me.

And when I can get my bullshit under control, I'm getting a new sister.

Let's not even get started about the whole Vixen's Lodge crap.

Fuck me! My brain can't cope with this information overload.

I spend the next thirty minutes pacing my room, chewing on my nails and effectively destroying the black Night Magic polish. I'm cagey as fuck. I want out. I could go. Slip out my window and make a run for it. It's not like I haven't done it before, but the whole Tyler situation is causing me to hesitate. Even though my 'rents haven't said so, I'm scared that I'll push them over the line, and they will expose Ty and go to the cops or send me away to live somewhere else, so I'm not their problem anymore.

The thing is, it's really fucking hard to fight my urges. The need to fuck isn't there, but the need to run into the arms of five particular males has me nearly screaming.

At some point, I start losing my shit and start dancing around my room to absolute silence.

Maybe I am crazy.

Even if I am, I'm not sure that I care.

I bounce on my bed for a while and try to nail a headstand, but never achieve that goal. Then I decide that perhaps an orgasm might help, so I go to my drawer and stare down at Big Jim.

"Hey big fella. You wanna play?"

He fucking doesn't answer! How fucking rude of the silicone masterpiece!

Ugh! I can't even get wet by looking at him. If I had my laptop, I could watch porn, but then I could also call my guys and have cam sex and fuck me; that sounds way better than Big Jim.

Oh my fucking God! Am I done with Big Jim once and for all? Have we come to the end of the line?

It's a devastating thought.

"Don't worry, Big Fella. I'll introduce you to my men. We will get you in on the action in no time."

Aaaaannnnddd, I'm talking to my fucking vibrator.

Cray-fucking-cray I am!

My tummy growls, and I freeze, listening for any sound in the house. I have no idea what time it is because I don't have a clock in my room. I've only ever used my phone. It's been dark for hours, and I can't remember the last time I heard a noise outside my bedroom door, the realisation making me grin.

Everyone is in bed.

I do an excited little jump because apparently, that's what the occasion calls for, and I dash to my door, quietly pulling it open. Silence meets my ears, and my grin broadens as I slip out and creep quietly through the dark house. I'm on a mission to find my phone. Or my laptop. Either will do at this point. I'm not picky.

In the main living area, I flip a lamp on and start searching quietly through every drawer, cupboard, bag, and hiding spot I can find. When I don't find anything, I move towards the front of the house and tiptoe through the home office. There are two desks in here. One for Cin and one for Will, and since it's off the same passage as their bedroom, I hold my breath as I pull open each drawer, searching for anything that will communicate with the outside world.

There's nothing.

That means they have my phone in their room.

I sneak up to their door and listen. I can't hear anything, but that doesn't mean they are asleep. What if I crack the door and see Cin riding Will?

Ew! No thanks!

I enjoy watching people fuck, but I don't *ever* want to see *them* in the act.

My shoulders drop in defeat as my tummy rumbles again. I may not be able to get to my phone, but I can get to some food. Being hangry mixed with frustration and heartbreak is a bad combination. If I can eliminate one thing, then maybe the others will be more tolerable?

I tiptoe back to the kitchen and rummage through the pantry and fridge, making myself a quick roast beef sandwich before turning the lamp off and returning to my prison cell.

I could just cry. I feel so helpless right now. And antsy as fuck. It's a frustrating combination.

After shutting my door, I place my plate on my bedside table right before I hear a weird noise.

Tapping.

Faint tapping is coming from my bedroom window. At first, I freeze, my heart in my throat because, helloooo horror movie! DON'T WALK TO THE WINDOW! But then, I get excited because I hear a hushed voice I recognise.

"Rhys, are you awake?"

I dart over to my window, reefing the curtains open wide to see my big guy standing on the other side of the glass, and a huge smile splits across my face.

"Garrett?" I whisper-yell, and he steps forward into the light flowing from my bedroom.

Then my smile drops.

His face. Each eye is bruised, and his nose looks a little swollen.

Moving quickly, I slide my window open and remove the flywire.

"Gar," I whisper, reaching my hand out to him, and he steps forward, lifting himself in through my window. I step back to give him space, but the moment he has both feet planted on my grey carpet, he pulls me against his chest in the tightest hug I've ever received.

This hug isn't for me. It's for him, so I squeeze him tight, silently showing that I'm here for him. When I go to pull back, his grip on me tightens, and my heart breaks because I know he's just been through an ordeal of his own.

Imagine if I had found a phone to call him on and rambled on about poor me, being locked in the tower, not able to get free. Of what? Loving parents who want to keep me safe? Yeah, my petty grounding situation doesn't even compare to whatever Garrett has endured tonight. Sure, he has a loving mum and two loving sisters, but his dad is back from prison, and it looks like he's out to make Garrett's life hell.

"Sorry." He whispers, slowly pulling back. "I would have called, but I didn't get a chance to grab my phone. I… kinda left in a hurry."

I gently cup his jaw, being careful not to hurt him, as I peer up into his glassy eyes. "You don't have to call before you come and see me, Gar. Not that calling would have helped. My olds have my phone. But you're welcome here any time."

A slight grin tugs at his mouth, and his shoulders relax.

"What are the chances I can crash here tonight?" He looks nervous as he asks, and I grin.

"You can stay here any time. Fuck, just move in. I won't complain."

His smile broadens. "I'm not sure your parents would agree."

I shrug. "For now, they don't need to know." I stand on my tiptoes and press my lips to his chin. "Let me get the window back together. Are you hungry?"

I move to step around him, but he grips my hand and lifts it to his lips, pressing a kiss on the back. "Let me fix the window. You go eat your sanga." He gestures his head to my bedside table, and I reluctantly nod as he moves back to my window to put everything back in place.

Before I do anything else, I move to my door and lock it. All I need now is for Cin to come and check on me, finding Garrett here. I don't really care what sort of trouble that will get me in. I'm more worried about her sending him back home to his dad.

I meet Garrett at my bed, and we both sit on top of the covers facing each other. I place the plate with my roast beef sandwich in between us, and I gesture my head.

"Have half with me."

Garrett studies me for a few moments, his icy-blue eyes roaming over my entire face. "I could have gone to Simon's. I know the code to get through his back door." He shrugs, looking nervous. "But I wanted to be with you."

I smile. "I'm glad you came here. Honestly, I've been going a little coo-coo without being able to talk to any of you."

Garrett grins back before dropping his eyes to the plate and picking up one half of the sandwich. I watch him, thinking he is going to take a bite, but instead, he holds the beefy goodness in front of my lips.

"Bite." He demands, and well, yes, we all know how that goes. Of course, I obey. Meanwhile, Kitty peaks her pointy ears up and starts to fucking purr.

Garrett watches as my teeth sink into the bread, taking my bite, and as I start chewing, he takes a bite of his own.

"Hmmm." He mumbles around his mouthful. "This is good."

I swallow my mouthful, something I'm good at, and nod. "Of course it is. I made it."

He chuckles, holding out the sandwich while I take another bite. "You always make a midnight snack?"

"Nope. Just tonight. I refused dinner, so I had to wait until everyone went to bed because I'm being stubborn."

Garrett grins at me, but then he frowns, looking down at the bread in his hand. Then he practically shoves it in my mouth.

"Eat." He demands, and since I have no fucking choice, I eat the rest of what he was holding. "No skipping meals, Baby Girl. You'll make yourself sick if you do that."

I roll my eyes but keep chewing on the food, feeling a little better as it fills my stomach. He watches me as I eat, grinning at the stupid moans I make as I chew, and when my plate is clean, I place it back on my bedside and return to face my big guy.

"I'm sorry about the video, Rhys, and what's happened with Tyler. I know I don't know him, but I can see how much you care about him. If I could fix it for you, I would."

I smile sombrely at Garrett and shrug. "It is what it is. I can only hope that things will improve and that he's ok."

Leaning forward, Garrett lifts my chin so my lips meet his, and I part mine, eager to feel his always consuming kiss. He doesn't disappoint. It's not a fevered kiss, but it is a hungry one. Hungry to express feelings that are perhaps too hard to speak out loud right now. I climb into his lap, wrapping my legs around his waist, and let myself get lost in the press of his lips and the stroke of his tongue. Garrett's big hands come up to tangle in my hair, and he grips the strands firmly near the roots, controlling my head to deepen the kiss.

We tumble to the side, crashing to my pillows, never once breaking our lip lock, and I'm helpless to control Kitty as she starts grinding over the top of the large bulge in Garrett's jeans. It's then that Garrett breaks our kiss, only to trail his lips down my neck.

"Grind on me, Baby Girl. Take what you need."

I mean, who am I to argue with his demand?

I do exactly as he asks and grind my Kitty over and over, the friction and clothing barrier between us fuelling me on. Kitty is gushing, my knickers soaked as I writhe against my big guy, and I know my big O is not far away. A good dry hump should never be underestimated, and dry humping the hard ridge of Garrett Cole's ginormous dick is a ride worth taking.

Garrett's kisses travel to my ear, sucking my lobe between his lips before he nips at it. My moan is loud, and I hope like hell that Char is passed out because she's not going to let me live it down if she hears. I can't seem to care, though. Not when I'm in Garrett's arms.

"Can I bite you, Baby Girl?" He rasps against my ear and then growls like a feral animal as if his control to bite me is waning.

"Yes." I pant. "Bite me good and deep. Make me bleed."

My words send him over the line he was hovering on, and with another growl, he pulls my t-shirt down past my shoulder and bites down hard on the exposed skin.

I'm a masochist, apparently, because the pain as his teeth break skin sends me skyrocketing, my Kitty tensing right before I explode and slap my hand over my mouth as I cry out.

"Fuck Gar." I pant as I feel his deep rumble through our chests as he growls again. He releases my shoulder and starts licking over the skin as I try to get my breath back. "Why do I react like that?"

Slowly, Garrett pulls back, shooting me a blood-stained toothy grin. "Don't question it, Baby Girl. Just fucking embrace it."

"Well, ok then." I grin back right before a knock sounds on my bedroom door.

We both freeze, eyes going wide as we listen.

"Rhys." Char's whisper floats through the door. "Please tell me you have company, and you aren't getting murdered right now."

I giggle at Char. Her tone tells me she's wearing a shit-eating grin.

"Not getting murdered. It's all g, Char." I whisper-yell, and she clucks.

"Is it vampire boy again?"

Garrett's brows shoot towards the ceiling, and I giggle.

"Yes. I'm with my vampire." I whisper-yell again, and she snickers.

"Okie Dokie. Try to keep it down. I'm not sure how to explain those noises to the olds if they hear them. Or the twins, for that matter."

"Ok," I mutter a little louder, and a few seconds later, I hear her bedroom door click shut.

Garrett grins. "Your sister is pretty cruisy."

"Yep." I nod, rolling my hips.

"Stop, Baby Girl," he chuckles. "I've already made a mess."

My brows lift this time, and his lips thin into a sideways smirk.

"Garrett Cole, did you cum in your pants?"

He chuckles. "I did, Baby Girl. Just like you did."

Chapter Eight

Garrett

My nose hurts like a bitch. It only bled a little after my dad landed his punch, but his nose pissed out with crimson worse than mine after I lost my shit at him. I still can't get the sound of Polly and Brittney's screams out of my head. They were terrified, and I fear it was of me. I tried to hold back, but when he said he would beat my mum for raising such a piece of shit like me, I saw red. There's no way I was letting him touch my mum.

I managed to bang him up enough that he had to go to the hospital. Because he's on parole, it will automatically get flagged, and the cops will pay him a visit. I also found what's probably Fox Pine's last remaining pay phone and made an anonymous call to the cops, hoping it gets my dad some extra attention that I know he's hoping to avoid. I don't know what else to do. He hasn't changed. He's angrier than ever. I have no fucking idea how he managed to get out of prison early.

Fleeing to Rhys was totally selfish. I'm fucking terrified that I'll be sent back to youth detention, or worse, prison, because I'm nearly eighteen. I don't even know if they can do that, but the mistake I made last time was not telling anyone what was happening, and when I snapped and beat my old man within an inch of his life, I was declared dangerous and got sent away for a little while too.

I won't let that happen this time if I can help it. Last night was self-defence, with a little added warning to my dad. I'm just worried that next time, I'll actually kill him, since I have trouble controlling my anger, and more often than not, it gets away from me.

A soft moan falls from Rhys' lips as she snuggles in closer to my side. I haven't been able to sleep a wink, but laying here with her in my arms is helping my anxiety. Her sweet scent, fruity almost, calms me. Grounds me. Wrapped in her scent, I feel like I'm home. A grin tugs at my lips as I remember what we did earlier. We dry-humped until we came. Fuck if that wasn't hot. There's something about the barrier of clothing, the teasing and wanting more, but not able to get it until you are both in a frenzy. It was fucking perfect. I can still hear her soft voice in my ear after I asked if I could bite her.

"Bite me good and deep. Make me bleed."

Fuuucck! I nearly came there and then. I gave her what she asked for, ignoring the throbbing in my nose as I latched onto her creamy flesh until it split, giving me her blood.

Her sister referred to me as Vampire Boy. I read a lot of vampire books a few years back, and have to admit, I don't hate the comparison. I'm not looking to drink her blood, but I do like tasting it. I love the look of its bright hue against her pale skin.

I kind of love that Rhys loves it as much as she does, and that she also doesn't understand why she loves it. I told her to embrace it, and I know she will. She did. It's why she is perfect for me. If there is a God, then he made Rhys George for me and my twisted desires. Strangely, I think he also made her for my mates, too. I'd never considered sharing a girl until I recognised her addiction. I wanted to help her and realised that sharing her was the only way.

A while after the sun starts shining through the crack in the curtains, noise floats in from outside Rhys' bedroom door. Everyone is getting up. I should probably bail and figure out how the fuck to sneak into my exam in casual clothes.

Running my fingers through the long dark strands of my girl's hair, I press a kiss to her forehead. "Baby Girl. Time to wake up."

"Noooo." She drawls out lazily, keeping her eyes shut. "Stay here forever."

I chuckle. "I wish we could."

The door starts banging then, my eyes going wide, darting to see it shaking.

"Rhysie, Mum said it's time to get up." One of the twins yells through the door while the other giggles.

"Yeah, Rhysie. Get up. You have that test thing again today." The other boy calls, and Rhys groans.

"It's called an exam!" She yells, and the little boys giggle again before the sound fades. They must have run off.

"Good morning, Baby Girl." I rasp against her hair as she wriggles closer to me.

"We have time for a quickie." She murmurs, and I chuckle as her head tilts back and those enchanting chocolate pools look up at me.

"I need to get out of here before your parents find me."

She shakes her head. "Not yet. I can sneak you into the bathroom to shower. Your jocks should be dry by now, too."

I chuckle again. Last night, after we finished grinding on each other, I snuck into the bathroom and washed my fucking jocks in the sink. I swear the guys will never let me live this down if they find out. Rhys was, as always, totally cool with the situation. Nothing about sex fazes her. She accepts the filth of it as naturally as she accepts oxygen into her lungs.

"I should probably go," I say again, and she sits up, frowning down at me. Her face is serious, but it's hard to see anything but a beautiful dark angel looking back at me. Her hair is a little messy. Her cheeks flushed pink. Her skin is natural and makeup free.

"No." She frowns. "Shower first. I insist."

I narrow my eyes at her, and she raises a single dark brow in challenge. I could argue all day with her just to see that fire in her eyes, but now isn't the time, so I nod, giving into her. If she wants me to take a shower before I leave, then I will. Hell, I probably reek.

At my nod, Rhys leaps up from the bed, somehow fuelled with enough energy to push ten trucks. She's so much like Simon in this respect. Balls of fucking energy and personalities to match.

"Come on, Big Guy. Let's sneak you into the bathroom again." She stands expectantly at the foot of the bed, so I roll my eyes and slowly ease out of her heavenly blankets.

Rhys peeks her head out the door first before sneaking out to the bathroom to make sure it's all clear. Then she dashes back in, grinning at me and snatching up my hand before leading me out. Within a few minutes she has me locked in the small bathroom while she returns to her bedroom, so I make quick work of taking a shower, using her soap to clean my body, not caring a fucking bit if I smell like a girl. It's a Rhys smell, and I'll gladly drown in it.

My jocks are still a bit damp but clean, so I slip them on and get dressed in my jeans and t-shirt again before using my fingers to style my hair. I don't know why I bother trying. My hair has gotten too long, and the curls are a wayward mess.

Once I'm done, I wait a moment by the door, listening to hear if anyone is on the other side. When it remains quiet, I unlock the door and swing it open, ready to quickly dash back into Rhys' bedroom.

I freeze, eyes wide, when I come face to face with my fucking school principal. Rhys' foster mum.

Fuck!

Chapter Nine

RHYS

M y mum follows me into my bedroom, looking at me warily, and once she is in, I quietly close the door behind her.

"What's going on?" Cin asks, her voice laced with concern.

I debated about what I'm about to do but came to the conclusion that honesty is the best policy with my 'rents. It's already worked in my favour recently, and if I want to remain in their good graces with the whole Tyler thing, I really need to prove to them that I'm mature enough to handle it.

"I need to tell you something, and I need you to please hear me out before you say anything. Please remember that I'm trying to be open and honest with you."

My mum's brows hitch, and I can see her mind ticking over at a million miles an hour, trying to figure out what the fuck has happened now. When she slowly nods, I relax a little.

"So, Garrett slept over last night."

My mum's mouth opens to speak, but I hold up my finger and raise my brows. She snaps her mouth shut and nods for me to continue.

"I don't want to break his trust in me, so all I can tell you is that his dad is back from prison, and things aren't good. You will know when you see him what I mean. Please don't react to his face. He needed a place to stay, and he turned up at my window. I was not and never will turn him or any of my guys away when they are in a crisis." I sigh, "Also, he wasn't able to get any of his things last night, so he doesn't have a uniform to wear to the exam today. Can you please make sure that isn't a problem and no teachers bug him about it? I just want him to have the opportunity to go to the exam and do his best."

When I'm finished speaking, I give my mum a nod, and she sucks in a big breath.

"Thank you for telling me, Rhys. I appreciate your honesty. I'll make sure he isn't bothered about his lack of uniform, but you know my duty of care means I will have to look into his family situation now that I know there is possibly something wrong. Do you think he will talk to me about it?"

I shrug. "Maybe. Can it wait until after the exam?"

My mum gives me a soft smile. "Of course." She steps forward, placing her hands on either side of my head, and leans in to press a kiss to my hair. "Please get ready quickly. I've made a big breakfast today, and I'd really like you to join us. Garrett too."

Well, fuck. My emotions nearly get the better of me, so I don't say anything, but I nod and smile, watching my mum open my bedroom door and leave. It's at that very moment that the bathroom door swings open, and I dart forward to stand in my doorway, taking in Garrett's deer in headlights moment.

My poor Big Guy.

"Good morning, Garrett." My mum's voice is cheery and lacks her authoritative school principal tone. "Breakfast is ready. I'll see you and Rhys in the kitchen soon."

"Uh... Yeah. Yes, sure. Thank you." Garrett stumbles his way through his words, and I have to bite my lip to stop from smiling. I fail, because as soon as my mum walks away and his icy-blues land on me, he grins back at me.

"What the fuck just happened?" He whispers, coming towards me quickly as if he's worried my dad will jump out any second.

I sure hope my mum is on her way to warn my dad to behave. I hope he's not going to react like he did with Ty. That was scary.

Garrett pushes me back into my bedroom, closing the door and presses me against the wall, caging me in.

"Uh. I may have told my mum that you slept over."

His eyes narrow at my words. "And?"

"And she's cool with it." I flutter my lashes, but he rolls his eyes.

"She is not cool with it. Aren't you meant to be grounded?"

"Well, yes, but under the circumstances…" I feel a pang in my chest as his eyes drop to the floor. Is he angry at me? "I didn't say too much. Just that things at home aren't good."

His eyes dart up. "It's ok, Baby Girl. I'm not upset. I just hate people knowing. It's hard enough going to a school for rich kids and pretending to be one of you. I'm not a fan of people knowing what happens in my family."

"Gar," I lift his chin until his eyes meet mine again. "I understand completely, and FYI, FP Catholic is not for rich kids. Just because you're there on a scholarship doesn't mean you don't deserve to be there. Hell, you deserve to be there more than most of the entitled fucks that attend the school. And as for my mum knowing. She only wants to help."

Garrett told me about what happened with his dad last night, not long after we snuggled up in my bed. He's worried about his mum and his sisters, but if he went back home last night, it may have made things worse. I'm so glad he came to me.

Leaning in, Garrett presses his forehead to mine, looking at me through the fan of his dark lashes. Then he cups my face and kisses me. Thoroughly. I love the way he claims me with each kiss, searing his invisible brand on me. It's intoxicating. His scent, which is fragranced with my own, wraps around us both, and I'm one hundred percent certain that I'll never be able to live a life without Garrett Cole in it.

Before his kiss can heat my entire body, he slowly pulls back and stares into my eyes.

"Thank you, Rhys."

I smile softly at him, trying not to shy away from his gratitude. I get the same feeling I get when someone compliments me, and I know I still have a lot to work on with my own self-doubts. I'm a work in progress, I guess.

After another few minutes of hugging, I dash into the bathroom to get myself ready and opt to leave my face fully make-up-free today. Sure, you can still see the bruising on my eye, but Garrett's can't be hidden, so I'm not going to hide mine, either.

When we join the rest of my family for breakfast, Char bites back a stupid smile while the twins bounce around excitedly to see Garrett, and my dad spends a good few minutes watching us as we dish up food onto our plates. We both pretend not to notice his eyes examining the situation, but when I finally make eye contact with him, he gives me a warm smile as we take a seat at the table.

"Good morning, Rhys. Garrett." My dad says, and I smile around the piece of toast I'm biting into.

"Hey Dad."

"Hi, Mr Rogan." Garrett's voice is softer than usual, but no less confident.

"Please call me Will. Mr Rogan makes me sound old."

"You are old, Dad." Archie snickers, and Conner joins in.

"Yeah. You are like one hundred and fifty."

"Gee, Dad. You're looking pretty good for a hundred and fifty." I smirk, and he grins back.

"Thank you. Good genes, I guess."

Even my mum laughs, and just like that, the mood is light, and we all enjoy a delicious breakfast.

It's about an hour later when we arrive at school, so many eyes taking in the fact that Garrett gets out of the principal's car and then walks hand in hand with me to make our way to the stadium for today's exam.

I didn't bother asking my olds for my phone back this morning, but I fully intend on trying to compromise with them tonight. When Shaun, Marcus and Simon see Garrett and me approaching, they look surprised. I guess the fact that we both don't have a phone for communicating has added to their confusion.

"Hey Rhys." Lexi's voice comes from my left, and she barrels into me, giving me a squeeze. "Are you ok?"

Smiling at the blonde beauty, I nod. "All g, I guess. Never a fucking dull moment in the Rhys George world."

She giggles. "That's for sure."

"How come you weren't answering my calls, man?" Marcus asks Garrett as they do some sort of fist bump handshake thing. "Did something happen?"

"My old man happened. I crashed at our girl's place. I'll fill you in later."

"Oh shit. Ok." Marcus claps him on the shoulder before directing his dark gaze to me.

"How are you feeling today, Rhee?"

I shrug. "Ok, I think."

"Rhys." Tillie barges into me this time, effectively pushing Garrett further away from me. Is it strange that I miss his touch only seconds after I've had it? "Bell is about to make an announcement."

I frown, looking at Tillie in confusion, but she's not looking at me. Her eyes are behind me, so I turn to see Bell standing on top of a picnic table as Tillie and Lexi link arms with me.

"Attention fuckers!" She calls out, and everyone turns to her. Some guys whoop while some girls curl their lips at her. "To the idiots that honestly thought it was Rhys George in the video, you're all dumb bastards. Just because there's some psycho chick out to get Rhys, you fucking idiots believe the crazy lady instead of looking at how fucked up it is that someone shared such a video in the first place. Not to mention how fucked up it is to be slut-shaming a fucking child!" She pops her hands on her hips and glares at everyone. "It was me in the video. That little girl was me, and that sick man is in jail, where he has been for years." Bell lifts her hands to her hair and starts to take out her dark Wednesday Addams braids while continuing. "And the fact that you all believe Eric fucking Carter, who, FYI, farts when he comes, means you are as fucking dumb as him."

Some of the girls in the crowd slap their hands over their mouths, and some nod knowingly at Bell's comment while the rest of the crowd roar with laughter.

"Shut the fuck up, bitch!" Eric Carter's voice booms through the laughing crowd, and Bell looks towards him as she combs her dark hair out, showing how long it is. Just like mine.

"Oh, Eric. That lady with the video lied to you." Bell pulls out a makeup wipe from her pocket and proceeds to wipe her thick, dark liner off. "And I can't let Rhys take the limelight here. I'm the star of *that* show."

"What the fuck is she doing?" I whisper, and Tillie tilts her head to grin at me.

"Confusing everyone."

"See," Bell calls, turning so everyone can see her make-up-free face and long dark hair. "Are you really sure it was Rhys in that video?" She points to her face. "We look like sisters, don't we? And yes, while Rhys likes to talk about sex all the time, ask yourself this. Is she really screwed up enough to have endured that as a child? Because she seems pretty fucking cruisy to me. I, on the other hand…" Bell leaves that hanging, shooting everyone a wide-eyed crazy smile, and I notice that everyone watching genuinely seems confused.

"Get down from the table, Miss Bishop!" Mrs Holland calls as she makes her way with a posse of teachers towards the crowd. Bell ignores her.

"Let me guess, Eric. You chose Rhys because she has four boyfriends, didn't you?"

"Once a slut, always a slut." Eric calls, and my heart seizes as my guys all fly through the crowd towards Eric.

"Wait! No!" I call to them as Tillie and Lexi hold me back. I don't want my guys getting in trouble. If Garrett does, it might make things worse with things at home. Simon's mum might drag him out of state before the school year even ends, and Shaun's dad will make him quit school for sure. Marcus can't afford to get in trouble for fighting again after what happened with Shaun last term, either. He has a police record now that I'll never forgive myself for.

Eric cries out in pain even before my guys make it to him, and people close in around him, blocking my guys from getting through but also blocking the teachers from being able to see.

What the fuck is going on?

I glance back at Bell, still standing on the table. She has the best view of whatever is going on, and when her eyes lock with mine, she gives me one of her rare smiles and shoots me a wink.

"Move out of the way!" Mrs Holland cries, trying to pry the crowd apart as other teachers join her. Their attempts are useless until a minute later when the crowd quickly moves apart, and Eric Carter comes into view.

I gasp, my hand flying to my mouth as a laugh bursts free. Everyone starts laughing at Eric as he stumbles to stand, his uniform slashed, his lip bleeding, and the top of his head shaved right down the middle.

Four sets of wide eyes turn back to me, amusement dancing across their faces as my guys slowly make their way back to my side, and Tillie steps out of the way.

Holy shit, this was planned. Bell. Tillie. Maybe even Lexi. I'm confused as fuck, but I'm not going to question it. Especially not now that my mum has shown up and students are being ushered into the stadium while Eric storms off with Mrs Holland at his side.

"What the fuck just happened?" Shaun voices the thought I had moments ago.

"I have no idea," I admit, turning to find Tillie and Lexi, but they're gone. Yep, those loveable bitches were totally involved.

"Fuck, that was… kind of epic." Simon chuckles, and Marcus joins him, nodding.

"It really was. I'm still gonna smash that fucker's face in the next chance I get, though."

"Same." Garrett growls.

"Guys. There's no need. Eric got what was coming to him, and I don't want you to get into any trouble. Promise me you will drop it." I eye each one of them, and my brows lift when they don't agree with me. "Fine. Can we at least wait until the summer break and get Eric somewhere that no cops can get to quickly?"

They all nod with satisfaction at that, and Marcus pulls me into his chest. "No one gets to speak that way about my girl and lives to take another breath."

"Oh, I do like fierce Marcus." I lift up on my toes and press a kiss to his smirking lips.

CHAPTER TEN

RHYS

I 'm over exams. I'm pretty sure I've failed each one now. After the whole Bell and Eric thing, I couldn't concentrate on anything but the clusterfuck that has become my life. I stared at my mum up the front of the exam hall for most of the time, and she stared right back, only occasionally looking around the room at other students. If she didn't already know that I've tanked year eleven, she does now.

The phone message from Julie that Char told me about is playing on my mind. I wonder if I ask Cin to play it to me, that she'll let me listen to it. I also wonder if I have to watch my back now. Julie said as much in the message, apparently. I'd be stupid to assume that the video reveal was the real threat. I just wish I could get to her first. Or at least wish the cops would hurry up and catch her. Lock her up and throw away the key.

It's not that simple, though, is it? If she is caught, then there will be a court case. I've been through that before. I don't want to go through it again, but I will if I have to. I'll do anything to end this nightmare.

When the exam is over, I don't get the same awful reception I received yesterday. No one calls me names. Those who look at me give me a smile, which are mostly from other girls. I stand from my seat, expecting to go to my guys, but my mum appears and takes my arm.

"What are you doing?"

"Will is waiting to take you home." She says as she leads me in the opposite direction to where I want to go. Looking over my shoulder, Shaun, Marcus, and Simon watch me while Garrett walks off in the other direction without looking back.

"Why are you so determined to keep me from them?" I turn back to my mum, reefing my arm from her grip. She sighs as she stops walking.

"Rhys, I'm not trying to keep you from them. You are *grounded* and therefore not allowed to see *anyone*."

"Yet you allowed me to walk in with Garrett this morning."

She sighs again. "I couldn't exactly tell him to wrack off, could I? Not after he has obviously been through his own ordeal. This morning was an exception. Garrett is on his way to my office now for a chat. I will help him, Rhys, but things haven't changed. You're still grounded."

I huff. "Why? Because I dared to fall in love with someone forbidden?" Tears pool in my eyes, and Cin's face softens as she looks around the hall to see if anyone can hear us.

"Honestly, Rhys, we only just learnt that you've been going to a sex club with adults. The thing with... you know who is a lot, but we aren't trying to punish you. We are trying to keep you safe."

I take a step back, frowning as I swipe at a tear that falls. "You think I'm going to go back to the sex club?"

She shrugs. "I think you will do anything to protect the people you care about. Even put yourself in danger."

She has me there. Isn't that exactly what I did by returning to the Feast?

"Rhys, we only want to keep you safe."

"Can I listen to the new message from Julie?"

Cynthia flinches back at my question, surprise lifting her brows. "How do you know about that?"

"It doesn't matter how I know. I just do. Can I listen to it?"

"Maybe. We can talk about it when I get home from work tonight."

I roll my eyes but nod at the same time and reluctantly follow her out of the hall. When I turn back, I'm expecting my guys to be gone, but Shaun is still there, his eyes on me, and before I step through the door, he blows me a kiss. My grin is wide, and I giggle, stopping in the doorway.

"I love you, Shaun Bossier!" I call out, my voice echoing in the stadium, drawing the attention of the handful of students and teachers remaining. Shaun beams at me, his teeth flashing as he chuckles.

"I love you too, Rhys George!" He calls back, and I hear my mum mutter out in the hall.

"For God's sake."

Nothing my 'rents can say or do will wipe the stupid grin off my face. Will's brows lift when he sees me, and when he looks to his wife for an explanation, she shakes her head and mumbles, "Don't ask."

The house is quiet when we get home. The twins are still at school, and Char is at work, and after a quick ham and cheese sanga, Will retreats to the home office to do his own work. I don't have another exam for a couple of days, and as much as that would normally make me happy, now I know I'm locked in this prison for two days without being able to see or contact my guys and nothing else to do.

I annoy Will for a bit, asking him questions about the house plans he is stewing over, and then ask him if he can buy me some paint so I can paint the walls of my bedroom. I was worried he'd say no, but he looked pleased that I asked, and he sat with me while I used his computer to choose a colour for him to pick up later. I tried to convince him to give me my laptop back so I could have a look by myself and take my time, but of course, he said no.

I busy myself for the afternoon, taking down my posters and cleaning my walls, dragging my furniture into the centre of the room so I can paint my walls as soon as my dad picks up the paint order and brushes. As busy as I try to make myself, my mind still wanders to my guys.

How did things go with my mum and Garrett? What is happening with his dad? Is Ty ok? Is he really alright about quitting his teaching job? What's happening with Sy's mum? Has she agreed to let him stay in Fox Pines? Will she pay for his schooling next year? How is Shaun's mum going? Is she doing any better or getting worse? Has his brother come out yet? If he has, does his dad accept that Derek is gay? Will his dad let Shaun finish year twelve before he forces him to work on their farm full time? Has Marcus tracked down Eric yet? What do his parents think of me since I'm the reason he smashed up the school office?

I have to say, having my mind consumed by thoughts of other people instead of my needy Kitty is good, but the only problem is, the more I'm away from my guys, the more my Kitty claws at me. I try to ignore her, but like always, it's impossible. She is missing their dicks as much as I'm missing their hearts.

By the time dinner comes around, I'm a grumpy bitch. I retreat to my room, not wanting to take my bitchiness out on the twins, and like last night, I refuse to join the family for dinner. I do, however, eat the plate of food the twins bring me because hangry me seems to be worse when my heart and Kitty are lonely.

Just like last night, I go kind of crazy, skipping around my room, and this time doing handstands against my bare walls. Will delivers me my paint and supplies by 8pm and is surprised when I get straight to work. But he doesn't question me or insist I wait until tomorrow. It takes me two hours to do the first coat of paint, the dark purple already making my bedroom feel more homely to me. I decide to do the second coat tomorrow and wash the rollers and brushes out by the back laundry door, tempted by the mild night air to just wander off for a walk to a place that houses one of my guys.

I don't go anywhere, though. I stay right where I am, going out of my mind.

It's after eleven when I can't take it any longer and sneak across the hall to Char's room. Tapping on her door, I slowly ease it open when she calls "come in", and she grins knowingly at me as if she were expecting me to drop by for a visit.

"How much do you love me?" I ask, and she rolls her fake green eyes.

"Shouldn't I be asking you that question? After all, you're here because you want something from me, aren't you?"

"Can I please use your phone? Just for a little while?" I beg, slapping my hands together in front of my chest.

Char huffs. "And what will you do for me *if* I let you use my phone?" Char asks, standing from her bed and placing a hand on her hip.

"I'll do your dish night for the next two weeks." I smile hopefully at her, but she rolls her eyes.

"Nope. Two weeks won't cut it. Make it a month, and you have yourself a deal."

I roll my eyes this time. "Fine. A month of your dish nights for an hour on your phone."

Char drops her hand from her hip and narrows her eyes. "Fine. But if you get caught, you say you stole it from me. I'm not going down for you."

I smile. "Deal."

Sighing, Char takes her phone off the charger and hands it to me. "One fucking hour, and that's it. And don't watch porn on my phone."

Gripping her phone, I grin and nod, darting out of her room to quickly return to mine.

It's easy enough to contact Shaun, Marcus, Garrett and Sy through SnapChat, but Tyler is a different story. I don't remember his number, but I scribbled it on my folder amongst all my other doodling a couple of years ago, so I rummage through my wardrobe until I find my old folder, opening it to find the number I'm looking for. Smiling, I close myself in my wardrobe, putting the torchlight on the phone so I can see and dial the number.

As it rings, my heart hammers in my chest, but as it rings out, my hammering heart dies. I open a message and key in the same number, sending him a text.

Unknown Number
Skipper. It's Kitten. Pick up when I call.

I dial the number again, and it picks up on the first ring.

"Kitten?"

Oh, my fucking God, that voice. Stupid tears wet my eyes just from hearing Tyler's deep rasp, and I have to swallow the lump in my throat before I can speak.

"Ty."

"Shit beautiful. It's good to hear your voice. I was getting worried when you didn't return my messages or calls."

"Sorry," I speak softly, not wanting to be overheard. "My parents took my phone. I'm using my sister's to call you. I'll delete the call and message once we are done."

"They took your phone?"

"Yes. I'm grounded, apparently. They've taken my laptop too. I'm not allowed to see anyone." Sliding to the floor, I lean against the back wall under my hanging clothes and draw my knees to my chest.

"Damn. They aren't messing around, are they?" His voice is light but strained. I can tell he's trying not to make me feel worse than I already do.

"Please tell me you didn't send me a dick pic? I'm not sure I'm comfortable with my mum looking at your dick, Ty."

He bursts out laughing, and I can't fight the grin that tugs at my lips.

"No, Kitten. No dick pic. Just concerned messages, asking if you're ok."

I nod, even though he can't see me. "They don't want me to see you again until I graduate." Saying the words I hate out loud sends a slicing pain through the centre of my chest. The thought of not seeing him until I graduate is excruciating.

"I thought as much, Kitten. Don't worry, though. If we can get through until you are eighteen, then I'll make sure we see each other in secret."

I smile at that. I kind of like sneaking around. It's fun.

"Are you still in Fox Pines?"

"No. I left yesterday. I'm at my house in Redfield. I'll lie low. Keep to myself for a bit. Hell, I'll change my name if I have to." His tone is light again. I can just imagine his face. He doesn't share his lighter side with many people, but I've seen it. It's seared into my brain.

"No way. I love your name."

"Really? I was kind of hoping to change it to Gilligan."

I giggle, probably a little too loud, but I can't help it. "Seriously? Gilligan?"

"Yeah. Why not? It goes with Skipper."

I laugh loud and slap my hand over my mouth. "Ty, you are going to get me busted."

He chuckles. "Sorry, beautiful. I'll keep Tyler for you. Ok?"

"Ok." I grin, wishing like hell that I could touch him right now. "I miss you."

"I miss you too, Kitten. You have no idea."

His words are raw and filled with sincerity, like he's been struggling just as much as I have.

"I love you," I whisper.

"I love you too, Rhys. So much." He rarely uses my real name, so I know he means the words he speaks.

"I should go, but I don't want to hang up," I whisper, feeling the burn at the back of my eyes again.

"Same, Kitten. Don't worry about me, though. I'm fine as long as you're fine. Ok?"

"Ok." I don't have the heart to tell him I'm not fine. I'm far from fine. I feel like I'm hanging by a thread that has already been severed halfway through.

We chat for a few more minutes and then reluctantly hang up. I take a moment, letting the tears fall before logging Char out of her SnapChat and logging into mine.

Straight away, I giggle at the name of the group chat with the guys.

Slaves to the Sex Kitten
Cherry AKA Kitten AKA Rhee AKA Baby Girl
Uh… what's with the name change?

The Hastinator
Cherry! You're alive!!

Cherry AKA Kitten AKA Rhee AKA Baby Girl
Kind of. Thanks to my big sis. I don't have long.
How is everyone doing?

The Hastinator
I'm fucking epic now that I've heard from you.
Life is so boring when you're not around!

Cherry AKA Kitten AKA Rhee AKA Baby Girl
And how were you before you heard from me?
Any updates about your mum and the move?

It takes a while for Simon to reply, but when he does, I can see why.

The Hastinator
I hate my mum!
I can't even get emancipated because Australia doesn't have such laws!
Can you imagine that?

Cherry AKA Kitten AKA Rhee AKA Baby Girl
What has your mum done now?

The Hastinator
She has already enrolled me in some snobby private school over in Perth. She thinks it will make me leave with her, but she's wrong.
I'd rather be homeless than leave you guys!!!

Marky Marc
Dude, we aren't ever going to let you be homeless.
We will figure it out. Bossi is working on a solution.

Cherry AKA Kitten AKA Rhee AKA Baby Girl
See Sy! It's ok. We are keeping you!
Hi Marky Marc! :)

The Hastinator
Thanks, guys!

Marky Marc
Hi Rhee. Did your olds give you your phone back?

Cherry AKA Kitten AKA Rhee AKA Baby Girl
Nope. I conned Char into letting me use her phone for a bit.

Marky Marc
Good idea! What do you owe her for that?

Cherry AKA Kitten AKA Rhee AKA Baby Girl
Her dish nights for a month!!
I think I've been outplayed!

Marky Marc
Hahaha, I think so!

The Hastinator
I'll come and help you do the dishes, Cherry :)

Cherry AKA Kitten AKA Rhee AKA Baby Girl
I'm not sure that's a good idea… You, me and kitchens seem to cause more mess!

The Hastinator
Only if you have cherry pie!

Marky Marc
I just threw up in my mouth, Hastings!

The Hastinator
Don't lie, Grady! You wanna see me naked and covered in cherry pie while our girl licks it off?

Cherry AKA Kitten AKA Rhee AKA Baby Girl
Ooooooooohhhhh!!!! I want to see that!
And taste that!
And feel your hard cock under my tongue!

The Hastinator
It's hard right now, Cherry.

Marky Marc
Do not turn this convo into a fucking sex chat!

Casanova
Don't mind me…
I'm just enjoying the entertainment!

Cherry AKA Kitten AKA Rhee AKA Baby Girl
Cass!! Hi!

Casanova
Hey Kitten. How are you coping?

Cherry AKA Kitten AKA Rhee AKA Baby Girl
Not the best, but feeling a little better now that I know you're all ok.
Wait… Where's Big Guy?

Marky Marc
You there, Gaz?

Casanova
Has anyone heard from him?

Cherry AKA Kitten AKA Rhee AKA Baby Girl
OMG! Please tell me you've spoken to him after the exam today?!?!?!

The Hastinator
Damn, no. Sorry, Cherry. I went to Bossi's after the exam, and we helped his brother repair one of the sheds.

Marky Marc
Sorry, Rhee. I went to Jared's place.

Casanova
I just tried to call him. He's not answering.

Cherry AKA Kitten AKA Rhee AKA Baby Girl
OMG!

Casanova
Calm down, Kitten. I'm sure he's ok.
He will reach out to one of us if he needs help.

I want to believe Shaun, but it's hard to when I feel this sense of dread in my gut.

Cherry AKA Kitten AKA Rhee AKA Baby Girl
I'm gonna give you my sister's number.
GARRETT or any of you, text her if you're in trouble or need help or need to get a message to me. She will pass it on to me.

While my head spins, my mind goes to dark scenarios of what could be happening to Garrett right now. I send through Char's phone number in the chat and debate if I should go and wake my mum. I could be overreacting, though… right?

I wrap up my chats with the guys as my hour time limit ticks over. It's ridiculous how emotionally attached I am to the device in my hand. Like taking it away will be the end of the world. It's a stupid reaction, yet it happens anyway, because that device is my link to my guys. I really need to get my phone back.

Just when I'm about to slip out of my wardrobe, Char's phone starts vibrating in my hand, and I glance at the screen to see the number. I recognise it but don't know who it belongs to exactly, so I take a risk and answer it.

"Hello?" I keep my voice low and wait for a response.

"Hey, Kitten. I hope you don't mind me calling. I really wanted to hear your voice."

"Cass." Tears well in my eyes as I give in to the ache in my heart. "I don't mind. It's so good to hear your voice."

"Yours too, Kitten." His tone sounds like he's smiling, and I imagine his chiselled features softening as his lips spread into his infectious smile. "I miss you like crazy. I'm tempted to break you out of that house."

I giggle quietly. "My knight in shining armour."

"Well, more like your Casanova in shining armour." He chuckles, and it sends warmth to the ache in my chest. "Kitten?" Shaun asks, his voice turning serious.

"Yes, Cass?"

"I don't want you to worry about anything. I know you will, but promise me you will try not to. Me and the guys will find out if Gaz is ok, and we will sort out those fuckers at school. We aren't going anywhere, so we will be pining after you for as long as your parents try to keep us apart. Keeping us apart won't extinguish the fire I have for you, and I know the others feel the same."

"Shit Cass. Come rescue me now. I wanna run away with you."

His chuckle is quiet. "Where do you want me to take you after I rescue you?"

"To your house. Your loft bed." I sigh. "That first night you took me there was so perfect. I felt so safe in your arms, looking up through the skylight at the passing storm. I want more of those nights, just the two of us in our own little bubble."

"Fuck, I want that too. I haven't even washed my sheets because they still smell like you, and I don't want that to go away. I love our group time, but I fucking miss the me and you time, Kitten."

"Same." My chest aches again. "We can do that soon, right? Just you and me?"

"I'll make it happen." Shaun declares, and I smile at the conviction in his tone.

"You should really wash those sheets, dude." I giggle, and his chuckle meets my ears.

"Not until I know you are about to dirty them up with me again."

"Maybe I can leave you with one of my t-shirts or something. You can cuddle it every night." I joke, but his voice is serious.

"I'd fucking love that, Kitten. I ache to be wrapped in your sweet scent again."

Swoon!

"My scent is sweet?"

"Yes. It's fucking intoxicating. I can't get enough of you. It's really fucking hard to share you sometimes." Shaun's tone is deadly serious, and it sends a pang to my heart.

"I'm sorry," I whisper.

"No need to be sorry, Kitten. It's natural for me to feel this way. I'm also a greedy fucker."

"A greedy fucker I love." I declare.

"This greedy fucker loves you right back, Kitten. So much so that I ache for you."

"Fuck, you really are good at this Casanova stuff, aren't you?" I tease, and he chuckles.

"It's not Casanova stuff. It's just my heart belonging to you."

"Shit Cass. When are you coming to rescue me?" My tone is serious because I know without a doubt that if he turned up to steal me away, I'd go with him in a heartbeat.

"I'll meet you in your dreams tonight, beautiful. Make sure you're naked."

I giggle a little too loudly and slap my hand over my mouth, stretching out my senses to hear if anyone is coming. When I don't hear any movement in the house beyond my wardrobe, I drop my hand and relax.

"I'm always naked in my dreams, Cass. Especially if you're there." I sigh. "I should get this phone back to Char before she loses her shit at me."

"Ok, Kitten. Take care of you, ok?"

I smile at the warmth and care in his tone.

"Ok, Cass. You too."

We say our goodbyes, and I hang up, wishing I didn't have to put an end to hearing Shaun's voice tonight. I feel like he's always there for me, swooping in to save me from my own emotions. He seems to always put me first, even before his mates a lot of the time. I kinda feel bad about that, yet selfishly crave his dedication to me. I'll never be able to get enough of Shaun Bossier. Ever.

After I take a moment to compose myself, I silently slip out of my room and step into Char's to see her cross-legged on her bed in front of her laptop, typing away. She glances up when her door clicks shut behind me, her eyes wide with excitement.

"Bec and Amanda have reached out… you know. The CEOs from Angel Org?" When I nod, moving to sit on the side of the bed, Char continues, "Well, they have suggested reaching out to Hush. She's an anonymous podcaster and TikToker. Her podcast is called Breaking the Silence, and she tells the stories of those who can't speak up for themselves because they need to remain anonymous. Not only does she tell their stories, but she name drops and image drops on her TikTok account. She creates hype until someone recognises the person or people she posts about, and the cops have caught heaps of shady fuckers because of her. That's why she hasn't been shut down. No one knows who she is, but she does the stuff that others are afraid to do in fear of backlash."

"Wow." It's all I can summon as my mind takes in what Char just said.

"Bec and Amanda think this is the best avenue, especially because there could be other girls that Julie is fucking with. It will hopefully expose Julie, or whoever she is calling herself these days, and perhaps also convince more of her victims to come forward. Someone might give up her location. You have to do it, Rhys."

Charlotte rarely gets this involved in my dramas, but as she speaks, I can see how passionate she is about this. It reminds me of the passion I saw in Evie Prattle's eyes, too. It's a cause they believe in, and hell, I think I do too.

"Can I think about it?"

Char nods, holding out her earbuds. "Here, take a listen to her first podcast."

Grinning, I shuffle up next to Char and accept the earbud, slipping it in my ear. A soft, husky female voice fills my ear, and I'm instantly drawn into the podcast as Hush tells a story about a young girl, only ten years old, who accidentally killed her step-mum to stop her step-mum from beating her dad to death.

CHAPTER ELEVEN

RHYS

S leep evaded me last night. With worry for Garrett, and the husky voice of Hush still dancing in my head, I tossed and turned most of the night. I had to stop myself from sneaking out to go to Garrett's to check on him, and from barging back into Char's room to take her phone and listen to more of what Hush had to say. Instead, I stared at my ceiling and wished for the sun to hurry up and rise.

At breakfast, I tried to play nice and join the family at the table, hoping to convince Cin to give my phone or laptop back. When she refused, I stormed off, having only taken a single bite of my toast, and locked myself in my bedroom. Again. Let's see if my olds can handle a hunger strike!

Not being able to contact the guys is eating at me. Especially my worry over Garrett. I have to assume the guys have it sorted, though. Char hasn't said they have contacted her, so no news has to be good news, right?

Marcus is the only one with an exam today, and it bums me out that I could be having a quiet lazy day with my guys if my 'rents weren't being all fucking parenty and shit. I spend the morning trying to keep myself busy, and I write my sick and twisted story on some crumbled pages torn from the back of my maths workbook to send to Hush for her podcast. It will need to be typed up when I can get my hands on my phone or laptop, since the only way to contact Hush is via email.

My writing tells the story of a little girl who went from foster home to foster home, each time hoping that the next one would be her forever home. All she wanted was for someone to love her enough to want to keep her and call her their own.

I explain what it was like living with Brian and Julie. How Julie would basically play the bad cop, so I would find comfort in the good cop, Brian. Then how Brian would play games with me and made me feel special and cared for, causing me to believe the games he played were normal for dads and daughters to play.

I explain how they groomed me and how Julie made sure to hurt me so Brian could make me feel good, which would result in me wanting more. I even went into some of the sick things we did together and how it never hurt but felt good. It confused me, as I was only eleven when it started. I didn't understand why the girls at school got so upset when I told them about one of the games Brian and I played. The *'nurse game'*, where I would make him feel better. The girls called me disgusting and ran off to tell the teacher, and I didn't understand why child services took me away. Not at the time, anyway.

Then there have been years of therapy, teaching me that what happened was wrong. I left out the whole sex addiction thing. It's not relevant to finding Julie. But then I described Julie's comeback into my life. The phone calls and messages. The prison visits, minus the involvement of the police. I included the name Julie went by while looking after me. Julie Bates, who currently lives in Allansdale, where she takes in homeless girls.

Once I'm done, and utterly exhausted from the emotions I revisited while delving into my memories, I fold the paper around a grainy photo of Julie from five years ago that the police had given me to memorise the other day. As if I needed to re-acquaint myself with her ugly face. I'd never forget that face. Ever!

Even though I feel emotionally drained after writing all of my darkest secrets on paper, I'm too antsy to sit still, so I paint the second coat of purple on my walls, leaving my window shut so I can get myself high on the fumes, then kind of regret it as a huge chemical headache hits.

Whoops.

Basically, my Tuesday is boring as bat shit. I have a big fat sleep when the exhaustion gets too much, and afterwards, I shift my furniture back into place with the paint now dry. I don't attempt to put any posters back up on my walls yet. I'll give it a couple of days to make sure the paint has settled before I go sticking stuff everywhere.

When Charlotte gets home from work, I take my story and slip into her room.

"Can't a girl get five fucking minutes?" She snaps, and my brows lift.

"Good day?" I stir, and she rolls her eyes, flopping back on her bed.

"Before you ask for my phone, no, you can't have it tonight. I'm staying over at Deena's."

"Oh, so you're getting some action tonight, then?" I smirk, and she lifts her head off the bed to glare at me.

"I wish. She wants to talk about *feelings*." Char screws her face up and flops her head back again.

I giggle. "Shit. That's fucked. You should tell her your sister needs you and stay home."

That gets a snicker from her. "Yeah, right. As if I'm choosing you over sex."

"I thought you weren't getting any action?"

She shrugs. "The payoff of all the talking about feelings is the sex afterwards. Duh."

I giggle again.

"Why are you here?" She sighs, sitting up.

I glance down at my hands, where I'm gripping the folded paper a little too hard. "Ah... I wrote down what I need to tell Hush." I shrug, feeling self-conscious as I look back up to my sister's green eyes. "I kinda need a phone or laptop to send her this." I lift the paper, and Char's brows lift.

"Yeah. Right. I keep forgetting that you have no way of communicating, even though I know you want my phone for your guys."

"Rhys?" Our mum's voice calls through the door, and I bring the paper to my chest, ready to shove it down my top.

"Yeah?" I call back, turning as the door opens, and I dart my hands with the piece of paper behind my back as Cynthia fills the doorway.

"Oh, there you are. I need to have a chat with you."

"Are you giving my phone back?" My eyes brighten hopefully, but she frowns and shakes her head.

"No. Come with me, please." Cynthia says sternly, and my shoulders slump. I'm not sure what to do with the paper, but before I move, Char's hand comes up and eases the folded paper from my grasp, coming to stand behind me as my mum turns her back on us.

"Want me to do it for you?" Char whispers in my ear, and I glance at her. She knows a bit about my past, but she doesn't know the whole story. I'd been scared for anyone to find out how depraved it was, yet now, as I look into my sister's green eyes, I know I can trust her. She's got my back.

"Yes, please," I whisper back, and she smiles and nods before I walk off to follow my mum.

Cynthia leads me through the house to the front office, where we seem to have the "serious" talks these days. Will is already there waiting for me, and I instantly feel anxious. These talks lately are rarely good.

"So we've been monitoring your messages and any phone calls coming into your phone," Cynthia states, and I glare at her because I hate that she is reading my private messages from my guys. The Julie stuff I don't care about, but what's said between my guys and me is private. "For the record, I'm not reading the messages from Marcus, Simon, Shaun, and Garrett."

"But you are from Tyler, right?" I hiss, hearing the venom in my tone.

"Well, I had to make sure his conversations weren't grooming you, Rhys."

I lift a brow. "And did you find anything like that from him?"

My dad growls under his breath then, and Cynthia shoots him a glare before turning her gaze back to me. "No. I didn't find anything that resembled Tyler grooming you."

My dad growls again, and I turn my venom to him.

"What's wrong, Dad? Disappointed that Ty is actually genuine in his feelings for me?"

"I'm still not convinced." He mutters, and Cynthia raises her hands in a calming motion.

"Let's not get off track here. I wanted to let you know that aside from the voicemail from Julie, there hasn't been anything else sent to your phone. My phone, however, has been blowing up every few hours with new video snippets of you at that sex club, and I've taken it all to the police."

"What!" I screech, my legs nearly collapsing from under me at her words.

"Calm down. I didn't tell them about the one of you and Tyler in the barn."

"A fucking mistake if you ask me!" Will snaps, but Cynthia ignores him, her dark eyes remaining on me.

"It's not just that." I blurt. "The man that sent the videos is a powerful man. He has connections high up. Probably has cops in his pockets. He could make things hard for you if you try to expose him."

"He can try." My dad hisses. "No one will stop me from protecting my daughter."

"Your dad is right. We don't care who this man is. Nothing will stop us from exposing him and anyone linked to him that has played a part."

I guess it's too late now, anyway. They have already handed the videos over to the cops.

"Why didn't you expose Ty?" Tears well in my eyes as the mere thought of him paying the price for me sinks in.

"I'm not sure exactly." She shakes her head, and I notice for the first time how exhausted she looks. "I don't condone what's been going on between you and Tyler, but I can't seem to bring myself to hurt you like that, Rhys. To expose you just so he gets punished."

Tears spill over as I plead with her. "Please don't punish him. He's a good person. I know it seems wrong to you, but it doesn't seem wrong to us. It feels so right."

"You thought things with you and Brian were right too, Rhys. How can you tell the difference? I don't think you can. I don't think you can see it clearly at all." My dad stands from his chair, frowning at me, his words slicing my heart in two.

"Because Tyler doesn't ask anything of me. He quit his job to be with me."

"He quit his job hoping he wouldn't get caught as a teacher sleeping with his student!" My dad roars, and I flinch.

"Let's not do this. It's not helping." Cynthia pleas. The pain in her tone almost makes me look at her, but I'm too angry to take my eyes off Will. He's usually such a mellow man, but this stuff with Ty and me has turned him into a lion.

"I love him." My voice is nothing but confident as I stare my dad down.

"Yes, and apparently, you love four other boys, too." There's sarcasm in my dad's tone, and I hate hearing it.

"Yeah. So?"

"So? So?" My dad rounds his desk to stand before me. "That's not normal!"

"Ding! Ding! Ding! And the winner is William Rogan for finally realising that his foster daughter isn't fucking normal!"

"Rhys!" Cynthia scoffs while Will takes a step back from me, frowning.

"It's true. I'm not normal. I never have been normal, and I never will be normal, and the sooner you accept that, the easier it will be to understand me. If that's not something you can accept, *Dad*, then perhaps I'm not meant to be a part of this family!"

I ignore Cynthia as she reaches for me, tears falling down her cheeks as I turn and flee from the room. If I were smart, I'd steal one of their phones and high-tail it outta here, but even though I said the words about not belonging to this family, my heart aches to be a part of it. It aches just as much as it aches for Ty and the other guys.

I lock myself in my room, once again refusing to eat, which sucks dog's balls because I fucking love food. The hunger doesn't do my state of mind any good either, as the darkness closes in on me, almost making me choke on it. Since I don't have access to my phone to play music, I lay the wrong way up on my bed, my head dangling over the end in the dark, and I sing every dark song I know. I don't care that I sound out of fucking tune. I sing at the top of my lungs, screaming at times as the unbearable pain of feeling alone consumes me. I ignore the banging on my door. Cynthia's threats of picking the lock. She can go ahead. I'm not moving off this bed, and I'm not going to stop singing like the crazy bitch they think I am.

I'm not sure how much time goes by, but my angry singing eventually turns into soft, sad crooning until all I'm doing is crying silently in the dark. There's so much pain inside me. How the hell does that work exactly? How do my emotions cause physical pain? It's almost unbearable. The kind of pain that you'll do almost anything to take it away. To end it.

This, too, shall pass.

Garrett's words flutter through my head. The words are so simple, yet so fucking powerful to me. This pain will pass. I just have to be patient. Julie will be found. My 'rents will unground me if they decide to keep me, and I will get to see my guys again. I will turn eighteen in less than four months, and then I can see Tyler as much as I like. It won't always be like this. I just have to be patient and strong.

I wish I had asked Cin about Garrett earlier when we had that fucked up discussion. I'm still so worried about him. Not knowing if he's ok is torturous. Have the guys heard from him? Is his dad still at his house? Ugh! I can probably kiss sleep goodbye for another hellish night. My thoughts are my worst enemy right now. I shouldn't be left alone with them.

A tap sounds at my bedroom door, and I pop my head up off my mattress to listen.

"Rhys, are you awake, honey? There's someone here that you might want to see." Cynthia's hushed voice has me frowning but also curious, so I roll off my bed and move to my door, unlocking it to peer out at Cin.

"Who?" I snap. It's probably the police or child services coming to take me away.

"Garrett is here, honey."

My brows shoot up, and I swing the door wide, ready to run out to find my big guy.

"Hang on." Cynthia holds her hands up. "Before you go barging out there, you need to know that he's a little beat up."

"What!" I screech, and she hushes me, sending a panicked look towards the twins' bedroom door.

"He's ok, Rhys. Your dad is cleaning him up in the kitchen now."

"But… why didn't he come to my window?" I glance over at it like it somehow betrayed me.

"When we had a chat yesterday, I told him he was welcome here anytime, especially if he felt unsafe or needed help. But I asked him not to come to your window. I asked him to come to the front door and to ask your dad or me for help. So that's what he did. I'm extremely proud of him for doing that. I can see how much he would prefer to keep his situation a secret, but he obviously knows he needs help."

I leap forward, wrapping my arms around my mum's neck, reminding myself that she isn't my enemy. That she cares about me and my friends and just wants us to be safe.

Cynthia hugs me back for a moment before pulling out of our embrace. "The best thing you can do for Garrett right now is to stay calm and be there for him. I have already put in a call to child services, so they know he is here and is safe. The police are already looking for Garrett's dad, and his mum and sisters are on their way as we speak with some officers to his aunt's house. One of their neighbours called the police as well, so there are witnesses."

"Doesn't Garrett want to go with his mum and sisters?"

"No." Cynthia shakes her head. "He doesn't want his sister's seeing him like this."

Her words sink in, and I push past her, running through the quiet house to the open plan living area to find Garrett sitting on a barstool facing the other direction while my dad dabs something on his face. I pull up short as I take in the tear at the back of his hoodie and the streak of blood that wraps around his head from the front.

Stepping forward slowly, I feel my heart start to fracture with each step as the side of his battered face comes into view. A gasp escapes me, my hand flying to my mouth as tears pool in my eyes.

My dad takes a step back as Garrett turns his head towards me, showing me that one side of his face resembles my big guy while the other resembles a bruised puffer fish.

"It looks worse than it is." Garrett rasps, and I shake my head.

"Liar," I whisper, and the good side of his face grins.

"Would it make you feel better to know that the other guy looks worse?"

I nod. "Your dad?"

He nods back, and my bottom lip wobbles.

"I'm so sorry." I push past Will and step close to Garrett, unsure if I should touch him because I might hurt him.

"I'm ok." He whispers, and his fingers link with mine.

I stare into his icy-blue eyes, noting the dullness in them tonight. He's trying to be strong right now. Maybe he's putting on a brave face in front of my dad, so I respect his needs, knowing exactly what it's like to feel the compulsion of wearing the confidence mask.

I don't let go of Garrett. Not when Will cleans up the rest of the blood from his face. Not when the police stop by to advise that they still haven't found his dad and to take his statement and some photos. Not when Cynthia leads us to the kids' zone, explaining that I can sleep in Charlotte's room and Garrett can sleep in my bed, even though she knows damn well that's not going to happen. And I don't let go of Garrett when I close the bathroom door in my mum's face, so I can help Garrett shower.

He sits on the edge of the bath as I ease his hoodie over his head, remaining quiet as he watches me. Then I ease his t-shirt off, taking in the bruising on his ribs.

"You've been crying." His deep voice is low and quiet, gaining my attention from his ribs.

"Well, duh. You come to my house beaten. Of course, I'm going to cry."

"No." He shakes his head a fraction. "I mean, before I came here. Your eyes are red and puffy. They were already like that before seeing me."

I roll my eyes. "Mr Observant. Aren't we?"

He chuckles before catching my hand in his and tugging me to stand between his parted legs. From this position, even though he's a giant, I'm a little taller as he sits before me. "Why was my girl crying?"

I shrug. "I've had a day."

"Tell me about it."

"Garrett, you've had a day, too. You don't want to hear about my bullshit."

"Actually, your bullshit is all I want to hear about. Please." His good eye gives me that puppy dog look, and I'm helpless to deny him.

"Fine." I huff. "I've been extra lonely today. I wrote down the shit that happened to me when I was younger, which has brought up feelings I don't want invading my brain. I gave myself a headache from paint fumes, hoping it would make me high. Which it kind of did, but the headache was the true result. I had a big blow-up with the olds. Especially my dad. Mostly about Tyler, of course, and how it's not normal to be seeing multiple guys." I shake my head, trying to clear away the memory of that clusterfuck of an argument. "The whole thing put me in a dark place, and because I don't have access to music, I had to sing the songs I wanted to listen to. And FYI. I was not put on this earth to sing." I sigh, my shoulders dropping as the darkness oozes back in. "Some of my singing turned into screaming, and eventually it turned into crying." I cup the good side of his face. "I was worried about you."

"Sorry, Baby Girl. I'm pretty sure my dad has my phone. And after going home yesterday after the exam, I decided I wasn't leaving my mum and sisters alone with that arsehole."

"So that's where you were? Just at home?"

He nods. "Yep. Thank fuck the girls slept through this." He gestures to his face. "He tried to make me cry out in pain with each punch he landed. It really pissed him off that I didn't make a sound. He even tried to keep quiet with each punch I landed on him, too. He wasn't as successful as me." Garrett smirks a little with the good side of his face.

I spend a moment studying his face. The bruised and unbruised parts and the in between. He may be battered right now, but all I see is a fighter. A warrior.

"Thank you for coming to my parents for help," I whisper.

"They're good people."

I nod. "Yes. I just wish they could accept me the way I am."

"They just need time." Garrett offers, lifting his bad hand to cup the side of my face.

"This too shall pass," I whisper, and his brows shoot up at the mantra he taught me.

"You remember."

"Yeah. It's honestly what got me through today." I smile, and he nods in understanding.

"Same."

As much as I want to kiss him, I hold myself back because he's sporting a fat cut lip, and I'm terrified of hurting him, even though it's something we usually like to do to each other.

Garrett showers while I hover by the door, and after a few minutes, he darts his hand out and drags me under the spray of water, soaking my t-shirt through. I squeal, but his hand slaps over my mouth as he pushes me up against the cold tiles in the shower.

"Quiet, Baby Girl. Let's not unintentionally invite your parents in here with us." Garrett rasps as he presses his body flush with mine.

I nod, reaching up to peel his hand from my mouth, and then I press my lips to the back of his fingers, where grazes mar his skin.

His long curls fall forward as the water rushes over his head, and I swear I've never seen him look younger. He looks very much like his age right now, despite his hulking size.

"I'm glad you came here, and not just because I was lonely. I want you to know you will always have a safe place to go."

He grins, awkwardly pressing the un-bruised part of his forehead against mine. "You're my safe place, Baby Girl. Nothing feels more right to me."

Damn. Those words are enough to make a black-hearted girl swoon.

So naturally, I do what any girl would do.

I drop to my knees.

Chapter Twelve

GARRETT

F uck. Those big chocolate pools peer up at me as she lowers herself to her knees, and in an instant, my flaccid cock is as stiff as a board. I reach for her, intending on tugging her back up. I'm not here for this. I'm not here just so I can get my dick some action. I'm here because I meant what I said. She is my safe place. She is home to me.

She bats my hands away, giving her head a shake as she shoots me a pointed glare. I can't help but chuckle and lift my hands in defeat. After all, who am I to deny my girl?

"You don't have to do this, Baby Girl." I rasp, and she shrugs.

"I know, but I want to do this for you. I want to worship you for once."

Doesn't she know that every naked encounter we have is her worshipping me? I'm about to say as much when she wraps her lips around the swollen head of my cock. My words die in my throat, and all I can release is a hiss as pleasure travels to my nuts and deep inside me.

Using both hands, she wraps them around my shaft and starts to work them up and down, squeezing as she goes to give me the friction I'm craving. It's fucking hard not to thrust my hips and penetrate her throat with the size of my dick. The urge is strong, and instead of gripping her hair to control her head, I slap my palms against the tiled wall to brace myself.

Her dark eyes haven't left mine. She has me in her trance as she pumps my dick and licks my tip before giving it a good suck.

"Fuck, Baby Girl. Your mouth is like heaven."

Her eyes flare like she would be grinning if my dick weren't taking up her mouth, and then she presses her head forward and takes more of me in. It's a stretch. I know that. My dick isn't small, and although most guys would probably love a dick like mine, it can be a deterrent. It's why my sexual encounters are minimal. Most girls balk at it when they feel it or get a look. Rhys George isn't most girls though, and she accepts me. All of me.

The moment she gags, my dick jerks. I instantly feel bad and pull out to give her time to recover.

She gasps, sucking in air, her cheeks flushed red as she keeps her eyes on me. "Such a mouthful." She pants, grinning up at me. "Give me more."

I chuckle as she eases my beast back into the heat of her mouth, and the way she moans around me shoots electric currents of pleasure to my balls. She picks up the pace, using one hand to stroke me, the other rolling my balls as she devours my cock.

It only takes another minute of her heavenly touch to send me fevered, and I sink my teeth into my forearm to stop from making any noise as I cum down her throat. My load is too much for her to handle, and the sick part of me loves how she can't take it all, needing to pull back so my seed jets over her face.

"Fuck baby." I pant, stroking the last remnants of cream from my cock as she uses her fingers to wipe up what the spray of the shower misses and licks her fingers clean.

"I don't need to worry about not eating while I'm on my hunger strike. You fill me up good, Big Guy."

My brows shoot up as I laugh. My girl never ceases to surprise me with her smart mouth and minxie ways.

"Come up here so I can repay you." I rasp, but she shakes her head as she stands.

"No need. I already came while I was choking on your cum. It's like magic orgasm juice or something." She beams, and again, I laugh.

Rhys George has a way of making a guy forget all about his worries. I know she fell to her knees for me on purpose. It's the only way she knows how to help in these situations.

We cuddle under the spray of the shower for a few more minutes before we get out and dry off, slipping into Rhys' bedroom with only towels wrapped around us. We hurry to climb under the covers, and although it hurts to have her pressed against my ribs, where I'm pretty sure one is cracked, I don't push my girl away. I fucking need her nearness right now. I need to feel the warmth of her skin, so soft and delicate and all feminine. I need to feel her chest rising and falling, feel her breath fan over my skin, and hear her breathing even out as she succumbs to sleep in my arms.

It's fucking perfect.

I try not to think too much about my old man. The way it pissed him off so much that his punches didn't pack what they did the last time he was living with us.

I try not to think about my mum and how much I look up to her, yet feel disappointed in her for not standing up and refusing to allow her abusive husband to come back into our home.

I try not to think about Britney and Polly and how scared they must have been when they were woken in the middle of the night to be rushed away to our aunt's house.

I try not to think about everything I had to reveal yesterday to Rhys' mum, my principal, and the look of sympathy she couldn't hold back. I fucking hate that look. It's one of the reasons I keep my bullshit to myself. The thing is, the situation with my dad doesn't just affect me. It affects my sisters and mum too, which is the reason I spoke up. They are the reason I wear these bruises, so they don't have to. And they are the reason I held back and didn't fucking kill my dad, because they need me, and so does this dark angel in my arms.

CHAPTER THIRTEEN

SHAUN

B eing apart from Kitten is a form of torture. I didn't realise how fucking boring life was without her in it. Not being able to see her or talk to her is the worst. Wait, no. What's worse is not knowing if she's ok.

My mama keeps asking if I'm ok, obviously reading my expression, but I don't want to worry her with my lonely heart when she is so clearly suffering in physical pain. Dad should be focused on looking after mama, especially with her condition worsening, but with the end of the year coming fast, he keeps asking me what my plans are after I graduate. Then he goes into a lecture about how finishing school is unnecessary because I don't need my high school diploma to learn the family business of running the vineyard.

I do love our vineyard. I just hate the pressure of feeling like I have no choice but to join my dad and Derek in running it. I kinda wish he'd give me a choice. I wish he'd tell me to go off travelling and learn who I am before settling down to run the family business with my brother.

Simon called an hour ago and said Garrett showed up at his house looking like he'd gone ten rounds in the boxing ring. Apparently, his old man tried to take him on last night and lost again. And apparently, he went to Kitten's parents for help in the middle of the night, and they took him in, giving him a place to stay and access to our girl. So now I'm on my way to Grady's house to hang out with the guys and find out from Garrett how Kitten really is.

When Derek drops me off, Garrett and Simon are already walking up the drive, passing through the gate that leads to the back, where the familiar sounds of a bouncing ball tells me Marcus is shooting hoops. As I pass through the gate, my eyes fall over my mates, which includes Jared. It's good to see him here. I think he's been feeling left out now that the rest of us have Rhys in common.

Our situation with Rhys has been on my mind lately. I'm not sure how Marcus is still talking to us after what we did to him. Or, more to the point, what I did to him. It's been playing on my mind more and more over the last few days that what I did to him was a pure fucking cunt's act. The hiding he gave me wasn't enough to make up for how much I betrayed him. Now, though, with these feelings I never thought I'd feel for a girl, I'm struggling with the fear that she will somehow be taken away from me. It's a fucking terrifying thought. I can't fathom it. And if I put myself in Grady's shoes and let myself feel a fraction of what he did when he realised his mate was fucking around with the girl he loved, the urge to kill every fucker in sight is almost overwhelming.

Marcus Grady is a better man than I'll ever be.

Fuck, my emotions are all over the place. Can guys get a male version of PMS?

"You look like you bit into a sour lemon, Bossi." Jared chuckles as I approach, and I frown.

"Aren't all lemons sour?"

Jared laughs, tossing the basketball towards me. I catch it, bouncing it a couple of times before lining up for a shot at the ring. The moment it leaves my hands, I know I've fucked up and I watch as the ball goes wide. Yeah, I'm off my game alright. The guys think my lack of skill today is the best thing, laughing at my poor display. I'm not laughing, though. Not as I take in Garrett's battered face.

"Fuck, man. Are you ok?" My concern makes Garrett frown, and he nods, too tough to admit if he weren't ok.

"We need to talk about our girl." Garrett avoids voicing an answer to my question, gaining the guys' attention.

"Since she's not *my* girl, do I have to be here for it?" Jared asks, and I nod.

"Yep, because once we are done, we're shooting hoops until I've kicked your arse, and you're begging for me to stop."

"As if." Jared chuckles, throwing the ball straight through the hoop.

"He's gonna kick your arse, Bossi." Hastings sings with a wide grin, and my lips spread wide, knowing it's the truth but not really caring.

"So, what do we need to talk about?" Marcus asks, and we all fall quiet, looking at Garrett.

"She's in a dark place. Understandably." Garrett frowns. "But when I went there last night, I could tell she'd been crying. Like a lot. She told me that the mantra I told her is what got her through the day, which means she's really struggling, and I know we can't hold her hand through everything, but I can't help wanting to." Garrett sweeps his hand through his curls. "Fuck, she'd sell her soul to the devil to save us. She basically did that for Tyler."

"Do you think her olds would let us see her if we turned up?" Simon asks, his playful nature gone as his concern for our girl worries him.

"I don't know." Garrett shrugs. "It's hard to tell. There's a fucking lot of tension between Rhys and her parents right now. They had a big argument yesterday. Something was said in that argument which has really dug under Rhys' skin. She seemed content when I was there with her last night, but when it was time for me to leave this morning, she got jittery and shit. Like really anxious. I didn't want to leave her, but the cops came, and I had to go with them to ID my dad in a lineup."

"Did they get him?" Jared asks, and Garrett nods.

"Yep. They didn't find my phone, though, so I still don't have any way to contact you guys. That's why I turned up at Simon's this morning unannounced."

"Shit, that's good that they got him. So he's locked up now?" I ask, and Garrett nods.

"Yeah, because he was on parole, he went straight back in. I'm not sure what happens now, though. I guess I'll find out soon."

"Are your sisters ok?" Hastings asks, and Garrett nods again.

"They're safe. I'm trying to avoid them, though. I don't want them to see this." He points to his face, and we all nod in understanding. He's pretty battered.

"Do you think Rhys' parents will let you go back there today? Or tonight?" I ask, and he shrugs.

"I can only try. It might be different now that my dad is locked up, though." He shrugs, and I nod in understanding. Rhys' parents were making an exception for Garrett with the problems with his dad, but now that his dad isn't an issue anymore, they may not be so quick to accommodate him.

We all fall silent, our thoughts with our girl or with Garrett, or probably even with the truck full of the crap we all have going on. When did everything get so fucking hard and complicated?

After a few minutes, Jared convinces Simon to shoot hoops with him, so I park my arse on the cool concrete path next to the drive to watch, and Marcus and Gaz join me. As I watch Simon, I notice the playfulness which typically lights him up isn't as bright today. His smiles are the fakest I've ever seen, and so are his laughs. I'm aware he often hides behind his humour, but today he isn't able to hide it very well at all. The stuff going on with his parents, and his mum wanting him to leave Fox Pines, is taking a toll, and with the end of the school year looming over us, Simon's time is running out.

I dropped a hint to my old man about having Simon live with us, and in exchange, he would work on the farm after school and on weekends. My dad made it clear that he won't be paying for Hastings to go to the uptight school I go to, but he's thinking about my suggestion of giving Simon a place to stay. I fucking hope he says yes.

"You're quiet, Bossi." Marcus nudges my shoulder, and I drag my eyes off Simon and Jared, wrestling for the ball, and take in the mate I betrayed, sitting next to me.

"There's a lot going on. I'm feeling… out of sorts."

He nods, his dark brown eyes shooting to the ground between us. "Yep. Same. Everything has changed in such a short time."

A lump forms in my throat as prissy emotions twist my gut. "I'm really sorry, man." I push the words out before I can cower, and his brown eyes flick up to mine again.

"What for?"

"What I did to you. It was a cunt's act." I take a moment to swallow down the bowling ball-sized lump in my throat before I continue. "Mates don't do that to each other."

Marcus frowns, tilting his head at me. "Why *did* you do it? Like I get that the first time you didn't know it was Rhys until it was too late, but you went back for more."

Even though he should sound pissed at me, he doesn't. Marcus just sounds curious.

"I was weak. I still am. I'm not willing to give her up for you or anyone else, but I still feel fucking awful about doing that to you."

He chuckles. "Yeah, well, I'm not fucking giving her up either, and honestly, I haven't thought much about the betrayal lately. Just Rhys, and how much I want to make her happy."

I nod in understanding. "I'm sure Hastings feels like shit about it, too. He didn't know about me and Rhys when things happened between them."

"Hastings was never going to be able to fight our girl off." Marcus glances over at Simon as Simon tries to get the ball out of Jared's grip. "I know she said it was just about sex, and I honestly think that's what she thought at the time, but it's always been more than that. I don't think she understood the difference between her attraction to sex and her attraction to each of us. She was drawn to us through the bond we'd already formed with her. Now she's learning the difference between the two, and I want that for her. I want her to feel that sort of love." Marcus shrugs and sighs. "Do I hate that I can't be the only one to give her that love? Yeah, it bums me out a bit. But sharing this with you guys also has an appeal. I feel like we are more than mates now."

I grin. "Yeah. More like family."

He nods, and Garrett leans forward. "I'm good with the family thing, as long as you keep your cocks away from my arse."

We throw our heads back, laughing, halting the game Jared and Simon are playing as they come over to us.

"What's so funny?" Simon asks, and Marcus answers.

"Garrett said he wants you to fuck him up the arse."

"I'm pretty sure my comment was the opposite to that," Garrett grumbles as I laugh harder.

"Are you guys like... hooking up, too?" Jared asks, looking mortified, and I can't breathe. Laughter stabbing my side like a stitch.

"What's wrong Crowley? Scared you're missing out?" Simon grins. "You want me to take you up the arse?"

The look on Jared's face is pure terror. "Stay the fuck away from my arse!" Jared hisses, and Marcus joins me in hysterics as Simon prowls toward Jared.

The moment Jared turns to run, letting out a squeal fit for a chick, we all fall into hysterics that I'm almost certain will cause us to stop breathing.

Chapter Fourteen

RHYS

I can't take it anymore. I feel like a caged animal, and Kitty is feeling my frustration to the core. I think about taking Big Jim for a spin, but I need more than the object. I need sound and visuals. I need a sex-filled atmosphere.

I haven't spoken to Will since the argument yesterday. I've avoided him like the plague, but today I'm feeling all sorts of bratty, mainly because I'm bored as fuck, and he is cock-blocking me. He also seems to have a problem with how *not normal* I am, so fuck it. I'm gonna show him just how not normal I am.

"Can I pleeeease have my laptop?" I whine, hovering by the kitchen table where Will is working today. I'm not sure why he isn't using his office. Probably to keep a better eye on me. "I reeeeally need it."

"No, Rhys. You'll just use it to contact people, and right now, you need a break from that." He doesn't even look up from his laptop. Ugh. He's so frustrating! Maybe I can snatch his laptop and keep it captive and see how he likes it?

"That's *nooot* what I want it *fooor*," I whine again, and he huffs, glancing up at me.

"What do you need a laptop for, then?"

"I wanna watch movies." I smile innocently, fluttering my dark lashes, and he shakes his head.

"Rhys, we have an expensive theatre room just down the hall. You can watch movies in there."

"Uh… I don't think you want me watching *my* movies in there." I shoot him a pointed look, waiting for him to get my meaning, but it goes straight over his head, which he shakes as he looks back down at his laptop.

"Rhys, you can watch movies in the theatre room or watch nothing at all. They are your options."

"Fine." I huff, spinning on my heel and storming off to my bedroom. Since the theatre room is my *only* option, I guess that's where this has to happen.

I go to my toy drawer and scoop up Big Jim, Little Jim and Peter Rabbit, as well as my largest tube of lube before I stop by the bathroom to get a towel because, you know, sometimes this sort of work can get messy. Once I have all my supplies, I stroll back out into the living area with my arms full of vibes, moving past Will towards the theatre room.

"Whoa. What are you doing?" Will's voice is high-pitched, and I bite my bottom lip, trying not to laugh as he chases behind me. I don't stop. Hurrying down the passage, I enter the theatre room, using my elbow to flick on the light switch.

"Rhys. What are you doing?" Will asks again, still sounding all panicky and shit.

I set my vibes down on the coffee table towards the front of the room, laying them out, biggest to smallest.

"I'm getting set up," I mutter to Will, pretending I'm too busy to pay him attention.

"I-I don't understand. Getting set up for what?"

I ignore him for a moment while I straighten and move across the space to the projector, turning it on and waiting while the web browser loads.

It occurs to me then that I could have been using the theatre to log in to SnapChat to contact the guys. *Duh!*

"Can you answer me, please?" Will snaps, and I bite back a laugh.

"What was the question again?" I spare him a brief glance, feigning distraction.

"What are you setting up?"

After the browser finishes loading and I type in the address, I watch as the projector lights up the screen before I turn and smile at Will.

"Porn hub." I gesture to the screen, and Will's eyes go wide as he takes it in.

I move back over to my beautiful toys that are waiting to be devoured by Kitty, and I pop the cap on the lube and start pouring it over each one.

"Stop, Rhys! What are you doing?" Will cries, and for a moment, I feel kind of bad for the guy, but then I remember how he brought this all on himself, and I forget to care.

"What does it look like? I'm getting ready to watch my movies." I say over my shoulder, knowing he can see everything I'm doing as I hold up Little Jim and flick him on, nodding as it comes to life in my hand.

"Stop! You can't do *this* in here!"

I sigh, turning Little Jim off but keeping him in my grip as I spin to face my dad.

"Jesus Christ, Dad. Make up your mind. I wanna watch porn and get some of this tension out. You won't give me my laptop, and I need a visual. You told me to watch it in here. So that's what I'm doing."

"I didn't mean, watch *that*." He cringes as he points to the screen like he's never watched porn before.

"What's going on?" Cynthia's voice startles me as she steps into the room, looking confused.

Shit. I didn't realise what the time was. Probably because I can't tell what fucking time of day it is without being able to check my phone. Sure, there's a clock somewhere in this house, but I'm yet to find it.

I sigh. "Dad is porn blocking me!"

"Fucking hell Cin, she wants to watch porn while… while…" He gestures to the table lined with my beautiful vibes waiting for some action, and Cin's eyes widen before she tries to smother a laugh.

"You think this is funny?" Will hisses at her, and she lets her laugh free.

"Oh, William. Can't you see? She's trying to shock you into getting her own way."

"Well, it's fucking working. She can have her laptop back!"

"Yes." I fist pump the air as Connor's voice makes me freeze.

"Are they new toys?"

"They look cool." Archie bounds into the room with his brother, standing before me, where I quickly hide Little Jim behind my back as Archie looks up at me. "What do they do?"

"Ahhh… they are rockets," I say cheerfully, and Will yells.

"No, they aren't! Go to your room, boys!"

Archie turns to frown at Dad. "You keep yelling at us lately. Maybe you need a time out, Dad."

"Yeah, Dad. Maybe you need a timeout." I agree, not so helpfully, and Will's face turns so red that I think his brain is about to burst through his ears.

"That's enough!" Cynthia yells this time. "Boys out now!" She points to the door before turning her eyes to me. "Rhys, put that stuff away. You're not getting your laptop back."

I pout. "My phone then?"

"No." She snaps as the boys slump their shoulders and leave.

"You really expect me to fuck these things and get any satisfaction without a visual? You may as well put a fucking chastity belt on me!" I'm irrationally angry now because I feel so out of sorts. It's torture having these things taken away from me, and while I'm trying to understand Cin and Will's mindset about it, I don't think they realise that it's having the opposite effect.

"Now there's an idea." Will pipes up and I glare at him before I hold Little Jim up and flick his switch on. As my vibe comes to life, buzzing in my hand, I hook my thumb in the band of my sweatpants and start to tug them down.

I know, I know. It's all sorts of fucked up to do this in front of my rents, but my crazy has kicked in, and I'm feeling so on edge that I'm almost scared another bender is about to consume me.

"Rhys! Stop!" Cynthia leaps forward and grabs Little Jim from my grip, tossing him across the room like he's meaningless before she spins to Will. "Get my bag. Her meds are in the side pocket."

I freeze, sweatpants at my knees, as my heart seizes.

"No! Wait! Please. I'm stopping. See!" I pull my pants back in place and hold up my hands just as the doorbell rings.

Cin and Will glance at each other, and I take that moment to bolt past them from the room towards the front door.

"Stop, Rhys!" Will yells, but I don't stop. I can't let them drug me. I can't let them take control over my body like that again. I didn't do anything wrong.

Ok, so maybe I'm being a brat, but it's not bender-worthy behaviour… is it?

I reach the door and swing it open to see four sets of familiar eyes staring at me before they widen and look over my shoulder. I don't think. I act and leap into Simon's arms like a spider monkey.

"Don't let them drug me." I whimper, actually feeling scared of Cynthia and Will. Maybe it's some sort of PTSD from the last few times that Cin had to use the drugs on me to get me into line. But those times, I was so far gone, I didn't even know my own name or care about anything but staying in my high. I'm not like that this time, so why would she want to drug me?

Because she's the same as all the adults in your life, Rhys. She wants to control you.

"What?" Garrett hisses, his voice a deep rumble that makes me jerk in Simon's arms, and I turn back to see Garrett step in between my parents and me.

"Rhys, it's not like that. It was just a threat. I wasn't actually going to use the meds. I just needed you to stop trying to use the vibrator." I would laugh at Cynthia's words if I didn't feel like she was lying.

She had every intention of using the meds to sedate me into a manageable zombie version of myself.

"Uh… Excuse me? You were going to drug her?" Shaun hisses this time, and my dad growls.

"This is none of your business."

"Actually, it is." Marcus growls this time. "Rhys is *our* business, and we won't stand by while you keep her captive and *drug* her." Another look over my shoulder shows that Garrett, Shaun and Marcus are now blocking my parents from getting to me.

"Oh my goodness. This is not how it seems." Cynthia sounds distraught. "She is just grounded. She's not being held captive. And the drugs were a threat. I would never use them on her unless she was out of control."

"She was out of control! She was going to masturbate in the theatre and watch porn while the rest of us go about our day around her. That's not normal." Will hisses, and I lose my shit, leaping off Simon and pushing through the wall of my guys as I scream.

"I AM NOT NORMAL! STOP TRYING TO CHANGE ME!"

My scream is piercing, echoing across the neighbourhood as everyone falls silent.

"What the fuck is going on?" Charlotte steps up, having pulled up in her car at some point to come home to this commotion.

No one speaks, so I do.

"I need everyone to stop trying to change me. Just because I'm different doesn't mean there's something wrong with me, and I refuse to be in the company of anyone who can't accept me the way I am." Even though I'm trying to be strong, a sob escapes as I push out the last word, and Charlotte pushes past Simon to hug me.

"That's exactly right, Rhys. People who don't accept you don't deserve a minute more of your time." She says loud enough for everyone to hear, holding me close as I bury my head in the crook of her neck.

"Charlotte. There's a lot at play here." Cynthia speaks, but Char shakes her head.

"You're making it harder than it needs to be. Making it hard for Rhys to cope with all of this stuff that she's drowning in. You need to take a step back and let her breathe. You're smothering her, and yes, it's because you care, but it's doing more harm than good." Charlotte rubs her hand up and down my back, offering me support as she continues. "You can't tell Rhys who to care about and who not to. It doesn't work like that. I can't tell you to not care about Will. If I say a bad word about him, you will feel insulted because you care for him so dearly. Each time you say something bad about someone Rhys cares about, you are pushing her away even more. Is her whole group relationship thing going to work? No one knows. All she can do is try. She needs to follow her own path, make her own mistakes, revel in her own wins, and know that no matter what happens, you will be there for her. Good or bad. Threatening to drug her to make her comply is not supporting her."

"I…" Cynthia is lost for words, and if I'm being honest. So am I.

I slowly pull back from Char, and she peers down at me with more care towards me than I've seen before.

"You are perfect just the way you are." She smiles, tears glistening in her green eyes as she brushes back some of my hair.

I nod because I can't speak, and we step away from each other to face the six sets of eyes watching our interaction.

"Here." Cynthia holds out a box, and my eyes widen as I take it in. "I want you to get rid of these. You don't need them, and I want you to trust that I will never use them on you again."

My guys step aside, giving me more room as I move forward to accept the box of potent sedatives, and I glance between my parents, knowing that I brought a lot of this on myself.

If only you were normal, you wouldn't annoy everyone so much.

"I'm sorry, Dad. I was desperate and acted like a brat, and I could have gone about that whole situation differently. I'm sorry it's so hard to understand why I need the things I need and why I care about multiple guys. People get scared when they don't understand something. I know. But that's who I am, and Char is right about everything she said." I swallow the lump in my throat, blinking back the hot tears that want to fall. "So, I'm going to go now." I take a step back, away from my parents. "I'll see you around."

Turning my back on everyone, I force one foot in front of the other as I walk down the dirty path at the front of my house toward the street. The sounds of footsteps behind me give me comfort, knowing they belong to my four guys.

"Wait!" Cynthia cries, and I stop as my bare feet hit the footpath that runs along my street. As I turn to look over my shoulder, I see Cin disappear into the house. While I wait to see what she wants, the warmth of Simon's hand comes to rest on my lower back, and I lean into it, needing the comfort it brings.

Cynthia appears again, passing Will, who looks rattled and confused, and she runs up the path holding out my phone.

"Please stay safe." Her voice is laced with so much worry as she hands me my phone, and I take it while watching her eyes pool with tears. "Your home is *here*, Rhys. Always. Come back soon, ok?"

My lower lip trembles as I give a slight nod, hoping her words are true, and before I can give in to the need to stay, I turn my back on her again and tears stream down my face as I walk away.

I don't even have shoes on, but the concrete path is warm from the mild spring day. My sweatpants aren't my usual get-up, and neither is the fitted superman t-shirt I'm wearing. I didn't actually think I'd be seeing anyone today, but oddly enough, I don't care about how I look. My hair is in a messy knot on top of my head while strays float in the breeze, and there's not a smudge of makeup on my face. I don't look like *me*, but right now, I feel more me than I ever have.

"Kitten." Shaun links his fingers with mine as we walk, and I glance at him through my tears, giving him a smile as I continue to cry silently. I don't have words right now, and he doesn't need to hear them. He just wants me to know he's there, and so are the others as we walk through my neighbourhood in silence.

I have no idea where we are going. I just walk and follow the direction the guys lead me until we eventually turn up at Simon's house. It makes sense. It's the closest to my house and school, and it's the biggest to accommodate our group. Garrett is probably still avoiding his house, and I don't think I'd be all that welcome at Marcus' house. Shaun's is out of town a little, so the only place for us to go is Simon's.

One by one, we pass through his oversized front door, ignoring his mum as she steps into the foyer, looking confused. None of us pay her any attention, and we head into the rumpus room, where Simon closes the door behind us, giving us privacy.

"What can we do, Rhee?" Marcus asks, and I turn back to look at the four of them.

Usually, I need sex. It was only an hour ago that I was setting my sights on my vibes, needing a release, yet now, that need is gone. In its place is something I don't really know how to voice.

"I just need... to be?" It comes out as a question and I know I'm making no sense.

"You want to be left alone?" Garrett asks and I shake my head.

"You want a hug, Kitten?" Shaun asks, and my bottom lip starts to seize while I slowly nod.

"You wanna hug and watch movies or something?" Simon asks, and I nod again, glancing at him as he approaches me. I swipe at my tears, wanting to see his face, which is normally so playful. The clown isn't here today, but as he cups my face and looks down at me, I feel like I'm seeing the real Simon Hastings for the first time. His eyes are raw with emotion, more green than hazel, as they stare into my soul, revealing the pain and fear that he has kept so well hidden. "We can watch anything you like."

I reach up, my fingers trembling as I return the favour and brush back his longish ash-blonde hair so I can see his whole face. "You're a beautiful person, Simon Hastings. Inside and out."

His face contorts like he's in pain before his eyes glass over. "Fuck Cherry. You're breaking down my walls."

I smile sympathetically, standing on my tiptoes to press my forehead against his. "Just like you've done to me. This is me. This is who I am. Messy. Flighty." I scoff at myself. "Bat shit crazy."

Simon chuckles, his hands sliding to the back of my head to grip my hair. "Just like me."

I nod. "Just like you. Maybe a bit more hella crazy, though."

"You're perfect. I wouldn't change anything about you, Cherry." Simon presses his forehead to mine.

"Good, because I want to watch Charlie and Lola episodes for the rest of the day."

Chuckles come from behind me, and Simon's face lights up as he pulls back in surprise. "Charlie and Lola? The cartoon?"

I nod. "Yes. And no one is allowed to speak bogan Aussie until tomorrow. We have to talk just like Charlie and Lola."

"You want us to talk British?" Simon grins, and I nod. "Deal." He beams while Shaun laughs, and Garrett mumbles, "Fucking hell."

Simon kisses me then, ignoring his three mates, claiming my lips in a soft, emotion-filled kiss. I melt into him, wrapping my arms around to grip his back and pull him close to me like I'll die if we ever part.

"Uh… what the hell is Charlie and Lola?" Marcus' confusion causes us to laugh mid-kiss, and our teeth clash as the mood lightens.

I used to feel like home was a place. A physical building with four walls and a roof. Now I know different. Now I know that home, for me, is the guys in this room, as well as the one who is missing yet still owns my heart.

Chapter Fifteen

Simon

Torturing my mum brings me a level of satisfaction I didn't know was possible. When we arrived home earlier, I'd locked the doors to the rumpus room so she couldn't just stroll in and annoy us. I also knew that Cherry needed some space and didn't need my mum coming in and being a bitch to her.

Even though I'd ignored my mum's knocks on the door and her calling my phone repeatedly, it was Cherry who insisted I not be a dick and see what my mum wanted. Turns out she'd ordered a heap of pizza for us and had it set up in the dining room. Did I feel bad about treating her like shit? Yeah, but she made up for it when we walked in, and she screwed up her nose at Cherry. She clearly didn't like the way my girl was dressed, but Cherry didn't seem to care, giving my mum a finger wave while she walked past, swaying her hips.

"Could you pass me a slice of the margarita pizza, please, Charlie?" The not so well done pommy accent coming from Cherry's mouth has my mum frowning in confusion as she sits at the table with us.

"Who is Charlie?" She asks, but we ignore her.

"Here you go, Lola. I've got you covered." Shaun's attempted accent is worse, and Marcus snickers as my mum's eyes bulge.

Cherry accepts the slice from Shaun and then looks to Garrett. "Excuse me, Charlie. Would you mind pouring me a glass of Chardy?"

I smother my laugh as my mum looks down the table to see who Cherry is talking to.

"Sure," Garrett mutters, and Cherry frowns.

"Excuse me, Charlie... Are you speaking a foreign language? I couldn't quite understand what you just said."

I laugh out loud now, no longer able to contain myself as Garrett rolls his eyes at our girl. He'd used his normal voice instead of trying to sound like Charlie off the cartoon.

"Sure Lola. Here's your Chardy." Garrett mutters unhappily, but probably with the best pommy accent of the lot of us, and he hands Cherry a glass of lemonade, which for some reason, she is calling Chardy today.

"Ohhh, my Charlie. What a deep accent you have." Cherry shoots Garrett a wink and bites her lip before my mum sighs.

"It's the cartoon, isn't it? Simon used to watch it when he was little. That Charlie and Lola one."

My brows shoot up at her understanding. "You mean you know stuff about me? Oh wait, that's right. You said when I was little. That must have been those few years before you decided to spend your life travelling the world with a man that you would end up divorcing while your child was raised by nannies."

The room falls silent as my mum's face turns red in anger, and I stare into her eyes, not backing down. The silence is long and drawn out, and my mum's glare falters, looking like she is biting the inside of her cheek.

"Yes, Charlie. You are right. I don't really know anything about you because I have been an absent mother."

Her British accent is on point, having clearly picked up the game we were playing, but her words are what stun me. I never thought she'd take ownership of her absence, and now I kind of feel bad for being a prick to her. But then again, if I didn't, maybe she would never have admitted it to me.

"Would you like to know more about him, Lola?" Cherry asks, staying in character, and my mum slowly shifts her hazel eyes across the table to my girl.

"Yes Lola. I think I really would."

Rhys beams at my mum's response. "Well, Lola. You already know how much Charlie loves Cherry pie."

"Don't remind me." My mum scoffs, but smirks at the same time.

"He also loves feet." Cherry continues, and I butt in.

"Ahhh… Lola, I don't think she needs to know *that* stuff about me."

Cherry giggles, and my mum bursts out laughing before Marcus tries to talk in an accent and tells my mum about school camp a few years ago. As the conversation flows in mostly bad accents, Rhys subtly smiles across the table at me and gives me a cheeky wink. I like seeing her like this. She has a way with people. An ability to take attention off someone else and put it on herself, even if it's negative. I can see she really wants everyone to just get along. And if there's a conflict or confrontation, she will throw herself in the firing line to take the heat off those she cares about.

I've never known anyone like her. She's so unique that I'm almost afraid she will disappear at any moment. The need to contain her is overwhelming, but you can't contain someone like Rhys George. She is the rarest of butterflies that needs to spread her wings and fly to wherever calls to her. I hope she realises that wherever she goes, Simon Hastings will be right there following behind.

We spend longer than I thought we would in the dining room chatting with my mum. I'll admit, it was kind of nice, but a part of me wonders if she's just trying to win me over in the hopes I'll stop giving her grief about moving away. There's nothing she can do that will make me leave my girl. Not now. Not ever.

"Please tell me we aren't going to watch more of that cartoon?" Garrett grumbles as we stumble back into the rumpus room with full bellies.

"Oh, fine! You can have your normal bogan accents back now."
Rhys giggles, and Marcus nods.

"I kinda like my bogan accent."

Rhys sidles up to him, wrapping her arms around his neck and tugging him down towards her lips. "I kinda like your bogan accent, too." Then they kiss.

I can't hide my grin. This girl is everything to us. She has each of us snared in the best way, and I fucking love how much she loves all of us right back.

When Marcus and Cherry break the kiss, she pulls her phone from her pocket, and I watch as the brief happiness that she'd been wearing for the last couple of hours falls from her face.

"What's wrong, Kitten?" Shaun asks, noticing too.

"Uh…" She looks up from her screen. "Char just sent me a link to a podcast… I, uh, need to listen to it."

"You can Bluetooth your phone to the speaker, and we can all listen, Cherry." I offer, but she frowns, looking uncomfortable.

"I'm not sure you guys want to listen to this."

Marcus wraps his arms around Rhys from behind and presses his lips to her head. "What is it, Rhee?"

Her chocolate eyes dart around the room before settling back on her phone. "It's called Breaking the Silence. The podcaster tells stories. Other people's stories that they can't tell because it will expose them. Then she uses her TikTok account to post info about the stories, which includes images of people who are bad and need to be caught." Rhys looks up again. "This podcast is of my story."

I can't speak for the other guys, but I think I stop breathing for a moment as the reality of what she said sinks in. Her story. The dark one that she tries to keep hidden. The one where she was taken advantage of as a child. The one that still haunts her to this day. I know a little about it, but not everything, and I only want to know everything if she wants me to.

"Cherry? I want to listen to it, but only if you're happy for me to. If that's not something you want, then I will respect your wishes."

Her smile is small yet warm as she looks at me. "Thank you, Sy."

Fuck, I love it when she calls me that.

"Do you want us to hear it, Kitten?" Shaun asks, and she turns her dark eyes to him and shrugs. "Is there something in particular you're worried about us hearing?"

She nods and takes a deep breath before she speaks. "I'm scared that when you hear the whole truth, you will think differently about me… and about what we have together."

"No way, Baby Girl. There ain't anything that will change how deeply I love you."

Fuck.

Garrett Cole is a broody, quiet mofo most of the time, but when he has something to say, it's always honest and meaningful.

"I'm with Gaz, Rhee. I'm all in no matter what, and if you don't want us listening to the podcast, then, like Hastings said, we will respect your wishes." Marcus turns Rhys in his arms and cups her face, looking at her with so much love that I have to fight back fucking tears. "Can I just say, though, that if we know everything about your past, it might make it easier for us to understand what's going on."

Cherry visibly swallows hard like she has a lump in her throat, her white teeth biting the corner of her lower lip as she stares up into Marcus' eyes. Then she nods. "Ok. Let's all listen to it." She declares quietly, and I silently sigh in relief, realising just how much I needed her to share this with us. To trust us with her truth.

While Cherry connects her phone to the speaker, I lock the door, so my mum can't barge in, and we all get comfy on the couch. Like earlier, when we had a Charlie and Lola marathon, we all surround our girl like she's the queen of our hive. Garrett grabs her by the hips before the rest of us can, dragging her to sit between his legs, tugging her back against his chest. I hover as I watch Shaun and Marcus take each side on the couch next to Cherry and Gaz, and I'm oddly ok with having the only spot left to be near her.

Her feet. I fucking love Cherry's feet.

As we all get settled, Cherry clicks the link on her phone, and a moment later, a soft, husky female voice comes through the speakers.

Welcome to another episode of Breaking the Silence. I am Hush, and today I have a dark and heartbreaking story to share. Please be warned, this story involves illegal acts with a minor that includes molestation and child pornography. As with all of my podcasts, the names of victims and some people have been changed to protect their identity, but the known names of the abusers and criminals will remain the same. This story takes place in Victoria, Australia. A young girl, no older than nine years old, getting thrown into the foster system after the death of her mother. Like with all of my podcasts, we will refer to this girl as V.

V thought foster parents were there to care for her. They certainly seemed friendly enough while the Child Services workers were with them and most of the time when they were in public. But behind closed doors, V was subject to a different version of her so-called carers. V was a victim to some of the most heinous acts while in the foster care system. One carer liked to slam V's fingers in the cupboard doors when she did something wrong. Another would force her to eat mouldy and off food while keeping the good food for herself and then forcing V to clean up her own vomit every time she got sick. One simply didn't feed her, and another made her steal for them. V says that the carers that would slap or hit her were almost better than the ones who would try to think up disgusting punishments like being put in timeout in the toilet room every time the carer passed a bowel motion.

Poor V was subjected to such vile things, and one day when she was maybe ten years old, she was put in yet another home, and V came across someone who was nice to her. She had only ever wanted to be loved. To be cared for. And while her new foster mum, Julie Bates, was nasty to her, her new foster dad, Brian Bates, was loving and caring. Every time Julie would lose her temper at V, Brian would protect her from Julie. He would take V and play games with her, take her to the park, feed her good food and buy her the nicest clothes she'd ever worn. She quickly relied on Brian and felt safe with him.

He would hug her when she was scared, upset, or just needed a hug. He would bathe and shower her, making sure she was always clean, and her hair was always smelling pretty. She loved Brian. She trusted Brian. Then one day, when she woke up from napping on Brian's chest with her arms still wrapped around him, not wanting to ever let him go, her dad, as she liked to call him at the time, seemed to be in pain,

which   caused   her distress.

Now I won't go into the finer details of where his pain was, other than it was in his groin region, but that day was the first day that he showed V how to make him feel better. It didn't feel wrong for V to help her dad when he was in pain. It made her feel important, and after she took his pain away, he told her that the things daddies and daughters do were a secret. Something that can't be done in front of other people and isn't really spoken about. Kind of like going to the bathroom. V thought because it involved private parts, that this made sense. Let's remember, she was only ten years old and had no other role model to teach her what was wrong and right. So naturally, she believed everything Brian Bates told her. Their interactions turned into games. Mostly, Brian liked to play the nurse game where it was V's job to make him feel better, and eventually, Brian started showing V that he could make her feel better, too. V didn't know it at the time, but when she was eleven, Brian Bates took her virginity.

V enjoyed her special times with Brian. He never hurt her. He always made her feel good, so when child services came to take her away from Brian when she was twelve, she was distraught. She'd been separated from the only person who had ever shown her love and care. She was confused and didn't understand why the police and therapists kept telling her that Brian was a bad man for doing that to her. How could it have been bad when it felt so good?

Five years on, and V understands now that what happened when she went into Brian and Julie's care was grooming. A case of good cop, bad cop. Julie kept her scared while Brian groomed her into his own plaything. Brian Bates went to prison for what he did to V, but Julie Bates fled and has been a ghost ever since. That is until V recently started receiving voice mails and text messages from Julie out of the blue. She started threatening V and demanded that she go and visit Brian in prison. If she didn't go, Julie was going to make her pay somehow.

Hearing from Julie brought up V's past traumas, and she was fearful of people finding out about her childhood. She explains her worries that the depravity of it will scare people away, which is why she went to the prison as Julie asked and saw the man that violated her as a child.

And guess what he did? He put his hand

down his pants! Brian Bates is a sick and twisted predator, and so is his wife, Julie Bates.

Together, they groomed V, and they filmed the molestation activities, selling copies on the black market. Julie has been trying to blackmail V with one such video, sending it to her school friends and challenging them to figure out who the little girl in the video was.

Well, Julie Bates, your time is up!

Here's what we know about you!

We know you live in Allandale, in Victoria, Australia, so you can visit your depraved husband in prison and that you have formed a very close relationship with two of the guards at the prison. We know you take in girls off the streets and give them a place to stay, and we know, by a source that I just received word from, that you have been soliciting those girls in exchange for a roof over their head and food in their bellies.

We know who you are, Julie Bates! Or should I say, Julie Clark!

TikTok Julie!

"Holy shit!" Cherry leaps up, grabbing her phone and pressing it to her ear. "Char, Hush found out the name she's using!"

While she talks to her sister, I sit back on my haunches, looking up at my mates. They are all wearing the same expression, which says, *what the fuck?*

"You have?" Cherry asks her sister. "What did Officer Zimora say?"

I take a moment to look at my girl. Like, *really* look at her.

I kind of knew the basics of her past, but hearing the details on how it came about is just so fucking heartbreaking. How can anyone do that to another human being? And Brian is her real fucking dad. That part wasn't mentioned on the podcast, so Cherry must want it to remain a secret, but how the fuck can a real dad do that to his child? I don't fucking understand!

"He made her enjoy it," Marcus whispers, loud enough for just us guys to hear. "She never felt forced."

"It's still rape." Garrett quietly grumbles, and I nod.

"It explains so much about her… needs," Shaun says in a hushed tone.

"Yeah. It explains why she thinks sex is the only currency in love and relationships." Garrett frowns, glancing up at Cherry, who is still talking with her sister.

"She doesn't think that way anymore." Shaun shifts to face Garrett. "She knows sex isn't the only currency now. When was the last time she even insinuated that she wanted sex?"

"Earlier today at her house. The whole vibrator incident." I add, and they all nod.

"Yeah, but that came from frustration and probably loneliness from the isolation." Shaun points out. "She's been around all of us all night and hasn't wanted an orgy. I think she's content with us. She feels safe and knows she doesn't have to spread her legs to feel that way."

Garrett nods, looking across the room to where our girl is pacing with the phone pressed to her ear. "When she says she loves us, she means it." He rasps quietly. "It's unconditional, just the same way we feel for her."

Chapter Sixteen

RHYS

I feel weird. My secret is out there in the world for people to listen to, and only those who I tell know the story on the podcast is about me. When I rang Charlotte after listening to it, she told me she had already sent the information about Julie Clark to the police. Then after I hung up, I went on TikTok to see the images of Julie that Hush posted. It wasn't just the image I'd passed on. There were more. Whoever this Hush person is, she has some serious investigative skills.

The comments blew up. And in them was the address of Julie Clark, residing in Allansdale, Victoria. I reached out to Hush late last night to thank her by email, and she replied instantly, telling me to stay strong and keep fighting. I don't know who she is, but I'm so grateful to her and what she does for people like me.

Me and the guys slept in the rumpus room at Simon's last night. They were a little quieter than usual after hearing the podcast, and of course, it gave me *insta'* anxiety. I tried my best not to think negative thoughts that they find me repulsive now, after learning the whole truth. It was hard to fight that bitch voice in the back of my mind telling me I'm not good enough, and at one stage, the need to flee was fucking consuming. It was the strong arms of my guys wrapping around me that eventually scared those negative demons away, and I slept soundly in their embrace.

Charlotte swung by this morning with my school uniform and stuff so I could go to my last exam, not looking like a homeless person.

She gave me a long hug before whispering in my ear to call mum. I want to call her. And Dad, too, but knowing we are likely to keep going in circles about everything has me hesitating to pick up my phone to make the call. I just can't bring myself to suffer through that exhaustion right now.

During the exam, I feel my mum's eyes on me. I avoid her gaze and try to focus on completing at least one exam this year, which I do, but I'm not sure it's done well. After it's over, the guys come to my table, their presence working like magic to calm my inner turmoil. When I stand from the table, Simon links his hand with my left, and Marcus links his hand with my right, leading me out behind Shaun and Garrett. As usual, all eyes fall on us and our unusual arrangement as we walk out of the school gates together to catch the bus to Shaun's.

The bus trip is longer than I'm used to, with Shaun's house dancing on the fringe of Fox Pines. It could honestly take five hours to get there, and I wouldn't care right now with how happy I am in the little bubble we create together. We take up the back seat of the bus, with me in the middle, of course, and I snuggle into Simon's side as Marcus slips an earbud in my ear before he presses play on his phone and the familiar sound of the Foo Fighters fills my ears.

A grin instantly tugs at my lips as I revel in the normalcy of this moment. Marcus is good at that. Making me not feel weird. Making me feel like I'm just a normal girl, living a normal life with normal friends. I know I'm not a typical normal, but this is my normal, and it feels so fucking right.

Tilting my head, I glance up at Marcus, who is wearing the other ear pod, listening to My Hero as well. His eyes are already on me, studying me even when I'm not aware.

"Thank you." I mouth, and he frowns a little before shifting his attention to his phone and turns the volume down. When he looks back at me, he leans down and eases the ear pod out before hovering his lips over my ear, his breath warm on my skin.

"What for?"

When he pulls back to look at me, I have to swallow a few times, chewing the inside of my cheek as my emotions tug at my heart.

"For accepting me."

My words are quiet for only him to hear, but the way Simon squeezes my other hand, I can tell he heard. Not that it matters. I'm not trying to hide this from anyone.

The big dark pools of Marcus' brown eyes fill with emotion, and I think what I'm starting to recognise as love, and he brushes the backs of his fingers over my cheek.

"Thank you for giving me the chance to see who you really are."

Fucking hell. Marcus Grady is certainly one with words. Fuck, they all are when they want to be. All I can manage is a smile, and I shift to hug him, Simon letting me go so I can share this moment with Marcus.

I don't care what anyone thinks about me and my guys. We fucking work.

After we get off at Shaun's stop, we wander up the long drive of Shaun's family farm, chatting and laughing at unimportant things, when Derek comes speeding up on a 4-wheeler and offers to take our bags on it. But screw that, I want on that thing, so I run up and climb on the back and yell for him to go as I laugh at the guys running after me. We speed up the drive, and I make myself *not* look over the paddocks to Vixen's Lodge before we pull into the large open shed that houses a tractor.

"You're crazy." Derek chuckles as he cuts the engine, and I climb off.

"You know it." I grin, righting my uniform as Derek jumps off.

"Come on into the house." He urges, gesturing his head to the adorable farmhouse. "Let's get a cold drink before the others make it back." I nod and grin, following Derek across the yard, and we head inside.

The house is warm, and the scent of cookies makes my tummy rumble, the fresh plate of baked treats calling my name on the counter.

"Hey Mama," Derek says to the short, frail lady standing over a pot in the kitchen. "You feeling good today?"

"Si." His mum replies, slowly turning from the stove. The moment her eyes land on me, they widen.

"Friend?" She asks Derek, and he chuckles.

"Mama, this is Rhys. Shaun's girlfriend."

"Ella es Hermosa." His mum says, and I pick up the word Shaun taught me.

Hermosa means beautiful.

"Uh… hi," I say nervously, shooting her the sweetest smile I can muster and giving her an awkward wave.

"Hola, Rhys."

"Who do we have here?" The deep rumble of a voice startles me from behind, and I whip around to see the balding man I know as Shaun's dad.

"Uh… I'm Rhys."

His brows shoot up. "The girl that has caused so much drama?"

"Allan!" Shaun's mum snaps, and his dad chuckles.

"I never said it was a bad thing. Although I'd rather Shaun and his mates not fight over a girl."

"You don't have to worry about that, Dad." Shaun's voice is a relief to hear, and I look around his dad to see Shaun strolling into the house with the others behind him. "We've sorted things out."

Shaun approaches me with a devilish glint in his eye, and he leans down, pressing a kiss to my cheek before moving on. Then Garrett does the same, followed by Simon and finally Marcus.

My cheeks are on fire as I drag my gaze from Shaun's dad, who seems to have a problem closing his mouth, and I take in Shaun's mum's face. She's grinning.

"Hurra! Maravillosa!" Shaun's mum cheers, and Shaun and Derek laugh.

"Mama is happy about our arrangement." Shaun grins, and I'm pretty sure I resemble a glowing red beacon right now.

"Would you like some help, Gabriella?" Simon asks, glancing over Shaun's mum's small frame to see what she's cooking.

"Si." Gabriella beams and starts talking quietly to Simon about whatever it is she's cooking.

"Have you thought any more about what I asked the other night, Dad?" Shaun asks as he leads me to sit at the kitchen bench and hands me one of the delicious-smelling cookies. I take it eagerly, biting into it, the sweet flavour bursting on my tongue, nearly causing a moan to escape.

As Shaun takes a seat on one side of me, and Marcus on the other, Garrett leans over my head and takes his own cookie, hovering behind my chair.

"Still thinking," Allan mumbles, moving to the fridge to pull out a carton of juice.

"Do you need anything done today? I could show Simon a few things. Start training him up now."

Allan turns from the fridge to glare at Shaun. "And who is going to pay for his schooling?"

Shaun shrugs. "We will figure it out."

"Are your parents going to pay for that?" Allan turns to face Simon, who I think was hoping to be left out of the conversation.

"Um… no. Not exactly."

"Right, so how do you think you are going to afford school? If you work here, I can't pay you. It's board and food in exchange for working on the farm. It's not easy work, boy. And you're a bit scrawny looking."

Gabriella growls something at Allan, pointing her wooden spoon at him with a furious look on her face, and Allan pales.

"We aren't a charity, Carino. We are struggling as it is." Allan approaches his wife with tenderness in his eyes, and I feel like I should look away.

"Mr Bossier… Sir. I'm not asking for charity. I will work hard for you to earn my keep, and I'm sure after a while of working here, I won't look so scrawny." Simon runs his hand through his longish hair. "As for school. I've already contacted Fox Pines High. As long as I can cover the costs of any school books, I don't have to pay tuition fees in public school. I will do my final year of school there."

I stop mid-chew, taking in Simon's words. He's already looked into this? Even through all the bullshit I brought into his life, he's been busy trying to figure this out on his own. As I stare at my adorable clown, I see the confident glint in his eyes. He's determined to stay here. Determined to make it work somehow.

Allan remains quiet for a moment, glaring at Simon, and then nods. "I'll think some more about it." Then he turns his gaze back to his son. "You lot may as well start cleaning up the staff quarters… Just in case."

Gabriella grins wide, turning her gaze to look up at Simon, and nudges her shoulder into his ribs. When Simon looks down at her, he smiles wide too, and they turn back to the stove.

We linger around the kitchen for a while, watching Simon cook with Gabriella. Turns out he actually knows what he's doing. I hadn't really thought much about where the food came from the night I went to his place for dinner, and he had a feast set up in the kitchen. Did he cook that himself? And why is that thought so sexy?

Images of chef Simon flash in my head, and I smile wide. Hell yes, that is sexy. I want chef Simon to cook for me.

"What are you thinking about, Kitten?" Shaun whispers in my ear, and I shoot him a sideways glance.

"Chef Simon."

Shaun chuckles. "You like the thought of chef Simon?"

"Hell yes." I grin, and Marcus chuckles on my other side.

"And what about that scenario do you like, Rhee?"

I grin wider and lower my voice. "So much delicious food play."

"So our girl likes food play and blood play. What else do you like, Baby Girl?" Garrett's husky whisper in my ear sends a shiver up my spine.

"Foot play, toy play, role play… as long as it isn't nurses," I whisper back, and I can feel the guys stiffen around me at the mention of that touchy subject.

"What about butt play?" Shaun leans in, speaking quietly after the tense moment passes and my grin returns.

"Maybe a little bit of butt play," I whisper back, shrugging as I turn to my Casanova, and he closes the distance, sealing his lips to mine. It's a short and quiet kiss because I'm sure the last thing he wants is to gain his mum's attention right at this moment, but it's a kiss that holds promises, and for the first time in days, I start to relax, feeling more like myself.

Even though things aren't perfect, my situation is looking up. Julie has been exposed. The cops will get to her soon, and I'll have one less psycho predator trying to bring me down. Things aren't great at home, but if I consider how circumstances had been at my other foster homes compared to my current overprotective parents, then I shouldn't really complain. Are they even overprotective? I don't really know. I don't have much to compare them to. Maybe they are just protective. Because they care.

I care about them too. So much more than I thought I would let myself. And I'd be happy to compromise. I understand that I can't just run off and do whatever. There are rules with everything, but there are just some things I can't live without, and unfortunately, my need to push boundaries and try new things is what makes most people uncomfortable.

That's why I needed a sex club. I needed to sneak around and keep it secret because most people just don't understand. Now my mum has involved the police. She has no idea who she's messing with, no idea that the people she's trying to expose have friends in high places. It's quite possible that if Master Hill starts getting heat about a sex club that allowed minors to partake in activities, he will pull strings and destroy my parents. I don't want that. I'd sooner die than let him ruin them, too.

My sombre thoughts turn me quiet again. Right when I was thinking things were looking up. Shaun notices and tugs me off the seat, calling for Simon to come with us as he leads me out the back door.

We make our way across the freshly mowed grass, past the large open shed and up the path that leads to the man cave shed we came back to after Halloween. Apparently, the staff quarters are upstairs, so after grabbing supplies from a cleaning closet, we follow Shaun upstairs to a large common area with a kitchenette and a long hall that has maybe six doors coming off each side.

Then we clean. I'm not really into cleaning, but then again, I've never cleaned with four super hot smouldering guys that take off their shirts and ripple their muscles all over the place. It's super hard to concentrate, and in the end, I'm pretty sure they do most of the work. What can I say? I'm only human!

The buzz of my phone distracts me from Garrett's rolling ridges, and I pull it quickly from my pocket, glaring at it for distracting me from the mouth-watering view of my guys. When I see the name flash across the screen, my face falls.

Fuck you Julie

I hesitate a moment, wondering if I should answer, but then I decide, what the hell, and hit the speaker icon so the guys can hear as well.

"What do you want?" I snap, and for a moment, the line is quiet. Did she hang up already?

"You fucking little whore! You think you can ruin everything I've worked so hard for and expect to get away with it?"

I feel the guys closing in as I place my phone on the old dusty brown table that sits off to the side of the common area near the kitchenette.

"I don't know what you mean." I throw innocence into my tone, and it just makes her angrier.

"You fucking little cunt!"

When Garrett opens his mouth to say something, I hold a finger up, shushing him, but shoot him an, *I'm sorry*, look as I let Julie continue.

"You know exactly what I mean! That fucking podcast! Oh, you told a version of your story, Patrice, but why didn't you tell them the truth?"

My brows shoot up. "And what truth is that, exactly?"

"That you're a dick-loving whore that fucking loved every minute that Brian touched you!" She scoffs. "Once a whore, always a whore. Isn't that right? You've been spreading your legs ever since you left our care, fucking anyone willing, probably using those special skills you learnt from Brian to make them cave!"

My eyes dart up to Simon's then, and when he notices, he frowns. *Shit. I did that, didn't I? To Simon. In the darkroom at school.*

I shoot my eyes back to the phone, feeling Julie's words oozing into my soul, reminding me of the depraved monster that lives inside me.

"Don't speak like you know a thing about me, Julie. You know nothing!" My voice quivers a little as I speak, which just pisses me off more. I don't want Julie to hear how her words affect me. I want her to think she means nothing.

"I know a fucking lot about you, Patty. I know all about those teachers at Redfield High. You know the ones you were fucking? You coaxed them in, didn't you? Just like you coax everyone in. They couldn't deny you because you didn't give them the chance to think twice. You lured them and trapped them, and their only way out was to flee. Patrice George, the teacher fucker." She laughs, pure evil in the tone. "How about that other teacher? What's his name? Mr-."

I quickly end the call before she can say, Foster. Tyler's surname. I should never have answered. I should never have provoked her. If she knows about the other two teachers, which is practically impossible, then she sure as shit knows about Ty. There haven't been any other teachers. Just those three, so the name she was about to reveal could have only belonged to one person.

"Ignore her bullshit, Kitten." Shaun wraps an arm around me from behind, tugging me against his chest as his spicy scent wraps around me.

I want to ignore her words, but they aren't bullshit, and Shaun is the only other person in this room that knows that. I never used to feel shame about my conquests, but I have been of late. The wires in my brain have changed somewhere between Shaun discovering that Skipper was Ty, and now. Before, everything was about sex. Now, Kitty has taken a backseat to my heart. When the hell did that happen exactly?

"Were there teachers?" Marcus asks, and I can't look at him. My eyes dip, and my shoulders slump, and I suddenly feel like the walls are closing in on me.

"What the fuck does that matter?" Shaun snaps over my shoulder at his mate, trying to protect me. But he shouldn't snap at his mate. Marcus and the others deserve to know the truth about my past. They should know who they are getting into bed with.

"It's ok." I grip Shaun's hand that is pressed tight to my belly, and I drag my shame-filled gaze up to meet Marcus' dark stare.

"Yes. There were teachers."

And there it is. The disappointment. Again. I saw it on his face by the fire at Lexi's after he found out about Shaun and Simon. And here it is again as he finds out another truth that's hard to swallow.

He doesn't speak. He just stares at me, lost for words.

"Did they like... force you?" Simon asks this time, and I suck in a deep breath, dragging my eyes from Marcus to meet the hazel eyes of my adorable clown.

"No." I shake my head, my voice quiet as my shame leaks through. "I seduced them. Julie didn't lie about that. In fact. She didn't lie about any of it. It's all true."

"Bullshit! Don't say that!" Garrett snaps, his eyes blazing with a fury that's fighting to be unleashed.

I pull out of Shaun's hold and turn to face the four of them. Heat pricks the backs of my eyes, my heart racing with dread as I take in their serious expressions. It's almost too much to bear. Are they finally seeing me for what I am? A whore? A manipulative predator?

"You know damn well how true that is, Big Guy. You know how I lured Simon into the photo lab that day?" I swallow, turning my eyes to Simon. "You hadn't even considered that we were going there to fuck, had you, Sy?"

He frowns. "I-I…"

"Think about it. When you asked to ditch class with me, did you think you were going to get laid?"

He frowns again.

"And we played the game. Remember? Simon Says. The Hastinator only plays games to get naked. You thought I was joking around at first, didn't you?"

"That doesn't mean anything. We were flirting, Cherry. I'd wanted you for so long, but I never thought you'd be interested in someone like me."

"I made it hard for you to say no, though. Didn't I? Standing there in my bra and panties. You were never going to be able to turn me down." A tear pops from my eye as I drag my gaze back to Marcus. "He was worried about you. He felt guilty. He didn't want to betray you, Marcus, but I gave him no choice. Julie is right. I used what I learnt from Brian. I'm a predator like him."

"We all use charm, Kitten. We all try to coax. What you're talking about is a form of flirting. A form of foreplay. Everyone has a choice. I know you think you gave Simon no choice, but he did have one. And I know what me and Simon did to Marcus was fucking wrong, but we made that decision, and that's on us. Not you."

"There was another teacher?" Marcus draws my attention again, quickly brushing off Shaun's words, his curiosity too strong to deny.

"It's all in the past now. There are no teachers I'm involved with now." That's a huge fucking blurred line of a lie if I've ever said one! Technically, Tyler isn't a teacher anymore, so that part of whatever we are is in the past.

"Does it really matter, Grady? Kitten is trying to move on. She's not the person she was a couple of months ago. Hell, even a couple of weeks ago." Once again, Shaun tries to defend me, and my heart swells, knowing he at least isn't judging me right now.

"It only matters because I think that Julie bitch is going to keep coming for you, Rhee. She's probably planning to out your relationships with the teachers, and it's going to ruin their lives."

I bite the insides of both cheeks as I suck in air, trying to push down my emotions. Marcus is right. Julie will totally use those teachers against me. And if she knows about Tyler, then Master Hill isn't our only threat.

CHAPTER SEVENTEEN

SHAUN

T hree hours. That's what it took us to get Kitten into a relatively calm and happy state again after Julie's phone call. I was sure I was going to have a fucking punch on with Grady after he was asking all of those questions when, in fact, he was just working through the information and processing what it meant. He's right, though. Julie will totally come at Rhys by using her hookups with teachers, and if she knows about those two teachers at Redfield, then she sure as shit knows about Tyler.

In order to help calm our girl, I had to beg Derek to get some weed off one of his mates. Aside from a full-blown sex party, weed was the next best thing, and I let her have a little before we joined my parents for dinner, which seemed to help. Afterwards, I let her have a whole lot more once we went out to the man cave, away from the parentals.

She seems happy again, especially after Simon declared his undying love for her in a song and then whispered some mushy shit in her ear afterwards. Then they started dancing, and Marcus, of all people, joined them, pressing Kitten between them and reminding her how much they care for her, no matter what.

Garrett has been quiet, but he's also been distracted by his phone, and I wouldn't be surprised if he's dealing with something to do with his useless old man right now. I'm about to ask him about it when my phone rings, and a number I don't recognise flashes across the screen. Cautiously, I answer it.

"Hello?"

"Where is she?" Relief fills me as I hear my principal's voice. For some reason, I was worried it was that stupid Julie bitch who was calling me.

"Hi Mrs R. She's safe." I move across the room, away from Kitten's ears.

She sighs with her own relief. "Can I speak with her, please?"

"Uh… Now's not the best time. She's only just started to relax. I can get her to call you later."

"Mr Bossier, I am freaking out right now! I had to hear from the police that Rhys got another call from Julie earlier today. You tell me she's safe, but how do I really know? How do I even know if you're treating her right?"

Mrs Rogan is hysterical. A mother distraught over the daughter she loves. A daughter that doesn't know how to accept the love because she's been burned so many times.

I fucking feel for both of them.

"We aren't the enemy here, Mrs R. We love Rhys. We will do anything for her. Anything to protect her. And I'm sorry the news didn't come directly from Rhys. She had some stuff to work through. It was hard enough for her to call the police and tell them."

"I know. I'm sorry. I just worry so much. Are you sure she's safe? Can you at least tell me where she is?" There's a pleading in her voice that I can't ignore.

"We are at my house. We've been cleaning up the old staff quarters for my dad, and we had dinner with my parents earlier. Now we are just trying to keep Rhys calm. The guys are trying to teach her snooker."

"Please tell me that's not a code word for a sex game? And please tell me you are all using protection?"

"Gee, Mrs R. Do you think all we do is have sex?"

"I know teenagers, Mr Bossier! Isn't that why you boys are hanging around Rhys?"

My brows shoot to my hairline at her question, which I find fucking insulting.

"You may think you know *teenagers,* but you don't know *us*. For the record, there hasn't been any sex tonight. I told you before, we love her. It may seem like a weird arrangement to you, but it's what we need. She needs us, and we need her. And I'm not talking about in a sex way. It's more than that. So much more. If you could only see how much she's changed."

Mrs Rogan sighs. "It's hard for me to comprehend the dynamics of the group relationship you all have. I'm trying."

"I guess it's hard for Rhys to talk about. She's still learning how to navigate feelings, but she's more to each of us than just another girl. Like, did you know that even though her and Simon are the same, clowning around all the time, she's brought a more serious side out in him? He's started opening up and talking about things he's never really spoken about before. His fun personality is just a mask to hide his pain. Rhys understands that because she does the same thing." I glance over at the girl in question to see her bent over the pool table, squeezing one eye shut, poking her tongue out in concentration as she lines up the ball. "Rhys and Garrett both come from hard childhoods. They understand each other on a level most can't. He can be such a moody bastard and hotheaded, but Rhys seems to mellow him. Hell, I don't think I've ever seen him smile this much, even though he's got his own crap going on. He's been determined to show Rhys that there's more to a relationship than just sex. She understands that now, mostly because of him." I grin as Rhys hits the ball and jumps up and down like she won the game, even though all she did was hit the ball. "And Marcus has been able to move past my betrayal and accept Rhys the way she is, sharing her with us because he loves her so deeply that he just wants her to be happy. He's so protective of her. He won't stand by and let anyone treat her badly, *even* his best mates."

"And you, Mr Bossier?" Mrs R asks. "What do you two have together? Sex parties? Secrets about your former PE teacher?"

Shit, she has me there.

"You're right. We do have *those* secrets, but only to protect both Rhys and Ty. That's not all we have, though. I'm in awe of Rhys. She embraces who she is. Even now, while threats are made against her, she holds her head high, owning who she is. She might struggle with how she is sometimes, especially when people try to drag her down, but she gets right up, head held high, and she stares them down. I admire how she stands up for what she believes in and doesn't give in to the pressure of social standards. Her individuality draws me to her." I run my hand through my hair, knowing I'm about to get really fucking honest with my school principal and the mother of the girl I love. "I never thought I'd be able to love anyone. I thought I'd be one of those guys who is still a bachelor when he's fifty. But she proved me wrong, Mrs R. Rhys has shown me that I can love and be loved and still get what I want. She's everything to me."

"And it's just the five of you?" Her voice is quieter this time, and I'm almost positive I hear resolve in her tone.

"Well, four of us, plus Ty. The other guys haven't met him yet, and they don't know who he is."

"But no one else? She's happy with just you boys?" She asks, and I scoff.

"Men. We are men, Mrs R."

She laughs a little. "Don't get ahead of yourself. You're only seventeen."

"It's just a number. It doesn't define us. Just because the law says we are children doesn't mean we are."

Mrs Rogan sighs again. "I guess you have a point."

"Can I ask you something, Mrs R?"

"I guess."

"How much do you know about Rhys' past?"

"Well, I read the reports before we chose her to join our family. She has told me some things. I'm sure there's a lot I don't know."

"Reports don't explain things from her point of view, though, so I'm going to do you a solid, Mrs R. There's a podcast called Breaking the Silence. Listen to the latest episode, and then ask Charlotte to show you the TikToks. I think you will learn more about Rhys."

"Uh… ok." She mumbles curiously. "Do you think there's any chance she will come home tonight? I know it's already after nine, but if she wants to come home, I can come and pick her up any time."

I look back up at Rhys, mellow as hell from the Mary Jane in her blood. I wonder if she'd like to go home and see her parents? I know she loves them. She's just scared, not sure who she can trust right now.

"If she comes home, are you going to take her only connection to us away?"

"No. That's a mistake I won't be making again." Mrs R grumbles, and I nod, even though she can't see me.

"And she's not a prisoner? She can come and go as she pleases within reason?"

"Yes. Of course."

"And you won't drug her? She flushed those other pills, but how do we know you don't have another box somewhere?"

She sighs. "I guess you don't. My word is all I have right now, Mr Bossier. And I give you my word that there are no other drugs, nor will I ever threaten to use them again."

"Can we negotiate?" I ask, and she chuckles.

"A negotiation? You want me to negotiate for my daughter to return home?"

"Yeah. I do."

Mrs R sighs. "Fine. What are your terms?"

"If I can convince Rhys to come home tonight, will you give your permission for us to take Rhys away for the weekend? This weekend."

"What?" She laughs. "You want me to let her run off with you somewhere that Julie can get to her?"

"No. The opposite, actually. It will be a secret location that only you and I will know. We won't go anywhere. We will stay at that location for the weekend."

"Why?" There is accusation in her tone.

"To celebrate the end of the year. A very hard year for most of us. Let Rhys come away with us and forget about the ugliness Julie and Brian have brought back into her life. She will be safe. I promise."

"You think she'll go for it?" Mrs R asks hopefully, and I grin.

"Yes."

"Fine. If you can convince her to come home tonight, I'll be happy for her to spend the weekend with you boys as long as the location is kept secret, and I know it."

"Ok. Give me some time. I'll get her to call or message you after."

I hang up the phone feeling proud as punch until I realise I somehow have to convince Kitten to go home to her parents tonight. I really want to take her away for the weekend, but if she doesn't feel safe going home, then she's staying here. I mean, I could just take her away anyway, without her mum's permission, but I don't want to burn bridges that Kitten will need. The last thing I want is to come between her and her parents.

I stroll back over to the others, and Garrett raises a brow at me.

"You had a good chat with someone?"

"Yeah, Rhys' mum."

His brows shoot up. "What did she want?"

"She's worried. Heard from the cops about the call from Julie. She wants Rhys to come home." I plant my arse on a rickety barstool and face Rhys and Simon. They have given up on snooker and are now spinning in circles to see who falls over first.

"Do you think Rhys should?"

I tear my gaze from the two clowns and look at my big, broody mate and shrug. "I only think she should if she wants to. I don't think her parents are a threat. I think they are just going crazy with the need to protect her. I made some negotiations."

A loud crash makes us jump, and I turn back to see Simon headfirst in the wood heap as he laughs uncontrollably. Rhys falls to the floor in her own fit of laughter, her hand pressed between her legs as she crosses them.

"Stop! I'm going to pee!"

We can't help ourselves and join in laughing at the idiots.

"Rhys won, Hastings." Marcus declares. "She gets to use the toilet first."

I frown, "Why is that even a competition? Can't Hastings take a piss outside?"

Marcus turns to me and shrugs, his face just as confused as mine.

"Ohmygoditsgoingtocomeout!" Rhys leaps up from the dusty floor and bolts towards the toilet, but Simon does too, and now they are both racing toward the small bathroom.

"It's kind of like having kids," Garrett observes, and Marcus and I chuckle and nod.

Rhys reaches the door first, shoving it open, and then nearly gets knocked out by it as it ricochets off the wall before Simon shoves past her, darting for the toilet.

"No!" She screams, grabbing the back of his hoodie and reefing him back, all while tugging her pants down. He goes flying back out the door, landing on his arse as she stumbles to the toilet with her white arse pointing our way before she spins and sits down, a look of pleasured relief washing over her face.

"Fucking hell." Marcus chuckles. "Hey Rhee. We can see you!"

"I don't care!" She yells back, keeping her eyes closed as her bladder empties.

"Fuck, fuck, fuck." Simon jumps up like he has ants in his pants and runs back into the bathroom, heading straight for the sink.

Kitten's eyes fly open, and a look of horror crosses her face as she takes in Simon, who is now pissing in the sink.

"Ew, Sy! I have to wash my hands in that sink!"

"You'll have to wait until I'm done, Cherry."

Marcus loses it, tumbling to the floor, clutching his middle.

"I gotta say, this is time well wasted." Garrett chuckles, and my smile stretches wider.

"Hell, yeah, it is."

Chapter Eighteen

RHYS

S haun Bossier has some serious negotiating tactics up his sleeve. Not only did he convince me it was a good idea to call my mum and go home for the night, but he did it without telling me what he negotiated with my mum. Sneaky fucker! I didn't even know there was a secret trip planned until my mum brought it up on the way home in the car. I think she was happy that I'd come home willingly after realising Shaun didn't need to bribe me.

She explained that my laptop and phone are mine and they won't take them from me, as well as assuring me that there are no drugs in the house. Maybe it was the Mary Jane in my system, or maybe I was just genuinely happy to see my mum, but either way, I believed her words.

It was late when I got home, the twins long in bed, and Char out for the night with her girlfriend. Will was up, though, and when I stepped into the living area and saw how frayed around the edges he was, I rushed up to hug him. Cynthia followed, and we all had a moment in a group hug, and then he said something I will never ever forget.

> *"Rhys, I'm so sorry for making you feel like you're not the most precious and exquisite thing on this earth. I let my emotions control me, and I need you to know that I love you just the way you are."*

Needless to say, I cried again, but this time, they were happy tears.

When I finally fall into my bed, sleep comes quickly. Again, probably because of the MJ. I'm so exhausted that I sleep past breakfast and wake a little after ten in the morning. My phone has a few unread messages from the guys. Just the usual good morning, we miss you, and we love you. It's enough to make this girl blush. I respond to the messages and then shower, making sure all the parts that don't need hair are silky smooth, and then I wash my hair before letting it dry naturally as I dress for the day.

It's another sunny day and mild outside, so I choose a t-shirt dress, rock chick style, charcoal with slashes and holes, and totally Rhys George. I keep my face free of makeup and piercings because I know the guys love seeing me that way, and the way their eyes light up like I'm the most beautiful thing they have ever seen is something I want to see over and over again. I slip into my black Docs, pack my bag full of lingerie that probably won't stay on for long, plus a few other boring items like clothes, make-up, and hair stuff. I throw in Big Jim because it's time he and Garrett sized up, and I carry my bag out to Will, who is working at the table again today while waiting for me.

Hearing me enter the room, he looks up, sitting back in his chair as he sighs. "Just so you know, I'm still your dad, and I have to do the dad thing."

"Uh-ok." I raise my brows as he stands from his chair at the table.

"*Don't* do anything you *don't* want to do. Maybe *don't* do everything you *do* want to do. And be safe. Always. I can't express how important that last one is."

Smiling, I step forward and throw my arms around his neck. "I love you, Dad."

He hugs me back instantly, squeezing me like he doesn't want to let me go, and for a moment, I don't want him to.

"I'm sorry about going cray-cray the other day," I say quietly, and he squeezes me tighter.

"I'm sorry we put you in a situation that sent you cray-cray."

I giggle at him, repeating my words, and he pulls back, smiling.

"Keep in contact with your mum. She worries too."

I nod. "Yep. I will."

Dad picks up a couple of shopping bags with food in it. Some pre-cooked by Mum to make sure I'm eating right, even though I'll only be gone for a few nights, and we head to the car.

Apparently, the guys are all travelling together to the secret location with Shaun's brother Derek, so Dad drives me out of Fox Pines and tells me as we are driving across the open countryside that our destination is Redfield Lake. I get butterflies at the mention of Redfield Lake because I've heard it's a beautiful spot where those with more money like to flock to over the summer. Cabins and luxurious houses hide in the thick bushland that wraps around the lake, a huge contrast to the more rundown, mill-style homes in the town of Redfield, where crime is high, and strip clubs are open twenty-four hours.

About thirty minutes later, we weave through a narrow bush-lined street, passing strange-looking letter boxes made out of tin to resemble an animal, or tree, or person, and we eventually turn into the driveway for number 37.

I can't help but bounce in the seat with excitement as we bump our way down the pot-holey driveway until a cute little log cabin comes into view.

"Ehhhh!" I squeal, and Dad chuckles. "This is so freaking adorable!"

As we pull to a stop by the wide steps that lead up to a wraparound veranda, the door to the house opens, and four of my five stud muffins stroll from the cabin.

I throw the car door open, leaping out and rounding the front, colliding into Simon at the bottom of the steps as we come together for a hug.

"It's so good to see you, Cherry." Simon pulls back, speaking quietly. "I know we only just saw you last night, but I bloody missed you."

"I missed you too, Sy." I grin and ruffle his longish hair, making him laugh.

"Let me help with that." Garrett's deep voice draws my attention, and I watch him move down the steps to help my dad with the bags. I take a moment to watch how my dad responds, seeing that he seems comfortable with Garrett. I guess he would after cleaning up the blood from his face the other night, although the confrontation at my front door a few days ago had me worried.

Shaun steps down from the veranda as well, taking the bags from my dad's grip, smiling at him, and my dad smiles back.

"You all healed up?" Dad asks Shaun quietly, and my Casanova nods. "I'm uh… sorry about… you know. Hitting you."

"All g, Mr Rogan." Shaun smiles. "It was an accident."

"Even so. My behaviour has been questionable of late. I appreciate you protecting my daughter."

I leave Simon's side then, sidling up next to my dad and slipping my arm around his waist as I look up into his light brown eyes. "You're not the only one that's had questionable behaviour, Dad. I've been pretty testing."

He leans down and presses a kiss to my forehead. "Have a good weekend, Rhys. Keep in contact, so we know you're safe."

"Okie Dokie, Daddio." I beam, and he chuckles before backing away, his eyes roaming over the guys.

"Oh, and boys, if anything happens to my daughter, I will fuck you up!"

I gasp, slapping my hand over my mouth as I try not to laugh at my dad, and I see a fierceness in his eyes that tells me he will do exactly what he said if something happens to me.

"Understood, Mr Rogan," Marcus speaks for the guys. "We will protect her with our lives."

My dad gives a curt nod before climbing back into his car and slowly backing out of the drive, leaving me with four of my guys. My heart pangs, longing for Tyler, so I promise myself that I'll video-call him later. Maybe I'll give him a little show, so he doesn't forget me.

"Come inside, Kitten. Check out our digs for the weekend."

I turn to Shaun, his grin infectious, my own lips tilting up as excitement rushes through me. I do a little jump and a clap and run up the steps and into the cabin, which looks a little rustic on the outside but has some modern-day furnishings on the inside.

There's a stone fireplace along the side wall, with a wide-screen TV above it and rustic bookshelves on either side, lined with books that I'm going to take some time looking through later. A rich timber square coffee table sits in line with the fireplace, and a long, cushiony beige couch faces the tv, with two armchairs along the windows that overlook the lake and a slim day bed on the other side.

"Whose house is this?" I ask, darting my head around to the guys to see them wearing slight grins as they watch me.

"It's an Airbnb." Simon answers. "I bribed Mum into shouting it for me for the weekend. She didn't care. She tossed me dad's credit card and told me to go for my life. I think what won her over was that the alternative was we spend the weekend at home, *and* I might have mentioned that there would be cherry pie involved. She was more than happy to help."

I giggle. "I can imagine your mum's expression, Sy." I turn to see a dark timber dining table with eight seats lining it, cushioned in the same beige as the couch, with a dark timber kitchen at the back of the room. It's not overly big, but looks to have everything one would need.

"So, what are we going to do all weekend?" I ask as Marcus shuts the cabin door, closing us in. An electric current shoots to Kitty as her naughty thoughts take over my mind.

Down Kitty!

"We have plans tonight. There's a little lakeside party we are going to." Shaun beams, and the guys frown, turning their eyes to him.

"We are going to a party?" Simon asks, and Shaun nods. "Cool. I love parties."

"Maybe Rhee doesn't want to go to a party, Bossi." Marcus points out, and Shaun looks back at me.

"You wanna go to a party, Kitten?"

I shrug. "Maybe. But what are we going to do *now*?"

"We can go and see if the water is warm enough to swim in," Simon suggests, and I shrug, turning to approach the bookshelf, running my finger along the timber.

"Or… We could watch some movies." I grin on the inside, my naughty Kitty ruling me right now.

"You want to waste this beautiful day watching movies?" Garrett asks, his icy-blue eyes latching onto mine.

I continue to walk slowly past the bookshelf to stand in front of the empty fireplace, turning to face my guys. "I mean, I don't think it will be *wasting* the day. They are some very good movies."

Garrett frowns, and Simon and Marcus look confused, but Shaun chuckles.

"Kitten. I'm not sure we can access *those* types of movies on this TV."

I pout. "Surely we can link a phone up or something?"

Garrett has a lightbulb moment, and his frown morphs into a grin as he shakes his head. "Really, Baby Girl? You wanna watch porn?"

"Yes! I wanna watch porn with you guys. It's fun watching porn. Seeing who breaks first to touch themselves. Let's play that game." I grin, rubbing my hands together and walk around the coffee table to sit on the couch expectantly.

The guys chuckle.

"I guess I'll see if we can hook a phone up to this TV," Marcus mutters and moves to the TV while Garrett comes to sit on the couch next to me.

"I think you're wasting your time, Grady. I'm pretty sure that TV isn't a smart TV."

"Ugh! I just want to watch porn! If that TV won't come to the party, then you guys need to give me the porn show. I love me a bit of guy-on-guy action."

Marcus swears, hitting his head as he tries to pull back from behind the TV, and Shaun and Simon, who are now standing by the bookshelf, look at me like I've lost my mind.

Let's be honest. I probably have, but they love me so….

"I've said it before, and I'll say it again. Keep your dicks away from my arse." Garrett grumbles next to me, and I laugh.

"What about your mouth, Big Guy? Haven't you always imagined what it would be like to slide a dick in your mouth? Let me watch you swallow a dick. All you need to do is imagine it's your own."

"What makes you think I need to imagine it's my own? Maybe my dick is long enough to reach my mouth."

My mouth drops open, and Kitty claws at me as the mental image of Garrett sucking his own dick pops into my head. I shift on the couch to look at Garrett next to me. "Omg, it fucking is long enough! Show me!"

"Fuck. Even I'd like to see that." Shaun chuckles from the corner, and I nod enthusiastically, fluttering my lashes at Garrett in the hope he will agree to show us. A moment later, my hopes are dashed when he shakes his head and chuckles.

"If I'm telling the truth, the only person I'll *ever* share *that* with is Rhys. *Alone*."

"I want to know what it's like."

Everyone stills at Simon's comment, turning our gazes to him.

"What? I'm not gay or anything, but I've fucking dreamed of sucking my own dick. If it has to be someone else's, then I'm up for anything once."

"I'm so wet," I speak the truth as I feel damp heat between my legs and Kitty pulses with need.

"The thought of me sucking dick makes you wet, Cherry?" Simon asks, and I nod with vigour. "Well, shit. Now I just have to find me a dick to suck."

Chapter Nineteen

SHAUN

Her face! There's just no way I'm gonna disappoint my girl when she looks so fucking hopeful and aroused. Fuck, my dick is hard just thinking about how much this idea turns her on.

Turning my back on Kitten, I pretend I'm looking at the bookshelf as Marcus sits next to Kitten, telling her we will find a way for her to watch porn. He's probably freaking out about Simon's declaration about sucking someone's dick.

"Shall we do it?" I say quietly, tilting my head towards Simon as he watches Rhys and Marcus argue about porn.

"What? You want me to suck your dick, Bossi?" He asks quietly, and my eyes finally flick to see the amusement in his hazel eyes.

"I want to give Kitten what she wants. Two guys."

Simon's brows shoot up. "You and me?"

"Yeah." I nod. "Those other two aren't gonna man up and do it."

"We're only talking about oral, right? Or are you talking about… like…" Simon leans in more to whisper, "you and me going all the way?"

I grin. "I'll fuck you up the arse if you want, Simon, but I'm not ready to be a receiver in *that* region."

Simon laughs, his eyes flicking back to Rhys and our other two mates. "Let's do oral." He nods. "I'll suck your cock, Bossi."

My dick jerks as my mate's words sink in, and I remind myself that I'm not gay. Sure, I've been in a massive orgy with hands that weren't female all over my skin, tugging on Thor until he came, but they were just hands. Tools to extract pleasure. It doesn't matter who they belonged to. This is the same situation. Right? Me and Hastings are mates, but it won't be weird or anything... I hope.

"Ok then, Hastings. Let's put on a good show."

Simon grins with mischief and moves to the couch to pull a cushion from behind Garrett, earning a glare from the big fella, before he hovers over Rhys, waiting to gain her attention from Marcus. She stops arguing about the best types of porn and glances up through those dark lashes of hers to look at Simon. He leans down and kisses her. It's a hot and heavy kiss, and she moans, grabbing a fistful of his hair before he breaks their lips apart, not saying a word as he slowly pulls back, her hand slipping free.

As Simon walks back towards the fireplace, I pass him, heading for my girl, and repeat what Simon did, taking her lips in mine. She tries to tug me down to the couch with her, but I pull back, chuckling.

"So needy, Kitten."

"Hell yes. My Kitty is ravenous."

I smirk. "Good."

I turn my back on her to watch Simon drop the cushion on the floor, and my heart rate picks up as I think about the line we are about to cross. Am I really going to let Hastings suck me off? I fucking hope Kitten likes this. It's all for her. Maybe a little for me, too, since I'm the one that's getting my dick sucked, but mostly it's for her.

"What are you two up to?" Rhys asks, her tone filled with curiosity as I stand at the fireplace with Simon and turn back to Marcus, Rhys and Garrett, all watching on.

I don't use my voice to answer Kitten. Instead, I show her by turning to face Simon while he faces me. We stare at each other for another beat, and then Simon drops to his knees on the cushion in front of me.

"Stop it! If you're teasing me, I'll cry." Kitten whines, and Simon answers her, his eyes level with my dick.

"We aren't teasing, Cherry."

I glance over at Kitten and my two other mates. Their eyes are wide. Kitten's with excitement, and Marcus and Garrett's with disbelief.

"I don't joke about putting my dick in another guy's mouth." I lock my gaze with Kitten's, hoping she can see the truth in my eyes.

"Oh hell! I'm gonna cream all over the place." Rhys rasps, her voice now huskier and a sure sign she is engulfed by arousal.

"Uh… Do I have to watch this?" Marcus' voice is higher pitched than usual.

"Yes, of course, you do. You like watching." Rhys nudges Marcus with her arm, but keeps her eyes on Simon and me.

"I like watching *you* with them." Marcus counters, and Rhys rolls her eyes.

"But I'm *really* into this." She turns to Marcus then. "Watch for me? Please?" She flutters her lashes innocently, which is amusing as fuck, because there's nothing innocent about Rhys George.

Marcus' dark eyes roam Kitten's face before he sighs. "I'll try. But I'm only watching for you, Rhee."

She beams.

"Can I bail?" Garrett grumbles, and she swings around to face him this time.

"No, Mr Cole! You may not!"

"Can I watch your reactions instead of what they're doing?" Garrett tries to compromise, but Rhys looks at him sternly.

"You can watch both, Big Guy."

Garrett growls but faces us, and we all know that if Gaz didn't really want to watch, then he wouldn't.

With three sets of eyes watching, I return my focus back to Simon. He glances up at me, raising a single blonde brow, and I give him a slight nod, urging him to get on with it.

My playful mate looks a little nervous as he reaches up to start undoing my jeans, and fuck, my heart starts racing with nerves, too. Ok, so there's some excitement laced with my nerves. Thor is hankering to be sucked after all, and I'm only human. I'm also curious as fuck to see if a guy sucking my dick is any different from a chick. I can't imagine that it would be too different. A mouth is a mouth… right?

My jeans slowly drop from my hips, and Simon eases them all the way down to my ankles while Thor strains in my boxer briefs. Simon's hazel eyes lock onto the bulge in my jocks and swallows deep.

"You don't have to do this, man," I whisper, and Simon's eyes dart up to mine.

"No. I want to… But what if I'm not good at it?"

"Just remember what you like and do the same. I'll guide you if needed."

I wait until Simon gives me a nod, and then I pull down my boxers and Thor springs free, bobbing in front of Simon's face.

"This is the best porn I've ever seen." Rhys singsongs, clapping, even though we haven't done anything yet. Meanwhile, Marcus grumbles.

"I've seen better."

Garrett chuckles at Marcus' comment, but I ignore them as I watch Simon's eyes staring at my dick.

"Fuck, Bossi. You have a good-looking cock." Simon grins up at me, and I smirk smugly because fuck yes, I do.

"Thor is a work of art."

"Thor? Jesus Christ." Garrett scoffs.

"Yes Thor." Kitten preens. "He's a magnificent specimen. I can't wait to see him sink into Simon's mouth."

"I'd be much more comfortable if it was Rhys about to take your cock, Bossi," Marcus comments, and I chuckle.

"Fuck, your tune has changed, Grady." I chuckle. "It wasn't that long ago that you wanted us to keep our cocks away from Rhys."

"Just remember this right here is only about sex." Rhys butts in. "It's not about feelings, just about arousal and desire and letting go. Imagine being so horny that you don't care who you fuck as long as it happens. It's like that sometimes at the clubs. Just giving yourself over to the carnal need."

"I'm ready to give in to my carnal need," I growl, my dick feeling like the skin is going to split any moment. Then I catch Simon's eye. "You sure about this, Hastings?"

Grinning, he moves his eyes back to my straining dick. "Simon says shut the fuck up." Then he wraps his hand around my cock and guides Thor's head between his lips.

My mouth drops open as the visuals and sensations take over, and I try to keep my eyes open to watch my dick sink into the heat of my mate's mouth. Rhys moans, and I glance over to see her put her hand between her legs. Frowning, I lift my finger and point sternly at her.

"Hands off, Kitten!"

"But…"

"No buts!" I hiss between my teeth as I struggle to keep my composure as the heat of Simon's mouth engulfs Thor. "You watch and don't touch. First one to touch themselves is the loser."

"But…" She complains again before Garrett's deep voice drowns her small voice out.

"Can *I* touch her?"

I lose my fucking ability to reply as Simon cups my nuts and sinks Thor to the back of his throat.

"Oh yes! More Sy. You can take more." Kitten encourages, and I glance back down at my mate, watching as he draws back, swirling his tongue around my tip. His familiar smirking eyes dart up to mine, wild with excitement. Fuck, he loves it. And fuck, I think I do, too. His mouth is bigger than Kitten's, and I don't even hate that occasionally I can feel the graze of his whiskers. He sinks me in again, releasing my balls, and his hands move around to grip each of my arse cheeks.

"Fuck." I hiss right before he forces me deeper, and he gags.

"That's it, Sy." Kitten's voice is breathy. "You can take him." She encourages again, her tone still husky as I watch Simon's face redden.

"I want to look away, but I can't." Marcus rasps.

"I'd prefer to look away," Garrett grumbles as my eyes dart between Simon's watering eyes and my girl's dark pools as she writhes with need, her hips lifting in search of friction that isn't there.

Simon picks up the pace, and Rhys keeps her eyes on us. Her lips parted, cheeks flushed as her arousal builds. Her hips rise to meet fresh air again, her body straining for some sort of friction to ease her ache. She's panting, biting her lip, her hands moving to touch herself, but then ball into fists at her sides as she fights the urge.

Fuck, this whole situation has me ready to explode, but I want it to last. I want to make her come and satisfy this fantasy she has. I also don't want it to end because there's just something about this forbidden act that I'm here for. Who needs a sex club when you can have your needs met in your relationship?

Of their own accord, my hips start thrusting forward, fucking Simon's mouth. The deep rumble of his moan nearly fucking sends me over. I squeeze my eyes shut, tipping my head back as I will myself not to cum yet.

Not yet, Thor!

But Thor doesn't want to listen as my nuts start to tighten. My eyes fly open. "I'm gonna blow, Hastings. Now's your chance to back away before you swallow my cum."

He grips my arse cheeks tighter, increasing his pace.

Fuuuccckkk.

"I wanna see you cum in his mouth!" Rhys cries, so I jerk back quickly, pulling Thor from the heat of Simon's mouth.

Gripping the base of my shaft, I squeeze as heat rushes over me, and I soar as I start coming hard. Simon moans again, leaving his mouth open to catch my seed, and Kitten cries out uncontrollably as she hits her own high.

It takes a moment for my heart to calm down enough so I can actually hear, and when it does, the room is filled with panting breaths.

"Holy fucking devil nuts! I just came without touching myself." Rhys cries, and I chuckle as I glance over at her.

"Well, I lost," Marcus admits quietly, his cheeks turning pink as if he's embarrassed that what he witnessed turned him on.

I glance between Kitten, Marcus and Garrett, then down to Simon as he finishes swallowing my load.

"I fucking love you guys!" Kitten laughs, her tone wild with excitement.

I beam. "Good. Get over here and ride Simon's dick then, Kitten." I figure he deserves that after what he just did.

"Oooh, I do love bossy Bossi." Rhys grins, standing from the couch. She's wearing a baggy dress thing, or maybe it's just an oversized t-shirt, but it has slashes in it that are nothing but tempting as it gives me glimpses of her creamy skin underneath, and I watch as she slips her hands up under the dress, and shimmies out of her knickers.

"Fuck, Baby Girl. Your panties are soaked through." Garrett leans forward, scooping her panties up with one finger, holding them up to us.

"I think I might have squirted a little." She admits with no shame. Fuck, she's perfect.

"I'm so hard." Simon moans, rubbing his hand over his straining cock in his shorts.

"Super Cherry to the rescue!" Rhys yells, fist-pumping the air.

It's so good to see our girl feeling more like her playful self. She's had so much darkness to carry. This, here, is exactly what she needs. She needs harmless fun. Time to forget her worries and just ride a high with people she feels safe with. I'm fucking stoked that she feels that way with us.

With mischief in her eyes, Rhys pushes aside the decorative bowl and candle thing that's in the centre of the coffee table and proceeds to crawl over the top like the kitten she is, poking her arse out, the dress slipping back to bunch in the centre of her back giving Marcus and Garrett a front row view to heaven.

Chapter Twenty

GARRETT

A m I really ok with what I just witnessed? Hastings sucking Bossi off… my mates… together? I feel like I should be more repulsed than I am. Sure, it was weird to watch two guys go at it like that. I've never watched gay porn, but I'm pretty sure I should be freaking out more after witnessing my mates doing that.

My worries fly out of my head as I watch Rhys crawl over the coffee table, pointing those creamy globes at me, her glistening cunt playing peekaboo as she moves. I scrunch her wet panties up in my hand and bring them to my nose, inhaling deeply.

Fuck, I'm hot for this siren of mine. I don't think I'll ever get enough of her. I'm hard as all fuck, and all I want to do is stand up and grip her hips and sink my cock into her hot cunt, but she has her sights set on Hastings, and to be honest, I think he deserves her attention after what he just did for her. I don't think I could do that, no matter how much she begs. Then again, it was fucking hot seeing how turned on it made her.

"Do you wanna fuck me, Sy?" Rhys asks in her fucking sexy husk.

"Fuck yes, Cherry. So bad."

"Where do you want me? Here?" She pats the tabletop. "Or on the floor? Or the kitchen bench? We can get some food out."

Simon's eyes light up. "That sounds fucking hot, but maybe later. Right now, I just want to feel you wrapped around Conan."

"Are you fucking serious?" Marcus grunts. "Conan?"

"What do you call your little peewee then, Grady?" Simon glares, standing from the floor where he knelt to suck Bossi off.

"I don't call it anything." Marcus snaps, and Bossi laughs.

"Of course, you have a name for your dick. Everyone does."

"Can we forget about the dick names, please? I just want one to fill me, and I'm getting impatient." Rhys whines, and I chuckle. I fucking love how honest she is.

"Simon says, lay back on the table." Simon hisses, and Rhys moans, loving the domination. Simon is usually such a playful guy, but right now, he looks fierce. He means business.

Rhys does as he commands, changing position to point her glistening pussy towards Simon as she leans back on her hands, spreading her legs wide.

"I'm all slick for you, Sy. Come and punish Kitty nice and good."

Fuuuuckkk. Her words make it almost impossible to restrain the beast inside me, the word *punish* calling to me like a moth to a flame. The need to claim her has me squirming, so I grip the arm of the couch, trying to calm myself as Hastings kicks off his shorts and stalks towards our girl with his dick pointing at her.

Shaun kicks the cushion Simon had knelt on earlier to the edge of the coffee table, and Simon nods in thanks as he lowers himself again, this time between Rhys' spread legs.

"You want me to eat you first, Cherry?" He asks, and Rhys shakes her head.

"No. Just fill me up. I'm aching to be filled." She admits, and Simon's eyes flare with excitement before he grasps each of her calves and tugs her forward to the edge of the table.

"Fuck, Cherry. I'm aching to be buried inside you." Simon moans.

He must be running his dick through her folds or something. I can't see from this position, but when she jerks and they both gasp, I know he just sunk into heaven.

Simon starts fucking her, pumping into her hard, his face a mask of pleasured pain, and his eyes dart from her face to where they are joined.

"More." Rhys gasps, throwing her head back, her dark hair flicking out, and Marcus leaps off the couch, kneeling on the table beside Rhys. He slides his hand between her and Simon, and she falls back on the table, her hair cascading over the edge as her head follows. With each thrust, her tits jolt, Simon fucking her hard, just how she likes, and now I can see Marcus working on her clit.

Her eyes fly open as she moans again. "More. I want more. Everything." She cries, and my eyes meet Bossi's as he shakes his head at me.

"You're not ready for everything, Kitten."

"Just fill me up." She cries, and fuck it, I'll fill her up alright.

Standing from the couch. I use my foot to push it back further to give me more room before tearing off my jeans and jocks, my cock straining heavily with consuming need. Looming over Rhys, I look down at her splayed out on the table. Simon on the opposite side of me thrusting hard, Marcus using one hand to circle her clit, and the other to tug on his dick.

"You want to be filled, Baby Girl?" My voice is deeper than it usually is, the desire coursing through my veins, taking control of my whole body.

"Yes, Mr Cole. Please fill me up."

My cock jerks at her, calling me Mr Cole. It makes me feel fucking powerful. Dominating. She knows how it affects me, using it to snap my control.

I kneel quickly at the end of the low coffee table, gripping the base of my shaft as I guide my cock towards my girl as she drops her wanton mouth open, her head dangling back over the edge of the table. From this angle, I will be able to slide my cock right down her pretty little throat while she stares at my nuts and arse in her upside-down position.

"You're gonna take all of me today, Baby Girl. I'm not going to hold back because my cock is too big for your little mouth. Today, you are going to let me force my way down your throat until you can't breathe."

"Yes, Mr Cole." She pants, her chocolate eyes meeting mine as I look down my body at her.

"Fucking hell. Don't kill her with your monster." Marcus glares at me over his shoulder, and I grin.

"You want my monster to destroy you, Baby Girl?"

"Yes!" She pants. "Yes, Mr Cole. Fucking destroy me."

I growl at her words and nudge her lips wider apart as I ease into the heat of her mouth. "Wider," I command, and she forces her mouth to obey as my wide girth pushes past her limits. As I near her throat, she gags around my cock, and I moan, but still.

"Give me your hand, baby."

She lifts her hand, no longer able to see anything past my balls, and I take it, pressing her hand to my thigh.

"Pinch me, and I'll stop," I tell her, and she lifts her other hand with a thumbs up.

Fuck, she's perfect.

"I'm not going to last much longer," Simon calls, but I ignore him, keeping my focus on watching the shape of my dick under Rhys' creamy skin as I force it down her throat. She gags, this time more muffled and gurgly, her body stiffening, but she doesn't pinch, so I keep going. I slide out, giving her a moment to suck in air, before sliding back in. This time she gags hard and deep, her whole body curling with the reflex, and Simon cries out, stilling as he throws his head back, slamming his dick into her one last time. Bossi is grinning like a fucking proud dad, watching on as we destroy our girl in the best way.

I ease out again, giving her a few moments this time to recover, and I look down at her.

"You want me to stop, Baby Girl?"

She shakes her head and grins. "Keep going. I can take it."

"Oh fuck. I don't think I can take it." Marcus hisses while Simon shifts back, and Bossi positions himself between our girls' legs. He holds up a finger in front of his mouth, telling me to remain quiet about him being there, so I shrug and line up my monster to Rhys' lips again. This time I slide in easier, her jaw already accustomed to the stretch, and as I ease past her throat, feeling her try to fight the gag, Shaun uses his fingers to spread her other lips wide, and he starts sucking on her clit. She arches, then constricts as she gags, and I sink in deeper until I'm fully seated down her throat. She gags again, and Shaun sucks harder, adding his fingers to the game, sinking inside her.

I feel her fingers start to pinch, but then they recede as she thrusts her hips a little, chasing her orgasm and fuck, I can't even control myself. I start fucking her mouth.

Over and over, she gags, and if I'm not careful, she'll likely throw up, but as her body stiffens and she comes hard, her moans muffled as I pump my cock faster down her throat, I explode. Rivers of cum shoot straight down her throat, but then she pinches hard, and I pull free quickly in time for some of my seed to come back up. She turns to the side as her body rejects some of it, barely a mouthful spilling free. She gasps and gasps, and for a moment, I fear I've gone too far. For a moment, I fear my monster is too much for her to handle.

But then she laughs hysterically, and I look up at the guys to see them looking as confused as me before she speaks.

"That was fucking epic. Let's do it again."

Chapter Twenty-One

Rhys

B lissful. That's how I feel right now. This is what vibrators *can't* do. They can't destroy you the way a man can. And by destroy, I mean fuck. Hard. Punishingly so.

It's the best way to clear my head sometimes.

Nothing before these guys came into my life has ever been this satisfying. They own me. I'm woman enough to admit that now. Previously, such a notion sounded absurd to me, but not now that I know what it's like to be worshipped.

We spend the afternoon recovering from our sex session. Kitty is asleep right now, and I had to take some ibuprofen earlier for the ache in my jaw and throat, but I can't feel it anymore. I'm pretty sure Garrett bruised my throat. Is that even a thing? It fucking feels like a thing, but it's mild and thoughts of what we did chase any pain away. The way he fucked my mouth so thoroughly made me come alive. It was a claiming of sorts, and I was there for it. For every slide of his monster dick. And what Simon and Shaun had done together, just to please me. I've fucking won the jackpot!

"Do we need jackets for the party, Bossi? Is it outside?" Simon asks, snapping me out of my daydream about monster cocks and guys-on-guys.

"The party is inside. You'll only need a hoodie or something to put on when we walk there and back." Shaun offers, and Marcus eyes him warily.

"Who's party is it?"

"A friend. She's nice." Shaun shrugs, not really giving us any information at all.

"What aren't you telling us?" I shoot Shaun a fake dagger, and he chuckles.

"Well, I was going to surprise you, but since you need to get ready, you'll need to know the dress code."

My brows shoot up. "I didn't pack much. Lots of lingerie and not much that can be worn to a party."

He grins. "Are you sure about that, Kitten? Your lingerie is perfect for tonight's party."

I frown, thinking over his words, and then a little rush of excitement makes me sit taller on the couch. "Don't tease me, Cass."

He beams. "I'm not teasing, Kitten."

I jump up, clapping excitedly. "Really?"

"Yes. Really." He beams.

"Wanna clue us in?" Marcus grumbles, and Shaun turns his attention to his mates.

"The party we are going to requires no clothing. Only masks."

"Eeeehhhhh!!!" I squeal, dancing around towards the fireplace.

"What the fuck?" Marcus hisses, and Shaun rolls his eyes.

"We said we would try the whole sex party thing for our girl. So tonight, we are. It's happening in the house right next door."

"It is?" I ask, my eyes widening as I move to the window to peer out, trying to see a house through the thick bushland.

Movement behind me makes me turn, and I see Marcus dart up from the armchair, his face red in anger. "We should have discussed this first! Together! Who the fuck are you to go and make this decision for us?"

"Grady has a point, man," Garrett adds, and my heart sinks.

"I'm cool with going to a sex party." Simon grins, and I skip over to him, pulling him up off the other armchair before throwing my arms around his neck.

"We can discuss it now." Shaun shrugs. "If you don't want to come, you don't have to."

"Right, but you and Rhee will still go?" Marcus snaps, and Shaun shrugs again. Marcus turns his furious eyes to me, and I pale, moving Simon in front of me and hiding behind his back. I'm trying to be playful in the hopes it will diffuse Marcus' anger a little. Out of all of them, I knew attending a sex party would be hardest for him to wrap his head around. "Rhee?" Marcus snaps, and I peek out from behind Simon's shoulder. "What if *I* don't want you to go? Will you still go anyway?"

Well shit. That's a tough question. I want to go to the sex party. But I also don't want to upset Marcus or any of the guys.

"Rhee?" Marcus asks again, and I sigh.

"I don't know." I poke my head out a little more from behind Simon. "I guess if you really don't want me to go, then I shouldn't."

"But you *want* to go?" He asks, and I shrug but nod at the same time.

"Aren't you ready to try it?" I ask, and Marcus frowns.

"I'm only just getting used to you fucking my mates. I don't think I'm ready to watch you fuck another guy."

"What if I stick with girls? Would you like to watch me with a girl?"

Marcus has no words, apparently, his brows shooting up and his face morphing to sheer confusion.

"I think his silence is a, duh yes." Simon chuckles as I come out from hiding.

"We haven't figured out rules for a sex party yet. Not really." Marcus finds his voice again.

"Actually, I think it was agreed to make those rules up as we go." Shaun offers, and Marcus shoots him a glare.

"Let's say I agree to go. What happens if we go there and I, or any of you," Marcus points to the guys, "can't handle watching Rhys fuck anyone, even a chick?" He turns back to me. "Does that mean you won't, Rhee? And how can we be sure that it won't just turn into a screaming match between us when we all have different opinions on how things should go?"

"Can you at least try to see if you can handle it? And to be honest, I have no interest in any other guys besides you four and Ty, so I don't think you have to worry about that."

"And girls? You interested in them still?" Marcus snaps, and my heart sinks. This is the part that people can't wrap their heads around about me because it's so different. I know I'm asking a lot of Marcus. Of all of my guys, but I really want them to at least try.

"Maybe a little scissor action will be fun?" I flash Marcus my teeth and bat my lashes at him, hoping to win him over.

"Now I'm hard." Simon snickers, and I turn to him, giving him a high five.

"Watching Rhys with a girl is something else." Shaun smiles at Simon while I return my focus to Marcus.

"What do you think, Gaz?" Marcus grunts towards my big guy, who is frowning. "You're fucking quiet about this."

"I think we need to have a safe word. If anyone has a huge problem with something, use the safe word, and we all take the sidelines and try to figure it out."

"And what if we can't figure it out?" I ask my big brooding monster-dick man, and he shrugs.

"Then it's time to come back here."

I nod, returning my gaze back to Marcus. "Wouldn't you like to see me with a chick, Marc?"

His eyes narrow at me for using my nickname for him. Damn, he knows I'm trying to butter him up.

"Maybe I would like to see you with a chick, but I'm telling you right fucking now, there's no way I can handle seeing you with another guy. You have five. That's enough!"

Is it wrong that Marcus' possessiveness gets me all hot and bothered?

"Ok, Marc. I agree. Five guys are enough. I will only fuck chicks."

"No kissing on the mouth. That's only for us." Marcus points a stern finger at me, and I grin, biting my lip as I approach him.

"Deal." I throw my arms around his neck, but he doesn't return the favour, instead glaring down at me like I'm nothing but a frustrating brat.

"Kiss me, big boy," I growl, and he cracks a smile.

"Stop it. I'm trying to be grumpy."

"Boo! Grumpy isn't sexy."

"Are you sure?" Marcus smirks as he finally wraps his arms around me, tugging me hard against his chest.

"I stand corrected. Grumpy Marcus can be very sexy."

"Can I ask a question?" Simon's head suddenly appears beside us, and I grin up at him, waiting. "What about us guys? It's a sex party, so what if we want to fuck someone else?"

My face drops, remembering how I felt when Cass was getting a BJ from Madam Vik. It fucking killed me.

"Is that question really necessary?" Garrett hisses at Simon, and he shrugs.

"What? It's a legit question."

"Simon's right. It is a legit question." I drop my arms from around Marcus' neck, and he releases me so I can take a step back. This is the part I struggle with. How can I ask them to allow me to fuck others, yet it fucking kills me to think of them doing the same thing? It's fucking double standards at its finest.

"Kitten?" Shaun urges me to say something, and I suck in a deep breath, hoping to calm my heart.

"I'll be honest. I'm probably going to struggle to watch any of you with someone else."

"I'll be honest too." Marcus takes my hand in his, capturing my attention. "I have no desire to touch another chick, Rhee."

"Same." Garrett's deep voice comes from behind me, and he presses his tall frame against my back.

"Same, Cherry. I just wanted to know what your answer was to that." Simon offers, lifting my hand to his mouth and pressing his lips to the back.

"Me too, Kitten. I'm only interested in you." Shaun smiles, but my heart sinks.

"But you did," I whisper, my eyes dropping to Marcus' chest in front of me.

"What?" Cass comes up to my other side, stroking my hair back behind my ear.

"At the Feast. I saw you with Vik kneeling between your legs." I turn to look up into those familiar steel-grey eyes and watch his brows shoot high.

"So… you saw her kneeling on the floor in front of me with her mouth open while I jerked off?"

My brows shoot up this time. "You were jerking off?"

"Yes." Shaun's face is deadly serious as he looks down at me.

"You weren't fucking her mouth?"

"Hell fucking no." Shaun's head jerks back. "I couldn't even get hard properly. I had to close my eyes and think of you to wake up Thor, and then that stupid bitch would go and speak, and he'd deflate again."

"Oh."

"Just out of curiosity," Simon butts in, "what about dudes on dudes?"

"What?" Cass frowns, looking over my shoulder to look at Simon.

"Well, we have established that we can try watching Cherry do some girl-on-girl action, but what if she wants to watch some guy-on-guy?"

"Stay the fuck away from my dick, Hastings!" Garrett hisses next to my ear, and I giggle.

Cass laughs, "you didn't get enough dick earlier, Hastings? You want me to bend you over? Is that it?"

"Do you want to do that, Sy?" I glance up at him through my lashes, hoping he can see how much this conversation is ok. This is a safe place.

"What? No!"

"It's ok if you do. Sex parties are places to explore desires. If you want to try something, Sy, then you should."

He frowns, keeping quiet.

"Kitten is right. I won't judge any of you if there's something you really wanna try that Kitten can't give you." Shaun offers sincerely, and I nod in agreement.

I kinda hate the thought that there's something I can't give them, though. "I mean… I'd honestly love any exploration to be with someone in this group, but if it can't be in the group, then we can find someone that can help out if you want, Sy. What are we talking exactly? Topping or…"

Simon huffs. "We aren't talking about anything. I was just asking where you stand on it." With a look of frustration, my playful guy turns and barges off into the bathroom, slamming the door behind him, leaving us in awkward silence.

"He obviously wants to try something." Garrett's deep voice is quiet. "I'm happy for him to do that as long as it's not with me. I love the guy, but I just can't go there."

"I don't think any guy could handle what you're packing, bro." Marcus chuckles quietly.

"I'll have a chat with him." Shaun looks over his shoulder at the closed bathroom door before turning back to me with a reassuring smile. "You go get ready, Kitten. I brought some of that face paint stuff you use at Vixen's Lodge. It's in the main bedroom." Shaun beams, slapping a wet kiss on my cheek before running off towards the door that Simon disappeared behind.

Chapter Twenty-Two

MARCUS

This is a bad idea. I know it is deep down, yet I'm curious as fuck, which is why I caved and gave in to Kitten, agreeing to come to this fucking sex party. I know my fucking emotions, though, and if any guy so much as looks Rhee's way, I'm going to lose my shit!

We weave through the trees, following the narrow path that connects the properties, my hand linked with Rhee's as she skips beside me. She's a fucking ball of energy. More so than usual. I have to admit, it's nice to see that spark in her step again. I wasn't sure I was ever going to see that confident, larger-than-life girl grace us with her presence the way she used to.

As we near the tree line, Shaun turns back to face us. "Masks on."

Rhee does a little jump with a clap, her painted mask glowing from the light filtering through the trees from the house just beyond. It's like a beautiful skull creation. I don't know what it's called, but most of her face is white, with black, purple and hot pink decorative detail around her eyes, nose and mouth. It's exotic, and even though she doesn't look like Rhys, I can still tell it's her by the way she moves and talks and how her soul calls to mine.

The guys tug their leather masks on, so I pull mine from my back pocket and do the same. It's all black leather, covering the top of my head and face, with holes for my eyes, breathing holes at the nose, and stops just above my lips to leave the bottom of my face free. All the masks are the same. Bossi got them for us because he planned this whole fucking thing without discussing it with us. I think I'll cock-block him all night. Make him suffer so he can only use his hand.

After I get my mask in place, making sure I can see properly, I watch my mates do the same, and Rhee does a whispered squeal.

"I'm so turned on right now!"

"We can ditch the party, Baby Girl. Instead, we can chase you through the trees and fuck you in the dirt once we catch you." Garrett suggests, and she freezes, her eyes wide with excitement as she looks around.

"Oh, fuck Big Guy. That sounds so hot."

"We can do that tomorrow night." Shaun chuckles, leaning forward to grab Rhee's hand.

Like the possessive fucker I am, especially tonight, I leap forward and snatch her hand before he makes contact. "She's walking in with me." I hiss, and Shaun holds up his hands, backing away with a smirk.

"Ok, Grady. You got it." He grins wider, which just pisses me off more.

"Are we going or what?" Simon snaps, turning his back on us and continuing up the path.

I glance down at Rhee to see the pretty skull frowning on her face, her eyes glued to Simon's back as he heads towards the house.

"Don't worry about him, Kitten. He's ok." Shaun offers quietly, and Rhee nods.

I can tell she doesn't believe it, and her hand starts to sweat in mine, so I squeeze it and tug her into my side. She offers me a small smile as she looks up at me, and the need to turn that slight tip of her lips into a full-blown cheesy grin is like a compulsion I can't deny. I just want her to be happy, which is why I agreed to this craziness. This group relationship.

"Come on, Rhee," I smirk at her past my mask. "I wanna see what this sex party stuff is like."

Her smile widens, and she nods eagerly, taking my hand in hers again to lead me up the path.

As we approach the house, I notice the Hamptons-style cottage has its shutters closed, blocking any chance of seeing inside. The light flowing from the house comes from the exterior lamps lining the veranda, and the faint thud of music filters from within, giving a hint that a party is underway. Other than that, the choir of crickets drowns out any other noises in the area, and unless you are as close as we are now, you wouldn't have a clue what's going on behind the closed door.

We follow Bossi up the steps and wait as he knocks. A moment later, the door swings open, and a tall woman wearing a pink flowery mask appears in the door.

"Moxie?" Rhee asks, and the woman smiles as she looks past Bossi.

"Hi, Kitten."

Rhee drops my hand, pushing past Bossi to throw her arms around the woman's neck.

"Holy shit balls, Mox! What are you doing here?" Rhee pulls back to look up at the woman, and fuck, I see the affection in this woman's eyes for my girl.

"Well, Kitten. I'm throwing a party. I'm so happy you can join us tonight."

Rhee's smile drops, "Join us? Who's us?"

"It's ok, Kitten. This isn't a Hill party." Shaun offers, and Rhee's shoulders instantly relax.

Then, the woman, Moxie, reaches out, cupping Rhee's face as she shifts to lean in. Holy shit, this lady is going to kiss my girl!

I barge forward, tugging Rhee away from Moxie, shooting her a glare when she looks at me in confusion.

"She only kisses us." I hiss, and Moxie's lips widen in a huge smile.

"Oh, how possessive. This is going to be fun."

Bossi chuckles, and Rhee giggles, and I'm about ready to fucking leave, but my girl tugs me in through the door and before I know it, we are closed in the house, and the sound of moaning meets my ears.

Ok. I'm man enough to admit that now I'm even more curious.

"The rules are, masks stay on at all times." Moxie turns to face us. "No phones. No real names, so make up a party name now if you haven't already."

Rhee turns to us, grinning. "Why hello boys, I'm Kitten." She holds her hands up to us like claws and sweeps them forward. "*Meow.*"

My lips spread wide because fuck, I can't even get annoyed about her using the same name as the other place she went to. Not when I can see she really is Kitten right now.

"I'm Casanova," Bossi states, drawing my attention from our girl, and I scoff.

"Real fucking OG, man."

"What are you going to be called, then?" Bossi snaps, and I shrug, glancing at Rhee.

"You name me *Kitten*." It's the first time I've called her Kitten. Shaun does it all the time, and that Tyler guy called her Kitten over the phone. I have to say, I don't hate it.

"Oooh. Ok." She bites her lip as she thinks, bringing a black painted nail to her purple lips. A grin morphs her painted face, and I can tell she's come up with an idea. "Caveman."

The guys laugh like it's the funniest thing, but I grin. It's fucking fitting. I did the whole caveman thing to her last term when me and Ayden went and stole her and Lexi away from a party. I threw Rhee over my shoulder and carried her out, and that was the first night we were together.

"Fuck yeah, I'm your Caveman!" I grin, and she grins back, nodding.

"I'm Barbarian," Simon mumbles, still moody.

"Monster," Garrett adds as Rhys beams at him, her eyes flicking back to Simon. She's still worried about him.

"Ok, now that's sorted," Moxie gains our attention again, her eyes lingering on Rhee's face a little too long for my liking. "The last rules are that you must ask permission to join any groups or individuals. No means no. And the safe word is Mississippi."

We all nod, me, Gaz and Hastings standing awkwardly, not knowing what to do next, before Rhee starts pulling her clothes off. Fuck, my heart begins beating wildly in my chest as anticipation grips me. It feels like it's going to burst through my rib cage, thumping so hard that I instinctually press my hand to the centre of my chest in the hopes of calming it the fuck down. This is really happening. I'm at a sex party with my girl and my mates.

When I notice the guys peeling off their clothes, too, I move quickly to do the same, following Shaun's lead as he dumps his stuff in a basket lining the wall. I dump my stuff in with Rhee's and look around, unsure if I should take my jocks off or not since Rhee is wearing her red lace bra and panties still. Oh, and let's not forget the lethal-looking red heels still on her feet.

"Do we keep jocks on, or?" My face flares with heat as the question passes my lips. I'm fucking glad I'm wearing a mask right now.

"It's up to you, man." Bossi shrugs. "I'm going in commando, but you can keep covered up until you wanna get your dick out."

"I'm keeping mine on," Garrett grumbles, and I take a moment to study my brooding mate. He's a fucking big bastard. He has muscles on muscles, tall, broad, and totally the monster he's named himself. And I'm not just talking about his cock. That thing is an entity of its own. I feel scrawny next to Gaz, even though I know I'm not, but all of a sudden, I feel self-conscious. Should I be here? Am I good enough?

"I'm going commando, too." Simon's voice draws me out of my inner turmoil, and I watch as he bends to peel his jocks off. His voice sounds a little lighter than it did a few minutes ago, and I can see the excitement in his eyes, peering out from the mask.

"I think I'll keep mine on for now." I nod, not ready to walk around a strange house with strange people with my fucking boner pointing at everyone.

Moxie turns and walks into the party, so I take Rhee's hand again, living up to my possessive Caveman name as we follow. Rhee sways her hips as she walks, her spine straight with more confidence than I've seen on her, probably ever. Her red heels click on the timber floors with each step she takes, drawing attention our way as we weave through the small space. There must be over twenty people in here, all in some sort of sex act. There are probably more women than men, but our presence evens it out a little. Gender doesn't seem to be much of an issue, though, with girls on girls and guys on girls and guys on guys. It's almost surreal to witness in the flesh, but fuck, my dick is instantly hard.

"Hey Tradie and Sheriff. You remember Kitten, right?" Moxie addresses two guys going at it as she passes them.

"Hey Tradie! Hey Sheriff." Rhee beams, wiggling her fingers at the two guys going at it. One has nothing but a cowboy hat on with a sheriff's badge, his lips curling up in a smile as he peels a hand off the globe of the arse he's pounding into. The other guy, who is wearing nothing but a tool belt, looks up, beaming back at Rhee for a moment before his eyes roll back, and he's lost to the pleasure he's experiencing.

"Hey, Kitten." Sheriff grunts. "Great to see you again."

"Fucking hell," Garrett says under his breath, clearly uncomfortable.

Moxie steps in our view, and I'm kind of glad for the distraction. I didn't want to watch, but the voyeur in me has a mind of its own, and I was about ready to pull up a fucking chair.

"Why don't you go into the main bedroom, Kitten," Moxie smiles at my girl, holding her hand out towards a door at the far side of the room. "There's something in there I think you'll like."

"Ohhh, ok, Mox. Thanks." Rhee preens and follows Bossi as he leads the way, tugging me behind her.

Glancing over my shoulder as we weave through the crowd, I see Garrett's eyes ahead, not looking at the porn scenes surrounding us, while Simon is grinning, staring at each one with interest. It's good to see the playful smile back on his face.

As we step through the bedroom door, Rhee stops in her tracks as a gasp escapes her lips. I glance past her small frame to see a big guy sitting in the corner of the room in an armchair, wearing nothing but a red leather mask.

Rhee squeals, dropping my hand and takes off towards the guy, who stands in all his fucking naked glory, his hard dick spearing out like a beastly weapon. My girl leaps at him, and he catches her as she wraps her legs around his waist and kisses him with only what I can describe as akin to desperation.

"What the fuck!" I hiss, darting forward, but Bossi, the annoying prick, steps in my way, his hands pushing against my bare chest.

"Relax, man. It's Skipper."

"I don't care who the fuck it is. She said it was only the five of us. NO ONE ELSE!"

Bossi grins. "Yeah. He's number five." He points his thumb over his shoulder. "Skipper is Ty."

Finally understanding, I glance back over to see the red masked man lying Rhee on the bed, his lips not leaving hers as they kiss like they're starved for each other.

Shit.

My heart sinks. I knew there was a fifth guy, and I knew he was older, but I wasn't prepared to see them together. I kind of thought we'd meet one day, like a long time in the future, at a barbeque or something. I kind of thought I'd get to know him before I had to see him claiming my girl.

"I need to taste you." His deep, gravelly voice floats across the room as I hear the door click shut behind me, and I stand with my four mates watching as number five leans back, grips her lace panties, and tears them from her skin like they were made from nothing but air. Rhys gasps, palming her lace-covered tits as the guy falls to his knees and buries his head between her thighs.

Rhee gasps again, her back arching off the bed, her head thrown back as one of her hands flies to the red leather wrapping his head to hold him in place.

"I don't know if I can do this," I whisper.

"Just watch her." Bossi's voice is hushed as he responds. "See how much she's enjoying this? She cares about this guy, just like she cares for us. Look at her face, man. Look how happy she is to be reunited with him."

I try to focus on the things Shaun tells me, and I keep reminding myself that this is the fifth boyfriend. This is the guy who I've been wanting to meet. I'm not sure what I'd been expecting, but it wasn't *this* guy. Ripped like he spends eight hours a day in a gym. Older. So much older, if the long stubble dusting his jaw is any indication. He has to be in his thirties, at least. And I guess the most shocking thing to me is that I didn't expect the two of them to look right together. But they fucking do.

I study him, trying to figure out if there's anything about him that I recognise, but I don't know any dudes with beards.

"Yes, Daddy." Rhys cries, and Skipper growls, tearing his mouth from her pussy and sneering at her.

"What have I told you about calling me that?"

"I don't know," Rhee pants, innocence lacing her tone. "What have you told me, D*addy*?"

He growls again, grabbing her legs and flipping her over, so she's face down on the bed. Then his hand comes down on her bare arse. Hard. I stiffen, ready to swing fists, but Bossi throws his hands out to stop Garrett and me at the same time.

"Oh, *Daddy*." Rhee moans. "Do it again."

He does it again, hissing through his teeth before tugging her arse high and lining his dick up before slamming inside her. She throws her head back, rising on all fours, her painted face showing only utter bliss.

"Fuck me hard, Daddy." She cries as he pounds into her while bringing his hand around to her front and working her clit.

"I think I understand the enjoyment of the whole watching thing you do, Caveman." Garrett's deep voice rumbles quietly next to Shaun, and Simon agrees.

"Yeah. This is something else."

Bossi chuckles as we watch our girl fuck one of her guys, and then Shaun grips his cock and starts fucking wanking. Jesus, the need to pull my own dick out is almost consuming, but I keep my hands balled into fists at my sides and watch this beast of a man pleasure our girl.

It doesn't take much longer before Rhee is screaming out in ecstasy, and the red masked brute is throwing his head back with his own release. Their panting fills the room, and after a minute, Rhee flops forward on the bed face first before lifting her head to look up at us, while number five stands tall, his dick slick from our girl.

"Ahhh… Guys." Rhee smirks. "This is Ty."

Chapter Twenty-Three

Rhys

M y heart is thrashing in my chest from excitement. I wasn't expecting to see Ty. We'd been texting and video chatting since I got my phone back, but he never once let on that I'd be seeing him anytime soon. Even when I told him I was going away with the guys for the weekend, he never gave a hint. Sneaky fucker!

"Get over here, Fuckboy." Tyler rasps from behind me, and I watch the smug smirk on Shaun's face grow wider as he leaves the others by the door and approaches us.

Propping myself up on my elbows, I glance back over my shoulder to look at Ty. I notice for the first time that his eyes aren't blue tonight. They are brown. He must be wearing contacts to further hide his identity.

It almost feels surreal to see him here. The lingering presence of his lips on mine isn't surreal, though. My daily dreams of seeing him again can't even compare to what it's like to be back in his arms. Part of me feels like crying because I legit didn't think I'd see him again for a long time. I'm too happy, though. I can't stop smiling because right now, I have all five of my guys in one room, and I desperately don't want this night to end.

"Hold her arms, like the first time at the Feast."

I freeze at Ty's directions to Cass. Even though that time with them both at the Feast was mind-blowing, the thought of having the control of my hands taken away shoots fears through me. After being restrained and gagged and then humiliated in front of the Feasters as my punishment, I can't bear the thought of handing over that sort of power to someone again.

"Stop!" My Caveman snaps and all eyes shoot to Marcus as he crosses the room. "Rh..." He stops himself before saying my name. "Kitten doesn't want this."

I glance from Marcus to Ty in time to see Ty frowning as he looks back at me, and it only takes a moment for the realisation to hit him. Then his eyes soften.

"Kitten." He reaches out his hand, and I roll over, taking it and letting him pull me up off the bed. I peer up, craning my neck to let myself get lost in his deep blue gaze, which is intense as he studies me. "You're safe with us. We would never hurt you. You will remain in control. It just lets us tease you more."

"Stop trying to talk her into something she doesn't want to do." Marcus snaps, and I watch as Ty's gaze shoots over my head. I'm expecting him to get angry. To tell Marcus to back off, but he doesn't. Instead, his eyes remain soft.

"I'm trying to help her. The best way for her to deal with those demons is to face them. She can do that by doing similar things with someone she trusts."

"Yeah, well, she isn't ready." Marcus snaps again, and I sigh.

I get what Ty is saying. I know it because I've done it before. I've re-enacted situations that Brian and I did, although the people I did them with were none the wiser. They just thought it was role-playing. I want everything with these guys, even the things that scare me. I trust them all, without a doubt, and I want to move past my fears, so there's no barrier between us.

"It's ok, Caveman. I can do this." I turn to him and offer him a smile. "You are always so perceptive of how I'm feeling. I love that about you. Thank you for watching my back."

"I love you, Rh... Kitten." Marcus rasps. "I will always look out for you. Even if it makes me look like a possessive fucker."

"You are a possessive fucker." Cass chuckles. "But we love that about you. You see things that we sometimes miss."

I nod, smiling reassuringly. "I want to face this fear, and I trust everyone in this room." I turn back to Ty. "No remote-controlled sex toys tonight, though."

Ty nods. "Agreed. No remote-controlled or vibrating toys. Just us and our bodies."

I smirk. "I do like the sound of that."

I feel heat at my back right before a body presses against it, and at first, I think it must be Shaun because he is familiar with Ty, but then Marcus speaks next to my ear.

"I will take her arms. Just tell me how you want me to hold them."

A shiver runs up my spine as anticipation fuels my blood, and Kitty comes to life again.

Greedy pussy!

"You're the one that likes to watch, aren't you?" Ty asks as Marcus' arms weave around my waist, tugging me back.

"I am."

"Good. You can watch me lick our girl clean."

I sigh and moan at the same time, images of Ty's head between my legs only minutes ago sending heat to my core.

"You like the sound of that, Kitten?" Ty grins down at me, and I bite my lip, my breathing a little shallow as I nod.

"Yes, *Daddy*."

"Fuckboy, show this possessive fucker what to do," Ty demands before glancing over to Simon and Garrett, who are still standing by the door. "I'm going to guess the big guy is the one with the monster cock you can't stop talking about, Kitten."

I giggle and nod. "Yes Daddy. He's the one with the monster."

"That must mean that Goldie Locks over there is the fetish guy."

"Cherry, do you tell this old dude everything?" Simon whines from behind me somewhere, and I giggle.

"Yes. How else am I going to torture him? I like to rile him up over the phone, so he can't help but take his big dick in his hand and-."

"Yep. Ok. We get it." Marcus grumbles behind me, and Tyler glares.

"You have a lot of spankings coming your way, Kitten. If you're not careful, you won't be able to sit for a week."

I scoff. "Please! You realise that isn't a punishment, right? I want you to destroy me, Daddy."

Ty's lip twitches as he lurches forward, his hand wrapping around my throat as he presses against my front, pushing me firmly into a Ty and Marcus sandwich.

"I'm going to fucking claim you." He growls. Like really growls like a deadly creature as it approaches its prey. And fuck if that isn't the hottest thing ever.

"You'd better not be hurting her." Marcus hisses at the way Ty is gripping my neck, and Ty chuckles against my ear, sending another shiver up my spine.

Ty shifts, his arm moving somewhere behind me. I'm not sure what he's doing because I can't see, given that I'm still stuck between him and Marcus, but then Marcus stiffens behind me, and Ty rasps at him. "You tell me if she's not enjoying this."

Hands nudge between my body and Ty's, and I feel him directing Marcus' hand down to my needy Kitty. The moment Caveman's fingers slide between my slick folds, we both moan, and I relax back into him.

"See?" Tyler chuckles low, and Marcus agrees.

"Yeah, man. I see." His voice is a sexy husk, and a moment later, his lips brush my shoulder, making my lids flutter shut as I melt into the feel of both guys.

"Fuck it. Let's do this right here." Ty states, and my lids fly open. "Lock Kitten's arms behind her back."

Marcus obeys Tyler, and a pang of guilt hits me, knowing that even though Marcus, Garrett and Simon have now met Ty in the flesh, they still have no idea that the identity behind the red leather mask is their old PE teacher.

"Make sure it's firm. We don't want her to get free." Ty orders, and even though the whole restraint thing was freaking me out only minutes ago, it seems to have vanished now. The thought of being at their mercy is making Kitty weep, and any worries I have about Ty and my guys float away.

Withdrawing his fingers from between my legs, Marcus grips my arms from behind and gently pulls them, locking my arms with his behind my back. The movement pushes my chest out, and Ty takes advantage of that by sucking one of my straining nipples into the heat of his mouth. Moaning, I tip my head back against Marcus' shoulder, and he brings his soft lips to my neck and nibbles on the sensitive skin just below my ear.

Ty's teeth come down on my nipple, and I yelp and jerk before he releases it and chuckles. "Spanking isn't the only way to punish you, Kitten."

I hiss at him, but there's no menace behind it. No fucking way am I going to refuse his punishments.

"Fuckboy and Monster dick, get over here and take a leg each." Ty orders, and as they each move to my sides, he continues, "Lift and hold her legs up, and open her wide for me."

"Fuck Daddy. I'm going to come before you even get started." I admit, in all honesty, and Ty grins.

"You don't come until I say you can."

I pout but am quickly distracted as Shaun and Garrett lift each of my legs and spread me wide open.

"Get over here, Fetish Boy." Ty snaps, and a moment later, the excited hazel eyes of my playful Hastinator come into view.

"My name is Barbarian," Simon mutters, and Ty chuckles.

"Nope. You're Fetish Boy. You can watch from here." Ty instructs, and Simon doesn't argue, his eyes roaming over my pink, parted flesh.

"You're fucking perfect, Cherry."

"Dude. It's Kitten." Shaun reminds Simon, who just shakes his head.

"Nope. She will always be Cherry to me."

I grin. I'm going to somehow learn how to bake cherry pies and then make a heap every week so me and Simon can get all messy and fuck in them.

Once Ty stops throwing orders around, he falls to his knees before shooting me a devilish grin. It's all sorts of sinful, igniting flames under my skin before he runs his tongue up between my parted folds. I gasp, the heat of his tongue a welcome sensation, and my body jerks against the hold Marcus, Garrett and Shaun have on me. I watch Ty as he settles in between my legs, his unusually brown eyes darting up to my face, taking in my reactions. His tongue circles my clit, and then brushes over it in a gentle torture that has me moaning for more.

Movement behind Ty gains my attention, and I see Simon's hand wrapped around his pretty cock, sliding up and down as he watches Ty eat me.

"Bring that dick over here, Barbarian." I rasp, and Simon's eyes dart up to meet mine. He looks a little confused, so I gesture my head towards my outstretched right foot and wiggle it in Shaun's hold, tempting Simon to come closer.

Licking his lips, Simon doesn't keep me waiting, rushing forward to pull my red heel free before Ty sinks three gloriously thick fingers into my heat while sucking on my clit. I moan and wiggle my toes until they meet the hot silken flesh of Simon's hard cock.

"Yes." I pant, both to Ty and Simon, and Ty picks up his pace, his fingers buried deep, working me from the inside while his lips and tongue play me like the strings of a guitar on the outside.

Simon presses his hard length against the bottom of my foot, and I curl my toes, trying to grip him.

"Wrap your hands around your cock and my foot," I pant to Simon, watching as he follows my order. "Now fuck it until you paint my toes with your cream."

Simon moans at my filthy mouth and does exactly what I ask of him, his eyes flitting between my foot and my restrained body. It's a different sensation to feel the skin of his cock piston against the sole of my foot as it works with his hands.

"I never thought I'd be into feet, but right now, my dick wishes it was doing that." Marcus rasps against my ear, and warmth fills my chest at the satisfaction of knowing he likes watching it.

"You think this is good?" Simon pants. "You should feel your foot sliding into her heat."

Moans fill the room as the guys take in Sy's words, probably conjuring their own visual of fucking me with their feet right now. Simon's words increase my wanton desire tenfold. I start to struggle against the restraint of Marcus' hold of my arms and Shaun and Garrett's hold of my legs. Kitty is starved, and my hips try to thrust harder against Ty's face, ready to swallow him whole.

"That's it, Baby Girl. Fuck your Daddy good." Garrett's deep baritone has the intended effect, causing my hips to surge harder against Ty's face. Meanwhile, Ty growls at Garrett calling him Daddy, and I'd laugh if I wasn't completely consumed with the need to reach my high.

"Your come face is on, Kitten. Are you about to give Daddy your juice?" Shaun taunts Tyler this time, and all I can do is nod as I feel the pleasured pain crinkle my face as my mouth drops open, and I lose myself to the sensations.

"I'm gonna blow, Cherry!" Simon yells, and my eyes fly open in time to see white rivers of cum shoot from his dick and ooze between my toes.

I explode. The scream that tears from me is animalistic, and my O is so intense that I feel like I might pass out. But then I realise Tyler isn't stopping, his eyes boring into mine, determination swimming in them as he keeps going.

"She's done, man." Marcus hisses, and Tyler pries his mouth from my clit, but his fingers continue to work me from the inside as I moan and writhe.

"One more Kitten. That's all I'm asking for, is one more. Trust that I will stop once I've milked that from you." Then his lips clamp onto my clit again.

I cry out as intense pleasure builds and builds, and I feel like I'm going to lose all control of my body.

"One more Kitten." Shaun nips at my ear while Marcus moves behind me.

I'm not sure what he's doing. I'm too focused on the deep blue gaze staring up at me from between my legs, but then I feel a hand on my nipple, and I look down, knowing those fingers belong to Marcus.

This time, when my climax hits, I do lose control of any restraint I had, and just like at the Feast on the night I was tortured through pleasure, my greedy little Kitty starts to spray. With Ty directly in the line of fire, his red leather mask turns glossy, and he moves back a little with his mouth wide, catching my flow.

I can't even hear my screams. My hearing is lost, and my vision blackens around the edges before my body eventually falls slack. I can tell I'm being moved. Three or four sets of hands are on my flesh, shifting me and laying me on the bed.

A strange kind of peace sweeps over me. A level of calm I've never felt taking over. It's a place of utter contentment that I've never found before until now.

"Shit. Is she ok?" I think it's Simon's voice speaking, but I can't be sure as my muffled hearing slowly returns.

"Kitten?" That's Ty. No mistaking his rich manly gruff.

Slowly, my lips spread wide. It's a lazy smile, but it's there.

"More," I whisper.

"More?" Marcus asks.

My eyes begin to focus, and I see five sets of concerned eyes peering down at me.

"More," I repeat, louder this time. "Keep going. Don't stop."

"Kitten, you nearly passed out." Shaun points out, but I continue to grin.

"More. Fuck me more. Every way possible. Consume me completely." I sigh. "If I pass out, don't stop. Just keep going. I want more of the five of you while we are all together."

Ty chuckles. "Baby, I don't think you know what you're asking."

I try to nod. I think I do, but I can't be entirely sure. "I know exactly what I'm asking."

Frowning, Ty stands taller, crossing his arms over his chest. "Really? *Every way* possible?"

I nod, feeling the action this time.

"Even your hard limits?" Ty asks incredulously.

"Yes." I pant, slowly dragging my hands from where they lay lazily on the mattress, and I cup my tits. "I have no hard limits with the five of you."

A round of curses sound and a couple of the guys disappear from view as they step away, seeming to not be able to handle my admission. I keep grinning, though. I'm not lying to them. I want it all from them. I want it all *with* them.

Still not believing me, Ty starts reeling off my hard limits. "Right, so are you ready to lose your arse virginity? You ready to drink our piss? What about double penetration plus arse, Kitten? What about pain, having your air cut off until you black out, being tied up and fucked like a spit roast? What about hardcore, rough, and humiliation?" Ty's voice is deep and commanding, and if he's not careful, the guys will recognise his teacher's voice. "I'm not saying we want to do those things, Kitten, but you need to be careful about what you ask for."

My limbs seem to be working a little better now, which is just disappointing. I liked feeling legless there for a moment. I liked being at their mercy.

Slowly, I prop myself up on my elbows and look around the room at my five guys. My chest fills with so much warmth when I take them in that I know without a doubt I absolutely love each one of them.

"I nearly passed out just now, Skipper. And I want to do it again. Pain is fine. I like pain. Monster makes me bleed good, don't you, Big

Guy?" I smile at him, and he smirks, shooting me a wink. "I've had double penetration with Cass and Caveman," I grin at them both, and they return it. "The spit roast thing isn't new to me, and I'm ready to lose my arse virginity. I've had a few samples. I'm hungry for more. As for piss…" I shrug. "I'm happy to give you mine, and I'm not ruling out having any of yours." I shake my head. "I can't explain it. I just know I want everything. And I know if I change my mind or want something to stop, that it will with you guys. You will never hurt me."

"Be more specific, Kitten. What do you want *right now*?" Ty's deep rumble re-ignites my insides.

"I want you all to claim me. Own me. Worship me. Use me until your dicks go limp and won't harden. And don't stop if I pass out. I wanna wake up to being railed."

Chapter Twenty-Four

Simon

Rhys cries out with another orgasm as she mashes her sweet pussy over Garrett's face, smothering him as Shaun works a larger butt plug into her arse. After the red masked giant pulled us aside for a game plan when Cherry announced what she wanted, it was decided we would keep fucking Cherry, keep ripping orgasms from her while we prime her arse to take a cock. And, of course, we were all on board for it. It sounded like a solid fucking plan to me.

I can't tell you how long we've been at it. We've all had a chance to fill her tight pussy with our cum. She's also drank each of our seed down, and we are on another round of eating her again. Garrett must be getting more than he bargained for, though, because with her positioned above him like that, she must be leaking what we left behind down his throat. He doesn't seem to care, though. I don't know how he can breathe right now, but he doesn't let up, gripping her hips tighter, not letting her rise up off his face.

Fuck, my dick is harder than it's ever been.

"She's nearly ready." Skipper announces, and Cherry moans.

"I am ready. Fill me up, every way possible."

My dick jerks at her husky voice. Her pupils are practically blown. She is so high right now on what's being done to her. I can see how easily she falls into her addiction, but for the first time, she is one hundred percent safe and being treated right.

I have no idea how we are going to work this next part logistically. There are five of us and only one of her. We all seem to be letting

Tyler take the lead, given his experience, so I have to hope he knows what he's doing.

I'm down for whatever. I'll fuck her foot again if that's what she wants. I fucking loved the feel of her toes and the soft sole of her foot rubbing against my cock. The added bonus was watching my cum ooze between her toes. I have no idea why I like feet so fucking much, but I can't seem to make myself care that it might be wrong. Cherry loves what we share, and that's all that matters.

My eyes are drawn to this Tyler dude. Like a lot. Not in a creepy way, but I get the feeling I know him. I've been listening to his voice, and at times it seems familiar, but other times it doesn't. I've studied him from all angles tonight. I can't see much of his hair, but the little I can see at his nape shows me it's light and short, which narrows it down to like, a million possibilities. He has a blondish beard, and its short length either means he likes to keep it short or he has only recently been growing it. Again, a factor that doesn't really help me figure out who the fuck this guy is. He's a big guy. Tall, athletic and ripped, and maybe if I went to the gym or something, I might know him because it's obvious he works out, like a lot.

Garrett's gasp for air gains my attention as he finally releases Cherry's hips, and she lifts off his face.

"You ok there, Monster?" Shaun chuckles, and Garrett nods, a huge grin spreading his lips wide.

Fucking hell. I've never seen him smile like that. He looks so playful right now. I love that Rhys brings this side out in him. She does that with each of us. She makes us happy and accepts us for who we are.

"Stay on your back, Monster Cock. Just shift to the edge of the bed." Tyler instructs, and fuck, his voice sounds familiar. It's not the first time I've thought it tonight, but I can't for the life of me figure out who it belongs to, or even if it belongs to someone I know.

Garrett does as he's told after Cherry climbs off him, and Cherry swigs down some water that Shaun offers her while Marcus holds her up. Her legs are trembling, but she's not showing any signs of exhaustion yet. She's utterly insatiable.

Marcus helps her move since she can't move properly with the plug protruding from her arse. I can't even fucking explain how hot that is. I want to tell Cherry what I've been doing at home at night. I want to let her know that I know exactly what that full feeling is like, but I don't. I keep my mouth shut like the coward I am. Just like earlier today at the cabin when I turned into a moody bitch instead of just telling them how I feel.

I know Cherry accepts us and our desires, but there's just something about admitting to wanting to be taken that way that has me confused and staying silent. I'm not gay, but if I were being totally honest with myself, I'd have to admit I'm not straight either. I think I might be bi. But then I don't really know if that's true either. I have these feelings when I'm with Cherry and the guys. Feelings that I've never had around other guys before, just these ones, and it only happened once the idea of sharing Cherry was put in my mind. I just want to know what it's like to be… filled. Consumed as our girl keeps asking for. And when I took Bossi's dick in my mouth earlier today, the feeling grew stronger.

Don't get me wrong. I love fucking. I love using my dick and sinking into heat and claiming, but I also crave to be the recipient. Maybe that makes me sick. I don't think Cherry would be put off by it, yet I still can't voice what I want. I think it would actually turn her on. But my mates… if they knew my thoughts, would they think I'm disgusting?

"You sure about this Kitten?" Tyler asks again, and she nods eagerly, grinning as she walks awkwardly with the plug sticking out as her fingers find her clit.

"I'm so fucking horny, Skipper. I'm desperate to be completely filled."

Fuuuck. My cock jerks again with the same need as Cherry.

Ty chuckles. "Ok. You asked for it." He takes her hands and leads her to Garrett. "Since he really does have a monster cock, there's no way I'm letting him take your virginity, so you're going to climb on top and sink your sweet pussy down on him and sit there while he stretches you for a bit."

Cherry moans. "Yes, Daddy."

Tyler helps her manoeuvre over Garrett, and with the plug still in, Garrett grips his dick as Cherry slowly impales herself. Gritting his teeth, Garrett's other hand moves to Cherry's hip, his fingers digging into her creamy flesh, helping her until he's fully seated. Her back arches, her head falling back as her dark silken hair flows down past the two perfect globes of her arse.

That's it, I can't take anymore. I give in and wrap my hand around Conan, giving him a good long squeeze.

"Ok, who's going to take her virginity?" Ty asks, and the rest of us look at each other. "One of you three." Ty points, and Shaun shrugs.

"I think it should be Caveman."

"Me? Why?" Marcus looks confused, but excited at the same time, his hand pumping his dick a little faster.

"Well, man. Me and Barberian owe you this." Shaun explains. "For being betraying cunts." He points to our girl. "That sacred moment belongs to you and Kitten."

I nod, knowing he's right. This *does* belong to Marcus. He loves her fiercely, and we hurt him in the most unbearable way. Sometimes I wonder why he forgave us, but mostly I'm just thankful he did. He's one of my best mates. He didn't deserve what me and Bossi did to him.

"It's yours, man," I say, gesturing my head to our girl, and Marcus slowly nods, his eyes lighting up with warmth and excitement.

"It's yours Caveman. Come and take it." Cherry purrs, and Marcus moves quickly, leaning down to kiss her. The action causes her to gyrate her hips, and Garrett groans as his monster dick takes the pleasure.

When Marcus breaks the kiss, Tyler slowly eases the plug free before pressing his big hand against Cherry's shoulder, pushing her forward to lean her over Garrett's chest. Her lips find Garrett's, and

I shift around to see Ty spreading her cheeks wider, the channel of her arse open and ready.

"Lube." Tyler demands, and Shaun jumps into action, pouring lube over Marcus' straining dick before pouring more over the crack of Cherry's arse, pushing some inside her. She moans at the feel of his fingers moving inside her now open rose, and then he grins, pulling back to clap Marcus on the shoulder.

"Have fun."

Marcus chuckles, and Tyler cracks a rare grin. I study him for a moment, something about Ty's eyes seeming familiar. I can't put my finger on it, though, and when he speaks, I decide to worry about that later.

"Ok, first, you're going to slide in slowly. An inch at a time. Then when you're in, you can fuck her slowly, so her body adjusts. After that, I'll get you to make room so we can get Goldie Locks in on some action too."

I ignore the way he calls me Goldie Locks because my dick is desperate to sink into something right the fuck now. Moving closer, my legs press against one of Garrett's as I watch Marcus line up his dick and slowly starts to ease inside Cherry's arse.

Her kiss with Garrett breaks, a needy moan escaping, and I notice her arse pressing back, seeking more.

"Oh God, yes." She pants, her hips moving slightly, unable to hold back her need to chase the pleasure.

"Fuck Kitten. It's so tight. Are you ok?" Marcus asks with a pained expression, and Rhys nods.

"She's ok, Caveman." Ty stirs. "The plug prepared her."

"Yes. I'm prepped and ready. Give me more, Caveman." She pleads, and he's helpless to deny her. The moment he sinks all the way in, she comes hard, and while she's coming, Ty tells Marcus to start thrusting.

Her orgasm lasts ages, and Garrett starts moving too, unable to hold back.

"Fuck. I can feel you, Caveman." He grits between his teeth, and Marcus grunts.

"Yeah. I feel your mammoth, too."

"This is a beautiful sight." Shaun's grin is from ear to ear, and our eyes lock over our friends' writhing bodies. Even though we are still wearing masks, I can see the excitement in my mates' eyes.

"How are you going, Kitten?" Tyler asks, moving to brush dark strands of our girl's hair from her face. She has fallen quiet now. Her face turned to rest on Garrett's shoulder as her body jolts with pleasure with each thrust from Gaz and Grady.

"I'm in heaven." She pants and a slight grin tips up her lips.

"Do you want more, or are you content with two cocks, baby?" Tyler asks, still stroking her hair.

"More." She pants. "All of you."

Tyler chuckles as Marcus grunts.

"I can't hold it." He pants. "She's too tight."

Marcus thrusts harder, his head tipping back, and a moment later, a guttural moan rips from his throat. Garrett picks up the pace then, too, his own roar loud as his release hits.

Marcus collapses on top of Rhys, both of them crushing Garrett to the bed. Lucky he's a big guy and can handle their weight. I can't help but grin. That must have felt fucking amazing. For Cherry and for Gaz and Marcus.

"Your turn blondie." Tyler chuckles at my expression, and I nod eagerly, ready to dive in. Marcus slowly eases out, staggering a little on his shaky legs, and then Ty helps our girl to climb off Garrett.

She turns in his arms, kissing Tyler like she's not in the least bit tired, and Shaun moves up behind them, pressing his chest against Cherry's back.

"Get over here, Barberian," Shaun calls, and I shake myself out of my ogling and move up to them. Shaun grabs my arm and pushes me between him and Cherry, my chest now replacing his at our girl's back. I run my hands over the soft creamy skin on her hips, and my lips nibble a path from her shoulder to her neck, biting down on her ear with just the right pressure to grab her attention.

"Sy?" She pants, forgetting to use my party name as she breaks her lip lock with Tyler.

"Yeah, Cherry. It's me."

"Oh, that feels so good." She cranes her neck to the side, giving me more access, and I glide my tongue up the curve of her neck, sending goosebumps across her skin.

"Fuck me, Sy." She pants again. "Fill me." Her arse presses back, giving my cock just enough room to settle into the ridge of her arse.

A thrill of excitement rushed through my veins as Shaun presses his dick against my arse, doing the same thing I'm doing to Cherry. I bite my lip painfully to stop myself from repeating what Cherry did and press my arse back with need. I keep still, kissing Cherry's searing skin, my hands slipping to Cherry's front, desperate to roll her nipple between my fingers.

"She feels amazing, doesn't she?" Shaun's voice is a low husk in my ear, his lips pressing close, and I struggle not to lean into him.

Would he freak out if I wanted his lips on me? If I wanted him to wrap his hand around my cock? Would he be happy to return the favour and let me slide my dick between his lips?

A desperate moan escapes me, and I still, almost certain I'm about to scare Shaun off, but then his hands are over mine, travelling the path between Cherry and Tyler to pinch her nipples.

Cherry arches her back, pushing her tits out, the movement pressing her arse back.

"More." She pants, and Tyler, who I kind of forgot was standing in front of our girl, steers us toward the bed.

"On the bed, blondie," Tyler orders, and Shaun leaves my back, his presence instantly missed.

I sit on the bed, my legs quivering a little in excitement as Tyler steers Cherry, and before I know it, she's wagging her arse in my face, looking over her shoulder with a fucking cheeky grin.

"Look at my arse, Sy. It's still hungry."

I can't help but look at her arse since it's right there. She parts her cheeks, showing me her deep channel and pre-cum leaks from my dick as intense need slams into me. I want to fill her up. I want to feel her squeeze me, and I especially want to experience how it feels to sink into *that* forbidden passage.

"Come here then, Cherry. Let me feed you." I grin, and she beams.

Shaun hovers over us, pouring more lube, drizzling it over my cock and her arse before I grip her hips, guiding her as she lowers herself down onto my dick. The lube is doing its thing, and she eases over my cock in a slippery but fucking amazingly tight squeeze.

We both moan and pant until I'm all the way in, and if I'm not careful, I'm going to show how fucking little experience I have and come before we even get started.

Fuck, that would be embarrassing.

I lay back more as Cherry leans backwards, and Marcus shoves a heap of pillows behind me, so I'm propped up, giving me support.

"You ready for dick number two, Kitten?" Shaun asks, and she nods eagerly.

"Yes Cass. Get in here."

Bossi's face is a mix of arousal, excitement, and determination as he climbs on the bed with us, and I feel his hands slip between my knees and push my legs wider. I didn't know it was possible, but my dick gets fucking harder, and as if she can feel it, Cherry grins over her shoulder at me and bites her lip.

Shaun settles between both mine and Cherry's legs, and his grin is mischievous as he looks at Cherry and then me over her shoulder. That's when I feel his hand cupping my nuts.

I moan, my eyes closing briefly as Cherry gyrates a little, and then Shaun runs his fingers over my perineum before pressing them to the pucker of my arse.

My brows hitch, and my eyes widen as he leans down close to me and Cherry.

"Feel that, Hastings?" When I nod, he continues, "I'm gonna fuck that one day soon."

I can't stop my moan this time or the way my arse pushes against his fingers.

"Ohmygodyes." Rhys pants as she starts moving over my cock.

My mate gives me a wicked grin full of promises. I want to look around the room to see how Marcus and Gaz are responding, but I can't take my eyes off my mate as he removes his fingers, grips his cock, and sinks into Cherry's greedy little cunt.

I feel his invasion, my dick lurching, nearly spilling before we have even begun, but Tyler's dick bobbing near my face distracts me, and I watch Rhys grip his cock and guide it to her mouth.

We all start fucking her then. I try to keep pace with Bossi, but it's hard with bodies pushing me into the mattress. The vice-like grip on Conan is extreme. It's also fucking addictive, and I know I'm going to want to do this again. It must feel fucking epic for our girl. Filled to the max, just the way she's been begging for.

Not only is the feeling epic, but the visual is too. That Tyler dude has a decent-sized cock. Like, it looks like his dick goes to the gym too. It's big. Not as monstrous as Garrett's beast, but fucking close. Garrett and Marcus have joined us on the bed, on the opposite side of Cherry, to where Tyler is kneeling as he fists our girl's hair and fucks her mouth. I peer over Cherry's shoulder to see Gaz palming Cherry's tit, while Marcus slips his hand between Rhys and Bossi and starts circling her clit.

A gurgled moan escapes her throat as she lets herself go to the sensations, and Tyler keeps his pace. I'm gonna blow, I can feel it in my balls, and as the pleasure gets so intense that I can no longer hold back, I start pushing as much as I can manage under everyone's weight, gritting my teeth and grunting as my dick is squeezed and rubbed from inside Cherry's tight back passage.

The moment is fucking perfect. I may not be the one being filled, but I'm consumed right now, crowded in, feeling the press of four other guys against me, with Cherry writhing in the middle.

The moment her walls start pulsing with her orgasm, I detonate, yelling loud as I shoot hot cum into her arse. I can't hear much, but my eyes don't miss the expression on Bossi's face as his release hits. Marcus doesn't let up on Cherry's clit, though, and another orgasm slams into her, causing her to release Tyler's dick and cry out.

"Keep going," Tyler commands, and Marcus looks up at Tyler to see that he's talking to him. "You too." He looks at me and then Shaun, and we start thrusting again, even though my dick is sensitive as shit.

As we thrust over and over, Marcus keeps up his pace and Garrett and Tyler work on our girl's nipples until a third orgasm hits her hard. She releases the most animalistic guttural scream of pleasure I've ever heard, and then she falls limp in our arms, her eyes falling shut as she gets her wish and finally blacks out.

Chapter Twenty-Five

Rhys

I've never been so sated in my life. My guys took me to new heights last night. Heights I didn't know were possible, and I know I'll only *ever* reach with these five guys of mine. Some might say I'm selfish, demanding, and an immature brat for wanting five guys. For not wanting to share them with anyone else. They would probably be right, but it doesn't matter what they think. All that matters is what we think. And as selfish as some people might find me, I'm not as self-centred as the Rhys George that was roaming the earth a few weeks ago.

She was a taker. It could have been from the so-called addiction, or it could have been because it was the only way she could protect herself, but she wouldn't have cared about her bed partners. Love them and leave them was her motto.

Now, though, I know I'd do anything these guys ask of me. If they ask me to never go to a sex club again, I will smile and say ok. Not that last night's sex party should be classed as us attending since we stayed in the bedroom all night until the guys gave me my wish and fucked me until I passed out. Then I woke in Garrett's arms as I was being carried through the trees that separate the Airbnb we are staying in, and the house Moxie's party was in.

I'd panicked at the time, thinking I didn't get to say goodbye to Ty, but he was following behind, still wearing his mask, and he helped the guys shower me, dry me, dress me in my Flyleaf t-shirt, and put me into bed.

We'd all had a deliciously rough gang bang, yet afterwards, they were so attentive. Their hands were gentle, with so much care with each touch. Their lips were soft, pressing love to my skin with each peck. And their words were filled with concern, compassion, and raw love.

It broke me. I started crying silently, and I had no idea why. Ty explained it's like a comedown, and he's right. It really was. My body was coming down from its high, and with it, my emotions crashed.

Even though the others had taken their masks off once back in the house, Ty kept his on, lying next to me on the mattresses lining the living room floor and telling me how much he's missed me and how he longs for the time that it will be ok for us to be together. Then he left.

I cried some more, each of the guys laying with me and cuddling me, taking turns to give me attention while the others showered and ate before we all finally settled into bed.

I'm sore this morning. Like everywhere. My muscles hurt from head to toe. Kitty is feeling raw, and my arse feels deliciously tender. A grin tugs at my lips as I remember the feeling of being consumed by my guys. There is honestly nothing like it. I've spent so much time searching for the next sex high, putting myself in vulnerable situations in the hopes of finding what I was looking for.

I've finally found it. I didn't know it was what I needed until these guys decided to show me. They are my ultimate in every way. My end game. And I finally realise that it has nothing to do with sex at all. It's about the ultimate trust and acceptance. It's about love.

With a full heart, I glance at Simon and Cass, who are still sleeping on either side of me, and I successfully slither myself out from between them without disturbing anyone. Garrett is sound asleep on the other side of Shaun, and Marcus is sleeping next to Simon. They all look like Sex Gods with their bare chests and tousled hair. Sex Gods sent to me to make me whole.

Jesus, my head is all girly and mushy right now.

I shake my head. I need a moment to myself.

I tiptoe across the room, heading to the toilet, before I slip into a steaming hot shower as my mind flashes with images of last night. The only thing that would have made it more perfect would have been if we were mask-free. I long for the guys to know exactly who Ty is. I know it will shock them and probably be a tender subject in the beginning, but when they come around and accept that what Ty and I have is serious, then I just know we can all be happy together. I hate keeping this secret from them. I hate lying to them about Ty's identity. It feels so wrong to keep this from them. To keep anything from them. I've never felt like that with anyone before. I've never felt the strong need to reveal all of my secrets.

"You ok, Rhee?"

My eyes dart up to see Marcus hovering on the other side of the glass. I flick the shower off, and as I open the door, he grins, holding a towel out to me.

"I'm ok." I smile. "You?"

He shrugs. "I'm tired but feeling ok. Especially if you are."

Using the towel to wring out my hair, I step out of the shower and into the chill of the bathroom.

"I'm tired too. But in a good way."

"Here, let me dry you." My brows shoot up at Marcus' words, and I let him take the towel from me, standing still as he glides it over my skin to soak up the water. I peer up at him through my lashes as he focuses on his task, and an aching pang hits me in the centre of my chest as guilt I have tried to bottle up rears its head.

"I'm sorry," I whisper, gaining his attention, and his dark eyes meet mine.

"What for?"

"What I did to you. How I treated you." Heat pricks the back of my eyes, "I'll never ever forgive myself for being such a heartless bitch. You deserve so much more than me." My voice quivers with the emotions I'm feeling, and I notice Marcus' eyes glass over, mimicking mine.

"You don't have to apologise, Rhee. I understand now."

I shake my head. "Just because you understand doesn't mean what I did is ok. Every minute of every day for the rest of my life, I will ache with shame for how I treated you. I'm not asking for your forgiveness. I just want you to know how *sorry* I am. I'm not saying this to try and make myself feel better for the hurt I caused. I'm saying it because you deserve better and because I love you. I think I always did. I just didn't understand it, and it scared me."

Wrapping the towel around me and tucking it in the front, Marcus reaches up and cups my jaw, lifting my chin so I have no choice but to look at him. "I love you too, Rhee. Nothing will change that."

I cringe. "Are you sure?"

He grins. "I am. You can't deter me, Rhee."

"Maybe when you find out who Tyler is, you won't think the same way."

His eyes narrow. "We know him, don't we? Sometimes I think his voice is familiar to me, but I can't quite figure out who it belongs to."

I grin, shaking my head. "I'm not saying anything, but when you *do* find out, try to remember that you love me." I plead with my eyes, and he shakes his head and chuckles.

"Ok, I'll try." A flash of uncertainty flicks across his expression before he tries to hide it. I don't say anything, though. I can't just spill the secret, at least not without talking to Ty first.

Marcus leans in then, taking my lips in his for a gentle kiss that is a language of its own, telling me how much he cares. The need to crawl under his skin washes over me, but not in a sexual way. I just want to be so close to him and never let go. I'm so terrified that he will walk away from me one day. So terrified that the others will as well. I can't control the future, though. Only hope that what we have is strong enough to last the distance.

When we finally emerge from the bathroom, Simon is cooking up a storm in the little kitchen, with Garrett helping, so I move to the living room and start tidying up, wanting to be useful. I need to get Simon to teach me how to cook. Maybe one day, I'll need to cook for my five men and have dinner on the table for them when they come home from work.

And where the fuck did that thought come from?

I've never thought much about domestic bliss before, yet here I am, conjuring up images of a large table with my guys sitting around it as I serve them dinner. I'd be the dessert, of course, which is a much more Rhys George way of thinking.

I turn back to take in my guys as I fold blankets. They are good mates. The best. They are each so different in many ways, and so similar in others. I love that even though we have this group thing, I have something special with each of them individually. I love that I can have tender moments with just one of them, and at other times with all of them. Ty is missing from the picture right now, but hopefully, one day, he will be here with us. I'm not sure how he will fit exactly, but I hope he does. I can't bear the thought of not being with him.

"Hey Kitten, what time is Ty picking you up?" Shaun asks as he sets the table.

"About five." I smile, but when I glance over at the other guys, they all look unhappy. "What?" I ask.

They remain quiet, turning their backs on me and focusing on what they are doing.

"Marcus?" I ask, gaining his attention. "What's going on?"

"Nothing, Rhee. All g." His voice is flat and nothing like the happy guy from the bathroom only minutes ago.

"Marc. Sy. Gaz. Communication is the only way this is going to work." I insist.

They remain silent.

Shaun sighs, looking at his mates. "If you aren't going to speak up, then I will." When the others don't respond, Shaun turns his steel-greys to me. "They are pissed about Tyler. They think they have the right to know who he is, and they're annoyed that you're ditching us to go hang with him on *our* weekend away."

I drag my eyes from Shaun to the others, who are trying really fucking hard to avoid eye contact with me. Shit, wasn't I just feeling like this was perfect? Did I get my wires crossed?

I take a moment to consider the situation. They are pissed that I'm ditching them, which is fair. I do feel bad about that, and I agreed to some one-on-one Tyler time, not even considering their feelings. Only mine. Shit, this is hard. I want to make them all happy, but how can I do that when things are the way they are with Ty?

I wish the guys would tell me their concerns instead of Shaun doing it for them. Why is he the only one that will speak up?

"Guys? Why won't you talk to me about this?"

"We are trying to avoid an argument." Garrett's deep voice rumbles as he mans up to answer, but he doesn't turn to face me, so all I see is his back. "We don't want to ruin the great night we had last night, Baby Girl." His tone sounds genuine, yet kind of hurt.

My heart twists in a knot. I hate that I'm hurting him. Them. But I nod slowly in understanding and try to compromise. "I'm sorry, guys. I know this is a shitty situation. How about I talk to Ty about it tonight? See if we can come to an agreement about you guys meeting him properly."

"You think he'd go for that?" Simon finally turns to me, and relief fills me that I'm no longer talking to his back.

I shrug. "I don't know, Sy. The four of you have been friends forever, but he doesn't have the same connection with you. It's risky for him. For all of us." I shrug again. "For what it's worth, I want him to come clean. I want the five of you to know each other. To build your own friendships with him. So I will speak with him tonight. I promise."

Simon and Garrett nod, seemingly happy with my response, as Garrett turns to look at me as well, but Marcus still avoids my gaze.

"Marcus Phillip Grady, stop avoiding me!"

His eyes dart up from the phone in his hands. "What?"

I place my hands on my hips, glaring at him. "Why didn't you tell me your concerns in the bathroom before?"

"I was trying to avoid your wrath." He shrugs with a smirk.

"Bullshit."

He chuckles. "Fine. We were having a moment, and I didn't want to ruin it."

My shoulders slump, and I shrug. "It *was* a pretty nice moment."

He grins. "Right?"

I sigh. "Guys, please don't avoid talking about your concerns with me. I'm trying to be all grown up and shit, and I know this will never work if we aren't open and honest." I look down at my feet for a moment as emotions swirl in my chest again. "And I really want this to work." I look back up at them. "I love you guys. I don't know what I'd do without you."

Simon drops the tongs in his hand and rounds the kitchen bench, keeping his eyes on mine the whole time as he stalks towards me with no hint of the clown in sight. I'm not sure what he's doing, but when he reaches me, he grips the back of my head and slams his lips into mine. I melt instantly, his lips a searing claim as they move over mine, doing the same thing that Marcus' did earlier and telling me how much he cares. When he pulls back, I gasp for air, a little taken aback by the serious expression on his face.

"I fucking love *you*, Rhys George."

I can feel the goofy grin spread across my face right before Simon dips me in his arms, bending me back to steal another kiss.

"The Hastinator's got moves." Shaun chuckles, and Marcus agrees.

"Who would have guessed?"

Simon breaks our kiss abruptly, my eyes widening at his still fierce gaze as he pulls me up to stand before he gives a single nod and walks back to the kitchen to resume cooking.

The guys chuckle while I'm left reeling and fucking horny because I like that side of Simon just as much as I like his playful side. When my eyes lock with Garrett's, he shoots me a wink and a smirk, and continues buttering the stack of toast in front of him.

I struggle to hold back my grin for the rest of the day. It's like it's permanently tattooed on my face, and fuck, it feels good.

Simon feeds me as we eat breakfast, and we go for a long walk along the water before lunch, where Simon teaches me how to make the best club sandwiches I've ever had. And yes, I get that a club sandwich isn't that hard, but a girl has to start somewhere!

After lunch, the guys reluctantly let me go next door to have a quick visit with Moxie, AKA Agatha. Things have been so up in the air since the night she let me, Shaun and Tyler into her house after the Feast. I haven't seen her, and last night wasn't the right place to chat about things.

Unfortunately, it's not until after I catch up with her that I kind of wish I didn't go to see her. After learning what she has to say, I think being none-the-wiser would have been better.

"So, are you living here now?" I sit down on the porch step of the small Hamptons-style cabin overlooking Redfield Lake and take a sip of the lemonade Agatha poured me.

"Yeah. I'm trying to lie low from certain people at Fox Pines. Only my closest bed partners know I'm here, so if anyone asks, you don't know where I am. Ok?"

I frown. "Why would anyone ask me where you are?"

She frowns back, studying me for a moment. "Wasn't it your parents that went to the cops with the videos?"

Wait? She knows about the videos Master Hill has been sending my parents?

I shake my head. "Those videos are of me. What's that got to do with you?"

She sighs. "You know Tradie and Sheriff? Well, Tradie is actually a cop at Fox Pines Police Department, so he's seen the videos and gave me a heads up. Yes, the videos are of you, but I'm with you in some of them, and so is Skipper and a heap of others. The cops only know your identity, but they are putting together a team to try and track down the secret sex club and find the list of all the members." She frowns and shakes her head. "So, I quit my job, and I'm renting this house under a different name. If things get too crazy, I'll probably head to another state. Shane, that's Tradie. He's keeping me in the loop. I'm pretty sure he's freaking out about videos of him and Sheriff coming out, too. No one knows they are gay. They are just two best mates, Shane and Ben, to most people."

"Fuck Agi. I had no idea. I should have, though, right? I should have considered that the cops would want to go after everyone."

"Haven't they spoken with you about it?" Agi asks, and I shake my head.

"Not about that. I've got some other shit going on that I've been helping them with, but it has nothing to do with Vixen's Lodge."

Her lips thin. "I'm sorry to be the one to tell you."

I shake my head. "No. I'm glad. My parents are obviously trying not to involve me as much as possible. There's a lot of shit happening right now." I sigh. "Why did you let us come here?" I glance around. "That's risky."

She nods. "I know, but Shaun was trying to find a way for you to have all your guys in one place while protecting Skipper's identity." She grins. "Oh, I'm loving the whole reverse harem thing you have going, by the way. Just a tad jelly."

We laugh.

"Thank you. That's a huge risk on your part, though. I owe you one." I smile, and she shakes her head.

"Nah. I'm happy to help love find its way, even if it isn't mine." Agatha smiles.

"So, Tradle and Sheriff… aren't they the ones that helped get Skipper and me out of the lodge that night when Master Hill…" I can't finish the sentence and say punished me by public humiliation. Even thinking it makes me want to hurl.

"Yep, that's them." She nods.

"And they are Shane and Ben? Best buddies who are secretly gay?"

Agatha laughs. "Yep. Now they come here to maintain their secret."

I smile, even though I don't feel like I should, because that's just sad that grown men have to hide their relationship and only come together at sex parties.

My mood plummets because, yet again, I have something new to worry about. The police aren't just looking for the person who sent those videos to my parents. They are looking for the sex club and the member list to make everyone pay... All because of me.

CHAPTER TWENTY-SIX

TYLER

P aranoia has me jumpy as shit as I drive around Redfield Lake with my girl by my side. I'm fucking happy to see her, but it will only take one nosey arsehole to spot us together and ruin everything.

I'm wearing a cap pulled low on my head, and I haven't shaved in a week, so the blondish growth on my jaw helps to hide my identity. Even though I didn't ask her to, Kitten is wearing a cap too, her long dark hair shielding the sides of her face, and the big sunglasses help to hide her eyes.

She's quieter than usual. Rhys George is normally a chatterbox, so her quietness is making me even more nervous.

I don't speak while we drive. It takes about twenty minutes to drive around the lake to my house. If we went by boat, it would have taken me five minutes to cruise across from the other side. That's what I did last night, using my small fishing boat to sneak up to the small jetty on the waterfront near Moxie's rental house. I had my red mask on the whole time, just in case. There and back.

As we turn off the main road, my heart rate picks up. I'm not sure if I'm excited or it's the same fucking nerves making me paranoid, but bringing Kitten here is kind of a big deal. My other place above the gym in Fox Pines was a rental. This place I own, and I've never had anyone here before besides my sister and her daughter.

In my peripheral, I see Rhys sit up taller in the seat as she looks through the windscreen as my house comes into view.

"Holy shit. This is your place?"

I chuckle at her amazed tone as I pull the car to a stop and look at my house, trying to see it through fresh eyes.

"Yep. This is it. It's made from shipping containers."

"No way!" She screeches before pushing the car door open and leaping from my car. "That was a shipping container?" She points up at the house, glancing back at me.

Closing my car door, I nod. "Yep. Multiple shipping containers."

"It doesn't even look like it." She says in disbelief, and I chuckle again.

The house is three levels. A basement, a ground floor and a second story. It's a crisp white elongated box shape with black window frames and edging around the roofline. The second story has a protruding box-like room sticking out to look over the water, encased in windows and black trim, and there's a large stone-paved patio that sits below it with stone steps rolling down to the sandy bank.

I smile. I do love this place. I'm not even mad that I have to hide away here. I'd been over teaching for a couple of years. I only stayed because I needed a purpose. Even though I enjoyed teaching, it didn't mean as much to me as Rhys does. Even though it was a hard decision to make, I'm glad I did.

We make our way to the large glass front entrance, and I unlock the door, holding it open for Rhys to enter. She's quiet again, but I can see her curious expression as she looks around at the modern interior, taking everything in.

"Ty," she breathes, "This is so beautiful." She swings around from gazing at the small living space, and I chuckle because this is a floor I rarely use. She hasn't seen anything yet.

"You should see upstairs, Kitten." I gesture to the industrial-style staircase.

Grinning, she moves quickly, obviously eager to see what's up there, and I follow slowly behind, staring at my space as she peers around. Up here, the view of the lake is serene. The open plan living area spans the long wall of windows with a floating fireplace, the feature in the lounge area, and the gloss black kitchen and dining area off to the side.

"No TV?" Rhys asks, and I grin, moving to the coffee table to pick up a remote. A moment later, a hidden cabinet in the roof slowly lowers down next to the fireplace with the wide screen TV hidden within.

"Get out of town." She screeches and throws her head back, laughing. "I didn't realise teachers' salaries paid so well."

"They don't." I grin. "This is family money."

She stops laughing, and her brows shoot up.

"Are you like… rich?"

I shake my head, chuckling. "Barely. When my mum passed, I got some money from her estate. Most of it went into this house. I invested the rest and let it earn a small income. I'm no millionaire, Kitten."

"Good. In my experience, rich people are corrupt arseholes."

I laugh again. She's not wrong, although I'm sure there are many that are good people.

We fall silent for a few minutes. I watch as she walks around my space, looking at pictures on the walls of my sister and me when we were little and some of my niece. Then she stops to stare at one of me when I was probably the age she is now.

"You look different here." She points to it. "Chicken legs." Her grin is wide as she turns her head to look at me, and I smile. Fuck, I love having her here. I don't want her to leave.

"Where's your bedroom?" She asks, wagging her brows, and I shake my head, trying to bite back my smirk.

"Surely you are too sore to be considering bedroom activities after last night?"

She shrugs. "Maybe I just want to lie down and snuggle up in your arms and pretend I never have to leave."

Her words match my thoughts only a moment ago, and I love that she wants that.

"I'd keep you if I could," I admit, and her smile falls.

"When I'm old enough for you to keep me, will you?"

"If you let me, Kitten. I'll keep you forever and never let you go."

She closes the distance between us, tugging her cap off as she approaches, so I do the same.

"I let you." She whispers, standing on her tiptoes as she clutches the front of my t-shirt. "Forever."

I finish closing the distance, pressing my lips to hers as I wrap my arms around her small frame, tugging her close. As with every other time Rhys George is near, my dick goes impossibly hard, wanting in on the action. I ignore it, though. Tonight isn't about sex. It's just about us spending time together before I take her back to her four other boyfriends and she goes back to her life.

As I kiss her, I bend and lift her in my arms, cradling her to my chest as I make my way through the living area and across the glass-lined passageway that joins the main house with my private retreat.

You can't see this part of the house from the front where you drive in, but you can glimpse it from the water, nestled behind the trees.

Striding across my bedroom, I ease Kitten down on my bed and hover over her as she steals more kisses from me, each brush of her lips branding her name into my soul.

When I break the kiss, her chocolate eyes are lust drunk, and with her natural face free of any makeup, she looks absolutely stunning. Leaning up on one hand, I stare at her, knowing I'll never let her go. I'll fight for us to be together. Fuck the age gap.

"You're the most stunning woman to walk this earth."

Immediately she gets uncomfortable from the compliment, but I cup the side of her face and lock my gaze with hers.

"It's the gods' honest truth, baby. I will never lie to you."

Pink tinges her cheeks then, and I feel the heat of the blush against the palm of my hand.

"In the spirit of being honest, we need to talk about telling the guys who you are."

My brows dip in a frown, and I pull back, standing from my bed. "Not until you're eighteen, Kitten."

She sighs, sitting up before she is momentarily distracted by her surroundings.

"This is your bedroom?"

I look around at the greys and blacks that make my bedroom feel warm. The timber floor is a light colour, and the floating desk on the far wall has LED lights illuminating the underside of the cabinetry. There's a large grey armchair in the corner that looks out over what you can see of the water through the trees, and next to it is a small round glass table that has a book resting on top about finding the warrior within.

"Yeah. This is it." I nod.

"Wow, the girls must really love coming for sleepovers."

"If by girls, you are referring to my sister and niece, then yes, they enjoy their visits on the lower level in the guest rooms."

She giggles. "I mean your hookups, Ty."

"Would it surprise you to know that you are the first girl I have brought here?"

Her dark brows shoot up as her mouth drops open.

I chuckle. "It's the truth, Kitten. The only person that has slept or otherwise in this bed is me. Now you are the first person other than me to press your arse against it."

She sits up. "Really?"

I nod. "Yes, really."

"But… why?"

I step forward, tucking my finger under her chin to make her look into my eyes so she can see the truth when I speak. "Because baby. I had to wait for you to come into my life."

Her eyes soften, and her head tilts to the side. "You're mine." She whispers, so I nod.

"Yes, I am. And you're mine."

Nodding, she stands from the bed, her expression serious. "That's why we need to be honest with the others. They aren't going anywhere, Ty. They care about me as much as I care about them, and this secret between us is toxic. They won't tell anyone. They love me too much to do that."

I wish I could give her what she wants, but it's too risky, and I know deep down she knows that. She's obviously getting pressure from the others. I don't want it to affect things, though, but it's still too risky right now. Maybe in a few months when things die down. After all, the cops are looking into Vixen's Lodge, and I might have to flee yet. It's better for everyone if they don't know my identity.

"Not yet, Kitten. We need to wait a little longer."

She sighs, nodding. She knows I'm right. It doesn't make things easier for her, though, since she's stuck in the middle.

"Come on. Let's make some dinner, and then we can have a bath in my tub and watch the sunset."

Rhys beams, the suggestion lighting up her eyes. "You do know I can't cook, right?"

I smile. "Well, let me teach you a basic. Tacos."

It turns out Rhys can cook. She simply doesn't like doing it. That is, until I pull her in front of me and lean over her as we prepare the salads and meat together. There's a mirror at the other end of the room, so I watch our reflections as we work as one, and I notice how she grins slightly throughout the process, thinking I can't see her. I fucking love putting that little smirk on her face. It's different from the big confident smile she offers a room when she walks in. It's slight. Delicate almost. She's not demanding the room's attention right now. She's not even demanding mine. She already has it, so there's no brazen attitude. Rhys is in a comfortable, quiet place right now, and I have to admit, I like this softer side to her.

So much of our time together has been about sex. It's what forced us together, but it isn't what makes me stick around. There's a side of Rhys George that doesn't have the opportunity to come out often, but when it does, it almost floors me. Under all that sass is a heart longing to be loved and accepted without conditions. Behind the addiction that normally controls her is a girl that longs to be content in her life and be free of the selfishness that comes from the consuming cravings. Now, though, she is accepting the unconditional love I am offering. She is accepting what her other guys are offering, and finally, she has moments of sheer contentment that reminds me our relationship is good for her. She needs me, us, just as much as we need her.

After we eat and clean up, I lead Kitten back into my bedroom, where I slide the heavy glass door open wide, creating an open space between my bedroom and my bathroom.

"This house really is the coolest, Ty." There's awe in her tone, and when I glance over my shoulder, I see her dark eyes are wide as she studies my bedroom.

"It's ok. It's a little big for one person. That's why I haven't spent much time here over the last few years. It just feels too empty."

The chill of the glossy charcoal tiles is refreshing on the soles of my feet as I pad across the room to the bath. It looks more like a miniature pool with its square box shape and the three steps that lead up to the small landing along the side of the bath. I flick the water on and pull the lever on the wall that pulls the plug in place before turning back to Kitten again.

She's leaning against the wall at the mouth of the bathroom, her chocolate eyes following my every move as if she's studying me.

"Like what you see?" I bite back my grin and cross my arms over my chest.

"Like is the wrong word." She deadpans.

"Oh, really? I thought you were checking me out just now."

A grin tugs at her lips. "Oh, I was." She pushes off the wall and slowly approaches me.

"So, what's the right word, then, Kitten?" I raise a brow.

She takes her time perusing me as she draws near. "The right word is love. I *love* what I see, Ty." Her big eyes peer up at me through the fan of her dark lashes.

"You *love* what you see? Or you *love* me?" My grin breaks through this time, and it ignites her own.

"Both." She whispers before biting her lower lip.

Fuck, there's just something so hot about the way she does that. The way her teeth clamp down on the soft skin as her eyes darken even more. I can see she wants to reach out and touch me, but she's working hard to keep her hands in place.

"Good," I growl, reaching out to fist the silky hair at the back of her head. "Because I fucking love you, Rhys George. And I'm fucking salivating at what I see when I look at you."

Her lips part as a breathy moan escapes her. "Jesus, Daddy. You know just the right words to make a girl weak at the knees."

I grin before I close the distance, taking her lips in mine for a searing kiss. I love the taste and feel of her kisses. I fucking love the way her tongue brushes against mine like it's starved for me. And I fucking love how her tits strain against my chest, her nipples pebbling hard.

Breaking the kiss, I stare into her lust-drunk eyes for a moment before releasing her and moving back to the bath to add some bubbles to the deep cavity that is only a quarter full. While I do that, Rhys slips out of her clothes, returning to me as naked as the day she was born, and starts to peel my clothes off me.

I let her take control, revelling in the way her fingers brush against my skin, branding me with her touch. She fucking owns me. She probably doesn't know it, but she does. I'm helpless to deny her. Helpless to walk away from her. I know she's the one with addiction problems, but what she doesn't realise is I am completely and utterly addicted to her. Having her in my house is making my obsession with her worse. I fucking love having her here in my space. Love her lingering scent in the air and the visual of her presence in my room. Even her clothes that she left in a pile on the floor are a sight I crave to see more of.

I'm a neat person, but fuck, I'd love her mess all around my house. It would probably piss me off sometimes. I'd get snappy and demand she pick it up, then she'd be a brat and refuse. Then I'd have to spank her. And fuck, my dick hardens at that thought, which just so happens to be the moment she slides my jocks down.

Her dark eyes take in the sight, and she licks her lips. "Let me help you with that."

The little minx doesn't give me time to respond, wrapping her hand around my hard cock and giving it a pump. I growl in satisfaction, watching how her eyes stay locked onto my dick as she slowly sinks to her knees before me.

"Kitten, you don't have to…"

She grins up at me with mischief in her eyes. "I know I don't *have* to, but I *want* to." Leaning forward, she drags her tongue up my shaft, giving my straining tip a flick as she draws back. "You always take care of me. I want to take care of you for once. Let me be the one to worship you."

My brows shoot up because I wasn't expecting that. Nor is it something I typically do. I prefer to be the carer in these situations. The one who dominates. The one who takes care of my girl's every need.

Parting her lips, she sucks the head of my cock into the heat of her mouth, and I give in, allowing her to do this if that's what she wants. I never usually come before my girl has. I try to wait it out, make sure she has shot to her heavenly place a time or two before allowing myself to take anything. It's hard for me to not feel selfish right now, but it's also hard for me to fucking think too hard about anything as she takes my dick all the way in.

"Fuck, Rhys. Your mouth Is heaven."

She moans around my cock, one hand pumping my length in rhythm with her mouth, while the other finds my balls as she cups them. Fuuuck, I wanna fuck her mouth so bad, but I want to give her the control here to take the lead.

She releases my dick with a pop before dragging her tongue down my shaft until it glides over my balls. She looks up at me, and fuck if I don't love the sight of her down there. Then she slowly sucks one of my nuts into that heavenly heat of her mouth, and my hands ball at my sides as I resist the urge to fist her hair.

My blood is pumping loud in my ears, my eyes caught in the sight of her as my chest rises and falls more rapidly. She releases my nut, only to do the same to my other one as her hand pumps my dick with a tight grip.

The telltale sign of a pending cum explosion starts to make itself known, and Kitten must somehow notice because she pops my nut from her mouth only to replace it with my cock. Then she sucks and fucking devours it, her free hand sliding between my legs to slip between my arse cheeks.

I'm about to tell her to stop because I never fucking go there with anyone, but my dick has a mind of its own, jerking with fucking desperation, and I find myself widening my stance to let her finger press against the pucker of my arse. She draws back, her eyes a blaze of arousal as she looks up at me.

"I'm gonna finger fuck you here one day soon, Daddy." She presses her finger firmer against my arse before taking my cock deep into her mouth again.

As she pumps and sucks and licks and pushes herself too far, making herself gag, she presses harder and harder against my back passage. It sends me fucking crazy, and my little brat knows it, and before I know it, I'm fisting her hair and slamming my dick past the resistance of her throat as I explode.

A guttural roar rips from me as I throw my head back, feeding her my cum. It's fucking intense and drawn out and fucking perfect.

"Fuck Kitten. You give the best head." I rasp as I ease my cock from her mouth, a shit-eating grin crossing her face as she wipes the drool from her chin.

"Why, thank you. It's a talent."

I chuckle at my little brat before I remember the bath is still filling. Luckily, it's a deep bath because it's nowhere near full yet.

I help my siren up off the floor, dragging her into my arms for another searing kiss. I want to keep her here forever. I fucking wish she was just that little bit older already. I'm already going against her parents by meeting up with her last night and having her here today. I should know better, me being the adult and all, but my rationality is fleeting when it comes to how I feel about Rhys.

When the water level is right, I flick off the water and take Kitten's hand, leading her up the steps to help her into the bath. She moans as she sinks down, and I climb in after her, thankful I went all out and paid for this oversized tub when I built this place.

We get settled, me sitting behind her as we face the window that overlooks the west and the pink-tinged sunset. She feels so fucking right in my arms. Perfect, like she was made for me. I've waited so long for her to come into my life. I can't imagine I could ever have this connection with anyone else. Rhys George is my end game. It's her or nothing.

Chapter Twenty-Seven

MARCUS

It's fucking boring here without Rhee. She left hours ago, sneaking off through the trees to meet Tyler while Shaun kept us hostage so we couldn't follow her. Bossi is on my shit list for his part in all of this, and if Garrett's brooding is anything to go by, then he is on the same page as me. Simon is quiet, which is disturbing in itself, and I know Bossi can feel the tension in the air as he tries to distract us.

I'm fucking pissed at both Bossi and Rhee. This secret of who Tyler is, is going to create big fucking issues. Hell, it already has. Yes, most of those issues will be with me, but I can't fucking help it. I'm obsessed with Rhys, and this whole not knowing the identity but kind of recognising the voice of Ty is making me crazy. Who the fuck is he?

The guys have been gaming for the last three hours, and I can't seem to concentrate, so I make us toasties for dinner and do the dishes before I do the one thing I promised myself I wouldn't do.

I pick up my phone, open SnapChat and find Rhys' location on SnapMaps.

She shares her location with just us these days, and she's been sending a few snaps of herself pulling funny faces inside Ty's house, so her location is current. She's across the other side of the lake, and I move to the window, looking out over the water in the general direction that Rhys is.

She's just over there, somewhere along the bank in a waterfront house. So fucking close. My eyes move down to the small jetty that sits between this house and the one we were at last night. There's a small tinnie tied up, just waiting to be used.

"Are you gonna play again, Grady?" Shaun asks, and I drag my gaze from the boat to my mates.

"Yeah-Nah. I think I'm gonna get some fresh air." It's not a total lie. I will get fresh air. I just leave out what else I'll be doing.

"Whatever, man." Shaun shrugs, not taking his eyes off the screen, and I take that moment to make my getaway.

I just want to see who this Tyler guy is. I get that he's older and what they have going is illegal, so they need to keep it quiet. But I have no intention of dobbing him in. I just need to know.

After slipping out the door, I rush down the front steps and head straight for the jetty. I don't know who's fucking boat it is, but it's similar to the one my dad used to take me fishing on, and hopefully the owner has left the key somewhere on board like my dad used to.

The sun is setting, painting the sky pink, reflecting off the calm of the lake. It's beautiful here. Tranquil. I hope I can afford to buy a house here one day. I'd spend my days fishing, swimming and fucking Rhee without a care in the world. I want that for her. For us. A place where we can be ourselves, that we can call our own and do as we please. I guess I may have to share it with my mates too, but I could think of worse things.

I run along the jetty, climbing on board the tinnie and use the flashlight on my phone to see better in the fading daylight. Sliding my hand under the lip of the bow, I nearly fucking cheer when I find the magnetic box that contains a key. I pull it free and, to my relief, it's not even a key box that requires a code to open.

I set to work, untying the tinnie from its mooring and then start the motor up. The tranquillity in the air vanishes as the little motors revs cut through the silence, and I know without a doubt that the guys will be able to hear it.

Deciding not to second guess my irrational behaviour, I steer the little boat, taking off quickly in the general direction that Rhys is on the other side of the lake. Noise behind me drags my attention away from the water before me, and I see my mates bursting from the house, running down the steps and towards the jetty, calling for me to stop.

I know I should. I fucking know it, yet I don't. I turn my back on them and ignore their yells, pulling out my phone to make sure I'm headed in the right direction.

I just need to know.

It doesn't take me long to reach the other side of the lake, and the closer I get, the guiltier I feel. Yet do I turn back? No, I fucking don't!

There's a huge chance that if Rhys catches me, she will rip my balls from my body. I'm hopeful I can be stealthy enough to have a quick look before going back to the boat and heading back to the others. All I want is a look. That's it.

I've hit ignore on about fifteen calls from the guys, and I turn my phone on silent after I tie the boat up on someone's jetty closer to where my girl is on the map. As I make my way onto the bank, I re-check the map again to find the location, then head west along the waterfront. It's nearly dark now, with the last remnants of pink on the horizon helping to keep me hidden.

I walk about five hundred metres before the lights of a house come into view, and another look at the map tells me that is where Rhee is. I stumble my way through the dark, up some fancy stone steps to a modern-looking house that I think is light in colour. It's hard to tell in the dark.

As I round the side of the house, following the path, I see a car parked and then an entrance into the house, which is a huge glass door.

Sneaking up to it, I peek around the door frame, trying to remain out of view, but it doesn't matter. There's no one there to see me. The light that I saw from the waterfront seems to be coming from the second story, which royally fucks with my plan of peeking through a window to get a glimpse at this Tyler guy.

Without even thinking, my hand comes to the handle of the door and pulls down to see if it's unlocked. When the handle shifts all the way down, and the door clicks open, I fucking freeze. I honestly thought it would be locked, but it's not, and now I have a choice to make.

Do I go in, try to sneak a peek, or do I turn around and go back to the others?

Yep, you fucking guessed it. I go in.

The faint noise of a TV floats to me, and after I quietly click the door shut, I creep toward the light filtering down the staircase and sneak up the stairs. Every time a step creaks under my foot, I freeze, blood rushing past my ears as I try to listen to see if I've been made. And each time, no one comes to investigate, so I keep going until the second level comes into view.

Fuck, this place is nice. Modern. This Tyler guy must have a fair bit of coin. Is he like a sugar daddy or something? Is that why she calls him Daddy all the time? Fucking hell, how am I meant to compete with that? I have three hundred dollars to my name. My family gets by, but I'm pretty sure my olds live week to week with what they earn at their jobs. My uncle Peter is pretty well-off, though, but he earnt that himself through his recording studio in the city. There's no big inheritance coming my way.

Pushing aside my jealousy of this considerably well-off Tyler dude, I poke my head around the corner as I reach the top step. I find a big open living area with a comfy-looking couch and a really cool fireplace that looks like it's hanging from the ceiling. Next to it is a TV that also looks like it comes down from the ceiling, which is the source of what I could hear when I came inside.

Down the end of the room is a kitchen, but there's no sign of people. I step up into the room to get a better look and sneak towards the kitchen, where I can see another doorway. That's when I pick up the faint sound of voices.

My heart rate picks up when I hear Rhee's familiar giggle, and my feet steer me into a glass-lined passage that connects the living area to another wing of the house.

Turn back!

I should. I know I fucking should, but I've come this far. I may as well go through with it. I just need a quick glance to see if I recognise the guy, then I'll fuck off just as quickly and head back to our cabin.

I still have shoes on, so I take each step slowly so I don't make a sound, and before I know it, the glass-lined passage is behind me, and I'm stepping through a door to a luxurious bedroom.

My eyes dart around the space looking for Rhee, but the room is empty, and I can now tell the voices are coming from the opening at the end of the room. I study the space as I creep toward their voices. The bed is a little rumpled but not dishevelled, like I assumed it would be. As I step in further, I see a pile of clothes just by the opening to the other room. Rhee's clothes. My heart flips in my chest.

I'm so close now.

I have to see.

I peek past the opening to see a charcoal grey tiled bathroom. It's slick. Modern and masculine. Tyler has fucking good taste. I'll give him that.

Then my eyes fall on them. There, at the other end of the room, in a deep oversized bath, are Tyler and Rhys. They have their backs to me, their attention directed towards the window.

Maybe they watched the sunset?

I expected to find them fucking or something, but Rhys is leaning back against Tyler's chest, their hands up on the ledge, their fingers weaving and stroking together in such a normal affectionate way.

Their voices are low. He's saying something next to her ear, and it makes her giggle again, the sound making my heart twist with jealousy I thought I had a handle on.

Suddenly, Tyler stiffens, and Rhee squeaks as she is lifted off his lap before he leaps up to face me. Standing with water dripping down his athletic naked flesh, I come face to face with Mr Foster. My fucking PE teacher.

Chapter Twenty-Eight

RHYS

"**G**et the fuck out!" Tyler's roar makes me flinch back, which nearly causes me to slip in the bath as I take in the scene.

Ty stiffened under me moments ago as we sat in the bath, and in a split second before he lifted me off him, I saw what had caught his attention. The reflection in the window of someone standing behind us.

I'm pretty sure my heart stopped in that moment, but then it kicked in again when Marcus' familiar brown eyes came into view. It was fleeting, though. Because what the fuck is Marcus doing here?

"This is a fucking joke, right?" Marcus yells. "Rhee, get the fuck over here!" His voice is panicked, more than demanding, but I don't go to him. Instead, I try to get myself out of the tub so I can get a towel for Ty and me.

"What are you doing here?" I yell back, freaking the fuck out.

"Get out of my house!" Ty roars again, and again I flinch at the menacing tone.

"Rhee, get away from him. He's… he's… a fucking predator!"

Ty moves to leap out of the bath, but my hand on his arm stops him, and he looks back at me as I pass him a towel.

"Get dressed," I whisper, and he glares at me. "Obviously, we need to talk to Marcus about this."

"I'm not talking to this little prick! He fucking broke into my home!" Ty points a stern finger in the direction of Marcus, who hisses back.

"Technically, I didn't break in. You left the door unlocked. And fuck you, Mr Fucking Foster! I'm not talking with you about your paedophile ways!"

"Marcus!" I scold, but it falls on deaf ears.

"You don't know what you're talking about!" Ty's yell is deafening. I try to wrap a towel around his waist to cover him up, but I can't make it work, and he's not trying to fucking help me.

"Oh, so you, a fucking teacher, aren't fucking one of your students? A fucking seventeen-year-old girl!"

"This is the last time I will ask you to get out of my house!" Tyler's fists ball at his sides, his eyes laser-focused on Marcus.

Sounds come from within the house. Voices, footsteps. I start to panic and grab for Ty's arm, but all he does is try to shield me from Marcus.

"I'm not leaving without Rhee, you fucking paedo!" Marcus yells right as three puffing guys skid to a stop behind him, their chests rising and falling in exertion.

Shaun, Simon and Garrett take in the scene, their breathing loud like they've been running. Shaun's eyes meet mine, his expression an apology, while Garrett is looking more and more pissed as the seconds tick by, and Simon is re-enacting a fish, opening and closing his mouth in shock.

Shit. It wasn't meant to happen like this.

"What the fuck?" Garrett hisses.

"Mr F?" Simon asks, as Marcus dares to glance over his shoulder at his mates.

"Sorry, Kitten. He snuck off." Shaun offers, which just seems to make Marcus angrier.

"You're sorry?" He spins on Shaun. "What the fuck is wrong with you, Bossi? How could you let her go with this fucking sicko?"

"Hey, calm down, man. Ty is good." Shaun defends, but Marcus scoffs.

"Ty is good?" His raging eyes flick back to Ty and me before he points at us. "He is our fucking teacher! How is he good?"

"All of you, get the fuck out now!" Ty bellows and Marcus chuckles, and not in a happy way.

"Or what? You gonna call the cops? I'm sure they would love to hear how you've been fucking a student!"

"Marcus! That's enough! Ty isn't a teacher anymore, and there's a lot you don't know about us." I cry out, needing to stop this.

His blazing brown eyes shoot to me. "And *why* is that Rhee? You're the one keeping fucking secrets. Don't you think we should have at least known that we were engaging in a fucking orgy with our PE teacher? We should have been given an option. And I can tell you right fucking now that I would have said no fucking way!"

His words are like a slap to my face. He's right. He should have been given the option. They all should have known they were joining their teacher in a group session with me.

Oh my God. What have I done?

"Hey, back off, Grady!" Shaun hisses, reefing Marcus around by the shoulder to face him. "Rhys didn't know that group session was going to happen. I planned it, and you fucking agreed to go into that sex party, knowing it would be filled with adults."

"You're right, Bossi. You were the one to organise it." Marcus growls right before his arm coils back, and his fist slams into Shaun's face.

A scream rips from me, and I try to run towards them, but Ty grabs me around the waist, pulling me back into the tub with him.

Shaun stumbles back from the blow, and when he rights himself, I see blood oozing from his nose. His eyes darken as anger takes over. "That's the last fucking free punch you get, Grady."

Marcus chuckles. "Yeah? Fucking bring it!" Then he swings at Shaun again.

They both clash together, fists swinging as they stumble out of the bathroom and into Ty's bedroom while Simon and Garrett leap out of the way.

Hissing under his breath, Ty releases me and leaps out of the bath, darting towards the guys as they keep swinging fists, but before he makes it there, Garrett lunges for him, taking them both to the hard, tiled floor.

I squeal like a fucking girl. "Stop!" I scream, but no one hears me. I glance at Simon, who just stands back watching his mate and naked PE teacher wrestling on the floor, his face unreadable as he watches on. Is he comprehending what's happening?

"Simon," I call, but he doesn't hear me.

Marcus and Shaun disappear from view, still punching each other before the sounds of fragile things start smashing.

Fuck. I did this. I've caused two mates to fight each other and a teacher to quit his job and have to fight off one of his students who has come into his private home without permission. My addiction may have been getting better, but it's what brought us together, and it's what is destroying their lives.

"Stop!" I cry out again, and still, I'm ignored.

Tears prick my eyes, but I refuse to let them fall. If one of the guys sees them, then they will get worried and offer me sympathy. Sympathy I don't deserve. The time for tears is over. I'm angry. Angry at myself and my past that has tainted me forever.

Quickly climbing back out of the tub, I grab a towel and do a bad job of drying off before stepping around the tangled limbs of Ty and Garrett and pick up my pile of clothes. Moving to the corner, I quickly get dressed in my gym pants and hoodie. Shaun and Marcus are no longer in the room, but by the angry screaming and things smashing coming from the passage, I know their melee has moved to Tyler's living area.

I don't know where my shoes are, but I guess that doesn't matter. Nothing matters right now other than getting as far away from these guys as I can. They are better off without me. They don't deserve this bullshit in their lives. If I go away, then they can move on and find someone to have a normal relationship with. Someone who doesn't want to be shared. Someone whose attention is solely on them. They deserve that sort of love.

I can never give them that. Not now that my heart belongs to each one of them. And I just can't have one without the other.

Because you're selfish.

I shake off my thoughts, dashing from Ty's bedroom and down the glass passage to enter the living area. I skid to a stop, broken shards of glass lining the floor everywhere, making it impossible to cross without shoes. I have no choice, though, so I step over the jagged shards and ignore the sting of pain as my skin slices open with each step. I don't know what the hell they broke, but Marcus and Shaun are doing a great job of destroying Tyler's home. All because of me.

I continue to ignore the pain as I move. I ignore Shaun and Marcus as they wrestle near the fireplace. I ignore my heart when it aches so badly that I think it will stop altogether. Instead, I keep walking, moving carefully down the stairs, the soles of my feet bloody with each step, the pain welcoming as it takes my attention off my heart.

The door is wide open, so I leave it that way as I walk out and down the steps into the cool night air. Taking a moment, I glance towards the waterfront, but since I'm scared that a lake monster might live at the bottom, I'm not all that keen on trying to swim across the lake to get back to the cabin. So I turn and stumble up the driveway.

Even as the house gets smaller behind me, I still hear things breaking. Stopping, I turn back to glance at the amber hue flowing from the second story, where the five guys I love are probably killing each other, and my heart sinks.

What am I doing?

Even if the best thing to do is set them free, running away like a coward isn't the right thing to do here. I made this mess. I should stay here and face it. Stay here and do things right for once in my fucking life.

I limp back towards Ty's home, not entirely sure how to get them to stop fighting, so I sit my arse down on the steps that lead to the front door, and I wait. Maybe my absence will be noticed eventually, and that will make them stop.

It's the best idea I can come up with as the weight of what has happened here tonight settles in my gut, and hot tears threaten again. Instead of giving into them, I yell a guttural growl up into the night air, trying to release some of my self-loathing anger. I don't want it to consume me. I've come too far to let my emotions drag me back into that dark hole I've been hovering on the ledge of for so long. I'm not sure if it's possible to have my guys, but I do know that I want to live. Which is a fucking huge development I'm sure my therapist, Melia, would like to hear about in our next session.

I have parents that love me. A big sister who stands up for me, and twin brothers who dote on me. That will just have to be enough if a future with the guys I love isn't feasible.

My attention is drawn to the thick bushland sitting before me. There are so many noises out here. I'm fairly certain there are possums stalking me right now. And I know by the faint thump every so often that there are roo's nearby.

I really hope the guys miss me soon, or it's possible I'm going to die out here while I wait for them. Death by koala. I sure hope it gives me a koala hug before it ends me, though. I could really use a hug right now.

It's then that I notice it has fallen quiet inside. Shit. Have they killed each other? Frowning in concern, I sneak a glance over my shoulder at the glass door I left open, wondering if I should go inside and check, but then I hear the deep baritone of male voices again, followed by heavy feet as they travel through the upper level of the house.

My shoulders slump in relief at hearing they are still at least breathing, and I turn my eyes up to the starry sky, finding peace in the illusion of their twinkle.

The rush of footsteps pound the staircase inside, and I suck in a deep breath, mentally preparing myself for whatever the fuck is about to come, right before the air shifts behind me. Strong arms wrap around me from behind, the familiar scent of Tyler engulfing me as his warm breath dances across my ear.

"Why are you out here, Kitten?"

I should fight off his touch, but I can't. I'm prisoner to my heart. It wants him desperately, just like it wants the others, too.

"I was going to run off. Go home." I watch as Ty shifts around me to kneel on the step below the one I'm sitting on.

"But you didn't?" Ty's deep blue eyes find mine in the dull light, and I can see the worry in them.

Movement behind me tells me we aren't alone, but I don't look to see who has joined us. I'm just happy they aren't swinging fists anymore.

"Do you want to go home, Kitten? Is that what you want?" He rasps, and I shake my head.

"No," I whisper.

"Then why go?" His thumb brushes over my cheek. Back and forth, back and forth. So lovingly.

I shrug. "I thought leaving would make you and the guys stop fighting. Stop having to deal with the crap I've brought into your lives." I drag my gaze from his as I squirm under their scrutiny.

"You said you wouldn't do that again, Kitten." Shaun's voice comes from behind me, and I glance over my shoulder to find those steel-grey eyes that melt my heart. "You said we were enough."

I slowly stand from the step, brushing the dirt from my arse as I turn to face Shaun, and my eyes also find Marcus, Simon, and Garrett staring back at me.

I glance back at Shaun and shake my head. "I'm still here, Cass. I realised we need to sort this out. One way or another, this thing we all have needs to be discussed. So I sat my arse out here waiting for you adorable idiots to stop bashing on each other. I never intended to harm myself. I only meant I was going to go home and give you guys space. Let you live your lives without the drama I bring. Each of you deserves more than that. But I figure I at least owe you all that conversation."

"Don't talk like that. We aren't having any conversation that involves a world in which we aren't yours, Kitten." Shaun's tone is final as he frowns, and I shrug again.

"I'm not so sure I'm good for you. Any of you. I'm selfish. Too selfish, especially asking each of you to share me. Maybe if I walk away, you guys will get along again. Be friends, again." I look back to Ty. "You can go back to teaching. You can find someone to share your life with."

"Don't you get it, Kitten?" Ty steps closer, moving up on the same step as me. "I've waited my whole life for you to come along. You're my end game. There's you, or there's nothing."

"What?" My bottom lip starts to fucking seize, and I hear feet shuffle behind me.

"I'm not letting you push me away because you have it in your head that I'm better off without you. I'm nothing without you, Rhys." Ty frowns, glancing over to the others before looking back at me. "Maybe that makes me the monster Marcus said I was. I don't know. But I can't change the way I feel about you. And I don't see you as anyone but a woman who owns my very soul."

"Ty," I whisper.

"I love *you,* Rhys. Not just Kitten. All of you." Reaching out, he grips my nape before his lips claim mine, branding me, owning me, and I clutch at his hoodie, desperate to climb under his skin.

"I'm sorry. I still can't get over the fact that my PE teacher is kissing my girlfriend."

The guys groan at Simon's statement as Ty's lips slow against mine, turning up into a grin against my mouth.

"Honestly, what we just witnessed was beautiful." Shaun remarks, and Marcus snaps.

"Fucking hell, Bossi. Has Cole got you into those mummy porn romance books he reads?"

"Don't knock them until you try them, Grady." Garrett snaps, and Ty and I reluctantly pull away from each other.

"You aren't going anywhere." He points in my face, and I grin, even though I still feel like crying and that I'm responsible for all this mess.

"I've been a bad girl, Daddy," I say innocently, grasping at the old habit of mine of being playful and trying to push myself into being ok.

"Ok, I'm just saying, I'm still not fucking cool with this fucked up situation." Marcus snaps, and I reluctantly drag my gaze from Ty's deep blue eyes.

Upon closer inspection, I can just make out bruises and grazes on Marcus and Shaun's faces. Fucking hell. How are they going to explain that to their parents?

"We heard you the first time." Shaun mumbles, winning him a glare from Marcus. "I guess there are some conversations to be had?"

"You'd better believe there are some conversations to be had." Marcus snaps, and I glance at Shaun. Waiting for him to bite back, but instead, he nods.

I feel bad. Shaun has kept the secret of who Ty is, too. He seems to always be siding with me like he's trying to take the heat off me, but I don't want him to do that anymore. I know he cares about his mates. I know he hates going against them. There are so many conversations to be had between the six of us, and as much as the thought of that makes me uncomfortable, I know that if we don't have them, then these issues will never be resolved.

"Let's get you inside and clean up your feet, beautiful." Ty sweeps down and scoops me up in his arms. He steps towards his front door, which has a wall of my guys blocking his path, and I glance up to see him raising a single blonde brow at his former students, who glare at him, all but Shaun, for a few tense moments before stepping aside to let him pass.

As Ty carries me back inside his house and I hear the guys follow behind, I still have no idea how to sort out this mess and if it's even something that can be rectified. I just know that I want to make it work. Whatever it takes.

Chapter Twenty-Nine

GARRETT

W e are going round in circles. Shaun is trying to defend Tyler, but Marcus can't accept it. I have to admit, it freaked me the fuck out when I finally saw who Ty actually was. Never did I think it was one of our teachers from school. Yet here we are, in his lake house, trying to have a discussion on how to make this work.

Just remembering what we did at the sex party last night, remembering that I watched my teacher fuck my girl, and he watched me fuck her, too. That's sick, right?

In theory it is, but being there, watching the connection he has with Rhys is undeniable. They love each other. Like intensely. I don't think Mr F is into students. He just fell in love with someone who happens to be legally too young. As soon as she's eighteen, that won't be an issue anymore, and honestly, in the bedroom, Rhys is all woman and nothing like a teenager.

Outside the bedroom, she does have a naivety about her when it comes to relationships, and yeah, she can be a sassy little minx, but her love for Ty, for all of us, is real. There's no doubting that.

"I don't understand how you can be ok with this." Marcus grits his teeth at Shaun.

"I guess I'm more like Ty and Rhys than the rest of you are. I get their connection, and yeah, I was fucking shocked when I first found out, but then Rhys explained to me how it came about, and I understand Ty didn't seek her out. He avoided her for a long time. Until…"

"Until what?" Marcus snaps, pacing in front of the fireplace.

"Until they were forced together by Master Hill." Shaun stands from the couch and starts pacing. "Rhys was given two options. One was to go with Master Hill alone, down to his fucking sex dungeon. The other was to fuck Ty on the podium in front of everyone. They both chose it. She chose Ty because she's terrified of Master Hill. And Ty sacrificed his reputation to do that with Rhys because he knows how she feels about the Master, and there's no way he was going to let that happen." Shaun tries to explain, but it's like talking to a brick wall when Marcus is this worked up.

"You do realise how ridiculous all that sounds, right? She had a third option. It was to get up and leave that fucking sick place." Marcus snaps, his fists balled like he's ready to throw down again.

"You're right. It does sound ridiculous." I interrupt. "To us, it does. But not to the people who go to places like that. And not to Rhys. I don't mean to sound like a prick, but are you forgetting about her addiction, Grady? To Rhys, taking away that place was probably like asking her to never have sex again. She needed it, man, at least until we came along."

"It still doesn't make sense to me." Marcus huffs, finally dropping his arse on the couch next to Simon.

"It doesn't have to make sense to you. This isn't about you. It's about Rhys." I point out, and Marcus glares at me.

"It is about me if I take part in a fucking orgy with my PE teacher."

"You're right." Rhys' voice gains our attention as she limps past the kitchen to where we are seated on the couch. Tyler enters the room after her, having spent a good twenty minutes cleaning up her feet, but he hovers near the kitchen, giving us space.

"You should have been told who you were getting naked with." Her voice is flat. It's filled with shame, and fuck, I hate hearing it. She comes to stand in front of us, her eyes red from unshed tears. She seems unusually nervous, her hands fidgeting in front of her. "I've been selfish. I always have, I guess. I used to think it was my addiction. Maybe my selfishness is from that, maybe it isn't, but it doesn't make it ok, either way." She turns to Marcus. "I strung you along for weeks last term, telling you what I couldn't give you, yet not letting you go. I was so messed up because I wanted you, but didn't want to admit it. I couldn't figure out how a relationship with you would work, and I knew that I'd seek out sex from someplace else, eventually. Not because you aren't amazing, but because I'm sick and need things that aren't normal." She slowly drags her eyes from Marcus to Shaun.

"As soon as I realised it was you under that mask, I should have stopped you because I knew it was wrong. I knew it was a betrayal to Marcus." She takes a deep breath like she's trying to compose herself, and fuck if I don't want to walk over to her and lift her in my arms and take her pain away. "But I didn't stop because I let the need control me."

"But-." Shaun tries to speak, but Rhys holds her finger up, shaking her head, silently telling him not to say anything.

"I also had the chance to stop it from going further at school. But I was weak and a mess after seeing Marcus again, and with all the shit going on with Julie…" She shakes her head, looking down as she sighs. "So I took what I needed once again." She turns to Simon. "And you, Sy. Fuck, you deserved someone nice and sweet to take your virginity. Not a whore."

"Hey! Now that's enough!" Simon leaps from his seat and comes to stand in front of Rhys. "Don't you talk like that, Cherry. Ever. I won't have it, and I understand that you feel like you need to explain things, but you don't. We all understand what the situation was in the beginning, but that's not what it is now. You're different now, Cherry. We have *all* changed."

"I may have changed, but I'm still me. I'm still selfish. How can you say I'm not when I'm asking each of you to share me? How can you deny that when I hide a huge secret of who Tyler is from you? How can you even trust what I'm saying?"

"You never lied about Tyler, Baby Girl." I stand from the couch, approaching her as Simon backs away. She cranes her head back to keep her eyes on mine, and when I reach her, I cup her rosy cheek. "You were honest about not being able to tell us who he was. He was the one that asked you to keep his identity a secret, and you were respecting his wishes because of the legal ramifications."

"I feel like I'm as bad as a predator, though. I feel like I've manipulated you all into something you don't really want, and one day you're going to wake up and think, what the fuck am I doing? This isn't right," her lip trembles, "and then you'll leave."

"You didn't manipulate us." I brush her dark hair back off her face, staring into her chocolate eyes that are filled with so much torment right now.

"Yes, I did." She pulls away from me. "I manipulated Tyler. I basically blackmailed him. I-."

"Enough!" Tyler snaps, coming to join us in his living room. "The past is in the past. No more talk of it. We can't change it. All we can do is focus on now and the future." He eyes each one of us then, and I step away, giving him space with Rhys. "I'm not going anywhere. You may not understand it, but what I have with Rhys is real. I am happy to share her with you, only if that's what *she* wants. If it means she can only be with me when the both of us can be alone because you're uncomfortable with me, then that's fine. I won't ask any of you to do anything you're not comfortable with, other than sharing Rhys with me." He turns to Rhys. "None of us are perfect, and Marcus is right to be pissed. He needs time to think over things. But the loving you part won't change, beautiful. He loves you. I love you. The other three love you. I'm not going anywhere, and I get the feeling they aren't either. So, let's just figure out how to make this work."

Rhys nods up at him hesitantly before sinking against his chest and wrapping her arms around his waist, seeking comfort.

"What do you say, fellas? Are you willing to figure out how to make this work?" Tyler asks us over the top of Rhys' head, and fuck it. I nod because I'm not going anywhere.

"Yep. I'm definitely willing." I announce, and Ty gives me a nod.

"You know I am." Shaun offers.

"I'll admit, I'm still freaking out that I watched my PE teacher bang my girl, but yeah. I'm gonna make Cherry an honest woman one day."

We all laugh at Simon, and the words *get in line* are on the tip of my tongue, but I don't say them.

We all glance at Marcus then. His face is sullen but not fuming with anger like it was before, and he stands, puffing his chest out and making himself taller as he approaches Tyler, who still has Rhys in his arms.

"I'm willing to try, but I'm telling you right now," he points aggressively at Tyler, "do not get your dick out in front of me again unless I say you can. I'm gonna need a whole fucking lot of time to get used to this." He huffs then, dropping his hand. "But yes. I love Rhee, so I will try. *For her*." Marcus reaches forward then, snagging Rhys by the arm and tugging her out of Ty's grip, only to pull her to his chest and hug her tight.

She automatically latches onto Marcus, and with her head buried in his neck, he whispers quietly in her ear. It's not loud enough for me to hear, but she nods before pulling back and pressing her lips to his.

When they part, Rhys steps back from Marcus and glances nervously at each of us.

"I want you to know that, uhhh…" She hesitates, her cheeks flushing red as her nervousness shows. "The five of you are it for me. I don't want any more sex parties. I don't want any girl-on-girl action. I don't have the desire to seek sex from anyone else. You have each agreed to share me and just be with me, so I need you to know that I'm committed to each of you, too. And only the five of you. No one else."

My heart fills with so much fucking love in that moment, like it had been holding off from feeling its full power until those very words passed her lips.

I stand from my place on the couch, beelining for her. Her eyes widen as she sees me at the last moment, and I lift her in my arms, her legs wrapping around my waist as I claim her lips. I'm well aware that there are four sets of eyes on us, yet I can't find it in me to care. Not in this pivotal moment, where our girl finally announced her commitment to us.

Pulling back, I grip the sides of her head and press my forehead to hers. "You have no idea how much I've wanted to hear those words fall from these sweet lips, Baby Girl." My thumb brushes over her lower lips, and she grins.

We embrace for a few minutes before Caveman Marcus comes and snatches our girl from my grip. He gives Ty a wide berth as he moves around the room like Ty has cooties or something, and he takes another private moment for himself with our girl.

When I turn back to the others, Shaun is smiling wide, the look of relief and happiness engulfing his face, while Simon is smiling until his eyes land on Mr F. Then he just glares at our old teacher.

Tyler watches Marcus and Rhys, a frown creasing his brow. I'm not sure what he's frowning at, but there's a fair chance it has to do with how much we fucked up his house. I never had any intention of coming here, but once we realised what Marcus was doing, we had to come after him and try to stop him. Of course, we didn't make it in time, and when we finally got here, Marcus was already screaming.

I'm pretty sure we will laugh about what happened one day. I'm trying not to think about how I lost my shit and fucking tackled my PE teacher to the floor. While he was naked. Fuck, did his junk touch me?

Rhys and Marcus stop kissing again, and Ty takes that moment to tell us to get the fuck outta his house. We agree, but first I make the guys help me clean up the rest of the stuff we trashed. Simon whines but helps anyway, and Marcus stays quiet, his face in a constant scowl as his eyes frequently dart around the room in search of Ty and Rhys.

This group situation has a long way to go between the six of us. It's going to take a long fucking time before we are all ok with the whole Mr Foster thing. We seem to have come to some sort of truce about it, though, the five of us guys just wanting to make our girl happy. I just hope that's enough for us to move past the fact that our teacher is guy number five.

It's about twenty minutes later when we step out of our PE teacher's house and make our way down to the waterfront.

"Just so you know, I'm not going back with you guys across the water," Rhys announces before standing on her tiptoes to give Simon a kiss.

"Why not Kitten?" Shaun asks, slapping her on the arse as he walks past.

She lets out a squeak, her kiss with Hastings cut short. "Cass, if you're gonna spank me, make sure an orgasm is about to follow."

We all chuckle, and she shoots a cheeky smile over her shoulder, which is illuminated by the faint light coming from Ty's house.

"Your wish is my command, Kitten. I can take care of that right now if you like?" Shaun closes Rhys in, trapping her in between him and Simon, and Rhys moans.

"Caaassss, stoooppp. Now isn't the time."

I chuckle. Her request for him to stop doesn't at all sound like she actually wants him to.

"Come across in the boat, and I'll make you come under the stars." Cass nips at her ear, and she stretches her neck to the side.

"There's no way I'm getting on one of those boats. I'm not prepared to take on the lake monster tonight."

"Lake monster?" Simon chuckles. "The only monster around here is in Garrett's pants."

Rhys giggles, and we all laugh. All except for Marcus. He's still pissed. Understandably.

"No, you guys take the boats back. Ty will drive me."

"Are you sure, Cherry? We can play Simon Says."

Rhys laughs at Simon's offer, and although he has his back to me, I can just imagine him wagging his brows at her.

"Can we play when I get back?" She asks and Shaun drags his tongue up her neck before speaking against her ear.

"Only if we can *all* play."

Rhys moans again and starts wriggling like a worm to get free while Bossi and Hastings laugh and release her before she huffs at them.

"You two are a Kitty tease. I'll be coming to collect as soon as I get back. If you're asleep, be prepared to wake up with me fucking your face."

"Fuck. I'm heading back there to fall asleep, like now." Simon says in all seriousness, and Shaun just laughs, slapping a kiss on Rhys' cheek before heading down the steps to the sandy bank. Simon follows him, and Marcus takes his place, approaching Rhys.

"We need to talk when you get back, Rhee."

I should leave them alone, but I need to speak with our girl too, so I stand back and wait my turn.

"Is it one of those '*we can't be together if you keep seeing my PE teacher*' talks?" Rhys asks, concern clear in her tone.

Marcus peers down at her in the dark, taking a few moments to study her, or at least what he can see in this light.

"No." He finally responds, and Rhys' shoulders drop in relief. "I just need to get a few things off my chest."

Rhys slowly nods, taking a moment to look at her feet before she glances back up. "Right, ok." Her voice is so small. So not like our girl. She's been through hell lately, and Marcus, although entitled to have an opinion, is starting to piss me off. I don't like the way it's making Rhys feel.

"Hey." Marcus steps forward, cupping her cheek. "I fucking love you, Rhee. I'm not trying to make you feel bad, and I'd hold back if I thought it would do any good, but secrets in this group relationship will only destroy what we have. So, I need an honest conversation with you later, but it doesn't mean that I love you any less or that I want things to end. We just need to talk about stuff."

"I'm not good with feelings, Marc." She mutters quietly.

"Yes, you are. You're getting better at expressing them. At feeling them."

She nods. "Can we like… have makeup sex afterwards?"

Finally, Marcus cracks a smile. "Maybe."

That's all she needs to stand taller, her confidence coming back. "Challenge accepted, Marky Marc." She giggles, and he sweeps down, wrapping his arms around her and stealing another kiss.

I give them a minute, but then, because I'm impatient as fuck right now, I wrap my arms around Rhys from behind and sever their connection.

"Dude! Rude!" Marcus hisses, and I throw him a dagger.

"Go get the fucking boat started. I need a minute with our girl."

Marcus rolls his eyes at me, but blows Rhys a kiss and heads in the opposite direction to find the others.

"Baby Girl." I rasp against Rhys' dark silky hair, and she turns in my arms, wrapping hers around my waist.

"Big Guy. I feel like I keep fucking up."

"Tonight is on Marcus. Not you."

"Yes, but he must have been so worked up about not knowing who Ty was to steal a fucking boat and break into a stranger's home."

I nod.

While we cleaned, Shaun filled Rhys in on how Marcus stole a boat and pissed off on us. And how we had to steal a boat too to come after him.

"The situation is complicated, but it's happened now, so we have to deal with it."

Rhys pulls back from me, stepping out of my space. "I still feel I'm to blame. I can't help feeling that way." Her dark eyes are a little shiny in the warm light floating out from Tyler's house. I hate to see her hurting so much. All I want is to take her pain away, so her smile never fades and her heart always feels full.

"It'll pass, Rhys. Over time, the raw feelings you have will lessen, especially when me and the guys spend every day showing you how important you are."

She grins. "I don't know what I'd do without you, Gar. Or any of the guys, for that matter."

"We aren't going anywhere, Baby Girl. It's time for you to accept that. No more thinking we are better off. It doesn't work that way. Ok?"

She nods. "Yep."

"Now," I reach out and pull her against my chest again, "I have something that will make you feel better."

Her brows hitch high, and I pull out my phone, using one hand to unlock it and open the photo app. Then I show her my screen.

"Ooooh, what a pretty knife."

"You like it?" I ask, trying to hide my smirk.

"Yes. What's it for?"

"It's for me," I brush the corner of my phone down the side of her cheek, "and for you."

"What am I going to do with a big knife like that?" Her voice is husky, her body automatically responding to my touch.

"*You* aren't going to do anything with the knife. I, however, will be using it on *you*."

Her brows shoot towards the starry night sky. "On me?"

"Yes." I trail the phone down between our bodies until it meets her sweet spot, covered by too many layers of clothing. "I'll either use the hilt to fuck you or the blade to cut you."

Her lips part as I press my phone harder against her bundle of nerves, extracting a husky moan.

"What would you prefer?" I ask, and she shrugs.

"Why choose. Can't I have both?"

I can't hide my grin, and her eyes flare with desire. "Both it is." I nip at her lip and then, in a flash, push away from her and point to Tyler's house. "Go back in and finish your night quickly. I'm not a patient man."

"What you are is a Kitty tease, too." Rhys pouts as I back away, and I chuckle.

I know I'm leaving her hanging, but I'll pay up later, and in the meantime, she has Tyler to take her frustrated pussy out on.

CHAPTER THIRTY

RHYS

M y emotions are shot, and Kitty is ravenous. Two things that are the key ingredients for my addiction to take over any control I have in place. Each of the guys left me with promises I'm desperate to take them up on, and the moment I walk back into Ty's house, he can see it written all over my face.

"Don't look at me like that, Kitten."

I grin at Ty's expression. He fucking loves me looking like that. Unfortunately, his head is still with the fuckery that happened earlier with Marcus.

"I can't help it, Daddy. I need… *something*."

Ty's blue eyes darken as he watches me walk across his living area to where he's leaning against the kitchen bench. "Uh-ha. And what did your boy band say to you that has you so worked up right now?"

I grin and bite my lip, stalking closer to Ty. "Well, Shaun was talking about spanking, and Sy said we can play Simon Says when I get back. Marcus wants to… talk. But he didn't say no to makeup sex afterwards, so that's promising."

Tyler chuckles. "And what about Garrett? Did the big fella leave you with any promises?"

My face heats with a flush as I remember Garrett's words. He said he would use the hilt of his knife to fuck me and the blade to cut me. Call me a twisted bitch, but that shit right there turns me right the fuck on.

"Fuck, Kitten. What did he promise?" Ty steps away from the counter and approaches, coming to stop a couple of feet in front of me.

"He has a knife." I rasp quietly. "He's going to use it on me."

Ty's brows shoot up. "Blood play?"

I nod, my Kitty aching with need.

A deep growl rumbles from Ty's chest before his hand darts out, gripping my upper arm and dragging me against his hard body. "Does he like tasting your blood, Kitten?"

"Yes, Daddy." I pant, Kitty pressing against his thigh, seeking some friction.

Tyler grips my chin roughly as he lowers his face level with mine, our lips a mere inch apart. "Do you like tasting his blood, too?"

I nod. "Yes. More than I probably should."

"When you are both eighteen, Kitten, and if he can handle seeing me fuck you, I want in on your blood play." Ty slams his lips to mine then, and I climb him like a tree as we kiss, hard and deep, full of desperation. This is nothing like what we shared earlier. This is pure animalistic need, and fuck yes, I'm here for it. But then Ty rips his mouth from mine and pulls away.

"Get your clothes off and get outside." His demand is confusing, and he must be able to read it in my expression. "Take them off now, Kitten. I wanna fuck you under the stars."

"Oh." My heart leaps. Shaun had said something similar before. What is it with these guys wanting to fuck under the stars?

Unfortunately for Ty, I can't give in so easily. It's not how things work with him and me. "Well, Daddy, that sounds like fun, but I'm not feeling very obedient right now."

Ty growls. "Don't test me, Kitten."

"But not testing you is *soooo* boring." I pout, and his eyes darken as he steps toward me. With each of his steps, I take my own, backing away and ignoring the sting of the cuts on my feet. When he lunges for me, I squeal and turn to make a run for it. I make it maybe five steps before his arms wrap around me, and his hand cups Kitty as his teeth scrape my neck. Fuck, it feels amazing. It's just a pity for him that I'm not ready to give in yet.

I grind Kitty against the heel of his palm, letting him tug my hoodie off, revealing my black bra underneath, and as soon as his hands loosen on me, I push from his hold and run. A hiss of frustration leaves him, and the pounding feet behind me tell me he has taken chase. My heart leaps over and over as I reach the stairs and rush down as quickly as I can with my stinging feet. The door is in sight, but Ty catches up with me again, this time tackling me to the ground.

A squeal rips from my lips as I see the floor hurling towards me, but at the last moment, Ty turns us, so he takes the brunt of our bodies crashing to the timber floor. He's quick, though, not giving me a chance to flee, rolling himself on top of me and claiming my lips in another searing kiss.

Kissing Ty is something else. Each brush of his lips and swipe of his tongue carries experience and knowledge, and I can't even be jealous at knowing others have been on the receiving end of his lips. His kiss is just so consuming, like a brand telling me who owns me. His big hands are demanding, running down between our bodies before he hooks his finger in my gym pants and starts dragging them down.

If only I were that easy. I mean, I am easy, but it doesn't mean I have to give it up straight away, even though Kitty is clawing at me.

Claws back in, you vicious Kitty!

The moment Ty eases off me a little to work my pants down, I start struggling under him, trying to wriggle my way out.

"Fucking hell, woman. Would you stop trying to get away?" He hisses, and I giggle.

"What's the fun in that?" I start kicking my legs around, and he turns his focus on getting my pants off while I try to crawl away.

We wrestle on the floor, and the moment he reefs my pants and knickers off in one move, I have a brief window of time to flee. With nothing left on me but my bra, I bolt to the door, swinging it wide as I rush outside.

He told me he wanted to fuck me under the stars, and although I'm being a brat right now, I'm not totally heartless. He'll get to fuck me under the stars. When he can catch me.

As I rush down the stone steps towards the car, I don't hear him behind me. I quickly risk a glance over my shoulder, and I see no sign of Ty. But that doesn't mean he's not coming.

I take cover behind his car, feeling a little weird with so much bare skin meeting the chill of the air. My white arse is probably shining brightly under the glow of the moon.

A rustle in the bushes behind me makes me stiffen, and I turn around quickly, hoping to see Ty there. The sight of thick bushes is all I can see, and the rustling sounds again.

Fucking hell. Why is the Australian wildlife so fucking scary? Sure, it could be a possum. I'm sure they aren't killers, but what if I'm the first person they turn on? What if all the possums in the country are about to turn on the human population?

Don't laugh!

It could totally happen.

Fuck this! I'm not sticking around to get mauled by a fucking possum. Standing abruptly, I turn and run a few steps to the front of the car, looking over my shoulder to make sure death by possum isn't actually about to happen when I slam into something hard.

I squeal, and strong hands grip my arms, and before I know what's happening, I'm being lifted in the air, and my back comes down on the cold metal of the car bonnet.

"You can't escape me, Kitten." Tyler rasps in my face, his eyes wild with desire. "I will always come for you, no matter what."

He doesn't give me a chance to respond before his lips are on mine again, and I finally concede. The time to submit is now, and I take what he gives me as he pushes my thighs apart on the hood of his car. His kisses a trail down my neck and chest, making the journey to the place that is craving his touch the most. I drag my eyes open, stars above twinkling in the sky, and the moment his tongue sweeps over my clit, my back arches off the metal surface, and my moan floats up into the night.

"Yes." I pant. "Don't stop," I beg. Already so close to orgasm. The hunting game we played has already primed me.

One thing I have noticed since opening my heart to five guys is that reaching my highs is so much easier than it used to be. These guys work me up so much before they even touch me, making my O come crashing ten times faster and with less mental effort on my part. I don't even have to think. Just feel and get lost with them, and even though I used to think I had already found that with other people before, I was wrong. Nothing compares to these guys. I don't need a sex club anymore. I just need them. Always.

My fingers fist tight in Ty's hair as the pleasure builds, and by the time his skilled tongue and mouth have ripped an orgasm from me, my Kitty is grinding against his face.

Prying himself from between my legs, Ty smirks as he stands over me, tugging me to slide over the hood, closer to the front of his car.

"I fucking love eating your pussy, Kitten."

I grin back, cupping my tits, still hidden in the bra. "I fucking love you eating Kitty, Ty. Please tell me you're going to fuck me now? I'm desperate to be filled."

A rumble sounds from his chest. "Yes Kitten. I'm going to fuck you right here on the hood of my car, so every time I drive it, I'll think of nothing but your sweet cunt."

"I like the sound of that." I flash my teeth at him in a cheesy grin, and he flashes his back.

He's completely naked. He stripped at some point and now stands strong and confident in front of his car in the chilly night air. The only light comes from the moon and the amber filtering from the windows in his house, and it dances across his skin in some places while other places are painted in shadows. He looks utterly evil and absolutely addictive, especially with the way he fists his cock, pumping it as he directs his head to my entrance. Then he slams into me.

We both cry out, his a deeper rumble than my high pitch, and after a brief moment of letting Kitty adjust around him, he starts to thrust. Ty isn't gentle. Each time he slides out, he slams in until he's fully seated. With each slamming thrust, my body tingles, his cock the perfect size and length to ignite all of my nerve endings inside.

"Rub your clit, beautiful." He demands, and I obey, sliding my hand down the front of my body until I find the swollen bundle of nerves and start to apply circled pressure. "That's it." He rasps. "Fuck, you're perfect." His deep blue eyes pierce mine, his hand fisting the back of my hair as he continues his pace.

"You like fucking me, Daddy?" I pant, and his lips twitch.

"Yes. Fuck yes." He grits his teeth this time, picking up his pace.

"You like it when I call you Daddy, don't you?"

His eyes flare at me, and he slams harder, punishing me in the best way.

"No." He lies.

"Yes, you do. DADDY!" I cry, and he moves faster. "Yes Daddy. Fuck me harder. Fill me with your cream, Daddy. I've been such a bad girl."

His palm comes down hard on the side of my arse cheek, and I nearly come apart.

"Yes Daddy. Spank me. Fuck me. Make me dirty."

He hisses this time, his hand wrapping around my throat, holding me in place against the onslaught of his thrusts.

"Oh God, yes. Fucking own me Daddy."

His hand around my throat squeezes, and my inner walls tighten as the familiar feeling of ecstasy begins to wash over me. I think I move my fingers faster, chasing my O, but I can't tell because it slams into me hard as a lightheaded faintness creeps in.

A roar rips from Ty's throat as his hand releases mine, and I continue to soar.

It feels like an eternity passes before I regain my senses, and when I do, I find those hypnotising, deep blue eyes peering down at me.

"Did I hurt you?" Ty pants, a frown creasing his brow.

"Only in the best way."

He's quiet for a few long-drawn-out moments before he speaks again. "Make sure you use the safe word with me. Or just punch me if I go too far."

Pushing up on my elbows, I tilt my head as I study him. "Yeah, of course, but you know I love every single thing we just did, right? You haven't forgotten who you're fucking, have you?"

His face cracks with a smile. "Maybe I forgot for a minute there. It's hard not to worry when I love you so much. There's this fucking annoying voice in my head that wants me to be gentle with you and treat you like you could break at any moment."

My brows lift high. "There's a time for gentle, and there's a time for brutal. You can be assured I'm likely to want brutal ninety percent of the time."

He chuckles. "Which is why you are perfect. Well, your age isn't perfect, but after April, it will be."

I smile. "I can't wait for April."

Even though my birthday is over four months away, it reminds me that I need to finish my driving hours with my parents. I only have ten hours left to get to be eligible to go for my probationary license when I turn eighteen. I haven't driven in a couple of months, though, so I need to start putting aside more time, and figure out how to get myself a car so that when I turn eighteen, I don't have to rely on anyone but myself to go places. It will make it easier to visit Ty.

"Me either." Ty smiles before slowly easing out of me.

Instantly, I feel his hot cum ooze from me, and he uses his fingers to push it back in.

"Hey." I half laugh and frown as I try to squirm from his touch.

"I don't want it getting on my car." He teases, and I laugh.

"We have thoroughly defiled your car, Ty. It's too late to be concerned about your cum getting on the hood."

"Maybe I really just like knowing that you're walking around with my cum running down your leg."

"That sounds more accurate." I giggle before he sweeps me up in his arms.

Latching my hands around Ty's neck, I hold on as he carries me to the passenger side of the car and opens the door before lowering my practically naked body into the seat.

"What are you doing?"

"Taking you back to your boy band. Keep your legs closed. Don't let me leak out." He points a stern finger to my Kitty, so I give him a flipping bird salute.

"Yes, Sir Daddy."

He growls, but then presses his lips to mine before shutting me in.

I quickly put my seat belt on and watch Ty disappear back inside his house, only to reappear a minute later wearing his sweatpants and carrying my clothes. He puts my clothes on the back seat and climbs in behind the wheel, starting his car up.

"Uh-can I have my clothes?"

"No." He smirks, shifting the car into reverse.

"You want me to sit here naked, squeezing my legs shut, so your cum doesn't spill out on the seat?"

Ty nods. "Yep." He reverses the car, turning us around in his driveway.

"Why exactly?"

The cutest smirk I've ever seen on Ty's face is directed at me as he shifts the car into drive. He doesn't say anything, though, and moves his attention to the road as he drives.

"What was that face?"

"What face?" He grins, even though he's not looking at me.

"Ty! Give me my clothes, or I'm going to open my legs and dirty this seat up."

"Keep your legs shut, Kitten. You don't need clothes. Just relax."

He's fucking up to something, yet I can't find it in me to fight it. He's kind of playful right now, and it makes him seem younger than his thirty-two years. So, I relax back in the seat as much as I can while trying to keep my thighs clamped tight and watch the thick bushland pass by in the headlights as Ty drives me back to the guys.

The drive isn't too long as we round the lake, and I thoroughly annoy him by changing his music to Paramore, but he snatches his phone back, changing the music to Foo Fighters. I wonder what Marcus would say if he knew that Ty listens to the same music as him?

The song, My Hero, comes on, making me grin because it's the exact same song Marcus played for me on the bus. I know most of the words, but I mostly enjoy listening to Ty sing the lyrics next to me. His voice is a deep baritone, so it surprises me that he's able to keep tune, his voice going higher as he sings.

Fuck, that's hot.

I realise I still know hardly anything about Ty, but tonight alone, I've learnt so much, and I look forward to the new things I'll learn when we can be alone together again. It's weird to think that we can be so infatuated with each other with the little we know. Our attraction is undeniable, though. The love I have for him is immense. So much so that the thought of saying goodbye when he drops me off sends an ache to my chest.

We pull down the driveway of the cabin, Ty driving right up this time since his cover has been blown. Marcus and Garrett stand in the window watching while Shaun and Simon step out onto the porch as Ty cuts the engine.

"Can I have my clothes now?" I ask and he shakes his head, dragging his gaze from the cabin to me with a smirk.

"Nope."

"Why?"

"Because." His grin grows.

"Oh my God, Tyler. How old are you?"

"Old enough to want to stir up your other boyfriends."

My mouth drops open. "You evil fucker!"

He throws his head back, laughing.

"That's *Evil Daddy* to you." Ty darts forward, slapping his lips to mine, kissing me through our smiles. When he pulls back, I shake my head.

"You're a naughty Daddy."

He just offers me a shit-eating grin before getting out of the car.

"Fuckboy, grab Kitten's clothes from the backseat."

Shaun's face morphs into a frown, but he doesn't ask any questions as he moves to the car. I watch Ty as he rounds the front of the car, his eyes trained on Marcus and Garrett inside as they stand at the window. Ty slowly grazes his hand over the hood of the car where he fucked me not too long ago, giving it a little slap as he makes his way to me. The back door opens, and Shaun leans down, scooping up my clothes, his eyes finding me in the front seat and taking in my state of undress. Then he chuckles, cursing under his breath.

The passenger door opens then, and Ty scoops me up. "Keep your legs together for a little longer, beautiful."

I do as he demands, mostly because I don't want to leak all over him as he carries me. Using his foot, he pushes the car door shut and carries me up the steps of the cabin. My face heats as I see the anger on Marcus' face. Ty is playing with fire right now. I should probably put a stop to it, but before I can do anything, he has carried me inside and lowers me to my feet in the middle of the living area before backing away.

Frowning at him, I squeeze my thighs tight. "Ah, Ty. Can you take me to the *bathroom,* please?"

He fucking shakes his head. "No, Kitten. I've taken up too much of your time already. I'll let your boyfriends clean you up."

"Why the fuck is she naked?" Marcus snaps, and Ty frowns, looking from me to Marcus.

"She's not naked. She has a bra on."

I suck my lips in, trying not to laugh. This would be funny if Marcus wasn't about to kill Ty, so I need to hide my reaction.

"Fucking hell." Shaun mumbles.

"You wanna explain why you're returning our girl to us practically naked?" Garrett asks, his tone laced with the promise of violence.

"I'm just gonna go shower." I point over my shoulder and try to take a few shuffled steps with my legs together.

"No, no, Kitten." Ty grabs my wrist. "You stay here and let these gentlemen clean you up."

With that, he kisses me, his hand travelling down the front of my leg. When he breaks the kiss, his hand urges my legs to part.

"Legs apart, Kitten."

I'm weak. Totally slave to him, because I do exactly as he demands and I shift my legs apart. With a nod, he chuckles and walks out, leaving me with four sets of eyes watching Tyler's cum ooze down the inside of my thigh.

Motherfucker.

CHAPTER THIRTY-ONE

SIMON

T yler has a fucking death wish. He must, to have pulled that stunt. I was sure Marcus was about to grab a knife and go after him, but after Ty pulls out of the driveway, Marcus smirks and mumbles. *"Touché, motherfucker."*

Before anyone else can do anything, Shaun scoops Cherry up and takes her to the bathroom, where he helps her shower. He leaves the door open so we can hear them chatting and laughing, and eventually, they re-emerge, and our girl is clean and wearing Shaun's t-shirt.

For a moment, no one speaks, and Cherry starts biting her thumbnail. She doesn't do that often, but I've noticed her do it a few times. A nervous habit, perhaps?

Looks like it's up to the Hastinator to break the ice.

"Did he wear you out, Cherry?"

Her chocolate eyes find mine, and she drops her hand back to her side.

"Nope. You know me, Sy. I'm insatiable."

"So do you wanna play Simon Says, or would you rather have a quiet night? Maybe a movie?"

"Definitely, Simon Says." She grins, and I beam back at her.

I would have been happy with a movie night if that's what she wanted. I don't care as long as I'm with her, learning more about the inner workings of Rhys George.

"Ok. Simon Says, it's time for you to receive your spanking from Bossi."

Her brows shoot up, and she looks at Shaun before looking back at me. "Shaun is playing Simon Says, too?"

"We all are. There's been too much tension tonight. Simon Says we need to have fun since we are going home tomorrow."

Cherry nods, smiling before looking to the other guys for their reaction. No one complains.

"Where should we play?" Shaun asks, and I point to the floor.

"Right here. Simon says, Cherry, take the t-shirt off and bend over the coffee table."

The sexiest fucking grin morphs my girl's face. "I fucking love demanding Simon. Makes Kitty ravenous."

"Kitty is always ravenous," Garrett speaks for the first time, pushing the couch back a little to give Cherry room as she drops the t-shirt to the floor and bends over the coffee table, pointing her bare arse at us.

Fuck, my dick goes instantly hard. I love how Cherry isn't shy about showing her body to us. She even parts her legs, giving us a glimpse of her satin folds.

I glance at the others, and Shaun is grinning while Garrett licks his lips, tilting his head as his eyes lock between her legs. Marcus no longer looks angry, and he sits on one of the bar stools, readjusting his dick in his pants.

I clear my throat before speaking, my arousal affecting my voice. "Simon says, Bossi, give Cherry the spanking she deserves."

At my words, Cherry sticks her arse out further, like she's hungry to feel the sting of a palm on her arse, and Shaun moves forward to take his place.

"So, you said there better be an orgasm attached to the spanking," Shaun speaks to our girl as he runs his hand over Cherry's arse. "And there will be, but I won't be giving it to you. The orgasm, that is. I'll deliver the spanking, though."

Cherry glances over her shoulder at him. "Who will be delivering the orgasm?"

"You will," Shaun states as he pulls his hand back. "Brace yourself, Kitten."

She frowns as she turns back, preparing for the spank, and a moment later, Shaun's hand slaps down hard on her right cheek. I'm expecting her to cry out, but instead, she moans. Then Shaun does it again, harder this time. Cherry throws her head back, another moan escaping, and Shaun bends down to take a look between Cherry's legs.

Grinning, he stands up, moving out of the way so we can see, and he points to her glistening lips. "You're wet, Kitten. Are you ready to get off, or do you want my hand on your arse again?"

"Again." She pants, and fuuuuccck, my dick wants in, like right fucking now. I'll never get enough of this girl.

Smirking, Bossi nods before slapping her arse again two more times. By the time he's removing his hand from her cheek, Cherry is panting.

"Simon says, it's time for Cherry to come." I declare, and Bossi nods over at me with a grin as he pulls our girl up to stand from the coffee table.

"Into the bedroom, Kitten." He demands, and she eyes him warily for a moment before strutting through the living area to enter the main bedroom, where we put the mattress back on the bed earlier. Marcus and Garrett are quiet, but they follow Bossi and me as we trail Cherry, filling the small space.

"So, how exactly am I getting myself off?" Cherry asks, pouting. "You know it will be quicker if one of you do it. Kitty doesn't crave my touch like she craves yours."

I'm about to put my hand up to take one for the team, but Shaun beats me to it.

"You remember when you told me about how you got yourself off at home? And you said you used your bed?"

Instantly, Cherry's face turns bright red, and Shaun chuckles. "Yeah, you remember. I want you to show me. Show us." Shaun gestures to the rest of us. "How you get off on your bed?"

I'm a little confused. Don't most people get themselves off on their bed? A shower is probably the other place people do that. So, are we gonna watch Cherry masturbate on the bed?

"Seriously? I'm not sure that's something you want to see." She complains, and Bossi nods.

"Fuck yes, seriously. Show us exactly how you do it. I don't think any of us have seen that before. Not even on the porn we watch."

Cherry giggles. "You're not watching the right porn then, Cass."

"I'm confused." Garrett finally speaks, and Cherry nods.

"Let me unconfuse you then." She glances down at the bed, moving to the end corner, and she flips the quilt back, so all that is there is the sheet-covered mattress. Placing her hand on the corner of the mattress, she pushes down a few times before smiling. "Yeah, this will work well. It's nice and firm."

"Where should we go?" I ask, and Cherry turns back to me.

"Well, firstly, the four of you have on too many clothes. I'm gonna need a visual."

She doesn't have to ask twice. I move quickly, getting my gear off, and Bossi isn't far behind me. Garrett takes his shirt and pants off, leaving his jocks on, while Marcus just shrugs his shirt off.

Cherry's eyes rake over each of us, her eyes dark with desire as she bites her bottom lip.

"Naked guys on the bed. Half-naked can just watch."

Oooh, yesss. That's me. I'm Naked Guy. So is Bossi, so we both sit on each side of the bed as Marcus and Garrett hover behind Cherry.

"Hands on dicks, please." She grins, and, of course, we comply. I don't squeeze Conan too tightly, though. I'm about ready to burst.

Cherry leans over the corner of the mattress then, placing her hands on the mattress in front while spreading her legs and moving forward. Then she presses her sweet pussy to the corner of the mattress and starts to move her hips back and forth.

Yep. I nearly fucking explode.

Think of gross things. Think of gross things. Think of gross things.

My eyes dart from Kitten's face to between her legs, where her folds part over the corner of the mattress and shift back and forth. Fuck, I have been watching the wrong porn. This is hot.

"Sy." She pants. "Lay down in front of me."

Fuck yes, I move like a fire is under my arse and lay down on the mattress, watching her cunt as her pace picks up.

"Cass. Kneel on the bed next to Simon." She pants again, and I frown as the bed dips, looking up to see Bossi's cock bobbing above me as he moves. Fuck, Conan just got harder.

"What now, Kitten?" Bossi asks, and she grins wickedly.

"Cass, wrap your hand around Simon's cock."

My mouth drops open as my brows shoot up. I'm about to say no because I don't want Bossi doing anything he doesn't want to do. Sure, I gave him a blow job, but I wanted to do that. And receiving is very different from giving in this situation.

"Only if you're both happy to do that," Cherry adds quickly. "I'm not making anyone do anything they don't want to do. So, if you do it, it has to be because you want to, and not because you are just trying to please me."

My eyes dart up to Bossi, who's looking down at me, and he shrugs. "I'm game if you are."

"Ah…. Ummm…" Just fucking say the words, you coward! Say yes! Yes, Shaun, I want to feel your hand around my cock. Yes, I want to feel your mouth around it and see your face when you drink down my cum, and yes, I want you to sink that cock deep inside my arse. JUST FUCKING SAY IT!

"Sy." Cherry pants. "This is a safe place. *I* want what *you* want."

I nod and return my gaze to my mate, and push the words past my lips. "Yeah, I'm game."

Cherry moans loud, and Garrett curses behind her.

"I'm not trying to be a downer here, but I'm not ready to see that again."

Cherry looks over her shoulder and nods. "Sit on the floor behind me then, Big Guy. Sit nice and close so you can see all of me from the back."

Garrett nods, moving quickly behind her, and then bites her left arse cheek before disappearing from sight.

"Marcus? You good?" She pants and I look over to see Marcus sitting in the armchair in the corner, his hand down his pants as he watches on. "All g, Rhee."

"Ok. Let's do this." Cherry announces, picking up the pace as she rubs herself against the mattress.

My hand is already around my dick, so I jump when I feel Shaun's hand come over the top of mine.

"My turn." Shaun's voice is low, so just me and Cherry can hear, and I ease my grip, moving my hand to my side. Shaun is there, though, his bare thighs pressed up against my side, so I rest my hand on his thigh, and his hand tightens around my cock.

I hiss as Cherry moans, my eyes darting from the wet patch on the bed where she friction fucks, to my dick with the very masculine hand of my mate's wrapped around it.

"Fuck. I'm not going to last." I admit, and Cherry moans again.

"Yes. Fuck his hand, Sy. Let yourself go."

I want to do what she says and just let go, but I also don't want this to end.

"Fuck." Shaun curses, and my eyes lock with his. "I wanna taste it."

"Oh my God, yes." Cherry cries, and I nod quickly, knowing I'm about to fucking explode.

Shaun moves fast, shifting on the bed to lower his head, and a moment later, I watch his lips part, and my dick sinks into his mouth. My nuts instantly tighten, and as I feel the first wave of my orgasm, I feel the press of Bossi's cock against my hand. I don't think. I act and wrap my hand around it, pumping quickly as I groan through my climax.

Cherry is crying out next to me, and as the ropes of my cum die off, Bossi lifts his head, his eyes wide.

"I'm gonna blow."

"Yes!" Cherry yells, leaping on the bed next to me, pressing her face against mine as she lies down.

"Feed us, Cass." She begs, and as I continue to pump my mate's cock, he kneels over us and throws his head back as his cum shoots over our faces.

Chapter Thirty-Two

Rhys

I 'm still licking Shaun's cum from my mouth when I feel hands part my thighs. I'm so turned on from watching Simon and Shaun together that I don't complain because I need to come again. Pronto.

Garrett appears between my legs, holding up the knife he showed me a picture of earlier. It's not as big as it looked in the picture, but it sure looks sharp.

"I'm gonna fuck you with it first, Baby Girl. Ok?" He slides a blade cover over the sharp blade and then holds that part in his hand, showing me the hilt he said he would fuck me with.

"Yes, Mr Cole," I respond, and his nostrils flare. Garrett and Ty are similar. They are both dominating, in a different way, to Simon. He likes to order people around but be part of the fun. Ty and Garrett like to dominate until their subject is nearly spent before they take anything for themselves. I wanna have both of them alone in the bedroom one day, just like Ty suggested earlier. Fuck, to be totally consumed by them both would be the ultimate.

"You're going to fuck her with a knife?" Simon asks, and Garrett grins wickedly. He's like walking sin.

"You don't have to watch if you can't handle it, Hastings." Garrett rasps, his voice husky with arousal.

"Yeah-Nah. I'm not leaving. I'm here for it." Sy responds, sitting up on the bed next to Shaun.

"Are you still wet, Baby Girl?" Garrett asks, and I nod but turn my head to look at Sy and Cass.

"Here we go then."

I feel the cold metal of the hilt as Garrett drags it up the inside of my thigh, teasing me. I part my thighs wider, my eyes darting between Sy and Cass, with another request on the tip of my tongue.

"Say what you want, Kitten." Shaun knows me too well, and fucking butterflies fill my tummy.

"Kiss," I whisper, and they both frown, leaning in closer to me. The hilt of the knife presses against my entrance, and I dart my eyes back to Garrett to see him watching me and I nod as my chest rises and falls in anticipation. With another grin, Garrett eases the hilt inside Kitty.

A loud moan escapes me as the object hits deep. I dart my eyes back to Sy and Cass, and Cass raises his brows in question.

"Kiss," I say louder.

"You want a kiss?" Shaun asks, but I shake my head.

"You two." I pant. "Kiss."

Both their brows shoot high, and Shaun shakes his head. "Not today, Kitten. Baby steps, yeah?"

I nod. "Yeah, ok. I'll take the…" I moan as pleasure builds, and Garrett's tongue flicks over my clit, making it hard for me to speak. "I'll take the kiss."

Grinning, Shaun jumps off the bed and comes to the end, leaning over to kiss me as I gyrate Kitty, picking up the pace. His lips are soft and hot, and I lose myself in his kiss as I fuck the knife in Garrett's hand. When Shaun pulls back, I barely take a breath before Simon's lips are on mine. Their kisses are different yet ignite the same heat in me, and I fall victim to Sy's long tongue. I suck on it, wrapping my lips around it, causing him to groan. He starts moving it in and out of my mouth, in rhythm with Garrett's pace, and when Shaun latches onto my nipple, I crash hard.

I moan over Sy's tongue, still sucking on it, and moments later, I release him and look down to see Garrett slip the knife free.

"Chuck those towels over here." Garrett holds his hand out toward Marcus, and I watch as Marcus throws a bundle of towels to his mate.

"What are the towels for?" Simon asks, and Garrett grins down at me as he answers.

"Because things are about to get really fucking messy."

Garrett shoos Simon off the bed, and he lays out the towels before gesturing his head to them. "On you hop, Baby Girl."

I do a roll that sticks my arse right out as I go, and Garrett's hand comes down hard on my arse before I can make it over.

Kitty fucking stirs awake again like the ravenous animal she is, and by the time I've positioned myself, Garrett has pulled the cover off the blade.

"Dude, what are you gonna do with that?" Simon asks, and Garrett looks at me again as he responds.

"Make her bleed."

I moan, and he parts my legs, positioning himself between them. His fucking monster cock is as hard as stone, and pre-cum balls at the tip. I want to lick it, the thought sending flashes of yesterday when he fucked my mouth and throat, pushing me further than I've ever been pushed. I fucking loved it. I love his dick, and I love him. I think I'd let Garrett Cole do anything he wants to me.

"Is anyone else concerned about this?" Simon asks, and I shake my head.

"It's ok, Sy. You and me like some food and foot play. And Garrett and me like some blood play. No one gets hurt."

I glance up to see Simon hover over my head, his eyes on Garrett, so I look back down to Garrett. He's looking between my legs. Not at my Kitty, but at my thighs.

"I won't ask you to take your rod out." Garrett looks up then. "You need the contraception with all this cum flowing. So for now, this will have to do." He holds the knife up. "Are you ready, Baby Girl?"

"Yes, Mr Cole. Make me bleed."

Garrett lowers the blade as his other hand pulls my skin taut on the inside of my thigh. I can feel the moment the blade glides over my skin. It stings, but in a good way, and the warm sensation of blood trickles down my skin to the towel below.

"You going ok?" Garrett asks, his voice a deeper gravel than usual.

"Yes. Keep going." I breathe through my panting, and he does as I ask, returning the blade to my skin on my other thigh to make a fine but not deep cut.

I grab my tits, rolling my nipples as the pain increases, and when Garrett is done, he lays the knife on the side table. Anticipation grips me, making me impatient. I want to tell Garrett to hurry up, but I also never want this night to end, so I hold my tongue.

Garrett's fingers dip between my legs, and he starts smearing my blood over my thighs and up to my Kitty. He circles my clit, and I cry out as pleasure overtakes me once again. His growl is my only warning before his hot mouth latches onto my clit, and he kisses it passionately, his tongue devouring the blood from my needy little bud.

"Fuck, Gar." I moan, my hands gripping his hair.

His fingers join the party then, two sinking deep inside. I writhe and gyrate and seek more, always more. When he removes his fingers and his molten lips from my needy Kitty, I feel the loss instantly. Rising up, Garrett shows me his fingers, the two that were inside me. They are coated in blood and my juices, and he hovers them over my mouth.

"Open."

Oh yes, Mr Cole and Daddy are going to destroy me.

I drop my lips open and stick my tongue out as he eases his fingers inside.

"Can you taste that, Baby Girl? Your blood? Your pussy?"

I nod around his fingers, and he sinks them deeper.

"Did you like it when I choked you on my cock yesterday?"

I nod again, relaxing my throat as he pushes past my gag reflex. It's hard to fight it, and my body does what it must, the gag a gurgle around his fingers.

"Fuck, you're perfect." Garrett hisses before removing his fingers and sucking them into his mouth.

I suck in air, trying to recompose myself, but my big guy doesn't give me a long reprieve, and before I know it, he is pressing that mammoth beast of his at my entrance.

"Legs wide." He grits between his teeth, and I open myself more, doing as he asks.

It doesn't take much for his big dick to slide in with how slick I am, and overwhelming fullness sends me senseless as he starts to thrust. With the length and girth he fucks me with, I'm instantly helpless to do anything but take it and hold on. Over and over, he slides home, his icy-blues darting from my face to where he disappears inside me.

Another growl rips from his lips as he lifts me, spinning us around so he's sitting on the bed and I'm straddling him. I try to take over and move, but his big hands grip my hips, and he does all the work. His pace picks up fast, and all I can do is hold on for dear life as he pistons into me.

His hand dips between us, and he swipes up some more blood from my thighs before smearing it over my lips and chin. I do the same to him, swiping up more of my blood and smearing his face.

"You look fucking perfect." He growls before taking my lips in his. The metallic taste of blood mingles with our tongues, and it's all I need to start pulsing around his cock as another O hits me.

My orgasm milks Garrett of his, his guttural yell loud in the small space, and when we finally come down from the cloud we were on, I see Shaun and Simon cleaning themselves up after getting themselves off.

With my chest rising and falling rapidly, I give Garrett a moment between the two of us, kissing him again.

"I'm all in, Rhys. No matter what." His whisper against my ear makes me pull back, and I study his eyes as they study mine.

"Me too." I smile, and he brushes my hair back.

"Bossi, grab your phone," Garrett demands, and Shaun doesn't ask why. He darts out of the bedroom, only to return a moment later with his phone.

"Take a photo of our faces and send it to me," Garrett instructs, and I drag my gaze from him to look at Shaun. He has the biggest grin on his face as he holds up his phone, snapping a few pictures.

Turning his phone to us, Shaun shows us the pictures, and I see now what they can see. Blood smeared over my face and mouth. I look like an animal, much like that first day me and Garrett hooked up.

"Send me the pictures too, please. I wanna make it my background on my phone."

The guys chuckle at me, and for the first time in ages, Marcus speaks.

"She's mine for the night. You can go now."

My brows shoot up as Simon complains.

"Why do you get her to yourself?"

Marcus stands from the chair, still sporting a very hard boner under his sweatpants. "I'm struggling a little. This Tyler stuff is screwing with my head. I just..." His head tips forwards as he struggles for words. "I just need a reminder that Rhee loves me as much as the rest of you."

His admission is raw and honest, and I know it was hard for him to say.

"Marc," I say quietly as I climb off Garrett's lap. I ignore the warm fluid running down my thigh once again, and I cross the room. His dark eyes look up to meet mine, and I can see the emotion swimming in them.

"I'm sorry that I get so territorial with you. I'm sorry that I couldn't just fucking wait to find out who Tyler is. I almost wish I didn't go there tonight."

"Why?" I reach out, taking his hand in mine, and instantly our fingers entwine.

"Seeing him without a mask, his identity aside, I also saw how much the two of you love each other. I know you love all of us, but I'm scared that you'll love me the least because I don't try to dominate you the way Tyler does, or want to inflict pain the way Gaz does, or

298

be into different kinks like Simon, or adventurous like Bossi. I don't know if I'll ever be able to touch another guy the way Hastings and Bossi did for you."

"Marcus." My heart breaks at his insecurities. This must have been what he wanted to talk to me about. He's definitely pissed about not knowing Tyler was his PE teacher, but his feelings of inadequacy are at the forefront, and I hate that he feels this way. "You all have some things in common, and you all are completely different in other ways. Just because you don't want to slice my skin open, or kiss another guy because I'd like that, doesn't mean you're not a major contributor to this relationship. You are what keeps me grounded, Marcus. You are the quiet moments. The way you love to watch turns me on so bad. I love knowing your eyes are on me, watching my expression, studying how my body reacts. And you're possessive as fuck. I fucking love that about you. You make me feel protected. Safe. This isn't just about sex, Marcus. I love *you*. And if I'm being honest, I loved you back when the two of us were fooling around. You're the first person I've ever loved like that, and these insecurities you're feeling come from how fucked up *I* am. I'm sorry for every ounce of pain I've caused you, and I swear I'll spend the rest of my life showing you just how important you are to me."

His eyes glass over as he stares at me, and I wish I knew what he was thinking.

"Guys?" I call to the others, and Shaun, Garrett and Simon all say "*yeah*" at the same time. "Do you mind if I spend the night alone with Marcus?"

"Not at all, Baby Girl." Garrett's deep rumble comes from my left. "Grady needs you. We are a family now, so we need to work together to make sure everyone is happy."

I glance up to see Garrett, still smeared with blood, looking like a warrior. "Thanks, Mr Cole."

He grins and leans down, pressing his lips to mine before stepping back to let Simon get to me.

"Thank you." Simon's eyes dip to the floor as his face flushes red when he speaks.

"What for?" I frown, confused.

"Not being freaked out by the things I want to do in the bedroom."

My smile is wide as I lean forward and press my forehead to his. "Like Gar said. We are a family. Everyone's feelings and desires are important. This isn't just about me." And fuck does it feel good to say that. It's like I'm letting go of some of my selfishness.

Simon smiles and nods, giving me a quick kiss before turning his eyes to Marcus. "I get it, you know. Not feeling like you fit in or that you're enough. But Cole is right. We are a family now, and I think it's important that each of us is heard when needed and maybe even reminded that we are loved."

"Damn Hastings. I didn't know you were so deep." Marcus adds, and Simon chuckles, playfully shoving Marcus' shoulder.

"Yes, you fucking did."

They all laugh.

"Right, well, I'm happy to leave you two alone for the night." Shaun agrees. "If there's anyone here that deserves to have our girl to himself, it's you, Grady. I still feel fucking bad about everything."

"I guess Ty was right about one thing earlier tonight." Marcus shifts in front of me, running his hand through his thick, dark hair.

"What's that?" Shaun asks.

"The past is the past. We can't change it. We may as well focus on now and the future."

"Too right." Garrett agrees, and I shoot him a wink as I fight back my emotions.

A small grin tugs at Marcus' lips as he cups my blood-smeared face, gaining my attention again. "You look vicious right now."

Shaun, Simon and Garrett come to stand beside Marcus, taking me in too.

"She does." Shaun agrees. "Our Vicious Kitten."

Marcus nods. "Yes. Our Vicious Kitten."

Chapter Thirty-Three

RHYS

M y night with Marcus is quiet, loving, and nurturing. Something I didn't realise until recently that I needed. I was speaking the truth when I said Marcus gives me the quiet moments. He gives me aftercare. I don't think he understands how much I need that. After all the crazy freaky highs I try to reach through sex, I need to come down. And sometimes, the comedown is so hard that the only way I can deal with it is to seek the high again.

Cue addiction.

He also gives me a sense of security. Yes, he's kind of possessive, but that means his eyes are always on me, making sure I'm ok. He was the one that noticed I was having trouble with the guys getting too close when we first went camping. He could see my attempt to hide my panic each time they got close. I was so messed up after the humiliation at the Feast, and I couldn't fathom being touched intimately.

It's Marcus' possessiveness that led him to steal a fucking boat to hunt me down, and it's the same possessiveness that let him see how much Ty and I care for each other. Marcus is the rationality when I'm anything but, and I absolutely need him and love him.

When the guys left us alone last night, he took me to the bathroom and showered with me, not saying anything as he washed the blood from my mouth and used gentle hands to clean between my legs. He washed my hair and combed through conditioner, his gentle touch igniting my vulnerable emotions. He even handed me a toothbrush and washed his own hair as he silently watched me brush my teeth in the shower.

Once I was clean, he kissed me. It was soft. Gentle. Intoxicating. It stirred butterflies deep in my belly and ignited me from the inside. Then he made love to me right there in the shower. There's no other way to put it, and even saying those words now, I don't feel like cringing because it was fucking beautiful.

There's no doubt that I like to fuck. Dirty, sweaty, filthy sex in all the forbidden ways. It can be utterly consuming. Something I'm absolutely addicted to. Yet this, with Marcus, was just as consuming. I'd felt it before with Ty and even Shaun, but with Marcus, it was like I handed over the key to my soul.

I cried a little afterwards, feeling pathetic. Marcus didn't see it that way, though. He dried my tears and pressed kisses to my burning hot cheeks, and when I managed to pull my shit together, he dried me and took me to bed.

We chatted quietly in the dark for a while about crazy things, like the future. He told me that he's not sure what he wants to do when we finish high school, and he asked me about my photography and if that's what I want to do after we graduate. Then he told me that no matter what I choose to do with my future, he'll be right by my side, even if he has to share me. We talked for so long with my face nuzzled into his neck, our bodies bare and entwined under the blanket. His fingers ran lazily up and down my arm, and before I even realised, I fell asleep in his arms.

The sun is up again now, bright rays beaming in from the gap in the curtain. It's going to be another mild spring day, and the idea spreads my lips into a grin.

Everything feels right. Even though the events of last night at Ty's house weren't a good situation, I feel so much better knowing I don't have to keep that secret from the guys anymore. There are no secrets now. They know everything, and they are still here.

I feel... happy. I'm pretty sure that's what this feeling is. It's a powerful feeling. I know there is still the Julie and Brian stuff, and that stupid prick Master Hill and his threats with the videos to my 'rents. But you know what? Not even they can bring me down. The cops are on to all of them, and soon they will be just an ugly memory that I'll push to the back of my mind and never think of again.

"You're awake?" Marcus rasps quietly against my ear before he nips it.

"Yep." I giggle, turning my head from the filtering rays of sun to take in my possessive lover.

His hair is dishevelled, and I don't think I've ever seen Marcus Grady look sexier.

"You, ok?" He asks, his brow furrowing in concern.

"Actually, I don't think I've ever been better."

His white teeth appear as he grins. "Must be because you woke up next to me."

I laugh before he grips the back of my head and kisses me.

Unfortunately, our kiss gets interrupted by the door flying open, and Simon barges in, hyped up full of playful energy.

"You guys. Check this out." He bounds onto the bed, holding up a phone and throws himself down, causing us to separate as he worms his way between us, laying his head on the pillow. "Bossi was sleepwalking last night. I recorded it."

"What?" I gasp, my eyes wide. "He was sleepwalking?"

"Yeah. It was funny as fuck." Simon chuckles before hitting play on his phone.

Shaun is on the screen, walking around the living area in just his jocks, his dark curls in disarray, and his eyes looking distant.

"Squiggle toothpicks… in the butt holes… chicken trucks do it."

The familiar shuffled walk I saw the first night I stayed at Shaun's house when he was sleepwalking shoots a pang of worry through my chest. Yeah, it's funny to watch, but his brother Derek told me he only sleepwalks when he's really worried about something.

As Marcus and Simon laugh at the video playing, I notice Shaun hovering in the doorway, frowning.

"Come here." I sit up, ignoring the fact that my tits are now exposed with the blanket bunched around my waist.

Steel-grey eyes connect with mine, and Shaun steps into the room, making his way to my side of the bed. As soon as he's within arm's reach, I tug him down and climb into his lap, cupping both sides of his face.

"Talk to me," I whisper.

His eyes portray his exhaustion even though he offers me a sexy grin and his hands grip my bare arse.

"I'm ok, Kitten."

I squint at him. "Liar. You only sleepwalk when you are worried about something." I brush his curls back from his eyes. "Let me help you for once."

He shrugs. "I'm not entirely sure what's bugging me." He rasps quietly so the other two can't hear. "I just have a bad feeling. It could be from the stuff that went down last night. I was worried that it might split the group up."

I nod. "I was terrified of that happening, too," I admit. "We're ok, though. Things will work out."

"You still love us? All of us?"

My brows shoot up at Shaun's question. "Hell yes. More than ever." I press my forehead to his. "I will fight for us, Cass. You and the others are my family."

"I'm so fucking in love with you, Rhys." My heart melts hearing him say my name. It's always Kitten these days, which I love, but for some reason, hearing him call me Rhys means so much more. "I want a future with you. I never want to live a day without you in my life, loving me back."

I lean back to peer into his steel-greys, which are swimming with so much emotion. It's emotion I'm not used to seeing on Shaun. He's always so damn confident.

"Even after I take my last breath on this earth when I'm old and frail, my love for you will continue on always, Shaun."

His lip quirks at the corner, and I shoot him a smiling frown.

"What?"

"I'm just imagining you old and frail getting railed by us frail old men." He grins, and I giggle until I realise that by the time I'm old and frail, there might not be five guys railing me because Ty might already be gone from this world.

The thought sends wetness to my eyes, and my heart feels like it's about to splinter apart.

"Hey. Where did your thoughts go?" Shaun cups my cheek, his eyes dancing between mine.

"Ty might not be there by the time we are old and frail," I whisper before biting my lower lip to hold back my irrational emotions.

"Don't think about it, Rhys. It's a long time away, and by then, we would have all lived a full life together."

"I know it's weird to think about, but I can't imagine a world without any of you guys in it," I admit, and he nods.

"I get it. I feel the same way, but we have many years ahead of us. Even old man Tyler."

I grin at Shaun's cheeky expression. "I'm going to tell him you called him that."

He shrugs. "That's fine. I'll happily deliver you another spanking after you blab to him."

I throw my head back, laughing. And he leans in, catching my lips with his. Our kiss is slow and sensual and stirs Kitty awake in an instant. Even the girls are on board, pressing against Shaun's chest as my nipples pebble.

Breaking the kiss, Shaun leans back and glances down between our bodies. "It's really hard to ignore your nakedness right now." He gives my arse a little squeeze, which causes me to roll my hips with need.

I grin back and press my forehead to his. "I'm yours, Cass. Do with me what you will."

That ignites a huge smile on his face, and he nips at my lips.

"I just got a message from Lexi." Garrett's voice comes from the doorway, gaining our attention. "Ayden will be here in an hour to pick Marcus and Rhys up."

"Boo." I pout, and the guys chuckle.

"Derek will be here around that time, too. I guess we need to pack up and clean this place?" Shaun sighs, and my pout gets bigger.

"Yep. Let's get to it." Simon whines like he'd rather pry his eyes out.

So we do the mundane tasks of getting ready, packing our things and cleaning this place. The music Shaun plays through his Bluetooth speaker, and the singing attempts by Simon make the tasks less painful and more amusing.

An appreciation for the domestic nature of it warms my chest. It's fun doing these things with my guys. I find myself watching how they work together and the banter that flows, my mind picturing times like this in our future together. Older, with Ty joining in, as we live as a family.

I want that. So fucking much. It may not be what's perceived as normal or acceptable in society, but I don't care. It's right for us.

By the time we are done, and I'm waving out the window of Ayden's car to Shaun, Simon and Garrett, I'm feeling high on life. Confident, and dare I say it? A little invincible.

I snuggle into Marcus' side for the drive home, and as we eventually pull up outside my house, he gives me a kiss filled with promises. He wanted to walk me in, but since I only have one bag to carry, given that we ate all the food Dad sent me with, I insist that he stay in the car, and I wave from the portico of my front door as Ayden drives off with my Marcus.

I can't seem to wipe the grin off my face as I key in the code to unlock the front door. Inside is quiet, and a quick glance in the study and my parents' bedroom shows they are empty.

"Hello?" I call into the silent house and get no response.

Dropping my bag to the tiled floor, I unlace my Docs and toe them off before hoisting up my bag and moving to the kitchen. The dishwasher is running, and as always, the place is spotless. There's a note on the counter, so I lift it up to read.

Rhys, your dad, and I had a last-minute appointment to go to in the city.
We should be back before dinner.
The twins are at the Martin's for a sleepover, and Charlotte is out with friends.
I hope you had a good weekend.
Text me to let me know you're home safe.
Xoxo Mum

I smile at the note. I love seeing *Mum* written on it, and not Cin or Cynthia. The sight warms my chest even more, and I swear my smile grows wider.

Fuck, I feel emotional as shit, but in a good way. It's weird, but I'm totally embracing it.

I shoot Mum a text to say that I'm home and debate whether to message the guys to let them know I'll be home alone for the afternoon but think better of it. I'd love to see them, but I don't want to be too smothering either. They need their own time. And time together without me.

Maybe I'll call Tillie and Bell and catch up with them. I do feel bad for giving all my attention to the guys lately. Some girl time is overdue.

I shoot Tillie and Bell a message and take my bag to my bedroom before coming back to the kitchen in search of food. I'm rummaging through the fridge when a noise behind me makes me freeze. Frowning, I straighten, the feeling that I'm not alone setting off alarm bells in my head.

Snapping my head around quickly, I gasp at the figure standing mere feet away.

"Hello, Patrice."

"What the fuck are you doing here?" I hiss at my old foster mum, Julie, who looks all sorts of wrong standing in the kitchen of the home my parents have given me. Her hair is brown, not blonde like it used to be. It's shorter. Like a boy's cut hidden under the cap she is wearing low on her head. Probably to hide her identity.

"I'm here to see you. A visit that's well overdue. Don't you think?"

I curl my lip in a snarl. "Get the fuck out of my house!" I yell as loud as I can in the hopes that if a neighbour is near, they might hear me.

"Now, now. Haven't your parents taught you to be kind to guests? Where's your hospitality?" Julie laughs with a sneer.

"If you don't leave, I'll call the police." I hiss, and she laughs again.

"What with? This?" She holds up her hand, and there, clasped in her grip, is my phone.

Fuck! She must have grabbed it off the bench where I left it.

What do I do now? Think! Think! Think!

Julie laughs again, obviously reading my expression and loving the fucking reaction.

"Oh, Patrice. Do you really think you can smear my name on a podcast and TikTok and get away with it? Un-fucking-likely."

"What do you want?" I'm surprised my voice sounds as confident as it does, given how fast my heart is racing right now.

"I'm so glad you asked, Patty." She smiles wide, her smoke-stained teeth off-putting to her make-up-clad face. "I want *you* to pay. You took my husband away from me. Now you have ruined my lucrative business of whoring homeless girls and making illicit movies. So now, I've come to collect."

I'm not sure what she means by collect, but I know I need to get the fuck away from her, like now.

I dart to my left, rounding the kitchen counter before stabbing pain shoots through my skull, and I fly backwards, crashing to the floor. Julie leaps on me, some strands of my long dark hair in her grip as she swings her fist at my face. I try to block her blows, but some make it past my hands, and I realise I need to try to get away or fight back. This crazy woman is going to kill me.

Balling my fist, I scream as hers makes contact with my cheek, and I drive mine into her temple. It must have been a good hit because she tumbles off me, and I use her distraction to scramble up and bolt towards the passage that leads to the front door.

I only make it a few steps before a body crashes into me, tackling me to the floor. My head slams hard on the tiles, and darkness rims my vision as I'm flipped over, and hands wrap around my throat. I try to think past the haze. What do I do?

I've watched a heap of TikTok's about self-defence, yet in this moment, I can't fucking think. I need to get her off me. I need to remove her hands from my throat.

A memory seeps in, and I react, slipping my hands up to my chest, and I shove them up and out quickly, breaking her connection with my neck. The action makes her fall forward, and I move quickly to the side, rolling myself on top of her this time. Then I scream and punch.

I swing my fists over and over, landing hits wherever I can, wanting Julie to pay for everything she has done.

It's too late when I realise we aren't alone.

The rustle of clothing behind me is all I hear before a hand holding a cloth cups my mouth and nose. I try to scream as an arm wraps around me from behind. Instead, I gasp, which is the wrong fucking thing to do as the strong chemical scent wafts up my nose and down my throat, and darkness rushes towards me, holding me prisoner.

CHAPTER THIRTY-FOUR

RHYS

D arkness swirls through my head, sucking me into a black hole of nothingness. I should probably stay there in that darkness, but this Vicious Kitten isn't willing to give up. So I fight the darkness, reaching for the faint glow of light in the distance. It rushes at me, jostling me, sounds loud and distorted before the darkness sucks me back in.

This happens over and over. The jostling. The loud, distorted sounds. The darkness.

I fight against my body, demanding it to function so I can figure out what the fuck is going on, and as the light comes at me again, I internally scream at myself to hold my eyes open. They are heavy, making it hard to keep them apart. I can feel my eyes roll back, but I blink, fighting to wake the fuck up. The jostling is back and feels real. My body moves in jarring motions, confusing me because I'm pretty sure I can't move.

I blink over and over, willing my sight to return. For the blur to clear. Sounds start filtering in. They are familiar sounds, yet I can't make my brain connect the dots. The jostling sensation turns almost rhythmic, and I focus on it, wondering why I can't feel my limbs. I stretch my senses out, trying to find my arms and legs. Their presence is hovering just out of reach, but I know they are there.

"Fuck yes."

A voice! I hear a voice! It's familiar. It's male. I just can't figure out who it belongs to.

"Get this angle."

The deep voice speaks again, and I blink again.

Fucking *see*, damn it!

The rhythmic jostling seems to speed up, and I hear a grunt.

Like a kick to my head, my brain, eyes and body all wake the fuck up at once.

No!

The first thing I recognise is the full feeling of being fucked. The second thing is remembering who owns that fucking voice. And the third thing is the sight of Master Hill looming over me while he fucks me.

"Stop!" I scream, trying to move my arms and legs, but I can't. They are restrained, just like the night at the Feast.

"Welcome to the party, Patty."

My eyes dart to the side to see Julie holding a camera, her brown gaze wild with excitement.

"What the…" I must be fucking delusional right now. This must be a nightmare. I'm not really here being raped by Master Hill while my old foster mum, Julie, the wife of my birth dad who is in prison for grooming and molesting me, is standing there filming it. This can't be real.

The sensation of fingernails digging into the flesh on my hips draws my drowsy eyes back to Master Hill, and I watch his face as he slams harder into me, pain stabbing me deep inside as my body tries to reject his intrusion.

"This was worth the wait." He grits between his teeth.

"Stop." I whimper as the realisation that this is *not* a dream, sinks in. "Please, stop," I beg, sounding weak.

Julie laughs, ignoring my plea, and moves the camera closer to my Kitty.

No. No. No. This can't be happening.

Don't ruin this for me. Don't take this from me.

Hot tears blur my eyes, and I tug on my arms and legs, not able to move an inch.

It's just a body. It's a vessel and nothing more. He can't get the important things like the love I share with my guys.

Oh my God, my guys. They don't know I've been taken. I have no idea what time it is and how long I've been here. As I cry, I try to focus on something else. Looking around the room doesn't help. I know where I am. I'm underneath Vixen's Lodge in the Master's sex dungeon. I'm so fucking close to Shaun right now, and he has no idea I'm here on the property next to his, being defiled by his neighbour.

Someone will come for me. Eventually. My parents will realise I'm missing. They will find me. They have to. Right?

A loud roar penetrates my thoughts, and I make the mistake of looking back at Master Hill to see his face contorted into the sickest kind of pleasure as he finishes inside me.

I suck in the whimper that wants to escape. I won't let them see my fear. Fuck them. I'm Rhys fucking George. I *am* sex. If they think they can use this against me, they have another thing coming.

The sick fuck pulls out from me, and I feel his seed ooze between my arse cheeks to pool on the red leather surface below me.

"That was perfect, Terry. Got me all hot and bothered." Julie smiles at him, and then he fists his hand in her hair and drags her in for a kiss.

I nearly gag because *ew*!

The door swings open behind them, and my eyes widen when I see Madam Vik and Brock come through the door. I wait for her to be shocked to see Julie and Master Hill kissing, to see me chained to the sex bench, but they both smile.

"The house is locked up tight. Now we can all have some fun."

Madam Vik's words are like a slap in the face. I knew she was a sick bitch, but I never thought she was like this. Master Hill, yes. Absolutely, which is why I tried to avoid him. But Madam? No fucking way.

How fucking wrong I was.

Master Hill and Julie pull apart, and Madam Vik replaces the Master, kissing Julie deep, while Brock, sexy fucking Vin Diesel look-a-like Brock, starts pashing the Master.

Well, I've fucking seen it all now!

As they do whatever the fuck they are doing, I look up at my wrists to see what they are bound with. It's those leather cuffs that they used on me last time. I try to reach my right hand toward my left, but the chains are pulled taut. I can't move.

"Don't even bother trying to think about escaping, Kitten. There's no way out for you." Madam Vik's voice gains my attention, and I see the four of them looking at me while the video camera sits on the tripod off to the side. I know what the red light means. It's recording.

"Why are you doing this?" I ask, my voice raspy.

"You've made us wait too long, Kitten. I know your birthday is in April. What fun would it be for me to fuck you once you are legal?"

"You're sick!" I hiss, my top lip curling in a snarl.

"I'm sick? Really?" Master rounds the bench, coming to my side, reaching out and running his hands over my bare tits. "You're the one that used to enjoy fucking your daddy. You're the one that used to get turned on by sucking his cock. Sometimes you were so horny that you would rub yourself on his leg while Julie cooked your dinner in the other room."

My chest rises and falls as nausea sweeps over me. "Stop!"

"But it's the truth." Julie sneers. "You have always been a whore, Patty. It got kind of pathetic, you know. As soon as you got home from school, you wanted to play games with Brian. He could tell you to do anything, and you did it."

"Stop," I whisper as my bottom lip wobbles. I don't want to hear this. I'm not that person anymore.

"Remember the time when we came over for dinner?" Madam Vik turns to Julie and laughs. "She wouldn't get off Brian's lap, so he took her into the playroom, and we watched them play through the window? I think Brian would pretend to be a sick patient in the hospital, and Patrice was his nurse, tasked to make him feel better."

"Yes, that's right." Julie turns to me. "Do you remember the window, Patty? It looked like a big mirror on the wall, but it actually went into the room we used to keep locked so you couldn't go in. That's where the video camera was set up. A couple of times a month, we would let people come in to watch the show. Fifty dollars per person. We made a killing."

Oh my God. It's worse than I thought.

"Brock." I lock eyes with the Feast's bouncer. The guy who, for a time, I thought was my friend. "Help me, please."

He shakes his head. "No way. Master has me lined up to make a pretty fucking hardcore porn movie with you that's gonna make me rich. No fucking way am I letting that slip through my fingers."

"What?"

Master chuckles. "Yes Kitten. We have so many plans for you. Tonight will be your last night in Fox Pines because tomorrow, you are going to your new home far away from here, and you will do what you do best. We have the most fucked up stuff organised for you."

A sob escapes, and they all fucking laugh.

No. I can't let them take me away from here. Ty. Marcus. Shaun. Simon. Garrett. I don't want to be apart from them. Or my family. My mum. My dad. Char or the twins. Lexi. Tillie or Bell. Fucking hell, I can't let them take me away.

I would rather die than do whatever it is they have planned for me. I won't let them destroy me like that.

"Clothes off," Master demands and for a moment, I'm confused, thinking I already have my clothes off, but then I realise he's talking to the others in the room. They obey, moving to the sides to get naked, and panic rushes through me.

What the fuck is happening now?

Once naked, they move off to the side, talking quietly together, and I strain my ears trying to hear, but it's no use. I tug on the restraints again, wanting to scream when they don't budge. Instead, I keep it in, letting it fester with my building rage.

When they are done, and even Master Hill is naked, which is weird as he usually wears his suit, I watch him stalk towards me, coming to stand between my legs again. A repulsive tremor works its way up my body as I see his stumpy, wrinkly, foreskined dick point to the ceiling. The urge to tease him about his dick is on the tip of my tongue, but the fact that I know he'll make me regret teasing him has me keeping the thought to myself.

"Last time, you managed to get away before I could take this virginity." He runs his fingers over the rose of my arse. "Tonight, you won't be so lucky. I'm claiming it, and I won't be gentle."

I laugh. Yep, pretty fucked up for the situation, but I laugh like I'm fucking happy. I am, in a way, but also, I'm pretty sure I'm a little cray-cray right now.

"What the fuck is so funny?" Master hisses, and I laugh again. That is until Julie darts beside me and fists my hair tight.

"Why are you laughing?" She hisses.

I don't stop laughing, ignoring the sting of hair ripping from my scalp.

"You're too late, Master." I laugh again. "I gave my arse virginity to my boyfriend. He fucked me soooo good with his big dick. Not like your stumpy, wrinkly little thing. I probably won't even feel it."

Whoops. I fucking said it out loud, didn't I?

"So, *Master*." I preen. "Looks like you won't be taking away any of my virginities."

His face reddens, and his nostrils flare as he grits his teeth. "Unlike my brother, who took your virginity when you were what? Eleven?"

What the fuck did he just say?

He starts laughing wickedly this time, and the others join him.

"What?" I snap.

"Oh, you didn't know?" Master looks smug as fuck as he looms over my bare Kitty. "Brian Bates is my brother. We share the same whore of a mother but have different dads. That's why we don't have the same surname."

What. The. Actual. Fuck!

"That makes me your uncle." He's wearing a shit-eating grin now, and after a moment of staring at him, I lose it.

I scream and thrash, baring my teeth, shaking the sex bench as I turn into a madwoman. Master throws his head back, laughing and Vik claps while Julie and Brock just grin.

I'm going to kill them all!

In my fit of rage, my hearing fades, and my vision turns almost red as I continue to fight against the bindings that hold me there. A scream rips from my throat the moment Master shoves his stumpy dick in my arse, not even using any lube. I fucking hope he grazed his dick.

Brock moves to the side of the bench up near my head, and Julie moves to the other side, gripping my head, her nails digging into my temple as she turns my head towards Brock.

Brock's dick presses against my lips, and I hold them shut, refusing his entry. It's such a pity that he is involved in this. He has a pretty cock and all. I've had it down my throat before, and I didn't hate it, but that's because I consented. This I don't consent to.

"Open your pretty mouth, Kitten," Brock growls, and I shoot a dagger up at him, clenching my teeth tight.

Master keeps fucking my arse, the pain there building, but it's the feeling of him trying to push his fucking fist into Kitty that makes me gasp. As soon as my lips part, Brock shoves his cock in my mouth to the hilt, inducing a gag.

Fuck these arseholes. My gagging belongs to my guys. To Ty and Garrett. Not these pricks. Brock's mistake is thinking I won't use my teeth. There's no turning back for me now. They can kill me before I'll let them destroy me.

I close my jaw tighter, pressing my teeth into the hard flesh of Brock's cock and bite. He yelps, and an explosion of pain rattles through my face as his fist connects. A wave of nausea rolls through me from the pain and disorientation, but his dick isn't in my mouth now, so I call that a win.

I close myself off, sending my thoughts to the things that make me happy, but the pain of Master's fist trying to breach me is too much, and I scream.

Something hot starts to splash on my face, and the smell of urine engulfs me. I have no control over my body's reaction, my stomach lurching as I begin to vomit.

Julie screeches, and through the blur of my vision, I see her standing over me and trying to leap away as I projectile in her direction.

She fucking pissed on me.

She's scared of my vom, but that will be the least of her problems when I get free.

The pressure in my Kitty and arse vanishes, and I hear Master bellowing to open the door right before he gags.

I fucking hate vomit. Like legit, hate it. But right now, it's my saving grace. It's what's repelling them from me, and note to fucking self, if I have to keep hurling my guts to keep them at bay, then that's what I'll fucking do.

Chapter Thirty-Five

TYLER

"Tell me she's with you!" The panicked scream of Cynthia Rogan on the other end of the line makes me freeze.

"What?"

"Tyler, please tell me she's with you, and I'm not overreacting at what I've come home to?" She cries, and I'm on my feet, running towards the door.

"I don't know what you mean, but I'm on my way. Talk to me. Tell me what's happening."

"Oh my God. She's not with you. She's not with her boyfriends. She's not with her other friends. Please tell me this isn't happening!"

"Cynthia! Calm down and tell me what exactly is going on." I jump into my car, gunning the engine and kicking up dirt as I speed down my driveway.

"She's not here. Her phone is here, but she's not. She doesn't go anywhere without her phone. Tillie said she was meant to meet Rhys here earlier, but when she got there, Rhys never answered the door. She assumed Rhys had ditched her to hang with her boyfriends."

"Have you called the police?" I bark, and she whimpers.

"Yes. William is on the phone with them now."

"I'm on my way. We will find her, Cynthia. I promise."

I end the call and dial Fuckboy.

"Is she with you?" Shaun asks the moment he answers.

"No. Tell me what you know."

"Well, Ayden and Marcus dropped her home just after twelve-thirty. She messaged her mum to let her know she was home. Then she messaged Tillie and asked her to come over in an hour, but when Tillie got there, Rhys didn't answer the door, so she left, thinking Rhys had ditched her to hang with us." Fuckboy sounds every bit the child he is right now. Fucking scared.

"And none of you heard from her once she was dropped home?" I ask.

"No. We've been sending messages through to our group chat, but she didn't join in. We thought she might be sleeping or something since she had such a big weekend."

"Fuck." I rasp. "Have the cops caught that Julie bitch yet?"

"No. I just heard Will speaking to the cops on the phone. She's still at large."

Fucking hell. It has to be Julie. She has Rhys. I just know it.

Fuckboy doesn't have any more information for me, so I break a thousand fucking laws speeding from Redfield Lake to Fox Pines. I make it in twenty minutes, which is fucking impressive, but man, they have to be the longest twenty minutes of my life. I slam the brakes on outside Kitten's home and fly from my car, up the front path and straight through the open doorway. There are cops everywhere, and I ignore their stares and follow the sounds of crying until I step through the doors of a home theatre.

All eyes turn to me, which includes Kitten's boy band and her parents.

"Oh my gosh, Tyler, please tell me you know something?"

They are the words of a desperate mother. She knows I don't have any information for her, but she can't help but ask.

I shake my head, and she collapses to the floor, her husband, Will, falling to his knees beside her.

"Has she had any more messages from Julie?" I ask, and Will looks up from the floor.

"No. Not that we could find on her phone."

"Fuck." I huff, dragging my hand through my hair.

Where the fuck are you, Kitten?

"We've got a few things." A police officer announces, walking into the room.

Cynthia leaps up off the floor, her hands coming together in front of her chest like she is about to prey.

"We found a small trace of blood on the tiles just in the passage near the kitchen. It's being sent for testing now. We should know if it belongs to Rhys soon. But the interesting thing we found was video footage from the doorbell ring camera across the road." The officer moves to the projector, and the video footage appears on the large screen a minute later.

We all watch silently as we see a car pull up at 11:30am, its windows tinted dark, and a woman with short dark hair gets out of the passenger side, wearing a cap low on her head. The footage isn't good enough to pick up facial features, but really there's only one person it can be.

As the car drives off, the lady doesn't go to the front door but walks around the back of the house. There are no fences up around their home since it's relatively new, so it's easy for anyone to get onto their property.

It's around 12:35pm when Ayden's car pulls up, and we see Rhys climb out from the backseat. She waves, her smile visible on the footage, before she turns and walks up the path carrying her bag. Then she turns again, and waves as Ayden's car pulls away, and then she turns back, opening the door and going inside.

Then there's nothing until 12:58pm, when the same car that pulled up earlier stops again, and a man wearing a cap gets out of the car and walks around the side of the house. His head is dipped low, so it's hard to see, but he looks like a big guy. The type of guy that works out a lot at the gym.

He reappears at 1:07pm, gets into his car, and then the garage door lifts. He reverses his car into the garage, and the door lowers again.

What the fuck?

At 1:17pm, the garage door lifts again, and the car pulls out and drives off as the door lowers.

The only thing that can be made out is the number plate of the car.

"Who are these people?" Cynthia cries.

"Julie." I bark, and the police officer turns to glare at me before moving his eyes back to Cynthia.

"Yes. We think it's most likely Julie. We have an APB out on the plates of the car. We should know more soon."

Cynthia breaks down crying again, and I fucking feel like it's time to start smashing shit.

"Who exactly are you?" The police officer asks.

"Tyler Foster. A family friend." The lie falls so easily from my lips, and I have to hope like fuck that Will and Cynthia don't throw me under the bus.

The police officer eyes me warily until Cynthia speaks up. "Yes, Ty is a close friend. I called him earlier to see if he'd heard from Rhys."

The officer frowns. "Does Rhys often call this man?"

Cynthia's face morphs into Principal mode, and she looks at the officer sternly. "Mr Zimora, I don't like your tone. Tyler is a very close friend and has been helping me with the heavy issues Rhys has been dealing with lately."

"My apologies, Mrs Rogan, but we have to check everyone." The officer directs his eyes over my shoulder, and I turn to see Shane Kent, Officer Shane Kent, otherwise known as Tradie from the Feast nights. His eyes widen slightly as he recognises me too, but he knows the situation between Rhys and me, well, kind of, and he schools his features as he looks back to Officer Zimora.

"Kent, please run a background check on this gentleman. Tyler Foster."

Fuck.

Shane nods and walks off, and I return my gaze to Rhys' parents.

"Tyler is right. I think that woman is Julie." Shaun speaks up. He's trying to keep the heat off me. Isn't that sweet? I'll have to thank Fuckboy later.

Officer Zimora sighs. "Yes, it's most likely Julie."

"Shouldn't you be out there looking for her!" Simon leaps up from his chair, his blonde hair a dishevelled mess from running his hands through it.

"We have everyone out looking, Simon. I can assure you of that." Officer Zimora responds.

"Well, they aren't doing a fucking good job, are they? My girl is still missing!"

Fuck, my heart sinks. This is bad. Rhys is in real danger if she's with Julie. She won't kill Rhys. At least not until she gets what she wants from her, but the things she's capable of doing, is something I don't want my girl to have to suffer through.

Not again.

CHAPTER THIRTY-SIX

RHYS

Vik shoves me through a bathroom door with one of her clawed hands while her other one pinches her nose. I want to laugh. This vile woman can handle drinking piss but can't handle a little vomit? I mean, it is pretty gross, and normally it would freak me out more, but since it's working in my favour, I'm rolling with it.

"Get in the shower, you stinky bitch." Vik hisses as I stumble my way across the small space to the shower.

I make the mistake of sneaking a glance at myself in the mirror as I pass it. There's red swelling puffing out my cheek with a trail of blood from where my skin has split open. My eye looks bruised too, but I can't be sure with the brief glance I get. My dark hair is matted, wet from Julie's piss, and one side is caked in my vomit, both of which dampen the naked skin of my body.

Stepping into the shower cubicle, I turn the water on, waiting for it to get warm, but a hand at my back shoves me under the cold stream, and a gasp escapes me.

"Hurry up and get clean. Use the shampoo and conditioner on the ledge. I expect you to smell like a fucking flower garden by the time you're done."

I've never heard Madam Vik sound so callous.

I pretend I'm crying, mainly because I can tell it pleases her to hear me like that. I have no interest in actually pleasing her, just fooling her. I'm working on the theory that if she thinks I'm weak, then she won't expect me to fight back. Something I totally plan on doing as soon as the opportunity arises.

"Why are you doing this?" I sob, sneaking a glance at her through the rapidly fogging glass.

She rolls her eyes. "Besides the fact that you got my brother-in-law locked up years ago, I get great enjoyment from torturing you like this. The money you will make us is also a big factor, but that can wait until I've had my fun."

A shiver runs up my spine. And here I thought Master Hill was the predator to be fearful of. His wife is just as fucking sick as he is. OMG, I can't believe I've eaten her out. I gag at the thought, trying to shake it off, so I don't waste any of my valuable stomach contents if there's any left. I may need it yet.

With the water now practically scolding my skin, I feel the biting sting between my legs from the two places Master Hill invaded. A real sob nearly bursts from my lips as the reality of what he did sinks in. I could let it consume me, but that will only make me weak. I need to be strong and smart right now. I need to figure out how to get away from them.

I go through the motions of trying to rinse all the vom from my hair and then shampoo it three times before conditioning it. I use shampoo on my body, too, hoping it will clean off the vileness that has tainted it, but deep down, I know that no soap will ever penetrate enough to wash that away.

Madam Vik is wearing a satin robe, and through the steam of the shower, I see she has pulled a phone out from the pocket and is scrolling through it.

I need that phone.

I search the shower cubicle for something I can use as a weapon. There are only the small shampoo and conditioner bottles, neither of which looks remotely weaponizing. Not in a deadly way, though a thought crosses my mind, and I eye the shampoo bottle again. That shit stings when it gets in your eyes.

The sinister smirk that widens my lips should scare me, but I embrace that shit. Sure, it could backfire, but I'm not willing to cower for the what if. Fuck that and fuck them.

Marcus and Shaun's words come back to me.

Our Vicious Kitten

I want to be her, now. Vicious. Animalistic. A fucking shock to the sickos under the roof of this toxic house.

The image of me and Garrett pops into my head. Blood smeared on our faces, making us look like vampires, or wild warriors who just fought a battle. We looked vicious, and I felt vicious, so I channel that feeling, letting the fury seep into my veins and sweep over my body.

I am *Vicious* Kitten. Hear me *roar*!

While Vik is distracted by her phone, I pour shampoo all over my hands before using my elbow to flip the water off. Even as I step out of the shower, Vik is foolish enough to assume she is safe. Her eyes still cast down at her phone screen.

I take another step forward, which gains her attention, and the moment her head starts to rise, I lunge for her with my arms outstretched. She flinches back when she realises, but it's not enough to get away from me, and a moment later, my shampoo slimy fingers press into her eyes.

Her lips part as a yell travels up her throat, and out of nowhere, I react, retracting my hands and giving her a right hook in her throat. Her eyes widen at the impact before her face contorts into grimacing pain. I'm not sure if it's from my punch or the sting of soap in her eyes, but she's not able to make much sound, so I call that a win.

Her hands grab at her throat and then move to her eyes, and I notice her phone is now lying face down on the cream-tiled floor. I need to do something before she regains some control. If she alerts the others, I'm truly fucked.

The satin sash holding her robe together has come loose, so I quickly grab it, pulling it free. Maybe I can tie her up somehow. Keep her out of the way so she can't raise the alarm that I've gotten away.

I move to grab her hand, but my lack of planning ahead has cost me time, and Vik regains some of her control, her hand darting out to wrap around my throat. I gasp, surprised, and manage to shove her back, but it's fleeting because she lunges at me with her whole body, crashing us into the shower stall. I slip, falling hard, Vik tumbling down with me as she lashes her claw-like nails at my face. I've fallen in an awkward position, my neck pushed forward in the corner, while my back is screaming from the metal door frame cutting into my skin.

Lashing out with my hands, I try to fend her off, realising the satin sash is still in my hand, so I channel every action movie I've seen and start trying to loop the sash around her neck. Each time I try to get the sash over her head, she's able to slap my hand away, and I know my attempt is useless. Fury washes over me as the thought of her winning this fight creeps in.

I can't let her win. I need to get away.

I hiss in her face, baring my teeth and something takes over me. All of a sudden, my fisted hands have a mind of their own, my body igniting with a fire I didn't know it was capable of, and I fight. With punches blowing, nails clawing, legs thrashing, I somehow get the upper hand, rolling us enough, so I have room to slip out from under her. While she tries to turn over to see me, her hands slipping from the soap covering them, I drag the hand-held showerhead from its holders and hook the chrome hose over Vik's head and around her neck.

Her whimper is the only thing I hear before I pull tight, dragging her neck backwards as the hose cuts off her airway. My weight sitting on her back restricts her ability to move, and I tug back harder, choking the life from her.

It takes longer than I thought. The movies certainly speed up the whole strangled-to-death process because she's still fucking breathing after thirty seconds. It feels like minutes pass, her body thrashing under mine as I do the unthinkable. It's not until I shift on her back, using my knee to press her hard against the tiled shower floor, that I get the right momentum to yank back hard enough to seal Madam Vik's fate. And my own.

She is now dead.

And I am now a murderer.

Shit. The overwhelming urge to cry slams into me, a couple of hot tears escaping before I slap them off my burning cheeks.

Slowly, I back up out of the cubicle, my eyes trained on Vik's lifeless body in an awkward heap.

I killed someone.

I should be happy, right? This bitch deserves death. They all do. So why do I feel so fucking bad?

The vibrating buzz of a phone snaps my head in the direction of where Vik's phone lays face down on the tiled floor.

Get your head in the game, Rhys!

I dart over to it but struggle to pick it up properly with my slimy hands, so I wash them quickly in the sink before picking up the phone.

Terry
Is she nearly clean?
Downstairs has been cleaned up, ready for round 2.

My stomach rolls.

No.

Master Hill's message to his wife is a clear reminder of the danger I'm in, so I suck in a breath and focus on my goal of escaping.

Cracking the bathroom door open, I strain my ears, trying to hear for any sound nearby. When I'm sure I'm alone upstairs, I slip out the door and tiptoe along the bottle green carpet runner to the top of the staircase.

Again, I strain my ears, hoping to find the path to the front door clear, but the undeniably close voices of Master and Julie tell me I'm likely to get sprung if I go down there.

My heart sinks.

I need to find another way out.

Creeping back up the passage, I pass the bathroom and enter the girls' bedroom that I was in the last time I was here. Rushing to the window, I try to open it, but it's locked by a key lock.

Fuck. Fuck. Fuck.

This room is at the back of the house, overlooking the pool, so there's no ledge, anyway. Just a straight drop, which I'm pretty sure even if I could get the window open, the drop would leave me injured and unable to run.

Pushing away from the window, I rummage through the closet, finding a man's t-shirt. It smells of mothballs but is large and dark grey and perfect to cover myself up with, so I'm not running around completely naked.

Knowing I'm wasting valuable time, I slip out of the girls' bedroom and check each door to find more bedrooms, all with windows securely locked.

At the end of the passage, the double doors open to the master bedroom. I almost don't go in because the thought of Master Hill and Madam Vik sleeping here creeps me the fuck out, but again, they are emotions that need to be shoved right the fuck down. They have no place in this situation.

Once again, I move to the windows, which are actually doors. Un-fucking-fortunately, they are locked too, and the need to scream in frustration is overwhelming. My eyes pick up a bathroom and walk-in robe off to the side, so I quietly dart across the room, only to find the same issue.

Fuck.

So, I'm not escaping from up here, which means I need to get downstairs. I could wait and hope Master and Julie move to a different location in the house while they are waiting for Vik to clean me up, but it's more likely that they will be up here any moment to see what's taking so long.

As if he read my mind, the phone in my hand vibrates with another message from Master Hill, telling his wife, in not a nice way, to hurry up.

Fucking arsehole!

Think Rhys! How can I get downstairs without them noticing?

A distraction, maybe?

I glance at the phone, knowing I need to call the police, but I also need to get to safety, so I look around the master bedroom, trying to figure out how I can distract everyone downstairs.

There, on the bedside table, is a scented candle and one of those gas candle lighter thingys.

A fire? Sure, that could be a distraction, but I could also fucking die from it if my plan backfires. Unfortunately, since I'm all out of other options, fire it is.

Grabbing the lighter, I click it a few times and it lights. Ooooh, it's like a mini blow torch. Cool.

Just like in the bathroom, a fucking scary, sinister smile spreads across my face. I really think I should be more concerned by my reactions, but right now, they are filling me with courage I didn't know I had.

Turning to look at my surroundings, I move to the curtains, and I click, click, click, making sure the little blow torch catches onto the fabric at the bottom. The flames ignite, catching hold and start to travel north, so I repeat the process on the other curtains, then move to the wardrobe, eyeing those pompous black suits Master wears, and I click, click, click them too.

In the bathroom, I ignite the curtains in there, as well as the towels, and then before I leave the master bedroom, I light up the bedspread.

I hurriedly creep from the room, dashing into each bedroom and lighting the curtains on fire before closing each door behind me. Crackles from the fire burning through objects, and thick smoke starts to drift down the passage before the smoke detectors blare to life. Darting quickly back down the passage, I slip into the closet right next to the staircase on the landing and suck in a breath as I try to calm my racing heart.

Glancing at the phone still in my hand, I dial triple zero and press it to my ear while I strain my ears to hear thudding footsteps bounding up the stairs.

"Police, fire or ambulance?"

The female voice startles me, and I focus on the phone, knowing I can't speak loudly.

"Police," I whisper.

"I'm sorry I can't hear you properly. Did you say police?"

"Yes." I hiss a little louder.

"What address, please?"

The footsteps stomp past the closet, and I freeze, holding my breath.

"What address, please?"

"Vixen's Lodge, Fox Pines." I hiss quietly. "They are going to kill me. Send help, please." Then I place the phone on the timber floor, leaving it connected and crack the closet door open.

Yelling from the direction of the master bedroom meets my ears, and I take that moment to bolt. Pushing the door open, I dash to the stairs, taking two at a time as the foyer and front door come into view.

My heart is pounding in my chest, blood thrashing in my ear as the possibility of escape draws closer. When my feet land on the ground floor, I dart toward the front door, only making it a few steps when a hard body crashes into me, lurching me forward to crash to the floor right in front of the door. The wind gets knocked out of me, and for a few long-drawn-out moments, I can't breathe.

"I don't fucking think so, Kitten." Brock hisses in my ear.

No. I'm so close.

As soon as air fills my lungs again, I thrash under Brock, trying to squirm free from his pressing weight and his hand fists in the back of my hair, trying to hold me still. With my face smooshed to the timber floor, I reach my hands out, trying to find something, anything, to use as a weapon.

"Get off me!" I scream, the action sucking in the faint tinge of smoke in the air. Yelling floats down from upstairs as Master and Julie obviously try to put the flames out, but unless they have a fire hose, their attempts will be futile.

"What the fuck have you done?" Brock hisses, his weight lifting a little, his fist letting go of my hair.

The action frees me enough to strain a glance over my shoulder to see Brock's eyes trained on the top of the staircase, watching smoke rush across the ceiling.

My eyes dart around, trying to figure out a way free, when they land on a cast iron doorstop in the shape of a fucking heart.

Yep, that'll do.

Reaching forward, I manage to squirm enough to get a good grip on it, and as Brock turns back to me, I swing backwards with everything I have, the motion throwing him back before the heavyweight slams into the side of his face.

I gasp at the crunch I feel as the cast iron connects with Brock's head, and he flies back, giving me room to get up. With the doorstop still in my hand, I lunge for the door, tugging on the handle before I'm reefed back and fall on my arse.

I momentarily drop the doorstop but scramble to pick it up as my eyes connect with Brock's. Blood pours from his brow, and he blinks rapidly, trying to shake off a daze that my blow rattled him with.

He now stands in between me and freedom, with the door at his back. I could run through the house, but I know I'll only make it a few steps before he's on me again.

No. I need to fight.

Baring my teeth, I hiss at him. "Move!"

"Not going to happen." He mutters, frowning and giving his head a shake.

Shit, I really did shake his brain.

I make like I'm going to run for the dining room off to the side, and he lunges in that direction, stumbling a little. I don't think as I swing the doorstop at his head again. He grabs me as he tumbles to the floor, his head bouncing off the front door as he lashes his fists out. I rear back and swing the heavy doorstop again, feeling it connect with his hand and his shoulder before I find another opening to slam it into his head. There's a sickening crack, and blood sprays up over my face. A feral scream lurches from me as I repeat the action before his arms flop to his sides and his body falls limp.

A loud crack pierces the air, and something whizzes past my ear before a bullet lodges in the front door next to Brock's head. I scramble back, running for the dining room before another bullet splinters the timber frame of the door.

A scream leaps from my mouth, fear slicing my bravado in half. I run for the back door I used the other night, knowing it could be locked but willing to throw my body through it if I have to.

The door to my left suddenly swings open, and the hulking figure of Master Hill lunges through, slamming me hard against the wall, knocking the air from my lungs.

"You killed my wife!" He screams, baring his teeth, a waft of smoke engulfing us from the stench of his clothes. His hands wrap around my throat as I try to push him back, my fists flailing in desperation as he squeezes tight.

"Fucking kill her!" Julie screams as she nears us, my eyes darting to her in a desperate plea for help. She's not going to help me, though. She's the one that was trying to shoot me, the barrel of the gun now pointed at my head.

Loud pops fill the air right before the house creaks with a groan, straining under the engulfed second floor right above us.

I realise that this is it. I'm going to die here in this house of horrors as the ceiling starts to give way around us and flames lick up the walls. As Master tightens his grip and darkness dances at the edges of my vision, I grab hold of his shirt, hoping I can hold him there long enough for the flames to take him too.

There's no way I'm going to hell without him joining me.

Chapter Thirty-Seven

SHAUN

Rhys' sister Charlotte rushes into the room with the click of heels behind her. All eyes turn to her and the two blonde women who stroll in, demanding everyone's attention by their presence alone.

"Mum. Dad. This is Bec and Amanda Angel. They are the founders of Angel Org, and they have some information that could help us find Rhys."

Cynthia Rogan leaps from the theatre seat she crumpled in a few minutes ago. "What? What do you know?"

"Excuse me? Who are you exactly?" Officer Zimora asks, and the tallest blonde looks him up and down, raising a perfectly shaped brow.

"I'm Amanda, and we're the Angel sisters. Our organisation provides support services for girls and women, and we were recently made aware of the situation with Rhys."

"One of our consultants recently did a podcast that I believe gave you the location of Julie Bates." The other blonde explains, and I assume she must be Bec, since the other one is Amanda.

"Oh, yes." Recognition flicks over Officer Zimora's expression.

"Well? What do you know?" Cynthia practically yells, clearly frustrated with the hold-up.

My eyes dart to the guys as they stand, too, desperate for information that may help us find our girl. Tyler's expression is pinched. He looks like a scary fucker, his eyes dark with the anger he's trying to contain.

Bec steps forward, handing a manilla folder to Officer Zimora, and I swear we all hold our breath as we wait.

Then, four things happen at once.

I get a message on my phone. Officer Kent rushes into the room, holding a piece of paper. Officer Zimora's eyes widen as he looks over the information in the folder and a female officer runs into the room, nearly crashing into Officer Kent.

I take out my phone to read the message.

Derek
Vixen's Lodge is on fire, and we heard gunshots.

"Jason." Officer Kent barks. "We got a hit on the number plates. They belong to a guy named Brock Pappas."

My eyes dart up. Brock? As in Brock from the Feast? I turn to find Tyler, who is already rushing towards the door.

"Officer Zimora?" The female officer calls. "We have an open line on a call from a young female asking for police help out at Vixen's Lodge. She seems to have dropped the phone but left the call active."

Officer Zimora looks up from the folder, glaring at the Angel sisters. "This information is accurate? Terence Hill is Brian Bates' brother?"

That's all we need to know. I'm on Ty's heels, racing out of the house towards his car. He has tunnel vision right now, not even noticing me leap in the front seat and Gaz, Marcus and Simon climbing in the back before he peels off down the road.

"Derek messaged me just now." I pant, my heart in my throat as fear grips me. "Vixen's Lodge is on fire, and he heard gunshots."

My words cause Ty to plant his foot harder. Fuck, we'll be lucky to make it there alive with the way he's driving.

"Seat belts!" Tyler roars, not taking his eyes off the road. He obviously knows we are all here, yet he hasn't acknowledged us.

I glance over my shoulder to see the guys scrambling to click their seatbelts in place. Mine is already on, but it doesn't make me feel any safer right now.

Sirens blare in the distance behind us, and I glance in the mirror to see flashing lights headed in the same direction as us.

"Who the fuck is Brock?" Marcus hisses from the backseat.

"He's the bouncer at the Feast nights." I grip the grab handle above the door as we take a corner, and the car slides.

"The sex club?" Simon asks.

"Yes." I nod, releasing a breath as the car rights itself just in time to miss a fucking power pole.

"And Brian's brother is Terence Hill? That's the Master dude?" Garrett asks this time, and I nod again.

"Yes, although I didn't know they were brothers."

"Fuck!" Tyler bellows, slamming his hand on the steering wheel over and over.

"Calm down, man. We need to be alive to help her." I remind him, and he snarls but manages to calm himself. His face is contorted in pain, his nostrils flaring as he fights a battle inside his head.

"She's strong, Ty."

His eyes dart to me. "I know she is." He snaps. "Not the point! This shouldn't have fucking happened!"

His temper rises again, and I drag my eyes from him as my phone vibrates again.

Derek
More gunshots.

Shaun
Get in the house and keep mama safe.
Is Dad there?
Get his shotgun if you need to.

I don't know who is shooting over at Vixen's Lodge, and as much as I want Kitten to be safe, I also need my family to be safe.

Derek
Dad is heading inside now from the shed.
I'll keep them safe.
Mama is on the phone with the police.

"Derek just said there are more gunshots," I announce, and Simon loses it.

"I can't fucking take this." I glance into the back seat to see his hands fisted, tugging on his hair as his eyes fill with tears. "What if we are too late?" Simon yells.

"Calm down. We need to remain calm and level-headed so we can help Rhys properly." Garrett's deep voice rasps, his arm wrapping around Simon's shoulder as he holds him to his side. "Stay strong for our girl. She needs us. We can fall apart later when this is all over, but for now, we focus on how the fuck we can help her if someone is shooting."

"What if it's her that's shooting? Maybe she got hold of a gun?" Marcus offers, and fuck, I hope he's right. I hope she blows their heads right the fuck off.

The car slides as we take another corner, and I notice that the crowded town has already passed by, and the road is now lined with trees. I recognise this road and know we aren't far from my house, which means we aren't far from Vixen's Lodge.

My heart is about ready to fly from my chest from worry when my eyes land on something out of place. Over the top of the pine trees up ahead, a red glow illuminates black smoke billowing up into the darkened sky over the place where Vixen's Lodge sits. Tyler must see what I am seeing, too, because he accelerates faster, pushing the car to its limit.

We all fall silent as we get closer, dread sitting in my gut, as I'm sure it is with the guys as well. I feel fucking sick as we fly past my house, none of us even sparing it a second glance as the grape vines come and go, replaced by a thick pine plantation.

Tyler releases the accelerator, letting the car slow naturally as we approach the driveway for Vixen's Lodge, and he slams on the brakes at the last moment, snaking us up the dusty drive.

My heart stops as the colonial homestead comes into view. Or at least what used to be the homestead. Flames as tall as trees roar up from the debris that used to be the lodge.

Kitten.

My eyes fill with hot tears at the thought that she's in those flames. Trapped or worse, burning alive. Ty slams the car to a stop, throwing his door open and takes a few steps towards the inferno before the old tin roof caves in, pulling Ty up short as we climb out of the car.

No. Kitten.

"Rhys!" Tyler bellows, the sounds filled with agony, and a fucking sob lurches from my throat. "Rhys!" He bellows again, fisting his hand into his short, cropped hair.

Gunshots pierce through the air, and we all drop to the ground. All except for Ty. He starts running towards the side of the house, which leads to the backyard and barn area.

I get up off the gravel, bolting after him and hearing the other guys on my heels. By the time we make a wide berth around the burning house, we see Ty throw the barn door open.

Another gunshot cracks through the air, and Ty flies backwards from an invisible force, his body slamming hard to the gravel. We freeze for a moment, the guys stopping by my side as we come to the same realisation.

Someone just shot Ty.

I only hesitate for a moment longer before lurching forward, but as a silhouette steps out from the barn, Garrett's large hands jerk me back behind a tree.

"Stop, man. You'll get yourself killed." Garrett's deep rasp is right at my ear as we peer around the trunk and see the silhouette transform into a female that can only be Julie. The flames from the house send a flickering glow over her skin, and she comes to stand over Tyler, pointing a gun down at him.

"Ahhh. The school teacher. Maybe I should leave you alive and leak all the recordings we have of you fucking your student. That might be more rewarding."

Tyler tries to speak, coughing, and what looks like blood sprays from his mouth.

Fuck. No. Ty.

I can't fucking take this.

"What do you think, Patty?" Julie tips her head back, yelling. "Should I keep your teacher alive?"

A scream, kind of what I assume a banshee would sound like, comes from inside the barn, and before Julie even has a chance to turn, a dark, long-haired figure leaps from inside the barn like a monkey, clinging onto Julie's back. The flash of metal is the only warning we get before the raised hand slams it into Julie's chest from behind. Over and over, the blade comes out and then slams back in as this wild creature attacks Julie.

I don't hold back any longer, the sirens getting closer as I run towards the barn, skidding to a stop a few meters away.

Julie drops the gun as she gurgles for air, falling to her knees before face planting the gravel. The figure on her back doesn't stop, just changes tactics, slamming the blade into Julie's back instead, repeatedly.

"It's Cherry," Simon whispers beside me as the glow of flames dance over the wild creature.

Her eyes dart up through a mess of blood-matted hair, her teeth bared at us as she releases another gut-wrenching scream.

"Put the weapon down!" An officer yells from behind us, and I turn to see a gun directed toward my girl.

Simultaneously, me and the guys turn, spreading our arms and legs wide, blocking the officer's path to her.

"No! Wait!" Marcus yells. "She's the victim. Don't harm her."

Movement behind us gains my attention, and I see Rhys has now dropped the knife and has crawled through the blood-soaked dirt to Tyler's side.

"No! Help! Help him!" She screams.

"Get the paramedics up here now!" Officer Zimora's voice cuts through the growing chaos. "Weapons down. Do a sweep to see if there are any others out here."

"Ty. You'll be ok." Kitten cries, and I turn my focus to her, falling to my knees beside Ty. Rhys rips her t-shirt over her head, not fazed by her nudity, as she presses it to Ty's chest, where blood is oozing out. "You'll be ok. Ty. Please fight. Don't leave me."

The other guys fall to their knees beside me, and I feel Simon take my hand in his trembling one as we look on, feeling helpless as Ty bleeds out in front of us.

"I… love you… baby." Ty rasps, his voice slurred as he fights to speak.

"Help!" Rhys screams again.

I can hear the paramedics running up, telling us to move, but I fear they are too late.

Ty's lids slowly fall shut, and the hand Rhys is clutching falls limp as the life seeps out of him.

Chapter Thirty-Eight

RHYS

The tears won't stop falling. Unimaginable pain tears my heart from my chest as the ambulance speeds off with Ty in the back. Even though I don't have a scrap of fabric on my skin, I feel like I'm burning up.

"Rhys, we need you to calm down." Officer Zimora is here, looking at me like I'm the one to be afraid of. Maybe I am. Maybe I'm too far gone to be saved now.

I'm a killer. Three people have died tonight by my hand. I remember feeling remorseful after killing Madam Vik, yet now I feel nothing but elated that she, Brock, and Julie have been taken from this earth forever.

"Just give her some space."

Cass. He's here with Garrett, Marcus and Simon, forming a barrier between me and the police.

"Rhys!" The cry comes from the shadows, and I squint, trying to make out the form running up the gravel path towards us. "Rhys!" She cries again, and a sob escapes my lips as recognition kicks in.

"Mum," I whisper, my tears blurring my blood-soaked eyes as a womanly figure skids to a stop in front of my guys. When someone else stops beside her, I know my dad is there too. "Dad?"

My choking sob is all he needs to kick into action, pushing through the wall of muscle and tearing his jumper over his head as he approaches.

"Rhys, honey. I'm just going to slip this on and cover you up."

I nod, trying not to flinch at his touch, but failing. He holds a calming hand up before trying again, and I let him draw the fabric over my head, slipping my arms in and letting it fall to my knees.

"Rhys." My mum sobs, stepping past Garrett and Marcus to join her husband before me.

"M-mum. T-Ty got s-shot."

Slowly she reaches a hand out, an offering for my hand, and I place my trembling fingers against her palm.

"I know, honey. He's on the way to the hospital. They will take care of him."

My lip quivers. "W-what if…" I can't say the words. I can barely think them.

What if he dies?

"Sweetheart, he's in the best hands now. All we can do is hope."

Hope? It's not enough. I want guarantees. I can't bear the thought of living a life without Ty in it, and by the solemn look on Shaun's face, I think he feels the same. I don't know how the other guys feel. They don't know Ty the way Shaun and I do.

"We found someone!" The voice of a male gains everyone's attention, and I see a couple of officers helping a limping man dripping with water towards the second ambulance.

I see red. Rage washes over me as the partially burnt face of Terence Hill comes into view. In a hurry of movement, me and my guys all move as one, our eyes trained on the predator of Vixen's Lodge. I don't make it far. My dad wraps his arms around me, holding me back, but my guys get further, Garrett reefing Terence from the stunned officers as Simon leaps on him like a crazy man.

I can't tell what's happening after that. A sea of bodies swarming in to break up the attack as all four of my guys defend my honour. It takes a few minutes for the officers to drag my snarling guys back, and just when they think they have the situation handled, my mum steps up, a heavy shovel in hand, before she swings it backwards and then slams it into Terence Hill's manhood.

Everyone gasps. Even the officers are too stunned to intervene. As Terence Hill doubles over in pain, my mum whispers something in his ear before turning back and handing the shovel to Officer Zimora as she walks back to join me and Dad.

What the fuck just happened?

I don't know, but I fucking love her.

A third ambulance rocks up as the second one leaves with Master Hill in the back, handcuffed to the bed, and as firefighters work to extinguish the flames, my parents try to get me into the ambulance.

"I just want you to take me to Tyler." I plead.

"You will be at the same hospital as Tyler, honey. You need to get checked out. You have a burn on your leg." My mum points out, but I shake my head and walk towards Marcus.

"My leg is fine."

"Your mum is right, Rhys. We need you to come to the hospital, please." Officer Zimora steps in front of me, and I glare at him.

"Why? What can the hospital do that I can't?"

Officer Zimora shifts uncomfortably on the spot, raking his hand through his short, dark hair. "We need the hospital to do some tests, Rhys."

My brows shoot up. "Tests? What to see if I've been raped?"

I'll give it to Officer Zimora. He doesn't flinch at my forwardness. "Yes."

"Let me save you the trouble. Record this because it's my statement." I jut my chin up, feeling my cheeks heat. "Julie and Brock came into my house uninvited. Julie attacked me, and I fought, but apparently, I don't have the superpower against Chloroform."

My mum gasps, but I ignore it.

"Then I woke up, in the middle of being raped by Terence Hill. I was bound by my wrists and ankles to the fucking torture bed he has in his basement. Julie filmed it all before Brock and Vik joined us. Terence raped me again, then, in my…" fuck, I struggle to get this out, my lip wobbling, "back region." I say quickly, trying to ignore the roar of pain that rips from Garrett's lips. I want to go to him, but I have to finish this. I have to tell them everything, so they will leave me alone. "He tried to use his fist…" I huff. "You get the fucking picture, right?" I yell, anger and shame sweeping through me. "It was Brock trying to choke me with his dick and Julie deciding to piss on my face that was their downfall. Apparently, the stench of vomit was a turnoff, and they had to stop their assault so I could shower."

"Oh my God. Oh my God." My mum cries behind me.

Tears pour from my eyes now, the pain as I relive the memories almost too much.

"I never planned on killing anyone. I just wanted to escape, but Vik…" I shake my head, fisting my hands in my hair. "She fought me, and before I knew it, she was dead." I shake my head, swiping at the damn tears that won't stop falling. "I tried to escape, but the windows were locked upstairs, and Terence and Julie were downstairs near the door, so I created a diversion and set some fires."

I glance past Officer Zimora at the simmering inferno I created. "I called triple zero from Vik's phone, and when Julie and Terence were trying to put the fires out, I ran downstairs and tried to escape. Brock caught me, though, and we fought, and stuff happened, and I really never wanted to hurt anyone. I just wanted to leave. I couldn't let them take me away like they said they were going to do. They had plans for me. Dirty porn movie plans that would make them a lot of money."

I shake my head, remembering the crunch of Brock's skull against the doorstop. "Julie had a gun and started shooting at me, so I tried to flee, but Master got to me first and was choking the life out of me. I was sure I was about to die because the house started caving in." I frown, remembering what happened next. "I guess I should thank Terence for dragging me out of the fire. He went back to get Julie, which I think is when he got badly burnt. I wasn't sticking around, though, and I ran off, but I wasn't fast enough. Julie followed me into the barn and started shooting at everything to find where I was hiding."

I turn back to look at the barn, nausea sweeping over me as I remember seeing Ty fly backwards when Julie shot him. "Julie shot Ty, and then I stopped her from hurting anyone else." I shrug.

"We will still need the evidence, Rhys. I'm sorry. Will you please come to the hospital?"

"I don't want anyone else to touch me." I sob, backing up.

"Rhee?" Marcus steps forward, his big dark eyes swimming with tears. "We will come with you. Make sure everyone treats you right."

Simon nods, coming to stand next to Marcus. "Yeah, Cherry. We won't let anyone hurt you ever again."

"Ever again." Garrett hisses through clenched teeth, towering behind Simon.

I glance at Shaun, who remains quiet, but steps up to me, holding out his hand. I stare at it for a beat before sucking in a shuddering breath, and I reach out and slowly take it, letting him lead me to the ambulance.

Chapter Thirty-Nine

RHYS

The hospital is utter chaos. Yes, I'm mostly to blame for it, but I was serious when I said I didn't want anyone to touch me. By anyone, I obviously meant strangers or people I don't know well because I can't stop touching my guys, and I don't flinch from my parents.

Getting the evidence off my body for the police wasn't easy, for me or for the nurses. I know they were just doing their jobs, but I had no control over my reactions to their touch. At one point, a nurse came in with a sedative to give me, and before I could go all ape shit about that, my mum stopped it from happening. Then, she pleaded with me to try and endure it a little longer so they could get what they needed.

I couldn't have done it without my guys. Garrett cupped my face, pressing his forehead to mine, whispering to me.

"You're the strongest person I know."
"I've never met anyone as brave as you."
"It will be over soon. You've got this."

Even though he was calling me strong and brave, I still let silent tears fall, trying to remain focused on his deep baritone and not the invasive swabbing between my legs.

Shaun was practically sitting on Garrett's knee, holding my hand, his thumb stroking over the back, while Marcus sat on the other side, his fingers entwined with mine. Simon paced beside the bed, and when the nurses were finally done, he fussed over me, ordering them to bring me heated blankets while he covered me up and gave me a foot massage, being careful to avoid the healing cuts on the bottom of my feet.

The only problem was that staying in bed felt like I was doing nothing. My mum told me Tyler had been rushed to surgery, but that's all we know, and not knowing how that was going, was turning me into a caged lioness.

That's where the rest of the chaos came from. My attempts at getting out of the bed in the emergency ward and trying to run off to find Ty. Of course, I never got far. Shaun or Marcus always catching me each time I tricked them into taking me to the toilet.

After another hour of the harsh lights in the emergency ward, I was moved to an overnight ward, which gave me my own room and more privacy.

"I'm guessing that asking you boys to go home and sleep will fall on deaf ears?" My dad asks after the nurses leave me to get settled.

I'm about to tell Dad I don't want the guys to leave when Garrett speaks up.

"I mean no disrespect, Mr Rogan, but we aren't leaving Rhys until she asks us to. Even then, we'll probably ignore her and stay, anyway."

My tired eyes widen at Garrett's words, and I expect my dad to argue, yet he doesn't, simply nodding and looking around the small space.

"I'll see if I can organise some more chairs." He looks exhausted as he leaves the room. Almost as if he's aged five years since I last saw him.

Still lingering, with my legs dangling over the side of my bed, I glance at the open door across the room that leads into the bathroom.

"I want a shower."

"Oh, yes, of course. I'll help you." My mum steps towards me, but I shake my head.

"It's ok. I'll try to do it myself. One of the guys can help me if I need it."

She looks hurt, so I ease myself off the bed and close the distance between us. "I'm sorry, mum. It's nothing against you. I just need… them right now. And I really need to know that you're available for updates about Ty."

Nodding, my mum gently cups my face. "I can do that for you, honey. But remember, I'm here if you need me."

I nod back, biting back my emotions because, quite frankly, I'm fucking sick of them. I just want this all to be over.

My mum leaves to see if she can get another update on Ty, and I make my way into the bathroom to shower.

"What do you want us to do, Kitten?" Shaun hovers behind me in the doorway as I eye the open shower and the handheld showerhead. The chrome hose is similar to the one I killed Vik with, and I try to drag my eyes from it, but it's like a magnet pulling me in.

My stomach rolls, the only warning I get before it lurches. I twist just in time to make it to the toilet, and I crash to my knees, gripping the toilet seat to hold myself steady, my body heaving over and over, trying to cleanse the vileness from inside.

My stupid fucking emotions win out after that, my body collapsing back into Shaun's arms as I cry. So much pain, almost unbearable, ripples through my body as images flash through my mind. One minute I was walking on cloud nine after spending the weekend with the guys, and the next minute I was being raped by my fucking uncle.

Everything that happened was just so vulgar and violent.

"I killed them." I cry, hating that I feel so bad about taking the lives of such repugnant humans.

"You were defending yourself, Baby Girl." Garrett's voice floats to me, and I'm pretty sure it's his large hand holding one of mine. I can't see him through the blur of my tears, though.

"But I killed them. Vik with the shower hose. Brock with the doorstop. Julie with the knife." I shake my head, trying to will away the images, but they stay put. "I can still hear Vik's gasps for air. Feel the crunch of Brock's bones. The smell of Julie's blood."

"Shhhh. Kitten. It's over now. Try not to think about it." Shaun rasps next to my ear, and I lean in closer to him, wishing I could just climb under his skin and forget about what happened.

"Let's get her in the shower," Marcus speaks softly to the guys, and while I continue my gut-wrenching cries, my four guys work together to get me out of the hospital gown and under the spray of the shower.

I get passed between them, my eyes open but not really seeing. It's their scents and hands that tell me who holds me in their arms to wash me, or shampoo my hair, or rinse me off. Even though I feel bare chests, I also feel fabric below their waists, telling me they aren't completely naked, and for some reason, it makes me cry even more.

"Y-you g-guys a-are t-too k-kind t-to m-me." I sob, feeling rawer than I have ever before.

"We love you." Simon rasps quietly next to my ear, and I lean into the press of his lips as they flutter over my temple.

"No matter what." Marcus' voice comes from in front of me, and I blink away my tears just enough to get a blurry view of his kind face and sincere expression.

Exhaustion like I've never felt slams into me hard. It's like I've been drugged or something, yet I know nothing has passed through my veins.

"You ok, Kitten?" Shaun asks as my head droops, and I lean into Simon, needing him to hold me up.

"So tired." I slur. "Don't know what's wrong with me."

"You're probably having an adrenalin crash. If that's even a thing." Shaun suggests, and I want to nod, but I can't make my head work properly as my legs start to shake.

"Let's get her dry and into bed." Garrett takes charge, so I let them dry me off and put a new gown on me before Garrett sweeps me up in his arms and carries me to the bed.

"Ty." I push the word past my lips. My desperation to know how he's doing overriding my exhaustion.

"We'll check on how he's going, Kitten. You rest now." Shaun's voice sounds distant as my body sinks into a not-so-soft hospital mattress. A heated blanket gets tucked around my body, making me feel like the filling in a burrito, and I know it's Simon's doing.

"Love you guys." I slur again, my vision black, my eyes no longer able to stay open. I want to ask someone to cuddle me. Wrap their arms around me and make me feel safe, but I can't make the words form.

It doesn't matter, though. The mattress dips beside me, and a moment later, I feel arms around me.

They know.

They know exactly what I need.

As darkness tugs at me, the scent of my playful guy wraps around me, and I finally give in and let sleep take me.

When I wake again a number of hours later, it's because I can hear crying. Uncontrollable crying. My eyes shoot open, and I sit up, startled, in the hospital bed, trying to make sense of what's going on.

"Calm down, Cin. We can't understand what you are trying to say." My dad rubs my mum's arms, trying to calm her, but each time she tries to speak, she starts wailing, her face screwed up as she ugly cries.

"Ty?" I whisper, yet everyone in the room hears my words, all eyes turning to me as I stare at my mum to gauge her reaction.

She starts crying harder, her hand pressed to the centre of her chest like she's in pain.

I shift to get out of the bed, but Simon's arms wrap around me, stopping me from going anywhere.

"You need to rest, Cherry."

"No." I shake my head. "I need to know about Ty." I direct my attention back to my mum. "Mum?" I ask louder. "Tell me about Ty."

Again, she goes to speak, even trying to step towards me, but her tears rule her, causing her to shake her head in frustration.

My heart sinks. What is she trying to say? Do I even want to know?

I *do* want to know, though, so I shove at Simon's hold, trying to get free.

"Mum! Tell me! Is Ty ok?"

Pure blabbering spills from her mouth, but she manages to nod.

"Sit down, honey. I'll tell her." My dad offers, and my mum nods again, letting him steer her to a chair.

Sighing, my dad rakes his hand through his hair and turns to face me.

"He's ok, Rhys. There were some complications during surgery, but they managed to get things under control, and he's resting in the recovery ward."

A strangled cry leaps from my throat before I can stop it, and I slap my hand over my mouth as tears spill from my eyes.

"That's good news." Shaun beams, his own eyes wet as he looks between my dad and me.

I nod, now impersonating my mum with uncontrollable blubbering that makes no sense.

My mum scrambles off her chair and stumbles to me, Garrett moving out of the way just in time to avoid being bowled down by her, and she throws her arms around my neck in a fierce mum hug. The best I've ever had.

When I'm finally able to form words again, I pull back from my mum and hope she's not going to give me hell for what I'm about to ask.

"I need to see him."

She nods as if she expected me to ask and glances over her shoulder at Will, who gives her a shrug.

"You can, but it will have to wait until he's transferred to the ward," She leans in closer, dropping her voice to a whisper, "and Dad and I will have to head home to grab you some clothes. You know, because we can't actually allow you to have a personal relationship with him." She gives me a pointed look, and I get her meaning. They will turn a blind eye and pretend like they have no idea.

I beam at her and nod, happy for the massive olive branch, and sink back into Simon's hold as a tap sounds at the door.

My dad moves to answer the door while Mum hugs me again, and I let my eyes fall shut as immense relief over Ty washes over me.

It's the click of heels and the voice that oozes authority that has me pulling back from my mum. Glancing towards the door, I watch as two blonde women stroll into the room. Their confident aura screams power, and I realise I am in the presence of two very successful women.

Hellooo, lady boner!

"Mr and Mrs Rogan. Lovely to see you again." The tallest blonde smiles, giving my parents a nod, while the other blonde nods at my guys.

Do they know these women?

"Ms Angel." My dad does this awkward head nod bow type of thing to the both of them like royalty is before him.

"No need to be so formal. Bec and Amanda is fine." The shorter but no less authoritative woman smiles, and my dad gives her a nod. Then she turns her eyes to me. "Rhys." She moves past my dad and makes her way to my bedside, where my mum slips out of the way, joining my dad at the back of the room. "I'm Bec, and this is Amanda. And we are the founders and CEOs of Angel Org. I believe one of our volunteers in the local division told you about our organisation?"

I nod slowly, feeling weirdly Starstruck by the two women before me. "Yes. Evie Prattle."

They both smile.

"Yes. Evie is a very loyal and fierce supporter of what we do." Amanda moves up next to Bec, and all I can do is nod.

Why are they here?

"Cherry, these badass chicks were the ones that came to the cops with info that led us to where you were." Simon rasps quietly in my ear, and I turn to him with my brows tugged together, still confused.

"Ah, sorry. We haven't had a chance to fill Rhys in on everything that happened yet." My dad speaks from the back of the room, and Bec turns a warm smile in his direction, nodding.

"Let me fill you in." Amanda smiles and lowers herself to sit on the edge of the bed. "One of our consultants was able to get their hands on some information the police hadn't yet stumbled across. We were already up in the air on our way to Fox Pines when she sent it to us."

"Up in the air?" I frown.

"In our helicopter," Bec adds with another warm smile and my brows hitch.

Fucking hell. They have a helicopter?

"Anyway, we went straight to your house where the investigation was running from. The information we had helped the local law enforcement to find you." Amanda tilts her head as she speaks to me, her eyes not wavering from my battered face.

"Who's your consultant?" I ask, still playing catch up on whatever the fuck is going on.

"You know her as Hush. The podcaster from Breaking the Silence." Bec advises, and my eyes widen.

Hush is the person I sent my story to. The one who aired it in her podcast and TikTok and called Julie out.

"Hush is your consultant?"

"Kind of. The easiest way to explain her connection with us is to throw out the term, consultant." Amanda grins, and I nod.

Fucking hell. I really think I am in the presence of royalty. Or the mafia. Do we have a mafia in Australia?

"Anyway, we wanted to come and meet you and tell you about some information we just passed on to the police," Bec advises, glancing at Amanda, who continues.

"Our consultant has some of her own connections with skill sets that come in very handy. She was able to get her hands on the cloud drive that Terence and Victoria Hill used to store all of their recordings. The pre-recorded and live ones." Amanda gives me a pointed look, but I'm too enthralled to have the wit to keep up with the meaning of her words.

"They have a very vast database of recordings from the illegal sex club they have been running that span a decade. They also have recordings of acts against children which have been linked to copies sold on the dark web. And there is a video that was live streamed from the lodge while they had you captive, which gives the police all the evidence they need to throw Terence Hill in prison for the rest of his life." Bec's words slowly sink in, and while part of me is mortified that there is video footage of my rape, the other part of me feels immense relief because, finally, I know this nightmare is over.

"The live video was linked to a site on the dark web," Amanda adds. "We have a team working with the police to try and locate the viewers that paid a lot of money to watch. Hopefully, it will lead to more arrests and the end of a very big illegal syndicate."

"Holy shit," Shaun mutters, and I nod.

"Yeah. What he said."

"So has that Terence fucker been taken to prison, then?" Marcus snaps, clearly struggling with his emotions, and I glance over to him where he stands with Garrett by the window and I mouth, *I love you,* when his eyes find mine. His shoulders relax, and he offers me the smallest of grins.

"Not exactly." Bec glances over at my guys. "His burns are quite bad, so he has been taken to a high-security burns unit in Melbourne, where he is under police guard. As soon as they have him well enough, he will head to his new home in prison."

"It's over, Cherry," Simon whispers in my ear, and I twist in the bed, throwing my arms around him and burying my head in his neck.

It really is over.

Chapter Forty

TYLER

It's not the annoying beeping, or the pain in my shoulder, or the sledgehammer thumping in my head that wakes me. It's the sweet scent of Kitten.

My Kitten.

My lids feel heavy as fuck, but I try to open them over and over until the useless bastards kick in and light starts to fill my vision. I can feel the soft press of skin against my shoulder. Not the one that's throbbing like a bitch, thank fuck. I ease my head to the side, and a head full of long, dark, silky hair comes into view.

"Kitten?"

The body shifts next to me, and big chocolate eyes peer up, darting over my face in surprise.

"Ty." She whispers right before she bursts into tears.

My heart breaks for her as she comes apart, her cries filled with so much agony that it's almost unbearable. I ease my good arm around her, tugging her as close as I can before the door creaks open, and Fuckboy's head appears.

"All good in here?"

I frown but nod and rasp. "Yeah."

He gives me a smile and a curt nod before closing the door again, leaving me alone with my girl.

"I'm so sorry." Rhys wails into my neck. "I thought she killed you. I thought you were dead." She cries even more, the sound causing my own eyes to prickle with hot tears.

"I'm ok, Kitten." Fuck, my voice sounds like I'm a pack-an-hour smoker.

Rhys shifts in my arm, sitting up next to me as she swipes at her tears. I get a good look at her now. Her face is bruised up. She has a cut that runs through her brow that has stitches. Fucking hell, rage ripples through me in an instant, the need to kill rising to the surface.

"I killed her, Ty. I killed Julie. I killed them all, except for Master Hill, but he's in a world of pain in a burns unit in the city under police guard. Karma's a bitch, I guess."

"You killed them?" I lift my hand, which feels like it's made of lead, and I stroke the backs of my fingers over her cheek.

"Yes." She frowns. "I hate that I feel bad about killing Vik and Brock, but I don't feel bad about stabbing the knife into Julie.

Flickers of my memory nudge at me. I see Rhys' face, but it's covered in blood. Her eyes look huge and wild, almost crazed. I can hear her voice. She's screaming and crying, begging me not to leave her. I remember telling her I loved her, and the last thing I remember was her screaming for help.

A lump forms in my throat as the reality that I nearly died hits me. I was nearly taken away from my girl forever, right when I'd finally found her.

"Marry me."

"What?" My girl's brows head north, and mine do too when I realise what I just said out loud.

Fuck it. I'm not taking them back.

"Marry me, Kitten."

A laugh bubbles up her throat, and a horrified expression morphs her face before she slaps her hand over her mouth.

"I'm so sorry. That was rude." Her voice is muffled from behind her hand.

I chuckle. "Not really the reaction I was hoping for."

Rhys giggles, dropping her hand from her mouth. "I can't marry you, Ty. I'm only seventeen."

"So, we'll have a long engagement." I shrug, and she giggles again.

"Can we revisit this in about ten years?"

"No. Ten years is too far away. I want to make you mine sooner." I take her hand in mine, bringing it to my lips before trying to compromise. "Five years?"

"Five?" Her brows hitch again. "How about ten?"

I sigh, shooting her a frustrated look. "I'm trying to compromise here, Kitten. You gotta give me something. How about six years?"

She screws her face up. "Nine years."

"Seven years. Come on, seven years is enough." I plead.

"Yeah-Nah. Make it eight." She grins.

"Eight years? I'll be forty in eight years?" I hiss, and she shrugs.

"And I'll be twenty-five. Besides, what makes you think I can marry you and not the other guys? That doesn't seem very fair."

"You can marry one of the others. After I die when I'm like eighty or something."

She glances to the side as she considers what I just said before she nods. "I mean, if you die at eighty, I'll be in my mid-sixties. Still plenty of time to get hitched again."

My smile spreads wide. "Exactly."

Rhys throws her head back, laughing. "You're funny."

My smile disappears. "I'm not trying to be funny, Kitten. I'm dead fucking serious."

Her head tilts to the side as her fingers play with mine before she entwines them together. "Well then, *Daddy*. Looks like you'd better find a place in the world that will let me marry five guys, because if I marry you, I'm marrying the other four as well."

A rumble vibrates my chest at her use of the word, *Daddy*. It's fucking weird that I like it so much. It's like each time she uses the word, she puts me under her spell. Little minx. My little minx.

"Fine. But if I have to share you with them, then we will revisit this conversation in five years, and the ring you wear on your finger will be mine."

She smirks. "Deal."

I relax, finally. I've never considered marriage before, but fuck, if I don't marry Rhys, then I'm not marrying anyone. She's it for me.

Unlocking her grip on my hand, I reach out and gently cup her face, being careful not to hurt her bruising. "Come here, baby."

She relaxes into my hand before shifting forward and giving me what I want. Her lips. It's a soft kiss. The softest we have ever shared. It's like we are both scared of hurting each other.

I want to ask her for more details about what happened at Vixen's Lodge, but I can't bring myself to ask her to relive that, so when she falls asleep at my side a little while later, and Marcus Grady slips through the door looking all possessive and shit, I take a risk and ask him.

"Is she ok?" His concern for her runs deep. His brown eyes roaming over her body, looking for something he's missed.

"She's ok." I rasp quietly, hoping not to wake up my girl.

"We've held the nurses off for long enough, but if we don't let them in, they are going to call security." Marcus sounds pissed off. At first, I think it's at me because of who I am in this situation, but then I realise as he glances at our girl that he's pissed off that the nurses are going to annoy Rhys.

"Ok." I mutter, "But before we wake her, can you fill me in on what she went through before we got to Vixen's Lodge? I didn't want to ask her to relive that."

Marcus stares at me, his expression unreadable, so I let down my walls and let him see how our girl affects me. Then he sighs.

"That Master fucker raped her. Brutally. She has grazes…" Marcus gulps, tears flooding his eyes, "between her legs. At the front and back."

I growl, my body vibrating with rage as his words sink in.

"Julie pissed on her, which made her throw up. That's what saved her from enduring any more of that brutality. Then she fought back when she was alone with the dude's wife. She strangled her with the shower hose thing." Marcus shakes his head as he thinks. "She started some fires upstairs, trying to distract them. Had a run-in with that Brock guy and used a doorstop to smash his head in. She said Julie was shooting at random in the barn trying to find her, and she saw you get shot, and that's when she found a knife and stabbed Julie over and over until she died." Tears spill over, and Marcus bats them away. "I'll die before I let anyone else hurt her."

I nod. "Yeah. Me too."

We fall quiet for a few moments, our eyes remaining on the girl we share before Marcus speaks again.

"Sorry for being such a prick when I found out who you were."

My brows shoot up, and I dart my eyes to him. "You don't have to be sorry. I'd be pissed off if you actually just accepted it straight away. It's a fucked up situation. Don't think I'm not aware of that. If I could make myself younger, I would." I scoff. "Hell, if I could turn these feelings I have for her off, I would, but I fucking can't."

He nods. "Yeah. I know how that feels."

A tap sounds on the door, and Marcus sighs again, moving around the bed and shooting me an apologetic look before he leans down and strokes Kitten's hair back, rousing her from sleep.

"Rhee, the nurses need to come in, so we have to leave now and get you back to your room."

A small whimper of annoyance comes from Rhys, sending my lips north. She's so fucking beautiful.

"Tell the nurses to fuck off." She rasps. Her voice husky, probably from all the crying she's done.

Marcus and I chuckle, which causes her eyes to flutter open. The two chocolate pools snag onto my stare, and she shoots me a sad smile.

"I don't want to leave you." She pouts, easing herself to sit up.

"It's ok. I'll be alright. You go and rest, and I'll talk to you later."

"Promise?"

I grin. "Of course, Kitten. I promise."

Ignoring another tap on the door, Rhys leans forward, pressing her lips to mine in a brief kiss before pulling back. "I love you, Tyler Foster."

I grin back. "Love you too, my fiancé."

"What? Fiancé?" Marcus snaps, and I chuckle while Rhys rolls her eyes, sliding off the bed.

"Not for another five years, Daddy." She pokes her tongue out.

"Hang on a minute." Marcus says in confusion. "Fiancé? You can't marry him." Marcus complains, and she smiles up at him.

"Why not?"

"Well… what about me?" The puppy dog eyes Marcus sends our girl's way is worthy of an award, and I can't help but laugh.

"Oh, I'll be marrying you too, Marc. We are all going to live happily ever after together."

Even with all the bruises marring her creamy skin, Kitten looks downright mischievous. I can't wipe the smile off my face as she leads Marcus from the room as he tries to explain to her that she can't marry more than one person.

I just shake my head. Doesn't he know that if there's one person on this earth that can find a loophole, it will be our girl?

Chapter Forty-One

RHYS

P eople are staring. They can't fucking help themselves, and all it does is fill me with more happiness. They can stare all they want. They can frown and whisper about how unacceptable it is that I walk around holding the hands of two guys at once, while another sweeps in for a kiss every now and then, and another moves up behind me to whisper in my ear before sucking my lobe into the heat of his mouth.

What a scandal.

It's laughable to me because I simply don't care. I'm so in love with these guys, and they love me back just as fiercely. Nothing else matters but the way we feel for each other. Even our parents have come to terms with the situation.

Shaun's parents were the first on board, already aware of the arrangement, accepting us as a part of their family, although his dad stays relatively quiet about it. My parents are still supporting me and have accepted me for who I am, welcoming my guys as a part of our family. Marcus' parents have taken some convincing, but after they had us over for dinner last week, they've seen firsthand how we all just work, and Garrett's mum said she didn't care how Garrett lives his life as long as he is happy.

Simon's mum already had a glimpse into our relationship the day we spoke in British accents while we ate pizza with her. She obviously didn't realise how serious things were, and when Simon announced that we were in an official group relationship, she demanded he end things with us or she would cut him off financially. He moved out that day into the staff quarters at Shaun's house and has been learning the ropes over this last week on the ins and outs of working on a small vineyard.

Of course, Ty still isn't here with us, something that I really hate, and I'm counting down the days until we can stop hiding his involvement.

"So this is all of your work?" Simon asks as we stand in front of the display of black and white photos lining the wall in this part of the local gallery.

The school shows off students' work for a week at the end of each school year, and this time, my work has its own display since I've been given a creativity award for my Beauty in Darkness portfolio.

I smile with pride at the pictures I created, which hold a very haunted vibe. "Yes, it's my work, although some of the photos were taken by Garrett."

The big guy in question wraps his arms around me from behind, pressing his lips to the top of my head. I sink back into his hold, keeping my hands locked with Shaun and Marcus, who are at my sides.

When we went camping, Garrett used my camera to take some sneaky pictures of me. On display, I've included the one of me asleep with Garrett's face near mine, which was the night he shared the tent with me so I wouldn't be alone. He took a selfie of sorts, taken with an SLR camera.

There's also one of me on Simon's back, which was when he was pretending to be a horse as we hiked back to camp. There's one of me and Marcus out in the water at Ebony Falls. It's an intimate picture that only I know the story of, when Marcus was trying to calm me down after my panic that there were wildebeests lurking under the water.

Garrett even managed to capture one of Shaun and me sitting next to each other with the glow of the campfire lighting up our faces as we stare into each other's eyes.

Unbeknownst to most people, there's even one of me and Ty. You can't tell it's Ty, though, with the way I cropped most of him out, only leaving his lips and chin as he presses a kiss to my forehead. That picture was taken on Garrett's phone the night Marcus broke into Ty's lake house and busted us. Garrett showed me it just last week and said he took it for me in case I ever doubted Ty's love for me again. In the original picture, you can see the love in his expression, and *that* version is for my eyes only, at least until I'm eighteen.

"It's incredible, Kitten." Shaun praises me, and my chest fills with warmth.

"Rhys?" My mum's voice gains my attention, and I turn to look at her as she approaches us with someone at her side.

My heart stops and then flips, and I'm certain my cheeks have flushed red as I take in the sight of Tyler right next to my mum. A lump forms in my throat. I haven't seen him in the flesh since the day I left the hospital a few weeks back. My only visuals of him have been on our daily FaceTime calls.

"Breathe, Rhee," Marcus whispers next to me as we all turn to face them as a group.

My hands are trembling, I realise, and my mum gives me a look that tells me not to leap on Ty in front of everyone.

Damn it.

"Hi." Is all I manage, and Ty grins.

"Rhys. Congratulations on the creativity award for your portfolio. It's well deserved."

I nod. "Thanks." Feeling weird that I can't just talk to him the way I want to. He may not be a teacher at our school anymore, but everyone still looks at him as Mr Foster, the PE teacher.

"Did you see us up there? We look good." Simon chuckles, pointing his thumb over his shoulder. To an outsider, they wouldn't pick up the double meaning. Us, meaning Tyler as well.

His eyes flick over my head, and he studies the display again as I drink in his appearance. He's wearing blue jeans with brown boots, and his light blue shirt is obscured by the sling supporting his left shoulder and arm. He's been telling people he had a shoulder reconstruction, and because he's a sporty guy, they believe he must have an old injury that required surgery.

He looks good in casual clothes. I'm so used to seeing him in sports clothing that the visual before me sends heat to places that should be sleeping right now.

A grin tugs at Ty's lips as he notices the picture on display of the two of us, and his deep blue eyes flick back to mine, flaring with happiness.

"It's a truly beautiful display, Rhys."

I bite my lip, a full blush creeping over my face as my mum clears her throat.

"Well, Mr Foster has some more displays to look at." My mum bursts my bubble, and I want to growl at her, but then she speaks again, and I want to kiss her. "Mr Foster will be joining us at the family barbeque later."

"Oh?" My eyes dart from her smug face to Ty's, who nods.

"See you all later." He shoots me a wink, and I watch him walk away with my mum, stopping every now and then to talk to an ex-student, parent or teacher.

"Can the barbeque start now?" I ask and the guys chuckle before Simon bounds in front of me and slaps another kiss on my lips.

His playfulness extracts another weird girly giggle from me, something I've been doing more of over the last couple of weeks, as the dark clouds that have been looming over me slowly dissipate.

The guys continue to distract me throughout the event before we all leave to go back to my house. When we get there, the twins are chasing each other around with foam dart guns while Charlotte and my dad stand over the barbeque as they start to cook up today's feast.

While they're busy and my mum joins in to help, we sneak off to my bedroom, where we lock ourselves in, and the guys work together to help me move past some of the trauma that's been plaguing me since the night Master Hill attacked me.

The doctor hasn't given me the all-clear for penetration yet, but the grazes have healed, and each day over the last week, I've been letting go of my fears and steering Kitty back to Funtown.

"Ok, so we've tried clitoral stimulation, some tongue alphabet, dry humping, nipple stimulation, and visual stimulation. What do you want today, Rhee?"

"Do you have to make it sound so clinical?" Shaun complains to Marcus as he tugs me towards my bed, and I grin because these guys are just too good to me.

"It's all g. Sex talk, whether it's clinical or not, gets me going."

Shaun chuckles. "Of course it does."

"How about dirty talk?" Simon offers, "Or food play?"

I bite my lip. "Can I have a visual with dirty talk during the tongue alphabet?"

All four guys chuckle this time, and the sound fills my heart, so full of warmth and happiness.

"What visual do you want, Kitten?" Shaun asks, and I shrug.

"Gay porn. In real life."

All four groan because I haven't stopped trying to get them to step over that line. Honestly, I'd be surprised if they did, but it's fun stirring them up with it.

"What about a game? First one to come loses." Marcus suggests, and my brows shoot up. This guy is full of ideas these days, and I fucking love it.

"What does the winner get?" Simon asks as he ties his ash blonde hair up in a topknot like he's preparing to get dirty.

Marcus shrugs and looks at me. "What do you think, Rhee?"

I take my time, pretending to mull over the idea when I already know what I want to say, and then I speak innocently. "First penetration when the Doc gives the green light?"

Simon's eyes flare with excitement, and he starts tugging down his pants, ready to take on the challenge.

"I should probably bow out. There's no way I'm going there first and risk hurting you again." Garrett declares, and I frown. He has a point.

"If you win, you can choose who it will be when the time comes, and as an added bonus, I'll let you choke me with your cockzilla at the same time."

Garrett's smile is blinding in response, and Marcus nods, happy with that arrangement.

Shaun ducks out of my bedroom, grabbing some towels from the linen closet before returning and laying them out on the floor, and then the guys drop their pants, joining Simon and lining up shoulder to shoulder before me with their growing dicks.

"What if I come before you?" I ask, slipping my skirt down but leaving my pink knickers on. I'm thinking a little peekaboo action will rile them up real quick.

"You have to keep going." Shaun grins. "You don't get to stop until there is no one else standing."

"Mean," I whine like it's a huge inconvenience when really, fuck yes, I'm down with that arrangement. The guys chuckle, knowing me too well.

I lean back on my bed, parting my legs and rolling my hips. That's all it takes for Simon to start pumping his dick.

"Mmm, yes, Sy. Fuck your hand for me."

"Yes, Cherry. Anything for you."

I bite my lip, looking at the other three who haven't touched their dicks yet.

"You three aren't turning me on right now."

Again, they chuckle but join Simon, wrapping their hands around their cocks, which are now at full attention. The sight is beautiful, all four with their pants around their ankles and their t-shirts still covering their chest, but their hands fisting their hard dicks, stroking themselves. Them being partially dressed almost seems naughtier, like it's too risky to get completely naked.

"Touch yourself, Baby Girl," Garrett demands, and I feel the instant gush between my thighs.

I make an O with my lips, feigning surprise, and dart my eyes between my legs to direct their attention. Four masculine groans fill the air as the evidence of my arousal dampens my panties.

"Kitty likes how you command her, Mr Cole." I press my fingers over my panty-clad clit and give it a gentle rub.

A rumbling sound comes from Garrett's chest, and he takes his second hand and wraps it around his beast of a cock. Jesus, he really does need two hands to tend to that monster.

"Fuck Kitten. I want to lose just because I know if you see me come, you're likely to, as well."

Damn it. Shaun knows me too well. He's fucking right. I *will* come if he does. If any of them do. Just the thought has me increasing the pressure over my clit and picking up the pace.

"You know what will really make me come? Hard?" I ask, and Shaun smirks. He fucking knows what I'm going to say. "If you come in Simon's arse."

"Fuck. Stop Cherry." Simon hisses, strangling his cock, trying to stop himself from losing the game.

It's hard to stop, though, because the thought is sending me fucking insane with need.

"What about my arse?" Marcus asks, and my eyes dart to him. "You wanna see Bossi fill my arse up with cum?"

I moan, intense need hitting me hard, and I can't control how fast my finger starts to move. "Yes." I pant, more damp heat wetting my panties.

Marcus' eyes flare, so I give him more of a show, gripping the fabric and pulling it tight between my folds. They all moan, their hands working faster, and even Simon has joined back in. I'm so turned on by how turned on they are that I don't think I need anyone to blow their load to get me over the edge. We spend a few minutes working ourselves over. Them pumping their dicks, while I rub, circle, and tease my entrance through the fabric of my knickers.

I spread my legs wider, pulling back the fabric to give them a flash of flesh, and I see the moment when Shaun loses control, and I know he's not even bothering with the challenge. He's going to come soon.

"Rub your pussy, Baby Girl." Garrett grits out, and my hand does as he commands, rubbing over it from front to back to front again. The need to come is too much now, so I give in to the feeling and play my clit like a fucking guitar string and cry out moments later. As my Kitty pulses, I close my eyes briefly, annoyed to be losing the visual of my guys, but when I open them again, I see Shaun's face, contorted as he struggles to hold himself back, so I give him a verbal nudge.

"Remember when Skipper fucked me on the platform, Cass, and you came in my mouth?"

White rivers of cum jet from his dick as he throws his head back, and like the greedy little bitch I am, I leap forward off my bed and try to catch some in my mouth as I kneel on the towel in front of him. That's when Marcus starts too, so I throw myself down on the floor in front of him just in time to get my face creamed. I'm pretty sure I've just dirtied up my little white collared shirt too, but fuck, who cares. I fucking love this.

My body takes over now, and I give myself over to the Kitten in me. My hand slips between my legs again, mashing my cunt in desperation as I give in to my animalistic need. Marcus and Shaun step back while Simon moves to stand over my feet, and Garrett shifts to loom over my head.

"What a fucking spectacular view!" I sing as I stimulate Kitty, while darting my tongue out to taste the cum on my chin. I have no idea if it's Marcus' or Shaun's, and fuck if that doesn't give me an even bigger Kitty stiffy.

"Hey Cass," I pant. "Come down here and bend over so I can finger your arse."

"You're…not… playing fair… Cherry." Simon grits out, and I grin because hell no, I'm not. I'm surprised he's lasted this long, and he knows I'm trying to get him to lose. Only because I want Garrett to choke me on his cock while one of them fucks me. How could I not want that?

Shaun does as he's told and lowers down next to me, poking his arse out near my head. "Give me your finger, Kitten." He rasps over his shoulder, his voice husky with arousal, and I give him my middle finger. He takes my hand, leading my finger into his mouth, his tongue swirling and lubing it up with saliva. With my other hand on Kitty, I circle my clit slowly, keeping the slow build, and watch as Shaun bends over more, parting his arse cheeks for me as he waits for me to penetrate him.

I've never done this before, so my heart races as I press my digit to his puckered rose, and I slowly sink it in.

Before I know what's happening, Simon lowers himself down to my feet, picking them up in his hand and pressing the souls of my feet to his straining cock. With my finger deep in Shaun's arse, and my feet effectively wanking Simon, I explode again, not even needing the extra friction from my fingers. That's when Simon loses his load, using my feet to catch his cum.

"Fuck. Why is this all so hot? Am I gay?" Marcus pants, his hand around his dick again, and I shake my head.

"It's just sex. And it's so hot because it's just us." I pant.

"I win." Garrett grits between his teeth, and my eyes shoot up to the sight of his heavy balls swaying as Garrett pumps his dick with two hands.

My finger is still in Shaun's arse, and I can feel him pushing back against my hand, wanting my finger to do more, so I take a risk and ask for help.

What's the worst that will happen?

"Sy, come take over for me here." I gesture my head to Shaun's arse.

Shaun's eyes dart back over his shoulder to meet mine, and I raise a brow in question, giving him a chance to say no, but the sexy fucker grins.

"You want me to..." Simon points to where my finger is disappearing into Shaun's arse.

"Yeah. If you want to? Cass doesn't mind. Do you, Cass?"

"Nope, I just want someone's finger up there."

I moan, my eyes falling shut as Kitty takes over, famished after hearing Shaun's words.

"Move, Hastings. I'm hungry." Marcus hisses, and my lids fly open again to see Simon shifting back and Marcus kneeling between my legs. Fuck yes. I don't even care how needy I look when I lift my hips to close the distance between Marcus' mouth and my Kitty.

He sweeps my knickers to the side, and the hot silk of his tongue glides up between my folds. I cry out, slipping my finger from Shaun's arse and fisting my hands into Marcus' hair. I'll have to remember to tell him to shower after this since my finger has just been in his mate's arse.

My eyes dart between the fierce brown pools looking up at me between my legs, to Shaun and Simon shifting in position next to me as Simon sinks his finger in his mouth in preparation, then to Garrett, whose nuts are now a lot fucking closer to my head now that he is kneeling.

I'm so close again, especially when I watch Simon sink his finger into Shaun's arse, and both of their expressions fill with so much lust that I'm surprised they are able to hold themselves back so well.

I can't believe Garrett hasn't come yet. One look at his expression shows me he is close, but he is holding it back. What for, I wonder? Maybe he loves the feeling of that build up, or maybe he loves edging himself. Fuck, that's a hot thought, but since I know lunch will be ready soon, I do the one thing that I know will make him spiral.

Pressing my teeth into the healing cut on my palm, thanks to my knife-wielding with Julie a few weeks back, I split the scabbed skin and don't stop until I taste metallic on my tongue. Then I reach up over my head and rub my hand over the tip of cockzilla, sliding it down the shaft before pulling away.

Garrett hisses, and I watch his face turn into the monster lurking underneath, his eyes flaring, his teeth snarling as he takes my offering and smears it over the taut skin before he explodes. The hot streams of cum that shoot from him feel more like he has unleashed a hose on me, spraying hard into my parted lips, then over my chest, completely drenching my shirt, then down near my bare flesh that is being worked over by Marcus.

I scream, my orgasm hitting me hard and fast, and a hand slaps over my mouth, but it does little to muffle the sound ripping from me. My hearing wanes, and it takes a few moments to return to hear the last parts of multiple male groans as more cum is spilled in my bedroom.

Shaun is panting, a pool of white creamy goodness sitting below him as his face quirks into a small grin. Simon is behind him, his chest rising and falling as he slowly slips his finger free of Shaun's arse, and I notice trails of more white creamy goodness painting the golden globes of Shaun's arse.

Holy shit. I wonder how close Sy was to replacing his finger with his dick?

And now Kitty is awake again.

FFS!

"Rhee. You ok?" I glance down at Marcus, who is using one of the towels to wipe up his cum, and then he presses it to his cheek where some of Garrett's reached.

"Yes." I rasp, my voice husky. "I'm extremely ok."

CHAPTER FORTY-TWO

SIMON

W e all needed to shower after the session in Cherry's bedroom. When we opened her door, we realised someone had closed the door to the living area where the kids' bedrooms are. There's a fair fucking chance we were too loud. It starts to worry me that her olds will kick us out or something, but when we emerge sometime later, showered, and re-dressed in a new outfit in Cherry's case, no one says anything.

Actually, that's a lie. Mr fucking Foster is there, glaring at us. My mind is still blown about that. Mr Foster is Ty. Lucky for him, I've always liked him. He was a pretty decent teacher, and the love he has in his eyes for our girl makes the whole thing easier to accept.

"You peewees better not be making her do anything she's not ready for." Tyler hisses between clenched teeth as he approaches us in the kitchen, away from Rhys' parents' ears.

"As if we would ever do that." Marcus rolls his eyes at Tyler, which wins him another glare made just for him.

"It's ok, Ty. I'm fine." Cherry offers, and I watch her link her pinkie with his. The way we are all standing shields anyone else from seeing the action, and I watch Ty visibly relax at her discrete touch.

Yeah, he loves her just as much as the rest of us do.

We haven't really discussed his part in this relationship since the day our girl was taken from us. It's like the events of that day cemented all of our relationships, no matter our age or who we are.

I still have fucking nightmares about that day. How fucking scared I was! I thought I was going to lose her, and even after we got her back, I was so worried about what new version of Rhys George we would get.

She's strong, though. Stronger than I could ever be. She's able to switch the trauma she's been through off somehow. We have been to a few of her therapy sessions over the last few weeks. Melia has been travelling to Fox Pines from the city to have long sessions with Cherry after everything that happened, and I've learnt a couple of things about our girl from those sessions.

One is that when she switches off the bad things, she's compartmentalising. Apparently, she has the ability to pick up those bad memories and put them somewhere else in her brain, so she doesn't have to think about them. Melia explained it to us, and also reminded Cherry that it's not healthy to lock her pain away. Cherry agreed and has been using her therapy sessions to release the memories, but as soon as she walks out that door, she switches it off again.

The other thing we learnt is that Cherry has arousal triggers as a result of the grooming she endured as a child. Melia believes this is where Cherry's need for sex came from, and she even explained, on behalf of our girl who was too embarrassed to say the words herself, that she was made to feel pleasure when she was groomed, which was why the video we saw of her didn't show a traumatised little girl.

My mind comes back to the present as I watch Cherry and Ty draw closer together like an invisible magnet is tugging at them. Without even realising, me and the other guys shift to shield Ty and Rhys even more from her family, who are outside the bifold doors on the patio. Ty takes the opportunity to lift Cherry's hand, pressing his lips to it before whispering to her.

"I miss you."

Fuck. I nearly tear up. There are just so many fucking emotions involved with this relationship stuff. I feel so… complete. My mates are my brothers. We are like our own little family unit, all with the same goal. To love Cherry and protect her until our dying days.

"Lunch is ready." Mr Rogan calls out, and we disperse from our tight group to stroll casually out onto the patio like we didn't just come all over their daughter less than thirty minutes ago.

We take our seats, and Cherry links her fingers with mine, tugging me to sit down next to her. I love how she does that. She finds time to make each of us feel special and loved. She's such a Queen. Our Queen.

Marcus takes the seat on the other side of her while Ty sits next to me at the end of the table, and Garrett and Shaun sit across from us.

"Oh, look at that." Cherry whispers so only we can hear. "I have Dad up one end of the table, and Daddy up the other." She snickers under her breath, and a low rumble sounds from Ty as she flashes a toothy smile his way.

We eat and chat. The food is fucking amazing, and the conversation is light and happy. Cherry and I work together to eat our food like a well-oiled machine. Somehow, she knows when I want to feed her something from my plate, and she turns her head, parting those pink lips for me. It's like we have been eating together for years like this. The idea of that filling my chest with warmth as I hope that in years to come, this is how we will eat.

"Can I have everyone's attention?" Mrs Rogan pushes her chair back and stands, her eyes roaming over everyone before she smiles down at her husband at the head of the table.

"Is this where you tell us that we are getting a new puppy?" Charlotte asks with a knowing smile and the twins gasp.

"We're getting a puppy?"

Mrs Rogan glares at Charlotte before turning her eyes to her sons. "No, boys. We aren't getting a puppy."

The twins' faces drop as their mum ruins their dream of having a puppy, and their little shoulders slump.

"Nice one, mum." Charlotte giggles, and I realise she's just as much of a shit stirrer as Cherry is.

Mrs Rogan sighs. "Simon?"

My eyes widen as all eyes fall to me, and I glance at Cherry to see her biting back a smirk.

"Uh-yeah?" I ask warily, glancing back at my school principal.

"I've been speaking with Mr and Mrs Bossier." Mrs Rogan smiles. "He advises me that you're living on their farm now and working on weekends. Is that right?"

My eyes automatically dart across the table to Shaun, noticing his broad grin. "Uh-yeah."

"I was happy to hear that. I was a little worried after your mother called to un-enrol you. She mentioned she was trying to get you to move with her to Western Australia."

My shoulders slump. I still can't believe my mum thought I'd leave my mates and my girl. Why would I go anywhere with her after she spent most of my life not wanting anything to do with me? It only took a week to sell our house, and she called my bluff, so I packed my bags and walked out. The staff quarters at Bossi's farm might not be luxurious, but it feels more like home than that stupid, oversized mansion ever did.

"Yeah. She left, and I stayed, and the Bossier's have been kind enough to put a roof over my head." My voice is flat because even though I am still here, I can't continue going to Fox Pines Catholic, as both my parents refuse to cover the bill.

"That's very kind of them." She smiles over to Shaun, who is nodding, proud of his family for not being arseholes. "Your mother mentioned that if you stay, you will have to attend public school for your final year."

"Yep." I nod, looking down at my plate.

"It's lucky I didn't finalise your un-enrolment paperwork then, isn't it?"

My eyes dart up to Mrs Rogan in confusion. "What?"

She turns around and takes some papers off a table behind her and then walks around the table to me, holding them out. "You have been granted a full scholarship to complete your final year of school at Fox Pines Catholic."

"What?" My eyes lock on the papers she's holding out, and with a shaky hand, I take them. My eyes roam over the words, and it takes a moment to sink in before I glance back up at her with damp eyes. "Really?"

"Yes, really." She smiles and nods, and I leap up from my seat, sending it crashing behind me. I throw my arms around her, and she stiffens, but I don't fucking care. She's getting a Simon hug, whether she likes it or not.

Cheers ring out around me, and I turn to Cherry, who is now standing, her lips spread wide in a smile as she watches on. I leap at her next, throwing my arms around her.

"I fucking love you, Cherry."

"I love you too, Sy." She rasps against my ear before we pull back.

I can't fucking help myself. I slap a kiss on those delicious lips in front of her parents, and the next thing I know, we are in a group hug, the guys diving on us to share in my celebration. We all start jumping around, linked together as one, but I realise someone is missing, so I break free of our group and approach Tyler.

His smile is genuine, and he stands from his chair, holding his hand out for me to shake. I shake my head at him and slap it away as his eyes go wide. Then I hug him too.

CHAPTER FORTY-THREE

RHYS

My cheeks hurt from smiling so much. Simon is so happy, and so he should be. He deserves to be happy. All my guys do.

I didn't even go to my mum and ask her to do this for Simon. She came to me and said that's what she was doing. I had to keep the secret for two fucking days. Holy hell, that was hard. I wanted to say something so many times, and in the end, I told Ty last night when I was alone on our daily FaceTime call. I get the feeling Shaun already knew, though. Cheeky fucker knows how to keep a secret.

"I have something else to say." My mum's voice gains everyone's attention, and we all return to our seats wearing the biggest, goofiest grins ever. Cynthia moves back over to the table she had Simon's scholarship papers on and picks up a large envelope. Then she turns her brown eyes to me.

"Rhys. We have something for you." She smiles down at Will, who stands from his chair and wraps his arm across her shoulders, smiling back at me. "We have actually had these for a while, but we didn't feel you were ready." She swallows like she has a lump in her throat and tears well in her eyes.

I stand, concern sinking into my chest. "Mum?"

She waves a hand in front of her face like that will make the tears disappear, and she shakes her head. "Maybe it's best if you just take this." She holds out the envelope.

I reach out across Marcus over the table and take the envelope, confusion swirling through my head. What the hell is going on?

Holding it in my hand, I glance back at my parents, who both nod at me to open the envelope, so I do. My fingers grip the papers inside, and I ease them out.

FAMILY COURT OF VICTORIA
ADOPTION ORDER

My lungs stop functioning. Air locks tight in my chest. My face heats, a flush washing over me as my eyes continue to read the document in my hand, picking up the most important words.

Mrs Cynthia Rogan and Mr William Rogan do hereby undertake to adopt Patrice Mauve George...

"Oh my God," I whisper, tears spilling free and my vision blurring. I want to look up, but I can't. I just can't. If I do, I know I'll break.

"Rhee," Marcus whispers next to me, and my bottom lip starts fucking seizing. My hands start trembling, so I slowly place the papers down on the table next to my plate and use the backs of my knees to push my chair back.

I don't look up. I keep my eyes trained on the ground as I walk on shaky legs to the end of the table where my parents are standing. Waiting for me to respond.

"Rhys?" My dad asks, concern laced in his tone.

Slowly I look up, using both my hands to bat my tears away as I let the meaning of those papers sink in. Their faces come into view, and even though they are blurry on account of my stupid tears, I can still see the love on their faces for me.

"I love you guys." I whisper, because there's no way in hell I can manage more than that right now. And then I throw my arms around them.

Cynthia starts crying too, all the emotions of the last few months catching up with her, and a few moments later, I feel more arms around me from behind, although these arms sit lower. Connor and Archie start crying, and then I smell the scent of incense that follows Charlotte around as she joins our hug, too.

Even though I'm in this bubble with my family, I can still feel the presence of my guys. It's like the Kitten in me can sense them. And by Kitten, I really mean my heart.

It takes me about twenty minutes to stop being emotional. Each of my guys gives me a good hug. Well, all but Ty, but our eyes gravitate back to each other so many times, and I can tell how desperately he wants to take me in his arms and show me how happy he is for me.

Neither of us are willing to push my parents' boundaries, though. The fact that they even allow me to communicate with him, to invite him into their house, knowing what we have between us, must be hard. I know they are thankful for Ty trying to save me. So we will take what they give us, and once I'm eighteen, things for us should get a little easier.

After all the tears and smiles, we all help to clean up, and then my guys, all of my guys, decide to kick a footy around on the vacant block next to us. We only have one neighbour so far, who are on the other side of our block, and we still don't have fences up, but with Christmas only a couple of weeks away, my parents have tasked themselves with the landscaping job while they have time off work.

It's fun watching the guys tackle each other and how they all try to take Ty down, Garrett being the only successful one. It's a little after three when my phone rings and Lexi's name flashes across the screen, so I answer it.

"Turn on the news," Lexi yells down the line.

I bolt up from my chair. "What?" My tone catches the attention of the guys and my parents.

"Turn on the TV. Channel Seven News. Quick!" Lexi demands, and I rush back into the house, fumbling with the remote to get the damn

TV on. It takes me a few tries, but eventually, the screen lights up, and my parents and the guys join me inside.

"What's going on?" My mum asks.

I ignore her, trying to figure that out myself.

Then I see it. The Breaking News.

> Mr Terence Hill from Fox Pines, who was recently charged for his role in a paedophile scandal in Victoria, has been brutally murdered under the noses of his police guard while undergoing treatment in a burns clinic in Melbourne. Sources say police are baffled as to how it happened, and video footage has not given them any leads.

"What the?" Simon mumbles behind me, and I spin to my parents.

"Tell me this isn't a joke. Tell me this is real?"

My dad nods, taking his phone out to make a call.

"It has to be real. Surely, they wouldn't name him if his identity wasn't confirmed." Marcus offers, his eyes wide in shock as they remain trained on the screen.

I remember then that I'm still clutching my phone with Lexi on the end of the line, so I press it to my ear again.

"Lex."

"It's over, Rhys. He's gone. They are *all* gone." She cries.

My heart sinks because they aren't all gone. Not yet. I don't voice that to her, though. She is excited for me. Happy that these monsters have been removed from existence.

I chat with Lexi for a little while longer, and when my dad comes back into the room, nodding and announcing that Officer Zimora has confirmed that Terence Hill has been murdered, I suck in a slow, steady breath and silently thank whoever the hell it was that stopped that oxygen thief once and for all.

I feel kind of numb. I'm happy he's gone. I'd been disappointed when the police found him near the pool, burnt to a crisp, yet still alive. He deserved death too, but now that it's been delivered, I kind of wish I'd been the one to send him to hell. I keep my thoughts to myself about that, though. I'm already seeing my therapist a couple of times a week at the moment. My 'rents will surely demand more sessions if they knew my line of thinking.

"Does this mean it's over?" Marcus asks, and I turn to see four sets of loving eyes on me.

I shake my head and sneak a glance at Ty. His lips are thin, and I know he's thinking the same thing as me, but it's Shaun who speaks quietly so my parents can't hear, and Ty takes a few steps closer.

"There's still the possibility that the police will find the member list for the Feast nights. If it's on the cloud drive that the police have access to, then me, Rhys and Ty will be put in the spotlight. It won't end well for Ty."

"Actually, I've taken care of that," Ty announces, and my brows shoot up.

"You have?"

He nods. "I reached out to Bec and Amanda and asked if their contacts could make our names and membership contracts vanish, along with a few others. I also asked them to find the video of us, Kitten. The one in the barn. It's all mysteriously vanished. The police can't get their hands on it."

"You sneaky fucker." Shaun chuckles, his face lighting up in a relieved grin.

"Lucky is what he is," Marcus mutters. He has accepted Ty, but I think it will be a while before he stops giving Tyler a hard time.

"So it really is over, then?" Simon asks what Marcus asked before.

"Not quite." Garrett rasps, and my eyes meet his. There's anger in them, but it's not anger towards me or anyone in this room.

"Brian," I whisper, and they each nod. "His time will come soon enough."

My words are sure and strong, and I do what I do best, shoving all unwanted thoughts to the back of my mind.

After things calm down, my parents retreat outside to lounge in the sun while the twins make a dirt track for their matchbox cars. The guys have had enough of the sun, apparently, so they move to the theatre to put on a movie while I reluctantly say goodbye to Ty and walk him out.

Our hands brush as we slowly walk down the passage that leads to my front door. I glance up at him to notice his eyes already on me as we delay the inevitable. I don't know how long it will be before I get to see him in person again. He's adamant about keeping his distance until I'm eighteen out of respect for my parents.

My heart sinks. The thought of not tasting his lips on mine until April is almost unbearable. I stop walking and glance back over my shoulder. My parents and the twins are out in the backyard. Char has gone to see her girlfriend. The guys are in the theatre.

"Kitten?" The rasp of Ty's voice is low, and I glance back to see he has stopped walking too, his deep blue eyes showing his confusion.

I bite my lip, dragging my gaze from his to peer down the darkened hallway off to my right, which leads to the garage and the guest powder room.

"Kitten?" Ty asks again, but this time it sounds more like a warning, so I grin and drag my eyes back to his.

"Daddy," I whisper, and he growls. He's about to open his mouth and say something else, but I shoosh him and snatch his hand in mine, quickly dragging him down the dark passage. He doesn't fight me. He lets me tug him toward the door of the small powder room, but when I go to step inside, he stops me, tugging me back and pushing me up against the wall by the door.

"You're going to get me into trouble, Kitten."

I shrug. "We *are* trouble, Ty. Why fight it?"

He chuckles quietly. "You make it impossible to refuse you."

"Good. It's best not to, anyway. I'm good at causing a commotion when I don't get my own way." I flash him a playful smile, and he shakes his head, his grin spreading wider. Fuck, it's really beautiful. I won't tell him that because I'm sure he'd have something to say about me thinking he's beautiful, but the way he smiled just now is the happiest smile I've ever seen on him. I want to see it more. Like every day.

"What are we doing here, Kitten?"

"What do you want to do here, *Daddy*?"

A low rumble comes from his chest, and I shoot him a wink.

He steps forward, closing the space between us and caging me in against the wall with his good arm.

"I can't do what I want to do yet, Kitten. You're still healing."

"There are some things I can do," I whisper, craning my head back to lock eyes with him as he hovers close, our lips a breath apart.

"No." He rasps. "Not here."

I pout.

"But," he grins, "I will steal a kiss." He sweeps down and presses his lips to mine.

My hands grip his shirt, tugging him closer, and he growls into my mouth as he tries to play nice and hold himself back. I want him to give in and just go with this, but I know he's trying to be respectful. I just really fucking miss him.

Our lips are searing against each other. The kiss turning hot and heavy in no time. He presses his body flush against mine, and I can feel his arousal through the barrier of our clothing. I grind my needy Kitty against his thigh, and I was hoping the action would push him over the edge to step inside the powder room with me.

Apparently not.

"Kitten." He rasps quietly, pulling back from me and biting his lower lip. "I fucking love you. I ache for you like you can't believe. I just don't want to risk things when we are so close to being free to be together."

I pout. "I miss you so much. Kitty misses your dick, and my body misses your hands, and my lips miss your kisses."

"And my heart misses your heart, Rhys."

My playfulness slips away as my emotions rise to the surface at his words.

"My heart misses your heart too, Ty."

He presses his forehead to mine, cupping my face and sweeping his big thumb across my flaming cheek. "We just need to be patient. We will be together again before you know it."

Slowly, I nod, knowing he is right, but selfishly wanting it all right this minute.

"I should go." He pulls back, dropping his hand from my cheek. "Your photo portfolio really is beautiful. You should definitely keep taking photos."

I blush at his praise and nod a little, feeling uncharacteristically shy all of a sudden.

"Thank you."

He chuckles. "That was hard for you, wasn't it? Accepting the compliment?"

My eyes narrow, and I slap his good shoulder playfully, causing him to laugh.

He gestures his head back towards the passage that leads to the entry of my house, and I sigh in defeat, scuffing my feet on the tiles as we exit the darkened passage. My eyes won't leave the sight of his face, so my first realisation that there's something wrong is when his face pales.

"Good decision, Tyler." My mum's voice is like a cold bucket of water, and my eyes dart to the side to see her giving Ty a stern look as she stands in the passage with her arms folded over her chest.

"Mum? Were you eavesdropping? What if we…"

"I would have stopped it before you did anything more, Rhys." She snaps, not at all happy.

"Uh, Cynthia. Sorry… I-."

"I know exactly what happened." My mum snaps again, shifting her gaze from Tyler to give me a pointed look.

"I miss him," I whisper, my emotions flaring to the surface, and my eyes plead with her to not make a big deal out of this.

She's quiet for a moment, but sighs and drops her arms to her sides. "I invited Tyler today because I know how much you miss him, and I wanted him to be a part of this special day for you. It doesn't mean I can turn a blind eye to certain things, though, Rhys. All I ask is that you please wait until you are of legal age to be with him in *that* way."

I nod, shooting my wet eyes to the floor, feeling like the child I am in the presence of two adults.

"I love her, Cynthia." Ty takes my hand in his, and I glance up to see his deep blue eyes already locked on me. "And when she turns eighteen, I would like to date Rhys and do things the right way." He drags his gaze from me to look at my mum. "If you will allow me?"

"I can see how much you both love each other, Tyler. There's no question in my mind about that. So yes, once she is eighteen, you can date her. But." Her principal voice slices through the air with her, *but*, "if you do anything to disrespect her, I will cut your fucking balls off."

A laugh bubbles up my throat, and I slap my hand over my mouth.

"I would expect nothing less, Cin." Ty gives my mum a nod, bow type of thing, and tugs my hand as we walk toward the front door.

I glance back to see my mum watching us, and when we reach the door, I turn back to see Ty trying to bite back a smirk. I grin back and stand still as he leans down, his lips hovering close to my ear.

"I love you, beautiful. Call you later." Then he gently brushes his lips over my cheek as he pulls back.

All I can do is nod and swoon because apparently, I'm that type of girl now, and I watch him walk out the front door.

When I turn back to my mum, I roll my eyes at her. "You're such a cockblock, Cynthia."

My teasing tone coerces a slight smirk from my mum, and she shakes her head.

"You have four cocks in the theatre. Don't act like you have it tough."

I burst out laughing at my mum's words. No teenage daughter would have ever heard those words pass their mum's lips before. But then again, no teenage girl would call their mum a cockblock, either. It's for this reason, amongst many more, that I know I truly have found my forever home.

Chapter Forty-Four

RHYS

Four Months Later

M y eighteenth birthday party was cancelled. Cancelled! And why? Because there is a virus sweeping the world, and the state government of Victoria has sent us into a lockdown. Seriously! What the actual fuck?

On a good note, we started the school holidays a week early, but everyone is freaking out because there are talks that the government is going to keep kids at home after the holidays for remote learning. What the hell is remote learning, anyway?

Like seriously? They want us to stay home?

Hell fucking yes!

The bad thing is that we aren't allowed, visitors. I mean, it would be bad if we obeyed the rules, but so far, my guys have come through my bedroom window every night, and when my mum and dad come into my bedroom, the guys try to hide, and my olds pretend like they can't see their feet poking out at the bottom of the curtains, or the way my bed has a big lump in it covered by blankets. They even gave me extra cake to take to my bedroom last night after the twins sang happy birthday to me for the millionth time.

It's only been a short time in this weird lockdown, but I can't say I hate it. Our house is full with Charlotte home every night, and we now share the kids' zone with the new puppy the olds finally brought home, even though she's really fucking quiet. And by new puppy, I mean I have a new foster sister who moved in just before the start of the school year.

All in all, things have been pretty fucking top-notch. My guys dote on me every day, and I've been focusing more on school, especially after having to re-sit my exams after I was granted special circumstances due to the kidnapping and threats leading up to the exams at the end of last year.

I've been attending my therapy sessions with Melia, plus an hour a week with the school counsellor, and I go to fortnightly meetings at the Youth Crisis and Addiction Centre in Redfield. I could argue that I no longer have an addiction problem, but that would be complacent of me. I've learnt the best thing I can do is continue working on myself. I may still be a crazy bitch, but I'm more self-aware now about my triggers and reactions.

"Rhys. Can you come here, please?" My dad's voice calling to me makes me roll my eyes. Since lockdown began, we have entered into a war of foam bullets, so no doubt, the moment I walk out into the main living area, I'm going to get shot.

Game on, Daddio.

I grin to myself, slipping my phone into my back pocket and snatch up the toy gun, loading a bullet in preparation as I leave the safety of my bedroom. My new foster sister, who is lounging on the sofa, raises a dark brow at me, but I just shoot her a mischievous grin and do an army roll across the floor of the kids' zone before standing and flattening myself against the wall by the door.

"Rhys?" My dad calls again, and I grin before I leap through the doorway, gun raised and ready to shoot.

The moment a tall figure shifts in my peripheral, I aim and shoot, but then gasp when I realise I shot someone *other* than my dad.

"Rhys." The deep voice rumbles, a smirk tugging at his lips.

"Ty!" I scream, tossing the gun to clatter across the tiled floor as I launch myself at him like a monkey.

I lock myself around him, all too aware that my dad is somewhere nearby, but I have no control right now. It's been four weeks since I've seen Ty in the flesh. Four fucking weeks. My lips claim his as he stumbles back, and I hear the muttered curses of both my mum and dad, so I reluctantly break the kiss and turn to yell over my shoulder.

"Look away!" I call before claiming his lips again, and he chuckles against my mouth.

"Kitten." He rasps quietly, trying to push me back. "I need you to hop down."

I pull back and pout, and he shakes his head with a smirk, his lips tugging north as he pries me off him. I sigh, annoyed that there are people around, and turn to see my parents with raised brows.

"What?" I smirk. "I'm eighteen now."

"Here." My mum holds out a bag to me, and I frown.

"Are you... kicking me out? Already?" My heart sinks as confusion swarms through me.

"Just for a couple of days. Go and enjoy your birthday at Redfield Lake." My mum smiles, and I look between Ty and my parents, trying to see if they are about to laugh and say *just kidding*. But they don't.

"For real? What about lockdown? I'm not allowed to leave the house."

"Then don't get caught." My mum smirks.

I run and launch myself at her, peppering annoying kisses over her face before slapping a wet kiss on my dad's cheek.

I don't linger, worried my olds might change their minds, and I drag Ty from my house with the bag my mum gave me, not having any idea what's in it, but not caring either.

Ty drives me out of Fox Pines, which resembles a ghost town now with lockdown, and he takes me to his lake house. Even though we have called each other daily and have seen each other for very brief moments over the last few months, I can't stop looking at Ty sitting next to me as he drives. It feels surreal. I never thought this day would come. The day that we can legally be together.

My parents have asked that we still keep our relationship relatively quiet until I graduate secondary school, but at least now, the police can't take him away from me. We aren't breaking the law. I was terrified Ty was going to get busted and taken to prison, so much so that I've had regular nightmares about him getting locked up in the same cell as my birth dad, Brian.

Now, I don't have to worry about that happening.

When we arrive at Ty's house, he cuts the engine and turns to me with a grin.

"Stay in the car, Kitten."

My brows shoot up. "Why?"

"Don't ask questions, beautiful. Just do what you're told." Ty rasps, and now it's my turn to grin.

"You do know I'm more likely to do the opposite, right?"

He growls low, his hand whipping out to grip my nape. "If you don't behave, I won't spank you."

I lift my hands in surrender. "I'll behave, *Daddy*."

With a satisfied smirk, Ty leans in and claims my lips in a searing kiss that holds dirty promises, causing Kitty to lift her tail in the air, eager and willing. He breaks the kiss by biting down on my lip hard, and I gasp as he chuckles and gets out of the car.

His playfulness is calling to the brat in me to do the opposite of what he asked, but the thought of not getting a good spanking from my man has me staying the fuck in the seat.

I watch as Ty runs into his house carrying my bag before coming back out a moment later carrying a single red rose. I've never been a flowery girl, but a single red rose is kind of sexy, especially when Tyler Foster is carrying it.

He darts around the car before opening my door and hands it to me.

"Happy birthday, beautiful."

My cheeks heat, and I smile, taking the rose before he leans in and claims my lips in another kiss that has flames igniting under my skin. I'm all set to get naked out here, not caring if anyone can see us. I haven't had sex with Ty since last year, and Kitty is dying to feel his stretch, so yeah. I'd be happy to roll around in the dirt outside the car if I have to.

Tyler has other ideas.

He sweeps me up in his arms, and a squeak flies from my mouth in surprise as he cradles me to his chest, carrying me into his house. It feels good to be in his arms and in his space again, his scent instantly wrapping around me, making me feel like I'm finally home.

"I've been getting the house ready." Tyler grins down at me as he takes the stairs up to the living area.

"Ready for what?" I smirk, my brows dipping in confusion at his playful tone.

"Ready for our future."

My brows shoot up this time. "Our future?" I ask, my eyes shifting from his face to take in the open plan living area, which looks the same as the last time I was here, except now there's a big dining table off to the side of the kitchen. "What does that mean, exactly?"

He chuckles, moving past the floating fireplace. "It means I've been making a few adjustments to my home to accommodate my new family."

My eyes shoot to his smirking face. "What adjustments?"

He shrugs, the movement pulling my arms with it since they are still wrapped around his neck. "I decked out the basement. It's now fit for a boy band to do boy band stuff in."

"What?" I screech. "You mean you're ok with the guys coming here?"

"Yes, Kitten. We all share you, so we may as well have a space that we can do that in once they are all eighteen. Assuming they are ok with it."

"Ty," I whisper, and he stops walking, his deep blue eyes connecting with mine. "You're really ok with them? You're really ok with opening your home to all of us?"

He smiles warmly, his eyes filling with emotion. "One day, I will marry you, and hell, if you have any say in the matter, you will probably be married to all five of us at once. I'm well aware that I'm the *old guy* in this situation, but it also has its perks. Like the fact I have a home for us to live in. Money to support you while you build yourself a career or do more studies. This house has always been too big for just me," he shrugs, "so having the others fill the space isn't that bad of an idea. As long as they stay in their boy band basement and stay the fuck out of my bedroom."

His growl is serious, matching his frown, yet I find it more adorable than anything.

"Show me the boy band basement."

"Later." He rasps, turning serious. "I need to show you something in my bedroom."

I giggle as he passes through the kitchen. "Is it your pretty cock?"

A smirk tugs at his lips again as he tries to fight it off. "Not exactly."

"Now I'm intrigued." I grin, studying his face as he carries me across the glass-lined passage and into his bedroom. He eases me down on his bed and slowly steps back, his eyes moving to the side of the room, so I follow his gaze.

There's some sort of timber frame running across the room from one wall to the other, with thick black rings hanging from it.

"Uh... What's that?"

Ty shifts nervously in front of me, glancing from the beam to me. "It's something I was hoping to try with you. I just installed it a few days ago."

"You didn't answer my question, Daddy. What is that?" For some reason, his nervousness is making me nervous, and I notice my hands going clammy.

Obviously seeing my discomfort, Ty falls to his knees on the plush carpet in front of me and takes my hands in his, locking his deep blue eyes to mine. "Have you heard of Shibari, Kitten?"

"Uh yeah, I think so. That's bondage stuff, right?" I frown as I speak, feeling a little more anxious. Garrett, Simon, Shaun and Marcus have been helping me work through my trauma from the day I was attacked, and things are relatively back to normal. All except the restraint thing.

Tyler nods. "Shibari is Japanese bondage."

My breathing starts to shallow as my eyes lock onto the black rings.

Keep calm, Rhys. Ty won't hurt you.

"You want to try Shibari?"

"Well, technically, I've tried it before, years ago at a club I used to go to, but I was hoping to try it with you now."

My eyes dart back to his, which are studying me closely. There's no way he missed the hitch in my breathing. A flash of embarrassment hits me, and for the first time with Ty, I feel insecure.

"I don't think I can," I whisper, feeling the flush of humiliation heat my cheeks. "I'm not ready."

Ty nods. "We can ease into it, Kitten. We don't have to do anything big just yet."

I frown as irrational anger fuels me, and I leap up from the bed as I pace. "What if I don't want to? Is this a deal breaker? Am I going to be depriving you if I don't do this?"

"What? No, Kitten." Ty stands from the carpet, stepping towards me, but I take a step back, and he instantly raises his hands in surrender. "This isn't for *me*, beautiful. It's for *you*."

My brows hitch. "Me? How is *this* for me?" I point to the structure. "I was restrained and raped, Ty. Why would I want to do it again?"

His face falls, and I instantly feel like a bitch.

"I haven't explained myself properly, Rhys. My apologies." His deep blue eyes plead with me, and he gestures to his bed. "Please sit. Let me explain."

I glare at him for a long, tense moment, my legs quivering under me as I try to calm my nerves. When I step back towards Ty's bed, his shoulders visibly relax, and he waits for me to sink back down to sit on the end before he lowers back to his knees, this time scooting up close to kneel between my feet as he takes my hands in his.

"Shibari can be therapeutic. I was hoping that by doing it with *me*, someone you trust, that it might help you. But I mean, if you would rather do it with one of the others, then that's ok, Kitten. It's understandable that you're no longer comfortable with me."

"What?" I frown again. "Why wouldn't I be comfortable with you?"

He shrugs. "Our time apart may have changed how you feel."

"Has it changed how you feel?" I ask, panic seeping in.

"Fuck, no, Kitten. I fucking love you. You're my end game. Remember?"

My panic recedes at Ty's words, so I focus on the bondage issue. "You think I should try this," I gesture to the structure, "and see if it helps me with my restraint fears?"

"The best way to overcome a fear is to face it, especially if you do it with someone you trust. Do you trust *me*, Kitten?"

"Yes." The word falls easily from my lips, and I reach for my man, running my hand over the blonde beard he's grown. "I'm just scared."

"I will never hurt you, Kitten, and I will always stop when you use the safe word." Ty leans his head into my palm, his eyes falling shut for a moment as he enjoys my hand on him.

"Cactus is the safe word." I nod, using the same safe word we used at the Feast. Melia, my therapist, told me I choose to use the same safe word as a sense of control now. Like if I say it now when I'm with my guys, they will always stop, unlike Master Hill, who dismissed the power behind a safe word.

"Of course, Kitten. If you say cactus, or no, or stop. I will stop for any of these words." Ty places his hand over mine and brings my hand to his lips, pressing a kiss on my palm.

"Will it hurt?" I whisper.

"No. Never. Shibari is about surrendering your control. Putting your complete trust in me. Once I have finished binding you, I will worship you, Kitten. And I won't stop until you tell me to."

I suck in a breath and look back over at the structure curiously.

"Ok," I whisper, and he smiles warmly as I shift my gaze back to him.

"Shall we do it now, or would you like to wait for another time?" He asks, giving me the control.

"Now," I say quietly. "The sooner we do it, the sooner we get to the part where you worship me." I grin, and he chuckles before pecking my nose as he stands.

Ty moves across the room and points to the ropes lined up on the window seat. "Which colour would you like?"

I stand, moving closer to inspect the ropes. "Does it matter?"

"Well, yes. I'm going to be creating a work of art with your body, so I thought you might like to choose the colour."

My brows shoot up, and I take in his lazy smirk, anticipation rearing its beautiful head.

"Purple is my vibe." I flash him my teeth, and he chuckles, nodding knowingly. "Uh, what are the scissors for?" I ask as my eyes land on the scissors sitting off to the side.

"A quick escape. If you need me to remove the ropes quickly, I can cut you free."

My heart races with fear at the idea of me needing to be cut free quickly. "Why would I need that?"

Ty turns to face me, taking in my concern as he approaches and cups my face. "You might panic. It happens sometimes, beautiful, and if it does, you can be assured that I will cut you free and take care of you."

I stare into Ty's eyes, feeling vulnerable but knowing I need to do this one last thing to help me move past my trauma.

"So I'll be completely restrained? Hands and feet?"

"Yes. I can leave an arm and leg free to start with if you like? We can work up to more on a different day."

Images of Shibari that I've watched on porn sites flash through my head. I have to admit, it's often intrigued me, but I've never considered it because there was just never the idea that I would trust someone enough to be *that* vulnerable with. Now though, with Ty, Marcus, Shaun, Simon and Garrett in my life, I have five someones that I could easily be that vulnerable with, and I have to admit, I don't hate the idea. Especially if it could potentially help me move past this last bit of trauma I've been struggling with.

"Let's try the full restraint." I grin. "Rope me up, Daddy."

A deep growl rumbles from Ty's chest, and then he claims my lips once again. I instantly get lost in his lips and tongue, feeling his arms wrap around me and tug me close. I'm almost tempted to tell him to just fuck me right now, but I want this new experience with him, so when he eases the kiss, I don't complain.

Ty takes my hand and leads me to a chair that's sitting near the ropes. Before I can sit down, he slowly peels my clothes from my body, his lips fluttering over my neck and arms as he goes. I see the moment his eyes land on some of my scars still lingering from that awful day last year. Aside from the scar running through my brow, I have a long scar running across my back from the metal runner that sliced into my skin when I was wrestling Madam Vik in the shower. Part of the scar travels around my side, and since Ty and I haven't come together like this since before the attack, he hasn't seen these scars yet. I also have a burn scar on my leg and a few random scars from who knows what.

In the beginning, just looking at the scars made my stomach turn, but now, after countless hours talking over things with Melia, I see the scars as medals of war. Signs of survival. Marks that tell a story of how strong I am. I fought, and I won, and aside from Brian, who is getting sicker by the day in prison, I'm the only one left standing.

I jut my chin up when Ty's eyes meet mine, silently showing him that the scars aren't bad, and something like pride fills his deep blues before he reaches out to run his thumb over my bottom lip.

"My warrior."

I smile, even when tears pool in my eyes, and when one falls, he catches it on his thumb before bringing it to his lips. His tongue darts out, tasting my tear, his eyes remaining locked with mine before he smiles warmly. He doesn't speak, just studies my face for a minute before stepping back and handing me a bottle of water.

"You need to stay hydrated, and you should probably go to the bathroom now because once we get started, we won't be stopping for a while."

I nod, deciding it's probably a good idea, so I have a guzzle of water before taking a few minutes to myself in his lush bathroom before returning to see Ty running the purple rope through his hands.

"Take a seat, Kitten."

Once again, my heart races with anticipation and I walk my naked self across his bedroom to sit on the chair.

"First, I'm going to tie a chest harness." Ty states as his fingers travel over my shoulder to my tits before taking my arms and lifting them up. "Hold them up here for me, Kitten."

I do as he asks, biting back my smirk as I watch him from this close proximity as he takes the rope and wraps it over my chest above the twins and around the back, where he starts to thread the rope between my shoulder blades.

"You ok so far, Kitten?" Ty asks, and I giggle.

"You just started."

He chuckles in return before pressing his lips to my shoulder. "Just checking. It's an important part of this, making sure you're doing ok the whole time."

I nod, relaxing a little more with how attentive he is, and let him move my arms in whatever place he needs as he binds my chest. At times as he works, our faces are so close that I find I really enjoy watching his concentration. This right here is a completely different level of intimacy. It should probably scare me, yet it doesn't. It somehow makes me feel closer to him.

After a few minutes, Ty gives the binding at my back a little tug before moving to stand before me again.

"There, Kitten, that's the chest harness. How's that feel?"

"Good." I smile, enjoying how soft the rope feels, yet how it also makes me feel secure. Almost like a hug. "Oddly nice, actually."

Ty grins. "Ok, now I'm going to bind your arms behind your back."

My heart flips at his words, and not in a good way, and instantly, I start to tremble.

Falling to his knees in front of me again, Ty runs his hands up and down my arms, offering me comfort. "It's ok, beautiful. I will never hurt you. You know that, right? Do you trust me?"

Even though I'm shaking, I nod. "Yes."

"Do you want me to continue?" He brushes my stray hairs off my face, and I nod.

"Yes."

Leaning forward, Ty presses his lips to mine, and I start to relax again, reminding myself that I'm ok and Ty will always look after me.

He wants to worship you, Rhys.

When he pulls back, Ty stands and takes my hand in his. "Let's give it a go." Then he cautiously moves my hand behind my back before taking my other hand and moving it there, too.

"Can you grab your elbows?" Ty asks as he lines my arms up to run across my back, and I stretch my hands out, seeking my elbows and gripping them. "Good. Does that hurt anywhere or feel too uncomfortable?"

"No, it's fine." I assure him, and he nods, "I'm going to bind your arms now." He instructs, locking eyes with me in question.

Sucking in a calming breath, I give him a nod, and he nods in confirmation before setting to work on the ropes again, binding my arms behind my back. It doesn't take him long to secure my arms, and once he's done, he moves to stand in front of me again, his eyes raking over my pebbled nipples and the way my chest strains in this position.

"How are you feeling, Kitten?"

"I'm ok, Daddy." I smirk, feeling more relaxed than I did before. It's strange because Ty has essentially tied my arms to my back, and there's no way I can free myself, yet I don't feel the fear I was feeling before he did it.

"Do you want me to keep going, or is that enough for today?" He asks again, and I consider his question, and more questions pop into my head.

"If you keep going, how will you do it?"

"Hmmm." Ty shifts, lifting his finger to his lips as he considers my question. "I was thinking, a leg opener." He smirks, and my brows shoot high. "First, I'd need you on the floor," he points, so I grin and ease off my chair, letting him help to lower me to the plush carpet. "Then I would bind each leg above the knee," he grazes his fingers over the flesh on my thigh, "and link the leg binding with the chest harness at the back and pull it tight to open you up to me."

Fuck. Kitty gushes at the thought, and a knowing grin crosses his face as he takes in my expression.

"What do you think?" He asks, and it takes me a moment to respond.

"Yes."

"Good girl."

Oh fuck. He went there, and now I'm gushing for praise kink.

Grinning knowingly again, Ty sets to work on the leg binding on each thigh before connecting them to the back somehow. From behind me, he leans over my shoulder, using his big hands to press my knees apart, opening my legs wide before pulling my feet closer to me, so my knees end up near my ears, almost like I'm in a sitting squat.

"You ready, beautiful?" Ty asks, and my heart flips as I nod, having no idea what I'm agreeing to but fucking eager to find out.

With a tug on the rope, it tightens at my back, effectively locking my legs open.

"Right." I giggle. "The leg opener."

Ty chuckles as he finishes securing my binds and then moves to face me again, his eyes locking onto my heavy breathing as my chest rises and falls before his eyes shift to between my legs, where my Kitty is practically weeping.

Yes, I am fucking turned on. I probably look ridiculous, but with the way Ty is eye fucking me, I don't really care. Need rushes through me, and I release a breathy moan because this whole binding part is a different level of foreplay, working a treat to get me riled up.

Leaning forward on the carpet, Ty kisses me gently, his lips nibbling mine like he's tasting a treat. It teases Kitty even more, and when I moan again, Tyler pulls back and grins wickedly.

"There's one last step before I worship you. Are you still going ok, Kitten?"

"If ok is really fucking randy, then I'm peachy." I grin, and he chuckles.

"I'd better hurry then. We wouldn't want you to have to suffer for too long now. Would we?"

"Hurrying is a fan-fucking-tastic idea, Daddy." I nod eagerly, and he grins as he gets to work.

I watch as he secures some sort of harness thing over my head to the black rings hanging from the beam, and then he gets another rope, threading it to the bindings at my back. Then, he moves me this way and that before he connects the ropes at my back to the harness.

"Are you ready, Kitten? It's time to suspend you."

My heart leaps in my chest, and I nod eagerly, not knowing why on earth I was worried about this before we got started. When Ty pulls on the ropes and does something I can't see behind me, a squeal flies from my lips as my arse and feet leave the carpet, my bound body slowly lifting in the air.

"This is going to hold me, right?" I ask nervously as I look up, my body swaying, moving higher as Ty secures my harness.

"Yes, beautiful. You're as light as a feather."

"I'm referring to your skills. You did it right, so it won't come undone, yeah?"

He laughs, "Yes, Kitten. Never doubt my skills."

I giggle nervously as I swing a little, and Ty shifts to stand before me.

"I feel like a pinata. Only, if you hit the right spot, I'll be the one to win the prize."

Ty throws his head back, laughing. "Trust me, Kitten, every time you win, I win."

I smile, watching how he watches me before he starts to strip out of his clothes. My smile turns into parted lips as his bare chest comes into view, and Kitty claws at me.

"Look at me, Kitten," Ty demands, and I draw my eyes from his abs, back up to his face. "I'm going to worship you now. Do you trust me completely?"

"Yes." I breathe.

"Let's confirm if there are any hard limits."

"Just no piss," I say quickly.

"No piss at all, or no piss on you?"

"On me," I say quietly, and he nods before grinning.

"So, if I fall to my knees before you," he falls to his knees, and I look down my suspended body to see him looking up at me, "and I ask you to piss in my mouth. Will you?"

I moan. "Fuck, Ty. You're making it hard for me to concentrate."

He reaches up and brushes his thumb over the centre of my parted folds, and I hold my breath, waiting for him to finally touch my needy clit, but he doesn't

"Answer my question, Kitten."

"Yes, I'll piss in your mouth if that's what you want," I growl, and he grins.

"What about here?" He moves his fingers to my puckered rose. "Have your boy band gone here again?"

I nod. "Yes."

"Are you happy for me to go there too, Kitten?"

Again I nod. "Yes, Daddy."

"Good. Let's get started."

Chapter Forty-Five

TYLER

She looks like a delectable dessert strung up in my bedroom. Dessert just for me. Fuck, it's taken everything in me to hold myself back and not just fuck her. The anticipation of what we are doing is like a crazy form of foreplay.

"Daddy, please," Kitten whines, her breath filled with desperate need.

I grin. Fuck it. I'm not waiting any longer. Fisting my cock in a tight grip, I shuffle closer to my dark angel, suspended in the purple ropes, spread wide for easy access. Her dark eyes are wide with anticipation as she watches me move in, hovering my mouth over her glistening cunt. She tries to move, her hips the only part of her that shifts, and she swings a little, right against my mouth.

That's the moment I break. My hands dig into the globes of her arse, and I sink my long tongue into her heat. She throws her head back, gasping and moaning at the same time, and I spend a minute just fucking her with my tongue, her slick juice rushing out more and more, coating my chin.

I fucking love it.

The moment I drag my tongue up to her clit, she explodes, already too worked up to last long. That's ok, though. I have no intention of stopping at one orgasm tonight. It's her birthday, after all. She's going to get exactly what she loves. To get fucked senseless.

As she comes down from her first climax, I swipe up some of her natural lubricant on my middle finger before gliding it to her arse, where I sink my digit in. It's so tight and hot, and she pushes back like the needy little sex kitten she is, seeking more.

"You want this hole filled, Kitten?"

"Yes." She pants.

"Filled a little or a lot?" I rasp before swiping my tongue through her parted folds again.

"A lot." She practically begs, and I chuckle against her clit.

"Your wish is my command, Kitten. Since it's your birthday."

I stand, slipping my finger from her back passage before giving her globe a little smack. She moans, her head tipped back to the ceiling as she hangs in my bedroom.

Moving to my phone, I shoot off a quick text message before picking up the lube and coating my dick with it.

"Is this my birthday present, Daddy?" She asks, not able to see me behind her.

"Yes, Kitten. And I have another surprise for you. I'll give it to you soon."

She giggles. "It's your dick, isn't it?"

"My cock is part of it, but not all of it." I move around in front of her, and she watches me as I hold up the lube and pour it over her cunt before I slap a handful to her arse.

I ignore the fact that my carpet is getting ruined. I've already organised to pull it up with the next part of the renovations I'm starting next week. Now that we are on lockdown, I have no choice but to stay here and work on things.

"Can I have a birthday every day?" She asks, and I chuckle.

"If by birthday, you mean worshipped, then yes, Kitten, I fully intend on worshipping you every day for the rest of our lives."

"Man, I like the sound of that." She moans, and I place the lube down and turn the harness so she is facing the other way to look out the window into the bushland beyond.

"I fucking love the sound of it," I admit, tugging on the harness to pull her body upright, which gives me a good angle to fuck her arse.

She squeaks in surprise since I didn't warn her I was going to move her, but then she moans when I press my dick to her rose.

"Ready, Kitten?" I rasp next to her ear, and she nods, so I use my hands to part her cheeks wide and nudge my cock to sink a little into her. "Relax for me, baby." I encourage when she tenses a little, and I take one hand, wrapping it around her front to circle her clit.

"Sorry." She whispers, slowly relaxing.

"You ok?" I ask as I push into her more, and she nods, panting. "Good, because I'm gonna fuck you now, Kitten. Nice and hard, just the way you like it."

She goes to nod again, but as I sink to the hilt, she forgets how to do anything but feel. Her arse grips my dick like a vice. A hot, wet vice I'm certain I won't last long in, so I lift my hand and wave my fingers forward, hoping our visitor is behind us, ready to step in. A second later, I see a tall body in my peripheral, so I increase the pressure on Kitten's clit, and rasp in her ear.

"Rest your head on my shoulder, Kitten, and close your eyes."

She moans, doing what I ask, and I nibble on her ear as I ease my dick in and out of her arse.

Our visitor moves then, stepping in front of Kitten, completely naked with his dick primed and ready. Our eyes lock, and I have a moment of, *what the fuck am I doing*, when I take him in, but quickly remind myself that he too is eighteen now. I could have kept Kitten to myself, but there will be time for that later. It's her birthday, and I want to give her one of her wishes.

Fuck, if I'm being honest, it's one of my wishes as well.

His icy-blue eyes assess our girl, roaming over her sweat-dampened skin to her weeping cunt, and he licks his lips. I give him a slight nod, careful not to give away the surprise to Kitten, and as he steps forward, I wrap my hand around Kitten's throat and tilt her head back to me.

Her eyes fly open, locking with mine, and I grin.

"Happy birthday, beautiful."

In one swift move, he grips her bound legs and slams into her.

Her eyes widen as shock morphs her face, and I release her neck in time for her attention to snap back in front of her.

"Oh my God." She squeals.

"Happy birthday, Baby Girl."

"Garrett. What are you-."

Her words are cut off as Garrett starts fucking her fast, and I work with him, keeping pace. With the way she is bound and strung up, she has no choice but to take what we give, and her moans sound more animalistic as she lets go of any control she has.

She's so close to flying already, her body filled to the brink with dick and as Garrett locks eyes with me again, and he gives me a nod, telling me it's time to take this one step further.

"Are you…" I pant as I thrust. "Ready for… more, Kitten?"

A strangled moan comes from our girl, and I start the countdown.

"Three, two, one."

Kitten screams as my teeth sink into the flesh on her shoulder, and Garrett's teeth sink into a patch of skin on her other shoulder. Our girl clamps around us as she explodes, and I taste her blood for the first time, flying right over the edge with her.

Chapter Forty-Six
Rhys

Worshipped. That's what I feel. Absolutely and thoroughly worshipped. I had no idea Tyler had invited Garrett to join us but fuuuuccccckkkk, it was the best present ever! I'm going to expect a lot every birthday from now on.

Of course, what would have made it better, if that's even possible, would be to have all my guys together again, but the other three aren't eighteen yet, so I'll have to remain patient until that day comes.

After Garrett joined the party and they both sunk their teeth into me, sending me crazy with lust, I bit them both right back. Fuck, by the time we were done, it looked like a massacre had taken place in Ty's bedroom.

Ok, so that might be slightly overdramatic, but we made a decent mess with the sticky blood.

Ty and Garrett checked on me every step of the way, making sure I was still coping ok with being bound up like that. After my initial panicked reaction to attempting Shibari, I found myself settling in relatively well, and I knew it was because of the trust I have with Ty. Throw in his little six-foot-six Garrett surprise, and I was there for it. Always.

After my body is thoroughly fucked and smeared with blood, Ty and Garrett work together to slowly lower me back to the plush carpet, where they unravel me from the ropes. It takes a while, and they each press their warm lips to the parts of my skin that had the purple rope digging into it, and the weirdest thing happens.

As the ropes loosen, tears start to fall. Emotions I didn't realise I'd been holding onto spill free, and I turn into a howling mess as the pain of the trauma I experienced last year comes out in a rush. I try to hold back, but I have no control, and I don't understand what the fuck is happening.

Flushed with embarrassment, I curl into myself, sitting on the floor, hiding my head.

"Kitten, why are you hiding your face from us?" Ty's voice is soft and calming, instantly putting me at ease like he has cast a spell on me.

"I'm sorry," I whisper, still hiding my face from them. "This is embarrassing. I don't know what's happening."

"Don't be embarrassed, Kitten. Remember how I told you Shibari can be therapeutic?" I feel the brush of Ty's warm, gentle hands over my hair. "This is part of it. It can be very cathartic. Like giving you an emotional release. Which obviously you needed."

I nod, peeking out between my fingers and whisper. "Thank you."

Ty's warm smile fills my vision as he ducks down, trying to see past my fingers. "Don't hide from us, beautiful."

His words wrap around me like a warm security blanket, and I slowly draw my hands from my face, blinking away the last tears to see my two big guys, side by side on the floor with me, watching with their own emotions glistening their eyes.

"What we did was kinda beautiful." I grin as I uncurl myself.

"It really was, Baby Girl. I hope we can do it again sometime soon." Garrett leans forward, cupping my face. "Thank you for trusting us."

I smile and lean forward, closing the distance to taste Garrett's lips for the millionth time today, and when he pulls back, Ty takes his place, his lips sending me into a sleepy state before he lifts me in his arms and carries me to his oversized shower.

Garrett and Ty talk in hushed tones as they both shower me, talking to me and each other. It should feel weird to have Garrett here with me and Ty. Aside from Shaun and the night they surprised me with Moxie's sex party, I haven't had them together like this. It doesn't feel weird, though. It feels perfect.

Once we are clean and dry, Garrett is the one to carry me to Ty's bed, where he eases me down in the middle before slipping under the sheets and settles in with me. I bite my lip, trying to hold back my happy grin as he shuffles close to me, and I watch Ty walk across the room naked before he slips in the other side.

"What are you grinning at, Kitten?"

"Tell me how this happened? How am I the filling in a Ty and Garrett sandwich right now?"

They both chuckle.

"Well, Baby Girl," Garrett nuzzles his nose into my hair. "Ty reached out after I turned eighteen, begging to get in on our blood play."

"I did not beg." Ty grunts.

"You did beg." Garrett chuckles.

"No, I fucking didn't. I don't beg."

I giggle at his tone.

"He did beg, and I said no at first." Garrett chuckles.

"You said no?" I turn my head to see the shit-eating grin he's sporting.

"Yeah, because he's greedy." Ty hisses from behind me, and Garrett rolls his eyes.

"I said no because I knew it would piss you off. Which it did. Well worth it, if you ask me."

"Mr Cole. You're such a tease. When did you give in?" I beam, and he winks.

"Last week, when he told me what he wanted to do for your birthday."

"I might add that I didn't need to add blood play to the bondage session with my girl. You should be thanking me for including you, Cole." Ty rasps, his arm curling over me to tug me back against his chest.

"First of all, she's *our* girl. And secondly, you have been desperate to taste her blood, so don't pretend like you were doing me any favours." Garrett grunts, linking his fingers with mine.

"I'm getting turned on by all of this alpha-arseholeness right now," I smirk, pressing my arse back into Ty's very obvious boner.

"Sleep, Kitten." Ty's breath flutters against my ear before he nips it, and I let my eyes fall shut, feeling exhaustion more than the need to spread my legs right now. Another reason this night is perfect because I am completely sated.

I sleep all night. Nightmares don't worm their way in. My mind is nothing but a blank calmness that has been rare to find but seems to be coming to me more often these days. My heart knows when my guys are near. It's like it switches my brain off and allows me to finally get some peace knowing I am being watched over and protected. It's utter bliss.

We wake early the next morning to the sound of Paramore blaring somewhere in the room. My phone is somewhere in here ringing, but I don't move to answer it. Not when I'm wedged between Daddy and Mr Cole. But then it rings again, and I frown before prying one lid open.

"I'll find your phone, Baby Girl," Garrett mumbles sleepily next to me, pressing his lips to my forehead before slipping from the sheets. He doesn't make it in time, the call ending before he takes two steps from the bed.

It's when it rings again immediately that I know something is wrong, and I bolt upright in the bed, the sheet pooling to my waist as I watch Garrett pull my phone from the back pocket of my jeans and he looks at the screen.

"It's your mum."

I reach my hand out for the phone, wiggling my fingers impatiently, but it cuts off again before Garrett can get it to me.

"Call her back, Kitten." Ty's husky morning voice wraps around me as he sits up too, and I take my phone and call my mum.

"Oh, thank God. I thought I was going to have to come and drag you out of bed." My mum sounds like she is walking briskly, and I take a look at the time on my phone. It's 7:24am.

"What's happened?" I ask, and she sighs.

"It's time, sweetie."

My heart stops for a moment as her words sink in. "It's time?"

"Yes. I'm on my way to get you."

"Uh. Ok." I mutter nervously. "Have you got the permit?"

"Yep. Got it. I'll see you soon."

"Ok. See you soon." I hang up the call and sit frozen for a minute, staring at the screen.

"Kitten?" Ty asks, his voice laced with concern.

I glance up at him and then at Garrett as I wrap my head around what I'm about to do. I haven't told the guys I'd planned to do this. I'm not sure why exactly. Perhaps I didn't want to worry them, or perhaps I was scared they would try to talk me out of it.

I didn't come to this decision lightly, though. I spoke with Melia about it and then to my parents, and they agreed to support me, knowing I needed closure.

"My mum is on her way to pick me up." My eyes connect with Ty's deep blue concerned gaze, and I cup his jaw. "I'm sorry, Ty. I need to go with my mum. But I'll come right back afterwards."

"Go where?" He places his warm palm over my hand, tilting his head into my touch.

I slowly drag my gaze from Ty to Garrett, then back to Ty. "I'm going to watch Brian die."

Ty's brows hitch high on his forehead, and another glance at Garrett shows the same expression.

"You're going to watch him die?" Garrett asks, and I nod.

"Yes. The cancer has been getting worse, and we have been waiting for the call that his organs are starting to shut down so we would have enough time to get there. It's happening now."

"Shit." Garrett rasps while Ty draws my eyes back to him.

"Are you sure about this, beautiful? Watching someone die is a hard thing to witness."

I nod again, heat pricking the backs of my eyes. "Yes, I'm sure. I need this closure. I need to see him die."

Ty studies me for a moment, his eyes dancing between mine, trying to read the truth in them. Then he nods.

"Ok, Kitten. You go and get that closure, and you come right back here because we have a little party planned for tonight."

"A party? With who?"

"The other guys." Garrett grins.

"But they aren't eighteen yet." I frown, and Ty chuckles.

"It's not a sex party, Kitten. Just a regular party with cake and drinks and music. If the boy band behave, I might let them stay the night downstairs, but I'm keeping you to myself tonight in this bed. It's been too long." He shoots Garrett a glare, and Garrett chuckles, holding up his hands.

"Fine with me, *Daddy*." He teases, and Ty growls at Garrett calling him Daddy.

My lips spread wide, and I leap on Ty as I grab Garrett's arm, pulling them both in for a hug before I drag myself up to get ready.

It's hard prying myself away from them, but I manage it with enough time to pee, throw some clothes on, tie my hair up and meet my mum as she pulls up.

The drive to the prison is long, but not as long as usual, since there are barely any cars on the road. It's eerie. So strange to go from the chaotic world we were living in last week to now, with only a car or two passing by and a police roadblock, checking permits to go into the city.

When we finally get there, we have to wear face masks and use hand sanitiser after we enter each section of the prison. We are led to the prison's medical centre, where Brian has been moved to for his final hours. If you ask me, they should have let him suffer in his cell and die on the cold, hard floor. Even a death like that doesn't come close to what he deserves.

As we step through the doors, my heart skyrockets with nerves, and my legs feel like they are going to vanish from under me. I'm not nervous about seeing Brian, but I am nervous about watching him die.

My mum stays behind me as I approach the bed with the frail man lying almost lifeless. His skin is ashen, and his chest rises and falls slowly, a groan leaving his dry, cracked lips every so often.

The beep of a heart monitor fills the room, and when I nudge his bed and his eyes flutter open, the beep picks up as I lower my face mask.

"P-Pat-ty."

I sneer at him. "I've come to watch you die, Brian. I've come to watch you drift off to hell where your brother Terence is. Where Vik is. And where Julie is."

At hearing me say Julie's name, his eyes flare a little.

"I wish you had seen it, Brian. The moment I killed your wife." The beeping increases. "I wish you had seen her face when my knife went through her chest and sunk into her heart. I would have liked to watch *your* face as you watched me take away your precious, vile wife. To see the life go out of her eyes." My lip curls as I glare at him. "That's why I'm here. To watch the life go out of your eyes, Brian, and then I'm going to fucking dance on your grave."

Brian makes a gargled noise, his hand flying to his chest as his face contorts in pain. The heart monitor is going crazy now, and I grin, knowing it's because of me. If Brian thought he was going to have a relaxing death, drifting off into nothingness, then he was extremely fucking wrong. I may not be able to plunge a knife into his heart today, but my words do that all on their own as the heart monitor stops beeping and starts blaring in a long-pitched alarm.

I lean in closer, watching Brian's eyes flutter open and lock onto me right before they turn black, and the light behind them goes out forever.

Epilogue - Rhys

Ten months later

"This is turning me on so bad right now." Simon's declaration sends us into hysterics as he grins mischievously while stomping his feet into the wide barrel of grapes.

"You wanna lick them off my toes, Sy?" I giggle, and he leans forward, tugging me closer and nearly making me fall over in the slush.

"You know I do, Cherry."

"Weirdly, I'd like to watch that," Marcus admits from beside the barrel, watching as me, Simon, and Shaun crush the grapes with our feet.

"Weirdly, I'd have to agree with Caveman." Tyler chuckles, and Marcus rolls his eyes while Garrett uses my camera to snap some photos.

"Are we doing it right, Gabriella?" I ask, looking over my shoulder at Shaun's grinning mama, who is sitting in a wheelchair, watching on.

"Si." She calls as Shaun's dad holds an umbrella up to shield her from the hot sun.

She told us it's an old tradition that her family used to do when couples fell in love. She wanted to make a new tradition, to crush the first grapes of the season in celebration of continued love. So it looks like we will be doing this every year, which is fine by me.

We graduated from school a few months ago, with a big celebration at the start of December, and as my school peers were getting wasted at the local pub, I was getting railed by my five guys.

What better way to celebrate? Am I right?

Simon has settled in well on the Bossier's vineyard. He even has muscles now, just like he told Shaun's dad he'd get if he worked on their farm. He's actually taken a keen interest in the running of it, and somehow managed to get Shaun excited about it, too. They've been working with Shaun's dad to come up with a new marketing campaign, but honestly, they haven't had to try hard. With the virus sending Australia and the world into numerous lockdowns, people have been extra needy for wine. Especially locally.

The other thing Simon has been doing a lot of is cooking. Gabriella has taught him some recipes handed down in her family, and he cooks up feasts for us all regularly, helping to take any pressure off Gabriella or her carers to prepare meals.

It's been great to see Shaun start to embrace his family business. He's actually a really good salesman, using his charm to make business deals and gain new clients. Having Simon here with him has helped a lot. Shaun no longer feels like he has to take over the business, but now he wants to, and it's stirred a fire in his belly.

Even during the lockdowns, he worked hard, networking online, having business meetings and dressing in suits to impress the clients over zoom calls. Of course, the fun part for me is taking the suit off when he's done. Aaaaand there may have been a few times I walked into his little office, which has been set up off the side of the man cave, completely naked while he was on a video call.

It's ok, though. The clients couldn't see me, but my sexy Casanova sure could. Did he spank me when he finished his meetings? Yes, he did, and I took it like a good girl.

Garrett started studying Psychology, and because of the virus, his classes are online for now, which means I get to keep him because he doesn't have to travel to the city for classes. Marcus is taking a gap year, having no idea what the hell he wants to do with his future, so he's been spending his days working at Maccas. And Ty has been building his personal training, offering services to the residents at Redfield Lake, which has taken off.

As for me, I'm taking my photography to the next level with online studies and selling some of my work on a website my new foster sister helped me create.

We introduced Ty to our families after graduation. Well, mine already knew, and Simon's haven't spoken to him since he walked out, so it was just Marcus', Garrett's and Shaun's families. Oh, and our friends, who were more accepting than I thought they'd be, but man, did Lexi and Tillie have a lot of questions about their old PE teacher.

Marcus' family still struggles to accept that we have a thirty-three-year-old man hanging around us, but they are polite to him when he's around, so I guess that's something.

Garrett's mum and sisters are fine with Ty, but Garrett's mum did take Ty aside and gave him a stern talking to, although Ty has never revealed what she said. We were surprised by her backbone since she lacked it with her husband, but she has been going to counselling, and the sessions have been helping her to overcome her fears. It's something Garrett is really proud of.

Shaun's family are fine with it, given that Shaun's dad is learning to accept all sorts of things these days, with Derek finally coming out of the closet last year. He even has a boyfriend now, which his dad acknowledges with a nod and a grunt.

It's progress.

"I'm not kidding, guys. Conan is hard as hell right now." Simon hisses so only we can hear, and I giggle.

"Keep him in your pants a bit longer, and I'll be sure to give him attention as soon as we are done."

"Promise, Cherry?"

"Yes, Sy. I promise."

He beams, lifting his feet up and down faster as Shaun leans into my ear to whisper.

"Wanna watch me take his arse virginity?"

My brows shoot high, and I jerk back to look at Shaun.

"Don't tease me, Cass."

"No tease, Kitten. It's long overdue. Don't you think?" Shaun winks, and I nod.

"Hell yeah, it is." I laugh and look back at Simon, who is too busy stomping in a circle to listen to our hushed conversation.

Concentrating on crushing the grapes gets harder as my mind goes to dirty places. Knowing my urgency, Shaun hurries us through the process before we finish up, and Derek and his fella take over. I give Gabriella a kiss on her cheek before we leave, and before I know it, we are pulling up outside Ty's house, which seems to be our main hangout these days.

Once inside and up in the living area, I shoot Simon a grin and approach him.

"Sy. Today's the day." I say quietly.

"The day for what?" He frowns in confusion.

"The day you lose your arse virginity."

This time his brows shoot high, disappearing under his blonde hair.

"Or not. It's completely up to you, but Cass is keen if you are." I smile and watch Simon drag his eyes from me to Shaun, who is approaching us.

"I'm up for it if you are, Hastings." Shaun nudges him with his shoulder, and Simon's face turns red, but he nods, and that's all the confirmation I need.

I know Simon has been wanting this for a long time. He finally opened up to me a couple of months ago, telling me he wants to know what it's like to be filled and completely consumed. I was so happy that he trusted me with that truth, and I've been giving him a couple of my fingers ever since, but it's not enough. To get what he truly desires, he needs a good hard dick.

"Ok, before you do this, I need to ask if you want to be alone with Cass? Because that's totally ok."

Simon's brows meet in the middle. "No, Cherry. I want you there. Always."

"It's ok if you want privacy, Sy. I can give you that if you want."

"Cherry, I may want to be filled, but I'm gonna need you as a visual. Plus, I can't imagine doing it without you. Anything I experience, I want you to be there for."

I close the distance between us and cup his jaw before stealing a kiss. He instantly slides his hand around my back, tugging me close, and I feel his arousal straining between us. Heat pools between my legs, and Kitty lifts her arse in the air, wanting in on the action.

When I pull back, I study his face, which is full of admiration, and I smile. "You want it to be just us three, then? Or are you happy for the others to watch?"

He shrugs. "They can watch if they think they can hack it." He wags his brows as Shaun throws his head back, laughing.

"Uh, guys." I ease out of Simon's hold, gaining everyone's attention. "I'm just gonna head down to the basement with Simon and Cass for some MM action. It's up to you if you wanna watch. Or join in. Whatever floats your boat."

Grinning, I take Simon and Shaun's hands, leading them towards the stairs before Ty steps in front of us and gives me a lazy smirk.

"Have fun, beautiful." He presses his lips to my cheek.

"You don't want to watch?" I ask, and his grin grows wider.

"Soon. You go have some fun first." He pecks my nose before stepping away, and I see Marcus rise from the stool he was on.

"I can't help it. I wanna see this."

Shaun chuckles. "Of course you do, Grady."

"I'll be down after as well," Garrett calls, and I shoot him a wink over my shoulder.

Simon is quiet as we descend the two staircases to get down to the basement. Ty decked it out last year so the guys would have a place to hang. It comes fully equipped with gaming consoles, a huge TV and state-of-the-art sound system, a couple of couches and chairs, and some games tables, plus an indoor mini basketball ring. The big one is outside at the front of the new garage that Ty built, which is also made from shipping containers.

I'm not sure why Ty did this for the guys, but I have the feeling it's more for him than them, so his part of the house upstairs remains clean and undamaged.

The lights come on, illuminating the room, and Shaun immediately connects his phone to the sound system, and music starts playing.

"Fuck. I'm nervous." Simon mutters, and I drop Shaun's hand and turn to Sy, cupping his face again and kissing him deeply.

"Just focus on the feeling." I rasp against his lips, and he moans, kissing me again. I walk backwards, leading him towards the back of the room, where a huge mattress rests ruffled with blankets. It's our fuck bench. Most of our group sessions happen here these days. It's easier to clean things up down here, and it keeps the beds upstairs neat for alone time with my guys.

Yes, I guess we have our own sex dungeon.

I run my hand down Simon's front, rubbing over his straining cock, which is eager to be freed from his shorts. Getting the tie undone takes more time than I'd like since we haven't pried our lips apart yet, and I'm doing it blind, but then two large hands join in, helping me to undress Simon, and when I open my eyes, I see Cass at Simon's back.

As Shaun pulls Simon's t-shirt over his head, I glance to the side to see Marcus in one of the armchairs, his hand already wrapped around his dick, stroking.

"Can I kiss you?" Shaun asks Simon as he runs his hands down Sy's bare arms.

Simon's eyes widen and he looks at me. I think he wants to know if I'm ok with it, so I nod, grinning. "That would make me so wet."

"One hundred bucks says you're already dripping, Rhee." Marcus chuckles from the chair, and I shoot him a wink.

"Uh-ok then." Simon agrees, so I slowly take a few steps back, dropping his hand when I get too far to keep it in my grip, and I watch one of my fantasies play out in front of me.

Shaun is already naked. He must have done that when I was busy kissing Simon, and as Shaun tugs Sy's jocks down his legs, I quickly tear off my clothes, needing no barriers to find my sensitive flesh. My hands pinch my nipples while Shaun steps slowly around to face Simon, leaning in to hover his lips in front of Simon's, so they are practically breathing the same air.

"Come here Rhee. Let me take care of you while you watch." Marcus' husky tone tells me he is just as turned on by what's about to happen, and I nod, moving to him and letting him guide me to sit on his lap, facing Cass and Sy.

The moment Cass closes the distance and kisses Simon, a gush of hot fluid leaks from between my legs, gaining Marcus' attention.

"Fuck, Rhee. You like that, huh?"

I moan in response as he slides his hand between my legs, cupping my Kitty.

Simon seems to get lost in the kiss, his hands wrapping around to grip the delicious golden globes of Shaun's arse, tugging him against his body.

That's all it takes. No more need to talk things through, just plain hot passion. Raw and animalistic with need, as they fight for domination. Shaun is the one to break the kiss, turning Simon in his arms and pushing him to kneel on the mattress.

Marcus takes that moment to slide two fingers inside me, his lips latching onto my neck from behind as he sucks. Any control I have is lost now, and I ride Marcus' fingers as I watch Shaun coat his dick with lube before paying Sy's arse the same courtesy.

"Lean forward on your hands." Cass rasps, pressing his hand to Simon's shoulder, and Sy does as he's told, moving to go on all fours. "You want me to fuck you here?" Shaun asks, his fingers running through the lube over Simon's puckered rose before slipping two fingers in.

When Simon told me he wanted to find out what it's like to be filled, he admitted that he'd been using butt plugs for some time, hoping to prepare himself for when the day came. Knowing that day has finally come for him fills me with so much happiness. And horniness. Let's not forget that!

Simon moans, accepting Shaun's fingers, and Shaun slides his free hand around to Sy's hard dick, giving it some attention too.

"Fuck, Bossi. I'm gonna come before you even stick it in." Simon groans, and I grin. I want to see him cum everywhere.

"Let's get to it then, shall we?"

Fuck, I love dominant Shaun. He's such a *go-with-the-flow* kind of guy, so it's nice to see him showing this side right now. It's just another turn on the guys throw my way on a daily basis.

A noise behind me tells me the four of us are no longer alone. I don't want to draw attention to whoever it is, though, so I keep my eyes focused on Shaun as he slips his fingers free and runs the tight head of his cock through the lube coating Sy's arse. Using his hands, he parts Simon's cheeks, and then he presses his dick to the forbidden passage.

A strangled yet pleasured moan fills the room as Shaun sinks into Simon's arse, taking that virginity from him like he's been longing for.

"Sit on my cock, Rhee." Marcus breathes against my ear, and my body obeys, having a mind of its own, spreading my legs wider as I ease onto Marcus' dick, reverse cowgirl style. The stretch is divine, and my visual is perfect, and when I see two figures pumping dicks on each side of my peripheral, I let myself go to every sensation there is right now.

As Shaun starts pumping into Sy, I watch both their faces contort into that always blissful pleasured pain expression, and before too long, Sy is pushing back hard against Shaun's thrusts, seeking the ultimate railing.

The moment Simon cums, spilling onto the mattress below, we all do. Shaun throws his head back, shooting his cum deep inside

Simon, while Marcus fills Kitty up with his, and Gar and Ty paint the floor with theirs.

The high we just reached is only the beginning because I lift off Marcus and go to Simon and Shaun, who then turn their attentions on me, and we spend the rest of the day fucking each other like tomorrow isn't guaranteed.

This is it. This is what I've been searching for, even when I didn't know I was looking. The ultimate trust. The ultimate acceptance. Both of which equal the ultimate love.

Most stories aren't like mine. Most girls don't wear their filthy heart on their sleeve the way I do. But that's ok because most girls don't get to spend the rest of their life with five guys who worship them like they are a queen.

Queen Kitty, that is.

I am Kitten. Hear me purr!

THE END!

HOLY HELL! WHAT A WILD RIDE!

Want more?

The next instalment in the Fox Pines Catholic Saga is none other than Jared's story.

Is he still pining over Lexi?

Will he find his own happiness?

Find out what dangers chase Jared, or if he's the one to run from, in

Silent Hush
Breaking the Silence Book 1

TROPES: MF – Tortured Souls – Secret Identity – Organised Crime – Assassin – Kidnapping – Violence & Gore (not between FMC & MMC) – Blackmail & Coercion – Non-con – Found Family – SERIOUS CONTENT WARNING!

Silent Hush - Book 1

https://geni.us/silenthush1

Are you in the mood for some next level filth
mixed with your danger?
Be sure to check out this standalone to scratch that itch
and learn more about Moxie!

SUBBING FOR SANTA

Meet our dominating Santa in this Dark Mafia Christmas
Romance with stalker vibes!

TROPES: MF – Stalker – Secret Identity – Mafia/Organised
Crime – Violence (not between FMC & MMC) – Found Family –
SERIOUS CONTENT WARNING!

https://geni.us/subbingforsanta

Sarah JDs Books

READING ORDER

SERIES ONE

THE HEAVY HEARTS SERIES

A DARK NEW ADULT ROMANCE

TROPES: MF – Tortured Souls – Kidnapping – Trauma – Violence & Bullying (not between FMC & MMC) – Blackmail – Found Family – SERIOUS CONTENT WARNING!

HEAVY (Book 1):
https://geni.us/heavyhearts1
DEEP (Book 2):
https://geni.us/heavyhearts2
BURIED (Book 3):
https://geni.us/heavyhearts3

SERIES TWO

THE INSATIABLE SERIES

A DARK REVERSE HAREM NEW ADULT ROMANCE

TROPES: RH – Some MM - Age Gap – Forbidden – Tortured Souls – Kidnapping – Past Trauma – Violence (not between FMC & MMCs) – Blackmail – Found Family – SERIOUS CONTENT WARNING!

INSATIABLE KITTEN (Book 1):
https://geni.us/Insatiablekitten
TAINTED KITTEN (Book 2):
https://geni.us/Taintedkitten
VICIOUS KITTEN (Book 3):
https://geni.us/Viciouskitten

SERIES FOUR

THE CRUZ KINGS MC SERIES

A DARK ENEMIES-TO-LOVERS MC ROMANCE
by B. Lybaek & Sarah JD

TROPES: MF – Motorcycle Club – Tortured Souls – Organised Crime – Kidnapping – Violence – Blackmail & Coercion – Dub-con – Non-con – SOMNOPHILIA – Found Family – Bets – SERIOUS CONTENT WARNING!

TEMPTED BY A KING (Book 1):
https://geni.us/cruzkings1
WANTED BY A KING (Book 2):
https://geni.us/cruzkings2
CLAIMED BY A KING (Book 3):
https://geni.us/cruzkings3

CHECK OUT ALL OF SARAH JD'S BOOKS HERE:

https://sarahjaneduncan.com/book-links/

Sarah JD's Books

Stay Connected

Want to find out all the Tea before everyone else?
Join my VIP readers list to hear more about Lexi and the gang, plus the other characters that join them along the way.

SIGN UP HERE!
https://sarahjaneduncan.com/newsletter/

Want to join the conversation about your fav characters?
Join my Facebook Readers Group
SARAH'S VICIOUS KITTENS

JOIN HERE!
https://www.facebook.com/groups/
sarahjaneduncanreadersgroup

For more information on books & book signing events
please visit:
sarahjaneduncan.com

STALK SARAH HERE:

SCAN
ME

STALK ME

Sarah JD

Sarah JD, also known as Sarah Jane Duncan, is a dark romance author living in Australia with Mr Duncan who stole her off the market back in high school.

Sarah can be found in her writing room plotting out her next smut filled romance filled with angst, violence, and themes so dark you should probably question why you love it so much.

Sarah writes about strong females who have to fight against the odds to find their power, their voice, and their truth. Her heroines possess the strength that only comes from being a survivor, and through their trauma, battles and struggles, they learn to trust again, and find love.

There's nothing easy about their stories. They are hard, gritty, and painfully heartbreaking at times. But what doesn't kill us makes us stronger, right? And when you throw in a swoon worthy guy, or an alphahole that you just want to slap, but also fall to your knees and obey, it's the recipe for a rollercoaster ride.

So buckle up. Read the warnings. And let yourself get lost in the dark stories Sarah creates.